Guests of Don Lorenzo ─────────────────────

ROBERT PICK

Guests of Don Lorenzo

A NOVEL

SECKER AND WARBURG
London   1950

MADE AND PRINTED IN GREAT BRITAIN BY
MORRISON AND GIBB LIMITED, LONDON AND EDINBURGH

Guests of Don Lorenzo _____

I

TODAY THE NORTHWEST of the Republic is no longer the unruly country it used to be as late as thirty, or even twenty-five, years ago. No longer do the dregs of outlawry, returning from the decaying rubber region, demoralize the pueblos, sack outlying haciendas, rob churches, or engage in shoddy dealings with disreputable alcaldes. The Expedition of 1930 —Lorenzo Requesens' "footling war," in the parlance of his detractors —put an end to the last vestige of such conditions. Today, Murcia, the most northwestern of the country's towns, dozes peacefully in the shadow of its twin-spired church. The poor are poor, and the rich are rich—though the wealth of even the most prosperous of them might only evoke pitying smiles from cattle breeders out East, Majamarca merchants, or the gentlemen at the Club Nacional in Huacho, the capital of the Republic.

Political changes such as take place there—Army putsches, rebellions, liberations from this or that accursed yoke, or whatever grandiose or belittling names are given to these affairs—reverberate but dimly in the Northwest. It is as if the drive of political passions were retarded north of Ulloa, the terminal of the Northern Railway, and hesitated to traverse the highway connecting that place with Murcia.

Now as to Murcia itself, it must be remembered that this town was in the center of the occurrences of 1930, and experiences of that kind leave scars on the minds of people. True, Lorenzo Requesens freed the neighborhood from the bandits, and did away with El Seringuero, their leader and a veteran of the rubber boom days who gilded his savage instincts with some high-flown catchwords. Yet Murcia's more substantial citizens no longer care to recall the gory justice meted out in their market place in 1930.

At any rate, the subsequent vicissitudes of Requesens' life were a

7

matter of near-indifference in these quarters. Had it not been for his own involvement in some of Don Lorenzo's activities, even Señor Adolfo Bundschuh, the man who was his host during the campaign against the brigands, might have given only small thought to the colonel's changing fortunes.

So it goes. There is no song about Lorenzo Requesens among the lowly, while there is one about El Seringuero. But since when are songs of any importance?

Surely the urchin who was humming that tune one evening—the early evening of a May day of 1945—in front of the gate of the Bundschuh hacienda had merely the vaguest of notions about the song's hero; and when he was shouted at from the inside of the casa, he must have simply assumed that the patrón did not like any noise round his house at this hour.

Yet it was the song, and not the singing, that annoyed Señor Bundschuh. 'El Seringuero, El Seringuero!' he repeated in his mind long after the child outside had taken to his heels, 'if there hadn't been any El Seringuero, or if he had perished in the forest, or never recruited his band, there wouldn't have been any expedition in 1930, and if there hadn't been any, I would never have met Don Lorenzo, and he would not have known of my existence, and could never have saddled me—fifteen years later!—with those three men. . . .'

Bundschuh stood at the opened front window of the ground-floor living room of his house. His arms—oddly short arms—were folded across his chest. He stared at the wall of masonry which, contrary to local custom, kept the front yard aloof from the dirt road and the grass and scrubland beyond. The gate was about a hundred meters to the right, with a spottily gravelled driveway leading to the inconspicuous wooden entrance door of the casa. A second pathway, its sand overgrown, branched off from the gate to its left in the direction of the so-called guest house—the present abode of the three men whose mental images occupied Señor Bundschuh.

He admitted to himself that their images vexed him more than the sight of them in the flesh. Looked at and spoken to, they were ordinary men, as foreigners went. But to think about them threatened to open the locks to the wildest imaginings. With all deference to their protector, Don Lorenzo, Bundschuh was well entitled to call them "an infernal nuisance." But such abuse was a poor outlet for his feelings. It seemed only to draw him closer to the awareness of their presence.

A young monkey cried in the distance. The lengthening shadows
of the bitter-orange trees had reached the wall. An Indio rode by on
his donkey; nothing more than his ragged straw hat was to be seen
above the wall, but Señor Bundschuh was sure he was not one of
his own men. He knew them all, and would laugh at the contention
of an occasional traveller stopping over at the hacienda that it was
impossible to remember the faces of Indians in this part of the country.
The truth of the matter was that the becalmed atmosphere of their
lives put a common stamp on their features. Bundschuh heaved a sigh.
In a roundabout way that thought had brought the three foreign men
back again to his mind. "Something will have to be done," he said
in a distinct undertone. He had heard his stepdaughter enter the room.

"It was one of Jacinto's children," the girl said.

"Who?"

"The boy who was singing."

"Those children should stop loitering around the gate. Why doesn't
Jacinto keep them where they belong? Well, how should you know,
Juana?" he added placatingly, whirling round and uncrossing his
arms. He walked quickly to the sideboard to pour himself a glass of
brandy, while he watched Juana lay the dinner table.

She was not beautiful, and the folds at the corners of her mouth told
of a premature seriousness. She was a tall young woman. Rich dark
hair crowned her very white face over deep-set blue eyes. "His wife
died last month," she observed in an explanatory tone, "and the child
may be afraid to stay near the hut. He must have overheard the grownups talk about the dead that return."

Bundschuh shook the bottle before uncorking it. "Not Jacinto," he
said, his voice following the rhythm of his motion, "a mechanic, a
driver, a man who can read . . . You know, when I first came to
Murcia, those superstitions were less offensive. Ingrown superstitions
are like those diseases that do no great harm to the Indios as long as
white doctors leave them alone. As soon as the fathers from Casaquiara
started their campaign against witchcraft, superstitions only grew
worse." He bent backwards, and drained his glass, closing his eyes
with a rapt quiver. "Any news?" he asked.

"The war in Europe is over," she said. "They surrendered, and so
the war is over."

He put his glass down, and gave a little grunt which indicated that
the news did not come as a surprise to him. He disliked radios in gen-

eral, and the syrupy voices of the two speakers of Huacho Broadcasting Station in particular; the one wireless set on the hacienda was installed in Juana's bedroom. Now he blinked toward the girl. "Is it not clever of Philibert to go to Huacho? To go there now—if you understand me. Go to Huacho! What I wanted to say was that it was pretty shrewd of him to get Requesens to meet him in Huacho, or anywhere, for that matter. The colonel is more likely than not to listen to him now. With the war over—if you understand me." He had reached for the bottle again, but withdrew his hand.

"You mean it would be easier for Philibert to stay in Huacho now? If that is what he wants?"

"Something like that," Bundschuh said. "Restrictions for aliens will be lifted. There always are restrictions in war times. It was the same in the last war, and life was miserable for aliens. I know it. Now with the war over . . ."

"You think that is what he'll ask of the colonel?"

Señor Bundschuh's voice fell to a murmur. "The best solution, no? The work I had in mind must be abandoned now. New projects must be postponed these days. So . . . so the idea just did not work out. That's all there is to it. Not sure they'd have been the right men anyway. . . . Best solution . . ."

This sort of vague talk in reference to the men in the guest house had, over the past four months, assumed an almost ritual quality between Bundschuh and his stepdaughter. He was not certain that she always grasped the unspoken rules of their game. But she had always complied with them. It annoyed him a little that she made no response this time. She would not have to touch on the reasons why the three men had come all the way to Murcia, to begin with, in order to say that she too was hoping they would leave, and for good.

Instead she only asked him whether he wanted the shutters closed. "I'll do it myself," he said, passing by her.

The great irritation in him of some minutes before had gone. What worried him was the openness of Juana's unconcern. Ever since the death of her mother he had felt a certain responsibility toward the girl. He had never reasoned her out. Sometimes he wondered how much common sense and how much content there were behind her quiet habits. And of late that feeling would in her presence translate itself into the reasonless notion that her attitude was, for good or for evil, something like a portent of the future.

II

THERE WAS IN Bundschuh a somewhat blurred fidelity to his past, which could not fail to include Colonel Requesens. Today's evil, as had been yesterday's good, was the outgrowth of an acquaintanceship that had begun in a perfectly natural manner.

It so happened that Don Lorenzo, in 1930, came into the command of the expeditionary force straight from a stay abroad of many long years. It was a delicate situation in various respects. Having lost what familiarity he had ever had with the ways of his country's provincials, the colonel was first attracted to the billet in Bundschuh's house by the depreciatory fashion in which the alcalde of Murcia spoke of "that *alemán*" and his indifference toward public affairs. The Bundschuh home, a two-storey building in a shadowy corner of the plaza, proved to be comfortable enough, and the skylight studio of its upper floor—Adolfo Bundschuh was a photographer by trade in those days—very well suited for doing mapwork. Perhaps Bundschuh's German origin was an additional incentive to Don Lorenzo for choosing these quarters, for he was to join the Republic's Berlin legation as soon as the Expedition was over, and knew next to nothing about his country of destination. So he moved in.

He often stayed in his lodgings at night, and sometimes he was alone, writing letters to his young wife, or merely resting after another strenuous day of stalking the bandits. At times he would not mind the company of his host. It may be doubted that Bundschuh's stories entertained him—as in the staff mess he said they did—but the apparent good humor of a man who, worsted by a prank of fate, had made the best of it seemed to touch a kindred chord in Requesens.

Bundschuh was flattered. But his real affection for the distinguished house guest had its source in the ease with which Don Lorenzo accepted the tale of his immigration. Very few people had ever as readily as

Requesens believed that a young man who, having wound up his peacetime service in the Kaiser's Navy, was residing in Alexandria, Egypt, could possibly have been so naïve as to board, in the autumn of 1914, a Greek freighter bound for South America, whose master had promised to put him ashore in a German harbor. Nor had many people ever given much credence to Bundschuh's account of his despair when he found himself "shanghaied" to, or "cast away" on, the other side of the Atlantic. Seen in the light of subsequent history, even a German's disinclination to join the Kaiser's war may not seem overly shameful today. But in 1930 a man's soldierly courage had still a fairly absolute value; and Bundschuh, whose reports of his futile attempts to be repatriated in 1914 and '15 had never impressed his interlocutors, was gratified by the affable credulity of Don Lorenzo.

According to his yarn, then, Bundschuh had begun to travel inland from the port of his debarkation some time in 1915, driven from one place to another—and from one country to the second, and finally to the Republic—in his pursuit of a livelihood, or else by the mounting enmity everywhere toward Germans. Take, for instance, his arrival at Huacho late in 1917. "Ha, *that* was a joke!" he exclaimed with the grim hilarity befitting a naturalized citizen in recalling this trying experience. "No sooner had my mother's son entered that fair city than the Republic declared war on the Reich, and he was in a proper fix again. . . ." From that episode on, the photographer's account was less detailed. But the colonel took it as it came. "You weathered the storm, my friend," he would say, "and that is the main thing."

The intimacy between the two disparate men soon attracted attention. It puzzled the officers. It was bound to make the worthies of Murcia envious. One day the local physician, a hard-drinking man of Irish-criollo descent, related to the colonel with a malicious overtone that "the whole town" used to wonder why Don Adolfo had "been sticking it out in Murcia" ever since allegedly he had found Huacho not to his taste. Requesens dismissed whatever aspersions may have been implied. He knew that at the time of Bundschuh's arrival in these parts travel northwest had been far from rare. Although large-scale rubber tapping belonged to the past even then, isolated adventurers, including foreigners, would turn up regularly in the region. As a rule Don Lorenzo did not care to discuss the rubber business of bygone times; yet one night he asked Bundschuh why, once "up here," he had not tried his luck in the forest.

Great enterprises did not seem to be in his blood, Don Adolfo replied, as he always had, to that query. Perhaps the stories issuing from the rubber frontier had repelled him, too. Had the señor colonel ever heard about the unbridled violence rampant there?

The colonel had. Yes, he said absently, Don Adolfo looked like a man who abhorred disorder.

"But not adventure!" Bundschuh went on in his unbidden self-defense. Ah, most likely he had been the first man of his trade ever to visit the wretched hamlets of the far Northwest, and set up his tent in their fairs. "What times, señor colonel, what hardships!" he said, with a half-humorous moan, pointing at the garish colored photographs on the wall of his studio. Did they not bear witness to the days when, with the ungainly box with his equipment fastened to his saddle, he used "to defy the burning sun of the summer and the torrential rains of the long months of winter"?

It took many a year before he was in a position to renounce his itinerant life. Now, he declared with a smile, the Indios flocked to his studio after Mass on Sundays. "Believe it or not," he told Requesens, "they've taken a fancy to having their photos, and even more so they like to display those of their departed folk. With them a piece of paper with a picture on it is not only a piece of paper. Sometimes I feel like a medicine man. Ha, ha!"

There was no true serenity in his loud-mouthed mirth. The colonel's presence—the daily sight of this paragon of success—had made Señor Bundschuh sorely conscious of his own melancholy career. How many years had he whiled away? Ten, eleven? Did he still hope to save money enough to exchange his toilsome métier for a position where others would work for him? Or was he for the rest of his days destined to toady to potbellied notables and ensnare illiterate peóns? Why *had* he put up for eleven years with the monotony of Murcia? Ah, those lonesome winter days with no one crossing the storm-swept plaza for hours! He would hate to tell this young colonel to what lengths he had gone in the futile pursuit of relaxation, and then of excitement again. When Requesens once genially referred to the picture of a comely Indian lass on the wall, Señor Bundschuh pressed his lips together, and made a vehement gesture of disparagement.

Gradually he shed his boisterous self-assurance in the company of Don Lorenzo. It had begun to dawn on him that the humor of fate which had brought this personage under his roof might have its meaning in the order of things. As it happened, a personal matter had—in the order of things—caused him much impotent anger of late. Step by step he found himself moved to reveal the source of his discontent to Requesens.

Voyaging half across the globe, a missive had reached the photographer, informing him of the death of an aunt in Westphalia who had bequeathed her estate, a handsome fortune, to her sundry nephews and nieces. But at the same time Bundschuh learned that his co-heirs contested his claims, and his letters to Westphalia had been of no avail thus far. In relating his story piecemeal, Bundschuh grew bold. He was bitterly outspoken about the consular service of the Republic. Would the señor colonel believe that those caballeros overseas had not lifted a finger to assist him in his righteous fight?

Don Lorenzo did not doubt the negligence of the ill-paid consular clerks in Berlin. But he had no advice to offer. As it was, he had no ear for the petty cares of his host at this moment.

El Seringuero had been captured at last; and while the populace of Murcia had stayed aloof from the fighting throughout the six weeks it had lasted, El Seringuero's impending execution produced an atmosphere of great tension. Out-of-towners had appeared on the streets, and their promenades taxed the nerves of the patrolling soldiers. But that was not all. On the past Sunday the silently milling assemblage had been augmented by four or five score of women, and that mob had blocked the way of the *cura* returning from Mass. "Mercy, *padrecito*," they had clamored, "mercy for El Seringuero!" They had been deaf to the padre's admonishments, repeating their plea ever louder; and had it not been for the carbines at last levelled at them, harm might have been done. It was very well to dismiss that near-riot, as sober citizens did, as an outburst of sentimentality on the part of "benighted churls." But in its Tuesday edition, *La Libertad,* Huacho's great daily, had promptly taken exception to the "hesitant tactics of the expeditionary forces in the face of the menacing spirit," and made a nasty allusion to "the peculiar situation in high quarters" to which "rather than to his strategic talents" Colonel Requesens owed his appointment.

Don Lorenzo knew what was meant. He knew that the General, averse to having one of the home colonels pick the laurels of victory, had recalled him from Paris and given him the command, determined to replace him himself, if he should fail. No wonder that Requesens was in no mood to discuss the Westphalian troubles of Señor Bundschuh.

Among the measures of which the colonel came to think in his desire to prove his worth, the plan occurred to him of displaying pictures of the hanging in every pueblo of the Northwest. He asked Bundschuh to take such photos. Bundschuh confessed to his repugnance to the grisly assignment, which he maintained might do damage to his business. Only when he realized that the colonel, apparently anxious not to be robbed of his thunder, was hesitant to apply for an Army photographer in Ulloa, did he allow himself to be talked into taking over the job. Meanwhile he had—in a candid exchange—made known to Requesens what he expected as a *quid pro quo* in the line of friendship.

Some days earlier the colonel had mentioned the post waiting for him at the Berlin legation. A gentleman's agreement came into being. Don Adolfo would do his duty as a patriot and furnish the photos; Don Lorenzo promised to straighten out the affair with the Westphalian court on the spot (with or without the help of the consul in Berlin); and of the legacy handed over to the heir in case of success, Don Lorenzo would receive a twenty per cent commission. About the security of that fee, the colonel was not worried. "I don't think you would cheat me," he said. "People in this country do not antagonize a Requesens. Nor, for that matter, do they discuss in public their dealings with him."

A month later the colonel broke camp. He left the theater of his victory riding the black stallion presented to him by Murcia's citizenry, behind him the band of the Eleventh (Ulloa) Infantry Regiment, whose brass easily drowned the cheers of the spectators lining the plaza. Bundschuh looked down at the martial scene from his studio—and for a whole year he was to ask himself whether the slight movement of Don Lorenzo's helmeted head as he rode by his home, eyes straight before him, was another seal upon their compact.

Sure enough, one beautiful morning the postmaster called him to his office to hand him a weighty letter; and soon word went round that the photographer's fortunes had changed. For in a flash of exhilaration and with a kind of defiance which seemed to take vengeance on all those whiled-away useless years, Bundschuh had, in the baffled postmaster's presence, hinted at certain grand plans of his that "must materialize now." He also had been heard to mutter something about a woman. The same people who used to shake their heads over the odd preference of the *alemán* for their township began now to whisper about some clandestine romance.

The truth of the matter was that, in the months since Requesens' departure, Bundschuh had come to covet the nearby property of a criollo woman whose husband, an educated German settler, had died a couple of years ago, leaving her his two-thousand-acre hacienda, plus an inordinate amount of debts contracted in his foolish efforts to establish a banana plantation. It was commonly surmised that the widow would have to sell out. Only the widespread lack of ready cash—this was 1931, and the economic world depression gripped the Republic—had theretofore discouraged attempts to make her an offer. Setting out to talk the thing over with her, Señor Bundschuh had every reason to foresee smooth going.

He had never had any respect for women. His appearance was not hewn out to attract them. His lumpy figure contrasted comically with the rapidity of his motions. The small eyes in his broad, yellowish face seemed to have adopted some of the stoniness of the Indios, and his lower lip had grown ever more drooping. A skin disease afflicted his bald head.

The widow cut short his overtures. No, she was not interested. She would never sell. Afraid of foreclosure? She would dare the alcalde to dislodge her and her daughter! She'd remind the *guardia civil*—if he should have the nerve to send them—of the Christian forbearance which even the bandits had shown her when they were raiding in the vicinity shortly after her husband's passing. And was he, Don Adolfo, not ashamed of trying to bring pressure to bear on her? On the widow of a man of his own racial stock? True, her late husband had done nothing to win his close friendship. But had he offended him ever? Surely they would have grown friends, had he lived to enjoy in some leisure the fruit of his labors. Don Adolfo might not be aware of the high esteem in which her husband had held his industry, his perseverance, his sober and even austere habits. . . .

Considering the customary pride of criollo women, such flatteries were unheard of. A bold thought struck Señor Bundschuh. He proposed to her three weeks later.

All turned out well. When, in July 1939, the señora Bundschuh succumbed to a poisonous snake bite, her second husband's bereavement was sincerely felt. It confirmed the opinion of better-class Murcianeros that family life and honest work on the soil had made a new man of the *alemán*. Notwithstanding an ugly rumor which sprang up years afterwards, the poor woman had in her agonies found tender words for Adolfo. She also may have felt some solace in her trust that he would be a good guardian for her Juanita.

It must have been the depressing mood of those days that prompted Bundschuh to apprise Requesens of the untimely death of his wife. With an emotional flourish foreign to his nature he assured the colonel on that occasion that "in sad days as in happy ones" Don Lorenzo's friendship was a matter of pride and comfort to him. Perhaps the mind of the mourner was fascinated by the notion that his present great sorrow was an indirect consequence of his dealings with Requesens, and hence this intimate letter to mark a cycle.

The two men had corresponded but rarely in the nine years past. Their intercourse had consisted exclusively of the annual New Year's wishes Don Adolfo would mail to Berlin; they were reciprocated sometimes and at other times weren't.

The extraordinary letter written upon the death of Señora Bundschuh remained unanswered. It may be that Don Lorenzo felt that the one-time photographer had overstepped his rank by so personal a communication. It also may be that the pressure of the colonel's work, in that autumn of 1939, kept him from attending to his mail. He may even have been absent from his desk at the Berlin legation in those days, participating in one of the Luftwaffe sorties over Poland—a foolhardiness which, together with some others, was held against him after his return to Huacho in November 1941.

Don Lorenzo's remiss habits of correspondence hurt Bundschuh, and in later years caused him a great deal of vexation. Even after their relationship grew closer again around Christmas 1944, and Don Adolfo had become the victim of his firm belief that one did not antagonize a Requesens, whatever his momentary status might be—even then he was kept waiting for endless weeks for the replies to his now more eloquent letters. This is why M. Philibert's success in persuading the colonel to meet him gave so much satisfaction to Bundschuh.

III

BOTH ELBOWS RESTING on his hunched-up knees, chin cupped in his hands, M. Philibert looked up at Don Lorenzo, who was pacing the ample room. A slight inflammation reddened the eyes of the man who had journeyed from Murcia. He had fidgety dark eyes, and together with the crisscrossed bags beneath their deep sockets, they gave to his face, despite the genially up-turned nose, a bird-like aspect. His greying hair was close cropped.

"You do not understand this country," Requesens had just repeated, talking in French. Although he spoke Philibert's native tongue as well, he insisted on talking in French. "Impatience is the thing which agrees least with this country. For *how* long have you been staying with my friend Bundschuh? Four months? Why, that is like four days! Do you know how long *I* stayed with my uncle out East without even once getting to Huacho? For three solid years plus three solid ·months. For thirty-nine months, that is, with my trip to Majamarca last January the one and only interruption."

"My letters gave you the wrong impression, colonel," M. Philibert remonstrated with civility. "It is not our stay with Bundschuh about which I complain, though Heaven knows it is not a pleasant spot, nor an easy one to keep a young man in line."

"Wasn't there talk of giving him some work to do?"

"If there was, nothing has come of it," said the other, drawing in his breath. "And there is the sick man, and the hacienda is not a good place to care for a sick man, colonel. But I am not complaining. Nor do I want to point out once again the dangers of our situation up there. My opinion on that point hasn't changed since January, and I still maintain that a crowded town would be preferable to the hacienda. That's what

18

I said in January . . ." M. Philibert shifted his weight, blinking against the midday light which pierced the obliquely drawn Venetian blinds of the one window.

Except for the colonel's footfalls, it was very still now. The house, on whose one-room upper floor the two men had been talking in this sparring fashion for the past half hour, stood on the northern edge of Carjavel, a thinly populated suburb of Huacho. The building belonged to Ramón, the former batman of Don Lorenzo.

"That's what *you* said in January," Requesens repeated belatedly. "And how about me, my friend? No, you do not understand this country. How much do you know, for instance, about El Huérfano? *You* said! How about what *I* said in January? Believe me, it did not give me much pleasure to have to tell you all this: that I was, to all practical purposes, an exile out East, that I had no longer any of the influence you had a right to expect me to have, that my erstwhile accomplishments in the service of my country no longer counted very much, that I had enemies, vicious enemies. . . ." He gave a laugh, rolling his lips under his long, straight, fleshy nose.

"You know what I came for," M. Philibert said with a tranquil snort.

Requesens pulled the wicker chair which stood near the door—the one decent piece of furniture in the room—up to his interlocutor. He crossed his long legs. "Yes," he said, and contemplated the shoe at the end of his crossed leg, "I know it. But I also know what you still have not learned."

"Which is?"

"That everything belongs to everything. Your concern, your sole concern is M. Philibert, is it?"

"Not my sole concern."

"Ah, it is," Don Lorenzo insisted. "And your specific concern at this moment is how you can get me to play your game, and play it according to your rules."

"*My* rules! Are these not everybody's rules?"

Requesens eyed his toes wriggling under the thin leather of his shoe.

"Do you remember where we met first, colonel?" M. Philibert asked sadly.

Don Lorenzo nodded.

"We had a talk about you after you left, our host and myself. I happen to recall that talk very well. And in particular there is one remark of our host's which I remember. I may say that I remembered it day and

.night on my Atlantic crossing, and later, when we travelled through those two countries on our way to Majamarca—"

"You did a good job at that," said Don Lorenzo.

"Perhaps I did a good job because I so vividly recalled that remark of our host's. It gave me courage. It gave me confidence in the future. Do you know what he said? He said you looked like a man with a passion for keeping his word. A passion. Which is something different from a belief, or the awareness of a duty. To me it seemed that a man's passion was something one could count on much better than on any awareness of a duty. That awareness may change, may vanish. A passion doesn't."

The colonel spread his hands. "I have no passion for danger," he pronounced at last. "Which leads us back to El Huérfano, the man you know nothing about."

"I know *something* about him," said the other, lifting his head, and for the first time his glum constraint seemed to desert him, "or at least I have heard his name. A little radical orator, isn't he?"

"Would you be greatly surprised to learn that this little orator had his share in what happened to me in '41? Surely you would be surprised to learn that his slander even managed to estrange the Army from me. How many officers do you assume were willing to give me a hand in . . . in teaching El Huérfano an old-fashioned lesson? One. One officer was prepared to go out to kidnap the fellow, put him into a sack, duck him into a sewer, and send him home soaked in filth. For that's what is known hereabouts as an old-fashioned lesson," Don Lorenzo threw in with a snicker. "And obviously one man could not do it all by himself. And why was there not one other officer itching to join me? Because I was *out* when I came home in '41! I was out before I could so much as open my mouth."

"British intervention?"

Requesens shrugged. "My head was a reasonable prize to pay to El Huérfano. The Government did not like the applause which he got in those days. And the Army—the General—went along with the Palace. . . . 'A ridiculous splinter party,' 'a faction mainly depending on the hue and cry of the illiterate and disfranchised,' 'street corner riffraff'—oh yes, these are some of the terms you may hear people employ when they talk about El Huérfano. Still he was strong enough— Now I do not want to overstate my case, and say that he alone forced me into eclipse. Still, without his ludicrous campaign I might have been left alone after the first shock blew over. In due time I might have gotten the command of a regiment, instead of having to cool my heels in bucolic retirement, so called." He brought up these matters without visible emotion. He had told Philibert earlier that his return to the capital coincided with the end of the "good long holiday" the Palace had suggested to him in November 1941. (He had, however, not breathed a word to the effect that his departure from the estate of his uncle had been precipitated by the news about the rapidly failing health of the General.) "I am telling you all this," he concluded, "to give you a glimpse of what *I* am up against."

"Up against! All that took place three and a half years ago, colonel."

"About three and a half years ago," Don Lorenzo confirmed. By way of an aftermath a great bitterness had seized hold of him; he had used El Huérfano's name merely as a stratagem; but now he realized that El Huérfano's attack had lost nothing of its cruel sting in his recollection.

It had been an outrage. Never up to then had El Huérfano shown an interest in foreign affairs; and therefore Requesens swore in those days that there was an understanding between the man and some foreign legation. But the puzzling thing was that El Huérfano concentrated on matters quite apart from the colonel's conduct abroad. He thought nothing of falsifying the history of the Expedition of 1930, and degrading it to "a barbaric manhunt culminating in an act of sadism." He dragged into the arena again the name of Lorenzo's defunct father. And he also began to amuse the readers of his despicable weekly sheet by bandying about minor gossip—and that had been the worst of it. Being ridiculed is the one unpardonable sin in the Republic.

How could this clumsy foreigner, this "M. Philibert," discern the underpinnings of public life and its subtle structures? The nerve of him! Coming here in this hour fraught with weighty decisions, and harping on matters as dead as the world he came from! "Yes, all that was three and a half years ago," Don Lorenzo said again. "But this is not a country of short memories. And I must also tell you that El Huérfano is on the stump again."

"Against you?"

"I am not sure. Perhaps not. Not yet. He does not yet know I am back in town."

"What are your plans for the immediate future?" Philibert asked.

"I suggest you go back to Murcia and try to remain on good terms with my friend Bundschuh."

"I was asking about your own plans."

"My own plans? Go back East, I presume."

M. Philibert let his chin sink down on his breast. "I forgot it is no longer up to me to ask questions. We used to discuss such matters in bygone days. We used to discuss them with mutual frankness. We used to." He took one of his hands away from his chin, waving it slightly.

Requesens stood up, and walked over to the window. It opened on a courtyard which had had its day as the patio of a colonial household. Now the shallow basin in its center, long emptied of water, served as a dumping place. The flagstones of the paving were strewn with crushed cardboard boxes, empty baskets, and faggots. A charcoal brazier stood under one of the dilapidated arcatures. "There is nothing to be frank about," he muttered, "at least nothing which concerns me directly." He let the fingers of his right hand run over the Venetian blinds, and accelerated the motion until the raucous glissando rang like the roll of a high-pitched drum.

"So there *is* something?" M. Philibert inquired. "something that concerns *me?*"

Don Lorenzo halted his drumming. Ramón had come out into the courtyard. He carried an almost fully unfurled flag over his shoulder, and jerked his head as the green-white-blue cloth with the three-headed serpent in its center field flapped against his ears. Then he stepped back again.

The colonel put his right hand into the inner breast pocket of his flannel jacket. "I am going to read this to you," he said without changing the inflection of his naturally hoarse voice. "I'll translate it for you." He held a newspaper clipping aloft, still without turning. "It's from *La Libertad.*"

M. Philibert got to his feet. Seated, he gave the impression of a very powerful man. But he stood no more than about five feet six, and the thinness of his legs, accentuated by the canvas leggings he sported, made him appear even shorter.

"I take it you *want* me to translate it for you?" Don Lorenzo continued. He had put on his glasses, and finally turning around, cast a tolerant glance toward M. Philibert, who said slightingly,

"If you want to."

"'Fairy Tales' is the headline of this editorial. It is a short piece. Here's how it goes. 'Certain malicious little men'—perhaps 'malicious' is too strong a translation—'little men seem to have been frightened of late by the loss of prestige which they suffered during the war. Now they try to worm their way into our political life again by whatever means are at hand. Recently one of them has chosen to question the attitude of the Government in the matter of such unwelcome guests as the outcome of the European war may bring to this continent. Now, as need not be stressed, a country like ours, without a coastline, is the last place on earth such fugitives would be able to enter. But even if they did, our would-be politicos may rest assured that the authorities would know how to deal with such unbidden callers. It is indeed beneath the dignity of any patriot to lend his ear to such spiteful speculations. They bank on the same streak of human imagination which in the dark days of our early history convinced the world of the presence of unicorns and Amazons in our woodlands.'"

"Why, that is *good* news!" M. Philibert burst out.

"I hope my translation was correct," said the colonel, taking off his glasses. He still held the clipping before him, daintily. "Good news? We in this country do not believe in directness, my friend. Now this may be a token of appeasement for El Huérfano. Likewise, it may be a left-handed pronunciamento to the address of certain foreign powers which cannot stop meddling in our affairs, a memento that, with the war over, the Republic is taking her destiny into her own hands again—Ah," he interrupted himself, "this thing here may mean practically anything, perhaps even good news. But if I were you, I would be on my guard just the same."

"Colonel Requesens," M. Philibert said, swallowing hard, "the sum is five hundred and eleven thousand North American dollars, roughly and without interest. I don't know how much the trifle you gave me in Majamarca amounts to in North American money. Nor can I estimate how much you are paying to Bundschuh for our upkeep. Roughly, as I said, the sum is five hundred and eleven thousand."

The colonel tore the newspaper clipping into small shreds, and tucked them into his pocket. "Whose money is it?" he asked.

"The understanding, as I hardly need remind you, was to deposit it under the name of François Philibert. Can anything—anything, Colonel Requesens!—alter that understanding between men of honor?"

"Nothing," Don Lorenzo replied, "nothing, except that, with El Huérfano watching my every step in those months and probably ever since, I did not feel like walking up to the Banco Oriental and telling them, 'Please open an account for a M. François Philibert, whereabouts unknown, and here are five hundred and eleven thousand North American dollars for deposit, and please mail all pertinent correspondence to my address.' Or could I? I was a fool in entering what you call our understanding. But I was not a big enough fool to make it public upon my return. Moreover, I do not think you would be here, if I had done any such thing."

The call of a bugle was heard, and grew more distinct. After a while the reverberation of the steps of a marching column fell into the silence which had followed Don Lorenzo's last words.

"But where *is* the money?" M. Philibert asked, twisting his face.

"Is it yours?"

"At any rate I don't think it is yours. Nor did you ask this question in Lisbon."

"The world has changed since, I daresay."

"We did not exclude such changes."

"*Such* changes?" Requesens said, and made a wide sweep expressing the magnitude of the actual changes and at the same time—through an awkward motion downwards of his spread fingers—their lamentable nature.

"Should those changes be great enough to alter a man's sense of honor, colonel? The sense of honor of a man who has a passion for keeping his word?"

Bugle and footsteps outside had died away. Don Lorenzo was leaning against the window sill. He was so tall he had to shove his feet forward a little on the floor. "Once more I urge you to have patience," he said. "This country is in flux—"

"The whole world is in flux! Which is an additional incentive for a man to clean up old affairs, and prepare for days to come."

Requesens, who had half turned again, was trying to pull the cord of the Venetian blinds to close them more tightly. "Give the future a chance," he said. "I cannot prevent you from committing all sorts of follies. But I can keep that money out of your hands and prevent you from making yourself conspicuous. It would be sheer madness. What would you gain by, let's say, buying Bundschuh, or the alcalde of Murcia, or perhaps even the Ulloa commander? You have known the real thing, my friend. Yours was a great experience. Do you want to play with marbles now? My advice is to wait, and bide your time."

M. Philibert said nothing. He shut his eyes to the glare of the sun. For in his attempts to pull the cord, Don Lorenzo had disarranged the Venetian blinds still more, and a solid beam of light made its way to M. Philibert who had returned to his chair. He could have shifted his body to elude the discomfort, or pulled away his chair. But he remained motionless. His thoughts had swung far away from the place and from the man at the window who seemed to talk on.

His eyes closed, M. Philibert saw the gaunt goateed captain stand at the chain rail of his conning tower, his hand stretched out half-downwards in a salute toward the canvas canoe about to be freed from the painter. In his mind M. Philibert lived again through that moment, an endless minute of tension, with the rocking bow of the U-boat threatening to scoop them out of the narrow bay and roll them back onto the deck. And again he watched, in his memory, the submarine glide off into the dark, a slowly merging, slowly dissolving structure of contours, the mute ghost of an eloquent shadow.

". . . if you were not a stickler for words," the colonel was observing, "I would be tempted to promise you that this is not the end." He stood near the door, one leg forward.

Dazzled by the sudden impact of light, as he looked up, the other was perplexed to find Requesens standing there: he had not heard him cross the room. "It's in my trusteeship," M. Philibert declared with provocative firmness. "Those five hundred and eleven thousand dollars are in my trusteeship. Does this satisfy you?"

"It makes at least some sense," Don Lorenzo answered, "and it might provide us with a basis for future negotiations. I am afraid I must go now, but I shall be back."

"Am I to consider myself—"

"—as confined to this room? It would be the wisest course to take. Your railroad ride was a great enough risk."

"That's one thing I cannot get into my head," M. Philibert remarked, raising his voice in exasperation. "You seem to think nothing of all the risks on the hacienda—that odd girl, Bundschuh's stepdaughter or something, who looks at us as if she'd like to rip us open, or the tight-lipped overseer they call the capataz, or the old cretin at the stables, or the Indios who live on the grounds, eighty or a hundred of them, or the two lorries that are driven to town all the time, or the postman who comes every other day, or the peddlers who stop by, some of them garrulous as parrots, and those ridiculous militia men who sometimes peer across the wall from the saddles of their mounts. . . . Ah, of that whole crew that sees us day in and day out you seem to think nothing at all, and are confident they've swallowed Bundschuh's silly story about his 'new agricultural experts,' and what not!"

Requesens had in vain tried to stop that outburst with fluttering gestures. "Murcia is Murcia, and Huacho is Huacho," he now said. "Not that I am happy about the situation up there. Not that I was anything like happy when three of you turned up on the River wharf in Majamarca in January, instead of only you, as agreed on. I promised you this refuge. I had to give it to your companions. Or at least I thought so. My sense of honor made me think so. But having made one false step, I need not make another."

"Talking about—"

"You know what I am talking about."

"About five hundred and eleven thousand dollars?" Philibert asked, tapping his foot at every syllable of the figure. "Refuge? You gave me refuge? You simply trapped me. You didn't want me to be at large. Or to put it correctly . . ." His face had grown ashen beneath its tan. "For really you don't give a hoot whether I am free or not— To put it correctly, then. You did not want me to be out of your reach. That's why you got me into your country. You didn't want me to be in a position to tell anyone about our business arrangements. Right? Right. You've trapped me, Colonel Requesens!"

Don Lorenzo was taken aback by that sudden plainness of speech. But he only raised his shoulders, and said, "That is what a man gets for keeping his word. Some day you will realize how greatly you've misjudged me. By that time you'll also have learned to grasp the merits of patience."

"Any time limit?"

"Isn't it the essence of patience to have none? Time limit! The time will come when men such as you can carry their heads high again, and if my guess is worth anything, that time—not entirely without thanks to the Huérfanos—will come sooner than some of the onlookers tonight may assume, or, for that matter, some of the protagonists of our great celebration of victory in a war we did not fight."

The colonel's words were not wasted on M. Philibert. He knew that lofty aims and selfishness both had room in a man's breast. An inseparable blend of patriotism and rapacity had animated him for a lifetime. He had always harbored a disdain for the pedantic asceticism of fanatics.

Originally he had regarded Requesens as just another well-groomed figure brightening the parquet of an *opéra bouffe* legation. Even when he came to know the attaché pretty well both as a military observer for the Republic and in their own dealings, he had not given much thought to the stuff such exotic colonels were actually made of. And surely the hush and feverish hurry of their negotiations in Lisbon—not to speak of the dazing briefness of their first meeting in this hemisphere —had not favored a coolheaded assessment of his character. Still, Requesens' brazenness and his stubborn greed did not shock M. Philibert now. They almost won his respect.

"Now let us be sensible, friend," Don Lorenzo broke the uneasy silence. "I cannot think that tonight's celebration would please you, considering the occasion."

"I get your point," M. Philibert said curtly.

"Good. I shall leave you now. I will see you once more before your departure. I really will," he repeated, pretending to interpret M. Philibert's arched brows as a sign of incredulity. "I could leave you with some high-sounding exhortations, to boost your morale, as the saying has it among minor people. The esteem I have for you is too great to engage in such nonsense." He had opened the door while he spoke, and closed it behind him.

On the ground-floor landing he stopped to listen upwards, but no sound issued from M. Philibert's quarters. 'Good man!' Don Lorenzo thought to himself, as he turned to his right toward the aperture which led to the patio. Bending his head, he lifted the curtain of varicolored wooden beads. Ramón was sitting on the flagstones, his back against the wall, his fat legs sprawling, the flag, rolled up again, resting athwart them. When the drowsy man made a motion to heave to his feet, Requesens motioned him not to get up. He snorted. "I see you're thinking of everything, Ramón. Yes, yes, victories call for gay bunting. Eh?"

"Indeed, señor colonel," agreed Ramón in his short-winded grating falsetto. "The flag will be up in time." He grimaced up at Requesens, who nodded at the obese man before he withdrew his head and straightened.

He crossed the hallway, and was out on the street. A file of Indios trudged along the downtrodden edge of the coarse grass facing Ramón's house. They did not raise their heads as Don Lorenzo inadvertently shut the door with a bang. Only their burdened burros quickened their pace and tossed their shaggy manes and kicked a little before they went on.

IV

THE STUCCOED THREE-STOREY structure of the Casa Requesens, dating from pre-Liberation days, stands on the western fringe of the Old City at the level end of a shadowy street which softly slants down to a narrow alley. From there the way to the Plaza is tortuous and takes about twenty-five minutes on foot. The new residential section of Huacho—an accomplishment of the glorious 1830's—lies at about the same distance farther west. Thus the Casa Requesens is situated half-way between the "throbbing heart of the Republic" and the dwellings of the wealthy, near-wealthy and once-wealthy that fancy themselves as its bloodstream. Since, today, what real wealth there is in the country is concentrated in the East, some of these residences have changed hands. Others are deserted part of the year, or even for some years in succession, and only now and then throw open their gates to teem once more with life and with youth.

Not so the Casa Requesens. For more than thirty years—in fact, up to this May of 1945—its inhospitable aspect constituted a sad landmark. Street vendors and beggars called it the "Casa Nobody-in," aping the cry v th which the old housekeeper, a goiterous half-breed woman by the name of Isabel, would answer their raps.

They may again call it the "Casa Nobody-in" today, and take their vengeance on Isabel by throwing pebbles at the windowpanes of the ground-floor sala, or else aim at the buzzards atop the roof or the crows which love to alight on the stone-dressed escutcheon above the panelled door of the building.

Perhaps it was a premonition of that future, and with it a feeling of impermanence and futility, which—on this day of May 1945— paralyzed the efforts of Doña Priscilla to bring some order into the interior of the Casa, where she and her husband had arrived very late on the previous night. She sat, only half relaxed, in one of the burlap-covered armchairs beneath the portrait of her father-in-law in the sala. The lips of her attractively large mouth were parted a little, while her translucent grey eyes watched the folds of the great flag beat softly against the window in the recess to the left of the vestibule door. Her angular features expressed a tension at the same time hardened and vapid. Now and then she readjusted the bandana over her auburn hair.

Perhaps it was also the onrush of recollections which made her so susceptible to the dreary surroundings. She had stayed at the Casa before. Upon Don Lorenzo's homecoming in 1941 his uncle, Don Esteban, had offered him the use of the mansion; and Priscilla remembered how greatly the idea of occupying it had appealed to her husband in the face of the humiliations he was exposed to. "They must be shown that a Requesens remains a Requesens," he would say, as though his defiance—directed at the Palace, at El Huérfano, at the General, or at his disloyal Army comrades—could soften the dismay of his wife. She would never forget her first entry into the Casa. Under the denuded beams of the ceiling the sala harbored droves of enormous bats; its splintering parquet was marred by their excrement and by mounds of dirt thrown up by termites; arrogant cats roved the corridors, coming to rest on the sills of windows impervious to the light of the day; piled-up furniture and rolled rugs blocked the arrivals' every step; and the tinkling of the great French chandelier, challenging its own tarnish, seemed to mock the return of the last of the Requesens. Thanks to Doña Priscilla's subsequent urging and the alarming report of Don Esteban's contractor, a sort of patchwork job had restored the house to a more livable condition in 1942. But the sounds from the crystal chandelier had not changed their tune.

Rationally, the element of surprise in her displeasure was as little founded on this day of May 1945, as it had been in November 1941. In the twelve years preceding her first view of the Casa, Lorenzo had hardly ever mentioned it—not even in that tenderly depreciatory vein in which decaying family houses are often talked about by men who, going into the world, have changed the scope of their concerns. And considering the fairly bright colors in which Lorenzo had painted the picture of his country from the very inception of their acquaintance, his reticence in regard to the Casa should have forewarned her.

Not that he had ever contended that his was a powerful country.

One of the first stories he told her—the account of his semi-diplomatic career—revealed to her the historical disaster which had crippled the growth of his native land. He had, so he told Priscilla, come to Paris as the secretary of the old gentleman who represented the Republic at the peace conference of Versailles. "Our participation in the World War amounted to nothing. Yet here we were, Don Salvador Leso and myself, sitting in at some of the conferences. Don Salvador did not breathe a word. Throughout those months his main occupation was to look forward to the actual signing of the treaty. He was fascinated by that prospect. As it happened, his father was among the unfortunate men who had to sign away our coastline (you must know that we once had an Atlantic coastline), and that pathetic piece of family history made him absurdly sensitive to what he'd call 'the unspeakable tragedy of the defeated.' Since we had no opportunity of even glimpsing the German delegation before the final act, he would send me out to get some information on what 'those poor wretches' were doing in their quarters. I still suspect that my success in bringing him news about them moved him to comply with my wish when I wanted to stay on in Paris. Oh, he was a darling, that Don Salvador of ours, and the classic example of the incompetence of our statesmen in those days."

The notable thing about such stories was the fact that their light-hearted irony did not include the country as such—though, again, Lorenzo did not maintain that it was a country far advanced in public enlightment, or blessed with the amenities of material civilization. Its worth, he gave her to understand, lay in deeper, more lasting values. "Fidelity," he would say, leaning slightly toward the girl, as he drove her through the French countryside, "the great fidelity to the intrinsic character of the country, to what exists and always will, to its spirit throughout the ages . . ." Or he would talk about "progress, so called," deride the "over-all yardstick certain observers love to apply to all nations alike," or again come back to "fidelity, man's loyalty to his ordained fate, his destiny, his guilt."

These were strange utterances to a girl moving in the circle of the foreign press in the Paris of the late 1920's. Only the haziness of Lorenzo's vocabulary cushioned its challenge. At any rate it blurred the backdrop of the stage which Lorenzo described to Priscilla. When he went on to tell her of the "upland evening hovering for the shortest of times over Huacho before plunging the whole plateau into black-

ness," or of the steep treeless slopes of the midlands, or of the cube-
shaped, "eternally shuttered" stone houses of the Eastern plains, or
the River jungle alive with mammals, reptiles and fowl whose names
evoked so many textbook pictures for her—then she felt as though
she were looking through the wrong end of a pair of binoculars which
she could put down at a moment's impulse. The company of the young
attaché was one thing, his faraway native land was another.

Priscilla had met him in the course of an assignment given her at
her press office chiefly to cover the uselessness of her presence. Her
talents as a newspaper woman were negligible. She had come to Paris
through the fervent wish of her mother, a scatter-brained lady living
in Evansville, Indiana, to "let Pris make something of her life," and
the generosity of her father who, not any too happy in the ticker-tape
turbulence of his Wall Street office, loved to think of the "grand time"
Pris was having. Probably his divorce had left him with a bad conscience
toward his only child.

Pris's first experience with the young attaché belonged undoubtedly
to that "good time." A brief and rather confused affair with one of
the young men at the office—followed, shortly thereafter, by an ugly
scene in the apartment of a French artist of repute—had frightened
Priscilla into the notion that physical love could give her nothing.
She learned differently with Lorenzo. "An exceedingly handsome chap
and all that, you know . . ." some of the women in Priscilla's "crowd"
would say when she introduced him to that circle. But the attraction
Lorenzo had for her soon threatened to grow beyond their mutual
enjoyment, and somewhat scared her. Lorenzo's manners were im-
peccable. He seemed to have nothing of the vainglorious volubility and
the exuberant or sentimental airs she had been warned against in a
"creole Army man of one of those picturesque republics." Priscilla was
accustomed to the unambiguous directness of her generation; now she
believed she had discovered that this pleasant spirit of matter-of-fact
comradeship entailed a thinness of emotion that always left her a beg-
gar. The very ambiguity about Lorenzo, the contradiction within his
nature—playfulness and determination, dexterity and dreaminess—not
only added luster to his company and aroused her curiosity, but also
gave to her life a new feeling of richness.

In a circuitous way she happened to learn that he made some extra
money by soliciting for a certain brokerage firm the accounts of wealthy
Latin-American residents. Her informants creased their noses a little

in imparting that gossip to her. Yet she mentioned it, perhaps by way of recommendation, when she answered her father's query in regard to the "conspicuous foreign beau" she had been seen with. About Lorenzo's veiled proposals she wrote only at a later stage. The man in Wall Street grew worried. He made inquiries in Huacho. He was informed that Colonel Requesens, owing to his late father's unwise investments, was dependent on his Army pay, except for such assistance as his uncle and only relative, a gentleman said to manage his ranch pretty carelessly, was able and willing to tender. It was not much information. But the language was eloquent enough for the recipient. No almond-eyed, shiny-haired Latin lounge lizard and fortune hunter would maneuver himself into his money! Urgent cables began to pour down on Priscilla, and their wordage increased with her half-hearted protests.

She was not entirely deaf to the voice from Wall Street. Why had Lorenzo never told her anything about his family, his childhood, his circumstances? "Why?" he countered. "Because I do not believe in wallowing in one's depressing remembrances in front of a woman, and especially not when this woman happens to be the girl I love." The sweep of his answer did not deflect her purpose. Depressing memories? Were they exclusively such? Oh yes, he had told her that his mother had died in childbirth. But had he not been devoted to his father, too? Was not his uncle a nice man? "My uncle is a very nice man," he said with an indulgent smile. "To my father the word 'nice' would not quite do justice. Devoted I was to him, my darling, and I still am to his memory." His father had not been in the Army, she presumed? "No." Had he been in business? "Not really," he replied with a ready sigh, and then, sitting up on the divan, and taking his head between his palms, he began, falteringly at first, his version of the great catastrophe which, some years before the war, had felled Don Julio Requesens.

He did not deny that financial losses, "invited by a foolhardy venture," had contributed to that fateful despondency of his father's which "must have deranged his mind in the end." Why should he deny those losses today, or belittle their magnitude? Or did she think he was afraid that the truth about them and what consequences those losses still had for his own situation . . . did she, in short, think that he feared his lack of funds might change her feelings toward him? As if—the other way round—she did not know that the rumored wealth of *her* father made not the least difference to his own feelings toward *her!* "But this is not the whole story, Priscilla," he continued, breaking her sympathetic silence, "not the real story. It was not only money. Ah, there is more than money to the story of Don Julio! In reality, he fell as the victim of political intrigues. He was on the eve of his election to the Presidency. . . ." And with that Lorenzo went off into the labyrinth of the Republic's domestic history. His report bristled with the names of people and places and Army regiments and their locations. The word "Otomayo" did not appear in it once.

Only much later—in fact, not before she came to the country—had Priscilla heard this word pronounced, and learned that to Don Julio's contemporaries it meant a great deal more than the name of a river coursing down from the glaciers of the Andes and forcing its way through semi-lit thickets, swampland and rot.

The upper Otomayo valley was practically no-man's land around the turn of the century. This, so the world said afterwards, was also the reason why well-meaning people, including a number of silk-hat financiers in London, were as slow as they were in ascertaining the crimes perpetrated by the rubber barons in those forests. These were misdeeds unheard of in those days: sixty thousand Indians, men, women and children, were within ten years plowed under by the "pioneers," as the exploiters of the *hevea* region were fond of calling themselves—"slave traders," "torturers" and "hangmen," as the civilized world, shuddering at the reports which came through in the end, was to call them. For after much squirming and fencing on the part of the three Governments involved, the British had succeeded in investigating the horror. In their final opinion, their own financiers, formally affiliated with the combine, were merely "culpably negligent."

So was Don Julio, Lorenzo's father. Surely he had never participated in any atrocities, and had known of them only vaguely. A gentleman of fairly unsettled habits, he had begun one day to try for the Presidency. He had always gambled. Now he depleted his funds to fill the pockets of politicos to the left and the right. To recoup his fortunes, he jumped into the rubber adventure. When shortly thereafter the crash threatened to catch up with the barons, he journeyed to the Northwest himself. It appears that, while there, he ran into the British investigators. In any case Julio Requesens' part in the world-wide scandal became known abroad, destroyed all his political chances, and at the same time added bankruptcy to his record at home.

"He died by his own hand," Lorenzo summed up *his* report, "and his enemies, the corrupt Liberals, won the day. It was to do them no good. But it was a hard experience just the same for a child to overhear grownups refer to his father's suicide as 'the last crime of those traitors.' "

It must be admitted that the atrocious story of the Otomayo valley would have been out of place in that hour. Priscilla reclined against the tapestry hanging over the divan, one elbow resting on a pillow. It was a mild night in October. The windows of her adjoining bedroom had been opened, the door was ajar, a slight draught stirred the curtains, and Lorenzo, sitting up more stiffly, could see the chimney-studded roofs of the city thrust against the shimmering horizon. "I take it," he said after a long pause, in an undertone at once grim and engaging, "your family does not approve of our plans."

"Father is a businessman, Lorenzo," she murmured.

"*We* aren't," he said.

"No, we aren't," she echoed. She felt a great tenderness at this moment, an affection which seemed to ennoble and legitimatize her attachment to the man. "We'll manage without him, darling," she declared.

They had to. For, twenty-four hours after that talk in Priscilla's Paris apartment the man in Wall Street was blotted out from the roster of moneyed people. He had never belonged to the great ones. His cables to Pris stopped overnight. He disappeared. He was rumored to have gone to Samoa, to China, to the Congo. His daughter did not succeed in ascertaining his whereabouts when, the year after, she spent some months in the States, while her young husband was warring against El Seringuero.

He had voluntarily agreed to that extended visit with her mother. Perhaps he wanted to spare Priscilla the tedium of Army routine to which he thought he had been recalled from the Paris legation. As soon as he had discharged his duty in Murcia, he joined her in New York. Thence they had sailed to Germany. He had never, in all the subsequent years, asked about her father's affairs.

"Your husband is not an offensively selfish man by any means," his uncle had once said to her, "but—now this may or may not flatter you, Priscilla dear— I truly think that his marriage is about the only thing he has ever done without balancing first all advantages against all possible risks. Ah, love, love . . . And you know, child," Don Esteban had continued, stopping the spiral motions of both hands with which he emphasized the puissance of love, "Lorenzito still loves you very, very much. As it is, you are the only being he loves." It would

have puzzled the old man, had he been told that what Lorenzo probably loved most in his wife was the fact that she was the living proof
of the high opinion he had of himself, the living proof of his honor.

And she? What did she love in him still? The proof of her surrender,
her weakness? What did she love in him after the sixteen years of
their childless marriage during which the antagonisms growing up
between them seemed only to have strengthened their intimacy?

"Women in your country run away from their husbands very easily,
do they not?" she recalled Don Esteban asking her shortly before their
departure for Huacho, "and the queerest thing I've been told is that
they also run away without a lover. What good can it do them, I
wonder. Freedom? Happiness? How can a woman be happy, how
can she be free, when she loves no one, and no one loves her, when
she needs no one, and no one needs her?" And while he went on to
enlarge on his meaningful nonsense, his raven-black small eyes had
wandered incessantly from the little madonna in her wall niche to
the spasmodically whispering fountain of the patio.

And suddenly Doña Priscilla remembered the four-room frame
house in Evansville, Indiana, and its genteelly restricted circumstances,
and the bespectacled old lady in it, all enmeshed in the cares of that
absurd sect which she had joined—and how, during Priscilla's visit in
1942, her mother had only once or twice groped back to reality, and only
to ask, "You *are* happy, Pris, aren't you?"

Priscilla had also gone to New York on that trip and seen a couple
of schoolmates and some friends of her "newspaper days" in Paris.
Nothing much had come of that. There had been a former Berlin
correspondent just back from German internment who had told
malevolent stories about Lorenzo's "great interest in the German
Army." She had returned to the Republic and Don Esteban's place
in a spirit of homecoming.

For all Don Esteban cared, Berlin was not on the map. He ignored
what he chose to ignore. "El Huérfano?" he would say. "Who is that
'Orphan' you keep talking about, children?" He refused to give any
sign that he knew what ill wind had brought Lorenzo under his roof.
How could he do otherwise, devoted to the General as he was?

According to Don Esteban, the General was still the backbone of
the country. He would see to it that "order was restored" after "that
silly foreign war" which had "imported all those outlandish ideas."
Lorenzito was thinking the General had lost some of his popularity?

Did he mean to imply that the Army put its stock in "the present occupant of the Palace"? Who else, pray, but the General was there to rivet one's eyes on? Fafreras, perhaps, the one-time sergeant? Or the Senator from Majamarca with all his money? Or one of those derelict Liberals in Dr. Zapeta's stupid coalition Cabinet? "See? You don't know the answer yourself! Ah, you don't know your country, Lorenzito. Your place is abroad, in Europe," he would declare in another exhibition of his wilful nescience, "and that's where they are going to send you after the war. Come, tell me again how that old cock of an Anastasio broke the bank in Monte"—or whatever item of dated Parisian gossip Don Esteban would deign to take up, and whose sum total he pretended to identify with Lorenzo's Continental experiences.

Lorenzo would talk about his uncle in a rather supercilious manner. But he never made the old man's devotion to the General the butt of his remarks. He also had spared him the bad tidings of the General's illness—an incident passed over thus far by *La Libertad*—and had asked Priscilla to do likewise. He himself had received the news through an officer of the Huacho garrison by the name of León Loyarte.

This was the same man who, back in 1941, had alone been willing to "teach" El Huérfano "an old-fashioned lesson."

Priscilla assumed that her husband had left the Casa this morning to meet him. She was certain Lorenzo was intent on regaining his former status, if need be by other means than the graciousness of the Palace and "the shameful *nihil obstat* of certain foreign legations." The prospect of being sent to some obscure post abroad held small attraction for her. She wished her husband would make an attempt to go into business.

She had never brought herself to take the Republic's political life seriously. It was still as though she had been looking through the wrong end of the binoculars onto a stage where men enacted a play, pathetically unaware of the littleness, the unreality of their preoccupations. But now that picture was no longer merely the backdrop of a faraway, foreign scene, as it had been in Paris, or amidst the madness of Berlin. Now it was as though Lorenzo himself had joined that diminutive world.

"Who's there?" she asked in a startled voice. "Is that you, Isabel?"

"It's me," Lorenzo's voice came with a chuckle.

"I didn't know you were using the back entrance."

"I don't as a rule," he said, emerging through the narrow door of the rear corridor leading to the patio, and came up to kiss her hand. "I wanted to scare old Isabel in her kitchen."

Priscilla got up. Again she could see the multi-colored festoons hanging across the archways on the opposite side of the street.

Lorenzo walked to the bronze statue which occupied the right front corner of the sala, a placid-looking youthful goddess in the nude—"Liberty"—and deposited his hat at her feet.

"I see they have put candles in the windows for tonight's celebration," Doña Priscilla said. "Would you like us to have candles, too?"

"Yes, let's have candles," he said, "by all means."

V

WHILE THE PLAZA and its approaches resounded with the shouts and the din of the celebration, the General lay in his ornate bedroom, breathing his last.

Around three o'clock in the morning, a group of revelers passing by his residence saw his famous Negro butler put new tapers into the candlesticks behind the central window. "Look, the General can't get enough of the illumination," said one of the men with a snicker, and some others tried to catch the butler's attention with ironic gestures. But the old Negro did not notice the drunks through the tears streaming down his face.

The orders which managed to withhold from the public the fatal turn in the General's condition had been issued, the night before, from the Palace. With great presence of mind Dr. Zapeta had perceived the danger: the sudden news thrown into the midst of the crowds on the streets could have resulted in a panic. When the Chief Executive, then, was informed of the new hemorrhage which had stricken his Minister of War, he instructed the latter's aide—as good luck willed it, the son of a second cousin of his—to allow no one to leave the mansion, to admit no one except the attending physicians and the priest, make sure that the telephone was used by no one except the aide himself, and, for the rest, to maintain at the front of the building the appearance of joining in the festivities of the night.

This act of Presidential wisdom had worked beautifully. When Dr. Zapeta stepped out onto the floodlighted, garlanded balcony to address the throngs, their unmitigated enthusiasm proved that no one was missing the General amongst all the gold lace and plumes surrounding the sober-clad speaker. Yes, Huacho put its trust in the "non-political

39

lawyer, *el hombre de las leyes,*" who had steered the Republic through the years of the global conflict.

The obituary with which *La Libertad* paid tribute to the General in its afternoon edition the following day was prudently worded. For when it went to press, it was no longer a secret that some hand-picked young Army officers, receiving a last-minute invitation to the Palace, had been asked to remain on the premises upon the conclusion of the ceremony—a courtesy extended over the whole night and the subsequent forenoon, and in fact barely terminated when the newspaper appeared on the streets. At that time the news of the General's demise had already been bruited about for a couple of hours.

To the Casa Requesens it had come in a rather undignified manner. At noon old Isabel waddled out of her kitchen to tell Don Lorenzo that the butcher boy swore he had seen *at least* five padres leave the General's mansion.

Lorenzo was still at the breakfast table, and when the housekeeper entered the dining room, he had expected her to announce Lieutenant Loyarte (or, as she was likely to call him, if he should not divulge his name to her, "a charming young caballero"). Late yesterday afternoon Loyarte had notified the colonel that he would call on him "first thing in the morning." The delay had already puzzled Lorenzo. "We all are in the hands of God," he now said in the direction of Isabel, while the unpleasant thought crossed his mind that, with preparations for the General's funeral sure to have started at the barracks, Loyarte might have to postpone his visit.

Isabel nodded at her master in silent mourning, the tips of her small fleshy hands touching each other across her stomach. When he disappointed her by falling silent again, she shrugged, and began to clear the table. From time to time she squinted up at the colonel.

She had been a little woman of astonishingly fair complexion when Don Esteban, defying the gossip about an intimate understanding of hers with his late brother, decided to leave her in charge of the Casa. Now she was fat, unkempt, ever-perspiring. She had outlived a good-for-nothing husband and an unknown number of children. She never addressed Don Lorenzo as "señor colonel," and he even assumed that to the few people who invaded her realm she talked about him as "Lorenzito."

"And the flag?" she was asking.

Absently, the colonel's eyes rested on the nape of Isabel's neck and its profusion of rebellious short hair. He was occupied with lighting one of the thin, longish cigars to which he was partial.

"I mean . . . the flag outside, Don Lorenzo," she insisted, still bent over the table.

He recalled the proud account she had given, directly upon his arrival at the Casa, of her presence of mind some hours earlier: as soon as she noticed the flags and streamers go up on the neighboring buildings, she had "all by herself" fetched the great flag from the attic and fastened it "all by herself" to the staff extending from the façade of the second storey. "Yes, that was a very thoughtful thing to do, my dove—as I told you before . . ." Don Lorenzo said, watching the first cloud of his cigar rebound from the tablecloth.

Isabel straightened. "But it must come down now, no? With the General's passing away it would not be fitting—"

"Again very thoughtful of you. I'll get you Ramón to take the flag down tonight. You must not work so hard. The two maids you've taken on aren't much help, are they? Yes, I'll get you Ramón to take the flag down to half-mast. . . ." Ah, Ramón would be free tonight. He must be free! The colonel was determined to pack off M. Philibert this very evening. He had been much too soft in their discussion, and much too candid. Had it been wise to impress on him the delicate nature of his own situation? Would not Philibert try to approach someone else in Huacho, someone less endangered and less stripped of power? Five hundred and eleven thousand dollars, or the prospect of a share in this sum, was not a bad introduction for even so tainted a stranger. There were men in Huacho, and on fairly high levels, too, who would not necessarily call the police. Or some of them might call the police, but not necessarily to arrest M. Philibert. Away with him, then, back to Murcia! An Ulloa-bound train left at six o'clock tonight. Don Lorenzo made up his mind to go to the house in Carjavel right after his siesta, whether Loyarte came or not. "Yes," he repeated, rising, "you can rely on me, my dove, I'll get you Ramón tonight."

Isabel deserted the dishes she had meanwhile piled up on the cupboard, mumbling something about "that cripple Ramón" and, carrying the coffee pot, waited for the colonel to open the sliding door to the sala.

He patted her shoulder, and gave a last soft push to the door behind her. Then he left the dining room himself, using the door to the rear. From the six- or seven-foot passage a narrow flight of stairs led to the second floor. As a child Lorenzo had always been made to come down this way, and not to use the great staircase; there had always been men to see his father in the sala, and no one had wanted a child to intrude on their weighty whispers.

Priscilla was in the "boudoir," an oblong front room, whose furniture had survived the decades of neglect with astonishing vigor. She was kneeling in front of an opened suitcase.

"He passed away," the colonel said, walking in.

Priscilla gave a conventional little gasp. "Did your young friend come?" she inquired after a pause.

"He may be celebrating with some of his more sensible friends," he replied. "Can I help you?"

She had got to her feet. "Celebrating still?" she asked, while she was crossing over to her bedroom, a bundle of lingerie in her arms.

Don Lorenzo contemplated the cylinder of ash on his cigar. He sat down on one of the once-gilded small chairs. When Priscilla returned, he said, "No, celebrating already. Loyarte wrote plainly enough, did he not? And more than once, too. He wrote quite plainly how tired the junior ranks had grown of the 'grand old man.'"

"Do you think you'll soon know how long we are going to stay, Lorenzo?"

"It might be a fortnight, that is, the time needed to get me the command of a regiment in the provinces. It might be three or four months, in case they want to send me abroad. Or maybe we'll stay for good, and I'll do service right here in Huacho."

"So you don't think his death will make any great difference?"

He drew his brows together. "Pris, Pris," he said with an attempt to lend a humorous inflection to his moan, "you know yourself that with him alive we might have been forced to return to Uncle Esteban, and on short notice, too. Or even . . ." A wave of his hand made the ashes of his cigar drop on the floor. "With him alive we might even have been tempted to go abroad, and live as private citizens." He bent down to sweep away the ashes with his handkerchief.

"Live as private citizens—on what?"

"Ah, I was only joking, Priscillita," he said as she stepped back to her suitcase. It was one of his secret pleasures to disconcert her by allusions of that kind. What would her face look like, he asked himself, if he were to tell her they could live as private citizens, or rather as distinguished expatriates, wherever they chose? The five hundred and eleven thousand North American dollars were hidden away safely.

The country southeast of the Republic was about the best place for a cache of this sort; and the provincial banker who kept the account was an old acquaintance of his, and not likely under any circumstances to violate the secrecy in banking matters upheld in that prosperous land. "François Philibert's" chances of discovering the location of those funds would represent a search for the proverbial needle in a haystack, even should he be free to travel all over the continent. . . . Still, Don Lorenzo reflected again, he would breathe more freely with Philibert in Murcia.

"Do you think Dr. Zapeta knows you are back?" Priscilla inquired, talking over her shoulder. "Are you going to see him?"

"You mean am I going to apply for an audience?"

"Are you?"

"I do not think so."

"Yes . . . what is it?" Priscilla asked. Isabel stood in the doorway. She had not knocked, and her sandals made her steps almost inaudible despite her great weight.

"Two señores—" she began.

"Two, did you say?" Don Lorenzo broke in.

"Two youngsters," the housekeeper said surlily, "and in dress uniform, too. And now here we are with the flag still up—"

"Two? They didn't say who they were, no? Tell them . . . tell them I shall be with them shortly."

Priscilla came over to him. "Anything wrong?" she asked in English while Isabel turned to sail out of the room.

"Nothing, Pris, nothing," he said, getting up and beginning to button his jacket. The pallor of his face had yielded to a flush darkening cheeks and forehead. "Nothing, Pris," he said again, and then he suddenly asked her whether she had thought of making her compliments to the American Chargé d'Affaires one of these days.

With an astonished glance she opened her mouth. But at this moment the bells of all the churches of the town began to peal, and so she only made a curt gesture that indicated the untimeliness of his question.

Probably the two young men in the sala had originally stood at attention, facing the sliding door through which the colonel was to emerge; it stood ajar about the width of a fist. But the plangent din outside had loosened their postures. Though they still held their plumed hats stiffly under their identically crooked arms, both had inclined their heads, and turned them toward the drawn velvet curtains of the windows. Don Lorenzo observed them for a long moment before he stepped in. Their tunics seemed to be crumpled: they must have set out in haste on their errand.

"What can I do for you, señores?"

They tossed their heads. Almost simultaneously they pronounced their names. The light left their countenances shadowed. Lorenzo hoped that whatever anxiety showed on his own face would be cloaked equally well.

He motioned the two to the bamboo settee opposite Don Julio's great portrait. Perching himself on one of the armchairs beneath it, he pronounced some words of excuse about the sorry state of the surroundings. He noticed that one of the two officers, a first lieutenant, of the cavalry, was a well-nigh perfect specimen of manly beauty.

"What a pity . . ." this handsome young man said, discreetly eyeing the hall, and with a kind of hiccup fell silent. Both held their white-gloved hands crossed over the hilt of their swords. They seemed hesitant to look at Lorenzo.

But his own glance did not flinch. Seconds of a nearly unbearable tension went by, while the colonel recalled the editorial which he had read the day before to M. Philibert—and in his heart he gave more and more credit to the authorities' earnest resolve to "deal with unbidden callers," together with their native protectors and hosts. Could not these two men before him be expected to leap to their feet at any moment, and ask him to follow them to the barracks?

"What a great pity," the lieutenant repeated at last.

His companion cleared his throat.

"I beg your pardon?" Requesens asked.

"His death finds the country completely unprepared," the young captain said somberly. "Do you not think so, señor colonel? The country, not only the Army. What will be done? Who will do it?"

Don Lorenzo, as if seized by grief, covered his forehead. He nodded several times before dropping his arm. His gaze came to a rest on the bronze goddess, and he began to study her with an intensity that seemed determined to separate her shape from the gloom of the corner, so much did he fear his face might betray the magnitude of his relief. Finally he murmured, "Yes, it is a great loss for the Republic."

"A great loss for the Palace . . ." the personable officer ventured under his breath. He leaned forward, attempting to detach the colonel's interest from the statue. The tasseled hilt of his sword touched his breast.

Don Lorenzo permitted the shadow of a smile to settle under his nose. Slowly he took his dark eyes away from the poised goddess, and asked once more, "What can I do for you, señores?" An eternity seemed to have passed since he had used the same words a few minutes ago.

The officers parted their lips in what resembled a concerted action. Had the señor colonel not heard?

The colonel had not, or rather, he did not know what they were talking about. "The fiesta last night while *he* lay in his last agony," he said with distaste, "that vulgar uproar in the Plaza—"

The visitors flung up their arms. The Plaza! What did the Plaza, what did the city know of the goings-on under their noses! "What happened," the captain continued, hushing his friend, "what happened during the celebration is this . . ." He faltered for a moment, as though, on second thought, he could not believe the news had not invaded every last house in Huacho. But since Don Lorenzo, as a sign of his preparedness to listen, opened his hands, palms upward, he started talking again.

Afterwards the incident which he related became known as the "Night in the Palace." But at this juncture it deserved no such full-sounding name. As Presidential tactics go in the Republic, it was not an unheard-of move. Nor, as he proceeded, did the captain treat it as such. In fact, Don Lorenzo wondered whether he did not in reality reproach Dr. Zapeta for his show of weakness in the end.

The lieutenant, taking over now, seemed already to ridicule the gravity of their "virtual imprisonment" in the Palace. He was willing to take an oath that the "provisional agreement" arrived at in the end between the President and the group of detained Army men had been a mere face-saving spectacle. To Requesens' mind it appeared that the impending death of the General had frightened Dr. Zapeta into a frenzy of energy which was not in his real nature. Whatever his more far-reaching scheme may have been, he seemed to have dropped it.

The two officers concluded their account with a note of irresolution. "Colonel Fafreras?" inquired Don Lorenzo.

Yes, he had been there. But damned if they knew whether he had been there as a guard or as a man detained like the others. Ah, the señor colonel had no idea of the confusion reigning over the small nocturnal assembly, in and out of the President's presence. The shame, the dismal shame! Had they been asked to name a successor to the Ministry of War—actually the young gentlemen and their friends had been asked no such question—they would have hesitated to offer the right suggestion, so little collaboration existed among the discontented, so inarticulate, through long suppression, was, as the callers put it, the voice of their hearts.

" 'The discontented'?" Don Lorenzo echoed. León Loyarte had been using that term in his letters. But he had never so much as mentioned a group, a junta.

To call it a junta was premature, to be sure. The simple fact was that the conduct of military affairs had greatly annoyed the lower ranks of the officers' corps. They knew, as did everyone else in the country, that the much-lauded coalition regime depended for its existence on the General's consent. But the deal had failed to pay dividends. One had hoped for an expansion of the shamefully obsolete air force; and all the Army had received from the great northern Ally was a bare score of outmoded fighting planes, together with four arrogant instructors. It was about the same with the tank corps. The increase in the officers' pay, practically promised when the Republic "entered the war" in 1942, had never materialized. The new foreign-made uniforms had created resentment "throughout the enlightened elements of the population," for the cut of the regimentals and the color of their material "virtually made colonial troups of the divisions." Some oldsters kept harping on the "refusal" of the General to grant air bases to the "co-belligerents"—pah, it was well known that the country's geographical position did not lend itself to the purpose in question. . . .

The colonel raised his arm to halt the alternating speech of the two. Their stories tallied with some of Loyarte's complaints. "Señores," he said, "again I must ask you: what can *I* do for you?"

"For the Republic, señor colonel!" the handsome first lieutenant exclaimed, while they both stood up. Their message, he declared with constraint, was a simple one. Would the señor colonel deign to join an informal gathering of some of his comrades? Would he condescend to discuss the situation with them?

"I am not on the active list," Requesens threw in drily. He knew it was not politic to inquire after the participants in the forthcoming caucus.

The other emissary gazed down. Was this the man, his pose seemed to express, whose blighted career had become a legend among the junior officers in Huacho? "Señor colonel," he said challengingly, "on the active list or not, you are a patriot."

"That I am, friend."

The captain raised his head. "The destiny of the Republic is at stake," he said gravely, and the other confirmed him,

"No less, señor colonel."

Requesens suppressed a smile. He pitied the two youthful envoys for their evident delight in the errand. They were not aware that their ordered mode of procedure only copied a time-honored pattern, and that the higher-ups in the budding junta were prepared to denounce them as wildcat rebels, should they fail in their mission and be given away by the man they had come to win over. Their faces were shining with the glory of a rare adventure.

One after another the church bells had ceased their chant. Only the lonesome thin-sounding ring of a single bell fell into the quiet.

The beautiful first lieutenant glared at Don Lorenzo, his eyes aflame. When he began to talk again, his high-pitched voice threatened to break. *Would* the señor colonel join the meeting, he asked, the select meeting they had been talking about?

Yes, said Requesens tranquilly, he would.

VI

THE LEVEL RIBBON of the road was unfolding itself in front of Bundschuh's Ford, and was rolled up again by its hood. To the distant left the endless stockade of grass glimmered in the reddening sun. Thatched huts came into sight and slid by.

"Indefinitely, then?" Señor Bundschuh asked.

"No, no. Not really indefinitely," said M. Philibert.

Bundschuh would have liked to ask him whether Requesens intended to stay on in Huacho. But he told himself that he must stick to his pretense that Don Lorenzo and he were in close contact. He had not talked much since the car left the Ulloa station. "Something will have to be done about your friend Roy," he began after another long silence. "He has gotten much worse. Did you bring up the matter in Huacho?"

"I don't believe in complaining."

"That is very commendable," Bundschuh said airily, "but something will have to be done."

"He may recover."

"I do not think so. He is very sick." In a gestured assurance of regret Bundschuh took one hand from the wheel. He had to slow down the car to let a boy fight it out with his mule on the road. Again he realized how much hope he had pinned on Philibert's meeting with Requesens, and felt very bitter toward Don Lorenzo.

M. Philibert gave a long sigh, and reclined as the motor accelerated. His knees trembled a little, unable to accommodate themselves to the ride over the uneven road.

Bundschuh did not have the heart to voice more of his thoughts about Roy. He recalled the far from eager manner in which M. Philibert had once, and once only, suggested that he call in a physician for Roy. It had been a disgrace. A sense of loyalty, one might think, would have survived even in a man so hardened as Philibert! His callousness had really shocked Bundschuh. But then, the only physician he could have called was the doctor in Murcia—the last person he wanted to have visit the hacienda under the circumstances. He himself would rather die than consult him. The drunkard! No, this old antagonist of his could not possibly be invited to come and see Roy; it was just as well that Philibert had not pressed the suggestion.

When Bundschuh yielded to the request of Don Lorenzo, and took in the three men—soldiers, soldiers whom Don Lorenzo wanted to "spare the ignominies of a long captivity"—he had relied on the tacit good will of the alcalde, a man he had always tipped generously. The alcalde had not disappointed him thus far. Murcia people are curious as magpies. A good thing for Bundschuh that peóns are not. He was certain that his Indios, if asked about the foreigners on the hacienda, were shrugging them off as a matter of no importance. They had seen white men, busy ones and idlers, come and go, as their father and grandfathers had, and whatever the newcomers' tongue and carriage had been, the Indio had to carry his burden as he had since Inca days. The Indios, Bundschuh decided once more, were safe. Still, he had to be on his guard, and doubly so now, with the prospect of an extended stay of the strangers before him.

"Did you see Roy during my absence?" Philibert asked.

Bundschuh made a sign of negation. Philibert should have known by now that he had made it a rule not to enter their quarters. "Why not face the facts?" he said gruffly. "I'd hate to have him die at the hacienda."

Suddenly a wall of packed yellow earth seemed to cut off the road, and only when they drove close up to it did M. Philibert see the bend. Bundschuh swung round it.

He was determined to free himself of the sick man. If need should arise, the other two could always be moved out of sight in a hurry. Some of the Indians, seasonal labor, lived ten leagues and more from the hacienda; and some of their womenfolk would recall his favors and his tempers, and none, neither man nor woman, was likely to ask any questions. If need should arise, Philibert and Ehinger, able-bodied men, could find their way to one of those hidden pueblos. But Roy? . . . Señor Bundschuh lowered his head to evade the glare of the sinking sun. He said, "Yes, this I would hate—to have him die at the hacienda. You may think the Indians are pagans. They are not. They are superstitious, but they are Christians. A contradiction? I do not know. But they are Christians, and never more so than when someone has died. They would not stand for a burial without the *cura*. They would think it an outrage. I would have to inform the *cura*—"

"I can't see your trouble," M. Philibert interrupted. "First of all, Roy happens to be a Belgian. There's no law in the Republic against Belgians travelling in the country; or is there?"

Bundschuh glimpsed the indecent grin on Philibert's lips. "As I was saying," he went on, rather pointlessly, "our Indios are Christians. Perhaps you've been misled in your judgment by those curios I showed you some time ago, those curios my predecessor collected, heathen stuff all right. But first, those objects are mostly from across the border . . ." He did not finish his sentence. This was another thing which he would not do in the future: lecture to his guests on the country's customs. The less he talked to them the better. Bundschuh checked his headlight by switching them on and off several times. "I have made up my mind," he declared. "Roy will have to be taken to Casaquiara."

"The monastery?"

"I know one of the fathers well enough," Bundschuh continued, animated by the lack of protest in Philibert's voice. "I may even say I know him very well. His name is Crisóstomo. I shall go and see him."

"When?"

Instead of an answer Señor Bundschuh cleared his throat at some length. He had left the hacienda early this morning with the idea of stopping off at Casaquiara. But then he had passed by the dirt road branching off the highway about thirty miles south from Murcia, and had proceeded to Ulloa directly. It would have been senseless to talk to Crisóstomo before knowing the outcome of Philibert's interview with Requesens. However, if he was to be frank in his reflections, he had to admit that this thought had hit him only afterwards, and not in passing the crossroads. How about going to see the padre now? But it would be fairly late in the evening. And could he drive to Casaquiara with M. Philibert in his car? No, he would have to make another trip. "Casaquiara happens to be a nice place," he said, and almost at once heard Philibert's ironical snort. "Is it settled? "Bundschuh asked, "Roy's transfer? Is it settled?"

"I'll have to talk it over with Ehinger," M. Philibert answered. "Roy is more his friend than mine, poor devil."

Bundschuh would have gone on to inquire why and in what respect Ehinger was closer to Roy, had it not been for his preoccupation with another subject which he intended to discuss 'right here and now,' as he repeated in his mind. He began by mentioning the "great youth" of Ehinger, and the demands human nature made on young men. Conditions were different in men of their own age. . . . Well, then . . . would it not be "an appropriate measure" to find some girl, a woman . . . ? "Get me right. What I am thinking of is some woman who'd visit him once in a while. That can be arranged without any consequences."

"My dear Herr Bundschuh," Philibert said rudely, "there would be no need to worry about the demands of nature, no need for you, that is, if your daughter would only stop mooning after Ehinger. I don't think—I don't think," he repeated, raising his voice to drown Bundschuh's indignant remonstration, "that Ehinger is that sort of young man. Don't you want to turn on your headlights?"

"Serves me right," Bundschuh said, "it does serve me right. That is what I get for being humane! As for my stepdaughter, I advise you to look for some other butt for your foul jokes. She is an educated young woman. Mooning after Ehinger!"

"Well, I am sorry," M. Philibert mumbled unexpectedly, yet Señor Bundschuh kept growling.

Had he not made a grave mistake when, in December, he employed so much deliberate haziness in informing Juana about his visitors? Requesens was to blame! *He* had counseled him to keep in the dark, even to the girl, whatever he "might be conjecturing about those war veterans from overseas." It was not too late, though. He would talk to her. A young woman of twenty-one could be talked to reasonably.

The car traversed a wooded stretch. Bundschuh turned on his headlights. A troop of screeching monkeys scampered, and one of them got entangled in the lianas, and its anguished cries sank down to an altogether human-sounding whimper, as the car rolled by, its lights reflected by the wide-open simian eyes which suggested a pair of diminutive lanterns swaying high up in the foliage.

M. Philibert laughed out loud. Boundless contempt for his country of refuge had grown in his heart. Whatever he saw aroused his scorn. Often it was as if what he saw stopped short of his retina, dissolved in a void. Was he not being driven through a void here? That idiot of an *opéra bouffe* colonel who thought that a hankering for the pleasures of life made him so impatient, and who had dangled the image of a future filled with activity before his eyes simply to deflect what he thought to be his rapacity, an appetite for mere living. The idiot! Did he not perceive the real plight of his captive? It was not—as Bundschuh advanced in his clumsy manner—his age that kept the merest thought of women away from his mind. It was the numbing hollowness of his present existence. He had never understood that fellow Ehinger and his vigor amid their stupid surroundings. His aimless alacrity was odious to him.

The road narrowed under the onrush of the wilderness on both sides. It demanded the driver's undivided attention. In the illumination of the dashboard, Bundschuh's face looked pasty and flat. The creases in it seemed only to ape the expression of worry. M. Philibert smiled wryly. Little man! Enslaved to that *opéra bouffe* colonel by his petty pride. Absurd little man, willing to act as a procurer for Ehinger!

A bizarre coincidence had lumped Ehinger with M. Philibert. While he was waiting in St. Nazaire for his passage in the summer of '44, Ehinger and Roy had arrived there by plane with orders to proceed to the Canal Zone. No sooner, however, had the three of them been put ashore than—with Roy beginning to ail—Ehinger shelved those orders, and decided to join Philibert on his trek. Philibert could have rejected their company. But the idea of leaving the two fellows adrift with the knowledge of his presence on the continent had not appealed to him.

Of course they knew nothing of his business with Requesens. "An old friend" he would call him in their talks, "a man with the real Latin sense of honor." Not one thing concerning his past history had his two companions wheedled out of Philibert. The makeshift comradeship of common perils had not gotten the better of him. He, on the other hand, had learned a lot about Ehinger's previous assignments, and could have learned more. He did not care. Those ledgers were closed. As for the Belgian Roy, Philibert surmised that he had been cast as the brain of the Canal Zone team. They had worked together before. Now their teamwork would be over in any case.

"We will be very late," said Bundschuh, "but there is no place on the road where we could spend the night."

"We might have spent it in Ulloa."

"We might have."

"Or were you afraid I'd play some trick on you?"

They came into the open, and of a sudden the macadam was smooth again beneath the wheels. "Trick?" Bundschuh asked. "Run away, you mean to say? Why should you want to run away? Where would you go after having broken with Don Lorenzo, as you would by making any such attempt?" He gave an angry tilt to his tweed cap. Some stars were out. "I am not your jailer. I am not even your keeper."

"So we are friends—right?" Philibert said with a puzzling brutality in his voice.

"You are my guest," Bundschuh countered, "Don Lorenzo's guest and mine. And you'd better not forget that."

M. Philibert extricated a cigarette from his pocket. He had some difficulty in lighting it. "I won't," he said with closed lips. "Guests. Guests and their host. Friends. Companions. Companions in misery, as they say."

"Who?" Bundschuh asked.

The other held his cigarette away from himself with a precious gesture. Then he put it back to his lips, puffed, and said, "We share a situation we both do not like. But whether we like or detest it, it's a companionship. It is even more."

The scorn in Philibert's speech did not escape Bundschuh. A pair of companions driving through the night, unwilling to halt at any human habitation! "Accomplices" might be the next word Philibert would use. If it was complicity to give illegal refuge to the three strangers, Don Lorenzo, not he, was guilty of it. Don Lorenzo's, not his, was the fellowship with those men. He, Bundschuh, had really nothing to do with them, and was merely doing a favor to Don Lorenzo; and considering Don Lorenzo's lessened influence in the country, that service rendered to him out of fidelity was something to be proud of, not to recoil from. . . . Bundschuh shifted gears. He said to himself that his curiosity about the three men—men he had nothing to do with!—was uncalled for, was unwholesome. He thanked God that he had not given way to his desire to crush the insolent armor of Philibert, make him talk, make him confess. Or could such a man be made to talk? Ghastly stories had come out of Europe about such men as his guests.

Except for the monotonous hum of the motor, no sound broke the stillness. The voices of the woods were long behind them. Philibert drew on his cigarette steadily. The intermittent reflection of its glow in the windshield alternated with the even yellowish gleam of the headlights.

How did such men feel? Bundschuh asked himself, as if testing his own imagination.

M. Philibert tossed the end of his cigarette out of the window. He sat deeper down. His lips made a smacking sound.

Now the highway crossed the rolling country which lies halfway between Ulloa and Murcia, stretching over more than ten miles. Whenever the Ford ascended one of the gentle slopes, the gleam of its headlights waxed brighter; and as the car came closer up to the ridge, that solid brightness was mirrored by the small pane in the rear, and in a dazzling forward-reflex thrown back again onto the windshield. And each time this happened, Señor Bundschuh glanced over his shoulder to see whether a motorcar was behind him on the road, trying to overtake him. But then his Ford would enter a downhill stretch again, and its headlights cast their weakened beams on the roadway. Behind him was blackness, and the baffling sorcery was wiped off the windshield.

VII

At about the same late hour that the two men arrived at Murcia, Lorenzo Requesens, at Huacho, returned to the Casa. The muted bang of the front door, as he entered the building, called Doña Priscilla back from her slumber. She groped for matches on her bedside table, for it took her a while to remember that the electric lights had been put back into working condition. Then she turned the switch of the lamp. She listened to Lorenzo's regular steps on the staircase. He seemed to hesitate on the landing. Priscilla let a second or two pass before she answered his rap.

The low-hanging Dutch chandelier—an affair rather out of place in a lady's bedroom—hid his head and the upper part of his body. "Priscilla," he said, as he advanced across the patterned straw mats, "Pris . . . it is me! It is me they're planning to suggest to the Palace. If I want it, it's me! They urged me to accept. They did."

She had not raised her eyes when Lorenzo walked in. Now she opened the mosquito net. "Did you think they would?" she asked.

"Nothing was farther from my mind," he said, his voice still not steadied. "Not even Loyarte had breathed a word to me. He must have been totally ignorant. Or else the idea came to them on the spur of the moment."

"Perhaps he was not in their confidence," she said. A small bluish spot on the tip of Lorenzo's nose gave it the air of being slightly crooked. She knew this sign of fatigue and excitement.

"I saw your light," he muttered apologetically, as he pulled a small stuffed stool up to the foot of her bed. He crossed his legs, and clasped one knee with both hands.

She asked, "So you did accept?"

"No. Not yet," he replied in a lively tone. "But it *is* good news, no? It is a good comeback!" Where did Priscilla think, he laughed out suddenly, where did she think the junta had convened? Where did she assume they had met, of all places? She would not believe this. At the Casa Ninon! At the bordello! That establishment had always been famous for its convenient rear entrance. Besides, no man entering that place would make himself conspicuous. Did she not think that such prudence augured well for the junta's future? Lorenzo did not expect her to answer. He went on to describe the meeting at the Casa Ninon. The party had gathered in an upstairs room whose walls and ceiling were literally covered with mirrors. "It was a little silly. With all those mirrors, it looked as if the entire officers' corps were present—endless rows and innumerable clusters of gentlemen in ill-fitting mufti—while everyone knew there wasn't a single officer from out of town at the meeting."

How did he know that? He didn't know the officers' faces, did he? Loyarte had told him so. Loyarte had, so to speak, acted as his aide in the beginning. Later he was tactful enough to step back (no need to publicize their friendship!) and also was sent dowstairs for a while. For Colonel Fafreras—he virtually presided over the gathering—had made it his business to order some of the younger caballeros to the ground-floor sala and its girls, to bring to perfection the semblance of a gay party. Again Lorenzo laughed out. Then he dropped a benevolent remark about the great naïveté of "good old" Fafreras.

The age-darkened silk shade of the bedside lamp admitted only a feeble light to Priscilla's face. But her eyes shone brightly out of the shadowed net, and Lorenzo recalled his uncle's exasperatingly chivalrous contention that no one needed lights with Priscilla's eyes in a darkened room. . . . It was comforting to be reminded of Don Esteban and the poor opinion he had of Fafreras. "Showmanship!" Lorenzo said disdainfully. "I am sure Fafreras regretted he couldn't appear at the Casa Ninon in all his usual splendor—with crimson breeches, and long sword complete with tassel, and brass shoulder pieces, and medals. But at least he had his famed mustachios."

"Did I ever see his picture? I think so."

Why should he report to Priscilla how puzzled he had been to find Fafreras at the assemblage, a clique of men on the average the colonel's juniors by twenty years? "Yes, I think you must have seen his picture somewhere. . . . Fafreras! Now I know perfectly well he might aspire to the office himself," he continued a little breathlessly, "and what's more, he probably would not need any junta to get it. But, first, he has risen through the ranks, and men who have risen through the ranks are shy of the responsibilities of high posts. Fafreras as War Minister! He is said to have learned how to read only as a sergeant." It took Requesens some time to think of another motive for Fafreras' attitude in the present crisis. "You see," he finally said, "he should have had a general's stars long ago, and would have received them, too, except for the jealousy of the 'grand old man.' There you are: Fafreras was as much a victim of the General's autocracy as I was myself."

"Could you pass me a cigarette, please? I am listening. Thanks."

Lorenzo did not put his lighter back into his pocket. He asked himself how much Priscilla still recalled of the events of 1930. Had he ever mentioned to her—and if so, had she grasped—the peculiar domestic situation which had helped him then to the command of the expeditionary force? To himself there was no denying that of all the officers passed over on that occasion none had felt more deeply hurt than Fafreras. But that was fifteen years ago. He leaned over sidewise to fetch a small metal ashtray from the dressing table, and put it beside her on her blanket.

"Thanks. You say Fafreras was harmed by the General, or offended. Which means you feel that he has a bone to pick with . . . with a shadow—"

"He has to live down an embarrassing memory."

"Whichever way you put it, Lorenzo, don't you think that the most rewarding course for Fafreras would be to take the General's place himself? Instead, he's pushing you into it. To take one's vengeance on a dead man by doing a favor to a living one—"

"To the dead man's living foe and his outstanding victim!"

"Even so it remains, shall we say, a noble gesture. Also Fafreras' nobleness comes rather suddenly. I don't seem to recall that he was anything like a helpmate of yours three and a half years ago. Nor has he written you since, or sought your advice. If he did, you forgot to tell me about it."

"He didn't."

"Did Loyarte ever refer to him in one of his letters? You hardly ever mentioned the name of the colonel. His love comes rather suddenly, don't you think so?"

"No one is talking about love, Priscilla," Lorenzo said with a ring of sincere persuasion. "As they put it tonight—Fafreras and some others—it was impossible in '41 to make an issue of the injustice I suffered. The poor fellows were in no position to challenge the General without at the same time challenging the Palace. And challenging the Palace would have meant opposing its famous pan-continental politics, its understanding with the Allies. There are such situations in politics, as there are in the field. You sometimes can't shoot at a given object because of what's behind it—you cannot stop the trajectory of a missile at a chosen point. That's Fafreras' coinage, by the way. Pretty good for a former sergeant and mestizo, is it not?" He kept tossing his cigarette lighter high up and catching it in mid-air. "We took it for granted that the wrong done to me was a matter of indifference to the Army. Actually, it appears that my person was a kind of symbol to them, all the time, a symbol of their own grievances. And do not think for a moment that I threw myself on their necks. I told them . . . why, first of all I told them in plain words how I felt about them in '41, and after." With a last sweeping snap he shut his fist over the lighter as he caught it once more before pocketing it. "I won't say they have been waiting to make amends. But I will say that once such an opportunity was in sight— Aren't you listening, Priscilla?"

"When is the funeral going to be?"

"Day after tomorrow," Lorenzo said, taken aback. "But how did you know—"

"What?"

"That there is, so to speak, a catch to the funeral."

"A catch?"

"Now this will sound grim to you," Lorenzo said with a hurried smile, "but it is an old custom, or at least it has been done before. If I accept . . . you see, in that case they'll refuse to let the General be buried before the Palace confirms my nomination and makes the appointment legal. He is embalmed, though."

"They will? And his family?"

"There is no family," he replied. The vacancy of the post, he went on, as Priscilla made no further comment, had occurred at a very propitious moment. The annual two-month session of the Senate was many months off. Nor was the House of Deputies, that "spineless body," likely to be called in before much later in the year. Public opinion, the opinion of the *gente decente,* was favorable to any move displaying the disinclination of the country to have its affairs interfered with any longer by foreign legations. Lord, he did not want to examine how much or how little those legations would savor his appointment; but the mere record of their previous sentiments toward him would give his appointment the touch of malice which public opinion at this time demanded in foreign relations.

"And Dr. Zapeta?"

"Dr. Zapeta will have precious little to say," he declared, "and that is not the least of my satisfactions."

"The touch of malice?"

She misunderstood the situation, he explained. In the case of the Ministry of War the "President's choice" had always been a theoretical provision. At least it had been so ever since the General's rise. Whenever the General found it advisable to relinquish the post himself, his own nominee had been confirmed by the Palace forthwith. In other words, what the junta aimed at was only the continuation of an old, well-nigh historical prerogative. Everything would go off in the most civilized fashion—

Would Lorenzo ask for Don Esteban's advice?

"In fact," Requesens said after responding with a toneless "Eh?" to her query, "Fafreras made this clear to some hotspurs who thought they had an axe to grind with Dr. Zapeta. They made quite some ado about their 'Night in the Palace.' Fafreras called them down on the spot."

Don Lorenzo disliked the memory of the "Night in the Palace" in a very personal way. He wanted to forget the grave apprehensions which had preceded his interview with the junta's two envoys. No thought of his guests in Murcia must thwart the liberty of his decision! It was painful enough that the reminiscence of that interview—an awareness of past dangers, lingering on—had caused an attack of downheartedness on his ride to the Casa Ninon. But then, so he told himself now, a middle-aged gentleman asking the driver of his cab to turn back, only to make him go ahead in the next second again, surely was a familiar type of fare on that particular road. His failing courage had had no witness.

"Or don't you put much stock in your uncle's judgment?" Priscilla persisted.

"Do you?"

"I've always understood him—"

"And haven't always understood me—is that it?"

"I think he is a great patriot. And he loves you."

He made an amiably disparaging gesture. "He loves the picture he has painted to himself of his Lorenzito. Besides, I don't think an aged man who has been sitting it out for thirty years out East could offer much counsel."

She gave him another long look, which made him think that this was a curious wrangle indeed.

Was it not as though he had to wrest the Cabinet post from his wife? He would have welcomed some greater, blunter challenge from her. The word "Berlin," no matter how lowly whispered, would at least give some substance to her unspoken protest.

Doña Priscilla did not pronounce that word. Long gone were the days when she beseeched him to tell her what his offense in Berlin, the reason for his removal, had been. Now, the mere memory of her inquisitiveness was tedious to her. And the mental image of Berlin itself and her years there was such a bore. Stale volubility, faded trimmings, madness that had run its course! Inevitably, Lorenzo's return to the Army, let alone his entering public office, would conjure up those noisome shadows once more.

"What are you thinking about?" Lorenzo asked, irritably.

"El Huérfano."

He folded his arms. "Don't you know there are people who call him a Communist?"

"Don Esteban says that no such party exists in the Republic."

"Anyway, his attacks should do me some good in the eyes of the right people in times to come."

"They didn't last time."

"There was a war on, remember? They pampered radicals in those days."

"Is that your idea, or did they say so, Fafreras and the rest?"

"No one had the bad taste to bring up El Huérfano."

That was not quite true. The officers' party had left the Casa Ninon one by one. But after a couple of hundred steps Requesens had been overtaken by Loyarte, and for a while they had walked side by side along the deserted, ill-lit, bleak road that leads from the isolated pink-colored villa to the commercial section of the town. And on that stroll, Loyarte had mentioned El Huérfano's name, and talked about "young intellectuals" ("upper-class boys, señor colonel!") who were said to "itch after political adventure, new style." If the señor colonel should "march with the Army," and all went well, as no doubt it would, he would be well advised to give some thought to the matter. They had been passing by the low fence of a tannery when the lieutenant made that spontaneous remark—and the stench of the place seemed still to hang on to the memory of Loyarte's warning.

Priscilla's upturned face gleamed in the purple light which had crept into the room. Her eyes, sparkling through the net, did not release Lorenzo. "You're talking of bad taste," she said in a belated answer. "It is not a matter of taste. How about your own thoughts? How about your own knowledge, Lorenzo, that it would be El Huérfano against you on the one hand, and Dr. Zapeta on the other? For you know that it would be that, don't you? Is it worth it?"

"The Army will be with me," he said stiffly.

"Is it worth it?"

"How seriously do you expect me to answer that question, Pris? Do you want me to hold forth on the Latin character, on Latin man's desire to be in the game? I'm afraid that 'Latin man' has grown somewhat shopworn between us."

"You aren't fair, Lorenzo."

"I said I did not want to bring up that sort of argument."

"I asked you a straight question," Priscilla said, staring at the ceiling. In the dawn she could see its peeling paint. Right over her head, the coating had coiled into scrolls of different sizes, which at inexplicable intervals would send down a thin spray. How tired she was of being the recipient of Lorenzo's self-deceiving confidences! And yet she was conscious of the fascination which his half truth was still exerting upon her. It was as if one were scratching the rough surface of a boil, torn between repugnance, pain and a sickly enjoyment.

Lorenzo watched her crush the cigarette. He removed the ashtray. Then he turned off the lamp. "I haven't succeeded very well thus far," he said. "One step forward, half a step back, another step forward, another step back. There were failures. I have to undo them."

"How can anyone undo past failures?"

"One can. Life is a continuous undoing of the past." He paused and went over to the casement farther away from Priscilla's bed, and opened it a little. The brass handle screeched. "I can't go on living with the past on my mind day and night, and telling myself that the present is nothing but a long dash after a period."

A stream of cool air rushed into the room. Priscilla pulled her blanket up to her chin. She saw the purposely sentimental smile on Lorenzo's face, as he kissed her on the forehead.

"Ah, my dear," he exclaimed, as he turned away, suddenly throwing up his arms in a winged motion, "things here are going to look different soon. I think, Pris . . . yes, I do think we are going to stay at the Casa."

VIII

THE UPPER STRATUM of Huacho is as a rule not given to lighthearted jokes. A definite gravity tinges even its wit. It is all the more remarkable, then, that a certain anecdote, first told in the middle Thirties, had so hard a time dying. It seems (so the story went) that one Friday night some of the gentlemen of the Club Nacional, upon leaving the library, found a copy of *La Semana*—El Huérfano's weekly, published on Fridays—sticking out of each man's topcoat pocket. Each one maintained that the cloakroom attendant had played an impudent trick on them, as indeed he had by removing the paper from wherever it had been tucked away in the coats, and putting the front page up for display. The innuendo of the story was obvious: what the attendant was supposed to have aimed at was to demonstrate that the caballeros were far more interested in El Huérfano's doings than they pretended to be. Yet an attack coming from him was a minor inconvenience in the middle Thirties. Its political consequences were nil then.

Viewed from the vantage of the Club Nacional, El Huérfano's savage onslaught on Requesens in 1941 was the highlight of his career—a beacon of far-off dangers, and at the same time the source of much hilarity. To the demagogue himself that campaign had brought no profit. His followers, while admiring his prowess, likely never grasped why he had picked a man without means as his target. They knew as little about the subtleties of foreign affairs in 1941 as they did three and a half years later.

After the Republic entered the war, a certain amount of prosperity among the laborers in Huacho had thinned out the ranks of the People's Party. The truce arrived at between the two great parties had created an atmosphere of tolerance that seemed to deprive El Huérfano's voice of its echo. What scandal he mongered in *La Semana* lost its color against the backdrop of the great events overseas; for, notwithstanding its resentment of the patronizing attitude of the great Allies, public opinion took much pride in the Republic's vicarious participation in the march to victory. During the closing stage of the war, El Huérfano's printed utterances, mainly consisting of oratory about the better world to come, had been downright boring. The gentlemen at the Club Nacional paid no attention to them any more.

Requesens' elevation to Cabinet rank revived their curiosity. The appointment had stunned non-military quarters. In one of the minor cafés of the town, a group of students on an outing from Majamarca had staged a spontaneous demonstration, and had come to blows with some regulars who insisted the conduct of those immature out-of-towners only served to prove the necessity of a strong hand. But that incident remained isolated, and was passed over by *La Libertad*.

What the great journal, first of all, did to meet the new situation —which seemed to have caught its staff napping—was to complete the obituary of the defunct grand old man, whose funeral it described in the most florid language. "Giving rein to historical conjecture," it was said in that piece, "we may be allowed to wonder whether our beloved country might not have been spared the loss of its seaboard had our forces in those fateful years enjoyed the leadership of a man of the General's stature." The enumeration of the armed engagements in which, directly or indirectly, he had had a hand was brought to a climax in a laudatory sentence on "the wise plans he laid down for the Expedition of 1930"—an historical remembrance which provided the writer with a fine transition to the military achievements of the General's successor in office. Requesens' diplomatic service abroad was covered by a couple of lines.

In the face of this truncated salutation to the new Minister of War, one was well justified in looking forward with gusto to El Huérfano's say in the matter. How would he comment on Dr. Zapeta's weakness in giving in at once to a junta whose alleged control of the Army was, when all was said, at least questionable? Would he cast aspersions upon the sincerity of the President's democratic credo? Would he dig up the old slander about Requesens once more? Come forth with a frontal attack on the Army?

But the issue of El Huérfano's paper which followed the swearing-in of Requesens contained not a single word on the event. A notice reporting the visit paid to the new Minister of War by a distinguished foreigner did not even mention Don Lorenzo by name.

To be sure, this foreigner, one of the first of His Excellency's callers, was not an ordinary person by any means. The landing of his monoplane at Carjavel Airfield was a challenge. A man of El Huérfano's persuasions was bound to find fault with it. The man's name was Mauricio Hojeda. Throughout the war years he had been prevented from making that "first-hand study of the Republic's economic possibilities" he was rumored to be embarking upon at this juncture. Otherwise Hojeda had not been idle through the years of the war. From his office, which was located on the Avenida de Mayo—the famous thoroughfare of the foreign capital—the tentacles of his business had reached many a place in this hemisphere as well as across the sea. Despite the obstacles which hindered neutral trade in a war-torn world, he had emerged from the holocaust a wealthier man than ever. It was pretty foolish to credit, as El Huérfano did, a man of his far-reaching cares with a scheme to "exploit the wage-earning multitudes" of a country with pitiable communications, no coastline, no mining, and no modernized agriculture.

But that was precisely what Hojeda wanted to have assumed in Huacho. In spreading word to that effect, he counted upon the patriotic vanity of the Republic's people; and observers in the Republic, including El Huérfano, swallowed the news hook, line and sinker. Hojeda went through the right motions: he conferred with some businessmen, peeped at their charts and into their ledgers, and put in an appearance at one or another of the modest plants at Huacho's outskirts. Though giving a wide berth to the offices of the British-owned Majamarca-Huacho Railroad, he called on the president of the Northern Railway, whose financial status had always been the object of pitying shrugs among those in the know. He also made his bow to the Minister of Commerce and Industry. On the third (and last) day of his sojourn he went to see Requesens. He let it be known that they were old friends.

Actually, he had met Requesens only once. He had come upon him, at some time in the middle Thirties, at the party of an exiled Russian noblewoman residing in Berlin, whose home was famous for the beauty of its female guests. Hojeda and Requesens had been the only Latins at the fête, and soon they engaged in a serious talk, oblivious of the ladies present. They had liked each other and found they had a lot in common. But Requesens had never seen Don Mauricio again since that pleasant meeting in Berlin, or ever received a communication from the Avenida de Mayo.

It was a gratifying experience to have Hojeda seated in front of him now. Requesens had just returned from an inspection at the De la Torre barracks. The welcome there extended to him had been highly satisfactory. The "warming-up period," as he spoke of these weeks to Lieutenant Loyarte, his aide, seemed to be well under way. It was an enjoyable midday. The sun played about the iridescent panes of the iron-barred windows of the Palacio Municipal, whose ancient structure faces Government House. The Plaza's street cries rose to His Excellency's chambers, holding their own against the horns of the isolated motorcars and the clatter of horses. The continuous buzzing of that chorus imbued Don Lorenzo with a sense of well-being. Heard from his desk, the howl of the "many-headed hydra," which, in reference to Huacho's populace, Don Esteban had mentioned in his note of congratulations, sounded rather humble. Don Lorenzo was leaning back in his swivel chair. He toyed with the brass buttons of his light-colored tunic. He had ample time to take his visitor's measure.

Hojeda was a talkative person. To think of all the water that had flowed in the River Plate—or, for that matter, the River Spree—since they had that inspiring confabulation! Ha, such was life: the young attaché of that night in Berlin had been transformed into the virtual ruler of his country ("Why object, Don Lorenzo? Your lamented predecessor *was* its ruler!"), while he, Hojeda was still peddling his wares, a simple tradesman. . . . Again and again he interrupted his verbiage with fits of self-appreciative laughter. When he turned serious, his upper lip tightened and uncovered a row of almost pointed incisors beneath the red clipped mustache.

How had Don Mauricio found conditions in the Republic?

"Fair. Fair, *mi amigo*. But a man of your insight must know that this is the beginning of a crisis. A world crisis. A peace crisis, so to speak, ha, ha!" Quite evidently his cheerfulness was intended to prove a great man's detachment from the vicissitudes of all crises to come. His conversation shifted from cattle breeding to railroad tariffs, from an airplane factory he happened to own "some shares" of to the "hopeless situation of one's assets in European combines." Throughout the interview his hands remained clasped across his stomach, and from time to time he gave it a short push upward.

Lorenzo followed his words with the required modicum of attentiveness. He was wondering how much of the purpose of Hojeda's trip his colleague at the Ministry of Commerce would reveal at the forthcoming Cabinet meeting. If there was money on Hojeda's palm, that colleague was not a bad person for Señor Hojeda to talk to. He himself was resolved to be deaf to all hints of financial rewards, whatever might be up the unexpected visitor's sleeve. He did not doubt that the old profiteer had come to see him in order to enlist his assistance.

But the talk had lasted well over half an hour now, and Hojeda had not referred to any business at hand. He enlarged on the economic changes in European countries, as he thought them most likely to develop. How would all the capital "freed from war enterprise" there behave in what remained of a "sane world"? "A jigsaw puzzle, Don Lorenzo! A puzzle of sanity and madness! Beyond me, my word of honor, beyond me!" And calling each subject he touched on "too funny for words" in the next breath, he gave to his call the air of a carefree social occasion.

His initial suspicion dispelled, Don Lorenzo grew livelier. He encouraged the tycoon to assess the situation in more detail. "Do let me have your opinion, Don Mauricio," he said. "How rarely we have the pleasure of listening to a man of your varied experience."

Hojeda complied. Such empty words were well fitted to smoothing the path to his goal. The genial chitchat had removed any possibility of unpleasantness. . . .

In outlining the scheme of his trip to a friend in his own Government, Hojeda had in fact promised to refrain from anything even resembling an unpleasant intrusion. "Let me try it my own way," he had pleaded with that high official. "I have an idea how to provide you people with a foothold in Huacho. That *is* what you want, no? It is," he had forestalled a protest, "it is, it is, and I know it, *mi amigo!*"

Hojeda had good reasons for trying to ingratiate himself with his Government. His war trade had gone rather far in its impudence. At one time the administration had shown a desire to encroach on his business and single him out to prove their neutral spirit to the world abroad. Things had not come to that pass. But official quarters had displayed, ever since, some reserve toward him. Hojeda was looking for an opportunity to recoup his loss of prestige. His chance had turned up on the day the firing ceased in Europe.

On that day a letter mailed at a Spanish resort was delivered to his office on the Avenida de Mayo. Its sender was another old acquaintance of Don Mauricio's, an elderly German financier whose advice used to carry weight with his country's rulers in the days of their glory. In that letter, then, mention was made of "a certain military man in one of the smaller republics who, having served with his Berlin legation, ought to have information on certain monetary transactions carried through some time in '40." It was the prudently styled communication of a man greatly intimidated by mishap; there was something beggarly in his tone, and only in the most modest fashion did he allude to his own claim to an unnamed portion of the funds reputedly transferred.

It would have taken Hojeda much time to make a good guess among all the one-time military attachés in question, or even to ascertain their names and their whereabouts. He was about to drop the affair when the General's death in Huacho brought into focus the picture, buried for years in his mind, of Lorenzo Requesens. Instantly he recalled the colonel's withdrawal from Berlin, that "flagrant case of Anglo-Saxon intervention" which in its day had been talked about quite a bit in Hojeda's country. No sooner had he started inquiries about Requesens than the news of his appointment reached the Plate, and that information strengthened Hojeda's resolve to go to the root of the matter. But soon his willingness to assist the old financier in Spain vanished; above all, he wanted to serve his country. "Let me, at least, track the game!" he exclaimed in the face of much reluctance on the part of his Government friend.

In the course of the present conversation Hojeda succeeded only partly in "tracking the game." For he left Requesens with no bigger result than a conviction that Don Lorenzo had engaged in some shabby deal during his stay overseas; and such a purely personal feeling had no value in business.

Except for his power of persuasion, it would not have been of much worth in matters political either. What was a "conviction" based on "impressions"? It was no mean task to convey their significance to the friendly Government man, to whom Hojeda reported upon his return. "Amigo! only a blind deaf-mute would have failed to notice how fidgety Requesens got in the course of my 'audience.' Only a perfect fool would not have perceived that the reason why he did not stop balancing a silly-looking paper knife on one finger of his outstretched hand was that he wanted to avoid my eyes. I concede that these may be small symptoms. But to an experienced negotiator such signs have more value than many a long-winded speech. What, if not a guilty conscience, made him break off the 'audience' under a flimsy pretext as soon as I breathed a single word about some 'hidden German assets in this hemisphere'? What, if not an uneasy mind, prompted him to tell me, the moment I rose to go, some stupid anecdotes about an aged uncle of his—an attempt, of course, to impress me with the distinguished position of his family?

"Keep after him!" Hojeda cried out in the end. "Probe the strength of his resistance. Probe it, and you will watch him stutter and falter and break down as soon as you drop the slightest hint at what you may safely pretend to know! You people go ahead and advance whatever suggestions you see fit to advance in Huacho. Advance them through their Ministry of War. Find something Requesens would have to act upon. I am willing to wager the nineteen horses of my racing stable, *mi amigo,* that the very nature of our half knowledge will do the trick with him. What am I saying about a wager? My head . . . my head is yours if the thing does not work!" Thus closing his patriotic appeal, the great businessman put the edge of his flattened right hand against the nape of his neck, as if to express his genuine preparedness to go to the axeman's block in case of failure. His bearing lacked completely the lightness which had marked his talk with Requesens.

In the latter's mental ear, the genial tone of their conversation held its own against ensuing doubts. Don Lorenzo convinced himself that no connection could possibly exist between Hojeda and Philibert: otherwise the desperate man in Murcia would have intimated so, long ago, or else, approaching Hojeda himself, provided him with more detailed knowledge. The simple fact was that any number of caches such as Philibert's (or rather such as his, Lorenzo's) could be assumed to be in existence in this hemisphere, with Señor Hojeda merely having a finger in one of those pies. The thought of being only one among many men who controlled such holdings—the thought of being in company—appealed to Don Lorenzo. For a week he was all courage.

He enjoyed his regular morning ride with muscular awareness. Returning with Loyarte, he often chose to pass through the narrow lanes of the Old City, and would, in an ironically self-indulgent way, relish the sight of the women, dishevelled and languid, throwing open their shutters and gaping at him. Sometimes there was also a small crowd in front of Government House when he dismounted. "To see them sweeping their hats off their heads," he said to Doña Priscilla one evening, "you certainly would not think El Huérfano has much of a chance with the common people. I tell you he practically no longer exists."

One day it so happened that a thick-set elderly gentleman of distinguished appearance was about to leave the building at the moment that the ragged assemblage broke into a cheer for Requesens. Loyarte, who was still holding the reins of both horses, whispered to His Excellency that this was the Senator from Majamarca. But Don Lorenzo only saluted curtly and strode by, while his aide, after tossing the reins to the groom, stepped up to the Senator, who shook hands with him perfunctorily.

Ascending the great staircase, Don Lorenzo was thinking that his A.D.C., being an Easterner, might have some family ties in Majamarca. 'I know far too little about my young aide,' he thought to himself. 'Except for his great loyalty to myself, I know nothing about him. And what do I know about his loyalty? From where does it stem? Where does it aim?' Don Lorenzo retarded his steps. The bust of the Liberator, squarely placed on the second landing, cast its enormous shadow in his direction. He could have talked to the Senator, it occurred to him, unusual though it would have been for a Cabinet Minister to have someone introduced to him on the sidewalk. With Colonel Fafreras transferred to Majamarca as its garrison commander —Requesens prided himself on the great wisdom of that recent move— it might be good politics to impress the Senator with the sobriety of his own judgment, and show the old politician that soldiering à la Fafreras, tasseled sword and all, was not the whole function of the Army. . . . Lorenzo absently stroked his hand over the dark folds of the marble toga of the bust. He would meet the Senator anyway at the Club Nacional.

Requesens preferred the polite indifference toward his rank manifested by the members at the Club Nacional to the heel-clicking stiffness he faced at the Officers' Club. Truth to tell, he had done nothing himself to ease the respectful formality which, shortly after his assumption of office, had begun to blight the exuberant spirit of the one-week junta. "Ah, it is just as well," he would say to his wife, "just as well for them to realize that the unspeakable infidelity of '41 has not fallen into oblivion altogether. My eclipse may have been, in fact it was, a legend with the caballeros. I am not. I am not a legend. I am alive, and very much so. And I intend to prove it to myself, not to them, first of all."

This sense of "being alive" was put to the test by an occurrence of the first magnitude in the second week of June. On the Tuesday of that week, the Minister of Commerce and Industry called on him, and laid a letter on his desk. In that neatly typed communication, the Chamber of Commerce of the capital of the powerful southeastern sister republic drew the attention of the Huacho Ministry to the lifting of the wartime embargo, concluding the message with a startling phrase about "a closer interweaving of interests to be striven for henceforth" between the two countries. That was daring language, not dreamed of since the Loss of the Seaboard.

When Requesens said he failed to see the document's importance for his own department, his colleague, smiling all over his face, drew a second sheet from his pocket: a certain company down there, "specializing in the disposal of Government surplus," offered fifty brand-new four-engine airplanes for immediate sale, and, "using these channels," asked the Ministry of Commerce and Industry in Huacho to find out whether the Ministry of War might be interested in this opportunity.

It might under certain conditions, said Don Lorenzo, but under certain conditions only. The offer's connection with Hojeda was evident. It was like Hojeda to try to kill two birds with one stone! Next thing, should the offer be accepted, Hojeda would turn up in Huacho again, sit here, hands folded across his stomach, and again ask questions. . . . But on the other hand there were the eyes of Don Lorenzo's officers that seemed all the time to remind him of the Army reforms promised in his pronunciamiento, and those other eyes, the tired old men's eyes at the Club which were saying, 'Having fun, Lorenzito? . . .' It was not an easy situation, to say the least. Here, in his very reach, was the spectacular first success he had been waiting for with so much impatience; and even if the Palace should not be amenable, his attempt would become known, and that alone would be a success with the Army. But here also, lurking for him, was Mauricio Hojeda. . . .

That night Lorenzo went to see the furniture at the General's mansion which had been put up for auction, rather hastily, as was observed in some quarters. On the Friday of the following week—at a time, that is, that Requesens had still not arrived at a decision in regard to the planes offered from abroad—the purchase by him of six Oriental rugs of varying size, together with an elaborately carved French writing table and a number of knickknacks, was reported by *La Semana*. Since this brief notice concluded by stating straightfacedly that "nothing of the General's personal apparel, not even his mantle," had been "auctioned off thus far," the *gente decente* had a good laugh.

IX

THE PROMOTION OF Requesens did not stun Señor Bundschuh. It had, at least in part, been Don Lorenzo's prophecies of a comeback which persuaded him to accept the three foreigners under his roof. Nevertheless it was one thing to be in the good graces of an influential staff officer—as such he had visualized Requesens again—and another to share a delicate secret with the Minister of War. Bundschuh's innate awe of successful people made him surmise that the first thing such men were bent on was a dissociation from the less glamorous acquaintances of their past. And as if to confirm his misgiving, Requesens had not acknowledged his congratulatory note, careful as Bundschuh had been to omit any allusion to their present joint concern.

Disquiet began to beset him. There was no cause for being alarmed about the arrival in Murcia of two squads of cavalrymen from Ulloa. This was June, and June is the month of conscription in the Republic. As is the custom, the captain set up his table right on the plaza, and had the young men step forward one after another from their uneasy cluster; peacefully drawing on his long cigar, he lolled in his chair and watched the doctor's performance. At night, laughter and shouts and strumming issued from the public houses. No sign of any sinister scheming was to be seen anywhere. Yet Bundschuh was haunted by vague images of some foulness afoot against him on Requesens' order. He interrupted his working schedule, and drove to town on several consecutive mornings. There he sauntered about the market place, stood a while in the nave of the church (only to turn his back as soon as he glimpsed the cloth of the *cura*), and entered the office of the alcalde to wish him a good day.

Bundschuh's trust in that dignitary was justified. Throughout the past months he had shown no interest in what might be going on at the hacienda. Vis-à-vis his worthies he had laughed off all rumors, and once had even rebuked the doctor for some frivolous intimation about Don Adolfo's "curious employes."

Bundschuh himself was defiantly ignorant of any such gossip. First, he had told himself that anyone trying to attack him would necessarily also anger Requesens, and that Requesens would know how to ward off such assailants. But now—would not Requesens leave him in the lurch, if and when in jeopardy himself? Some of the Army men must be envying him his advancement; he soon would have critics, and enmities would not be long in encroaching upon his exalted position. But now that Bundschuh, thus alarmed, grew sensitive to the rumors in Murcia, they stopped. They stopped because one recalled some fore-knowledge Don Adolfo had often voiced of Requesens' "great future," and the feeling prevailed that the name of someone so well informed on Huacho affairs had better not be trifled with.

Thus it was in ignorance—again—of actual public sentiment that Señor Bundschuh decided to carry out the one measure foremost on his mind: to rid himself of Roy, the sick man. He summoned Philibert and Ehinger to the casa and outlined his plan. He would drive to Casaquiara, and make an attempt to induce Father Crisóstomo to come and fetch Roy himself. The padres were efficient nurses, some of them were as good as physicians. And anyway, Roy would die soon.

M. Philibert, sitting opposite Bundschuh at the table, protested. His eyes were red and sleepless. Who was telling the señor that Roy was lost? True, he had been bedridden for more than three weeks, his appetite had failed him completely, and at times he talked incoherently in his pain. But had those excruciating coughing spells not stopped? And was this not a symptom of incipient recovery? And would that recovery not be endangered by the long drive to Casaquiara?

Bundschuh waited for Philibert to say something about a doctor again. But he said nothing of the sort. When he fell silent, looking before him with a scowl, Bundschuh turned toward Ehinger, who had re-mained standing. He had plunged one hand into the pocket of his breeches, while with the other he grasped the portiere which separated the living room from the alcove and its shelves crammed with curios. Set off against the scarlet fabric of the curtain, his large bony fingers seemed very white. Bundschuh grew keenly aware of his own excite-ment: the sight of Ehinger's face, his fair beard and the strong teeth whose ferocity was at variance with the undeniable beauty of his hazel eyes, evoked in him a recurrent feeling of constriction. "And you?" he asked. "Do you share the view of your friend?"

Ehinger clicked his tongue. It sounded like an acoustic shrug.

"The trouble is," said Bundschuh, "that the doctor in Murcia is no good." And as he drew no reaction from either of the two men, he continued, "I won't have to tell much about Roy to the fathers. Probably I'll tell them nothing at all."

"About what?" Ehinger inquired.

For a second it looked as if Bundschuh might flare up. But he merely said, "We'll make arrangements for you two to be out of sight when Crisóstomo comes to get Roy."

"Did *you* agree to Herr Bundschuh's proposition?" Ehinger addressed M. Philibert. "I didn't. I think it's a wicked shame—"

"To get the proper care for a sick man?"

"To put him out of the way."

"Requesens—" M. Philibert began, but Bundschuh waved his objection aside.

"A shame, eh? And you feel the shame is mine?"

"Let us talk the matter over in peace," Philibert said, and Bundschuh saw his mouth tighten in a warped smile.

"I could give you orders," he said. "Yes, I could simply order you to have Roy ready on a certain day, at a certain hour. Don't overrate my patience. Yes, I have made it a point to treat you as guests—"

"And friends!"

Señor Bundschuh passed his hand over the yellowish expanse of his forehead, and each time his fingers reached his temples he plucked for a while at the tufts of grey hair. "It is this way," he said at last, his eyes turning toward the side window. "A man knocks on your door. It is raining and a storm's going on. So you take him in. He calls you his friend. Naturally. And as he keeps calling you his friend, you begin to feel some friendship for him yourself. Man, after all, is man's fellow. But what friendship you may feel is for the man who has knocked on your door, mind you, the poor rain-soaked devil who has been begging for shelter. The man he was before he came abegging is a stranger to you. Thinking of him, imagining him in his own world, you start wondering what business of yours he is anyhow. The longer you think of *him,* the less friendship you feel for the man you've taken out of the rain. He would be wise not to remind you of the other fellow, that man you didn't know, don't know, don't care to know. . . ."

"And what has all that to do with Roy?" Ehinger asked. He contemplated Bundschuh's fist clenched on the table. "Here we are, friends or no friends. The three of us. The four of us. That's all there is to it. Orders, did you say? Isn't it you who've been taking orders all along, if only from Requesens?"

"His Excellency and I see eye to eye in the whole matter."

"Paying you how much?"

Bundschuh had started rolling one of his cigarettes. "If insolence gives you satisfaction . . ." he mumbled, his speech blurred as with his tongue he wetted the edge of the paper.

"A match, sir?"

Startled, Bundschuh squinted up to Ehinger who with a swift swish had lit a match on the wall, stepped up to the table, and held the flame to the crooked cigarette. "Thanks," he said, inhaling the first smoke nervously.

"You see, Herr Bundschuh," the young man said, while he walked back to the portiere, "I am not very good at taking orders."

"Still I must ask you to stay. We have to settle this affair."

"To kill a man," M. Philibert said, "that always settles an affair."

"You two go on 'settling,'" Ehinger threw in before Bundschuh could open his mouth. "I for one will have another look at your Indian curios in there. Do you mind?"

Bundschuh answered mechanically that he did not, and Ehinger drew the curtain behind him.

"I said—"

"Now, let's be sensible," Bundschuh interrupted harshly, "and let us discuss the transport to Casaquiara."

The so-called guest house was situated at about eight hundred steps' distance from the gate. It was hemmed in by an aloe hedge, gigantic ferns, and crippled wild seedlings of banana plants. The trail leading away from the ramshackle door of the one-storey structure seemed to get lost in a cluster of hardwood trees after a bare hundred meters. During the incessant cloudbursts in the first weeks of the sojourn of the three men, only a makeshift pavement of bamboo had afforded a precarious communication on that pathway. They had taken turns in bringing provisions and charcoal from the storehouse, until one day Roy collapsed, and the capataz seemed to take pity on him, and sent them a burro. They no longer had it; as soon as the rains were over,

Diego, the aged criollo in charge of the stables, had come and taken it away.

It was about the burro that Philibert now began to haggle with Bundschuh. The sick man, he declared, could not possibly be brought to the gate on foot. Or, since Bundschuh wanted the other two kept out of view of the reverend father, would *he* carry Roy pickaback down to the road?

"I might," Bundschuh said, eliciting a laugh from M. Philibert.

"I don't understand you," he said on a note of regret. "You don't look like a spiteful man and haven't acted like one in these months. . . ." He turned his head toward the alcove, where Ehinger had begun to hum one of the songs of the olden days. "Why don't you want to let us have one of your jackasses? This is the least we can ask of you in the line of ordinary decency. We could ask your overseer—"

"You'll do nothing of the kind. You know that you mustn't talk to any of my men under any conditions."

"We don't. I suggested it because you may be reluctant to commit yourself. I even think it'd be enough to ask the man at the stable."

Bundschuh shook his head slowly, like a man confronted with an insurmountable obstacle, or a child who feels something blocking a natural reaction without knowing the source of his inhibition. Commit himself! He *had* committed himself. . . . But he had nothing to fear from Miguel, the overseer. A middle-aged half-breed with reportedly some Negro blood in his veins, he was as taciturn and sober a man as ever had earned his bread in these parts; in fact, his tight-lipped disposition was not the least of his merits, for his monosyllabic commands cowed the laziest Indio into doing his work.

He had made his appearance shortly after the wedding of Don Adolfo. Miguel had come from nowhere, as it were—haggard and solemn, wearing a jacket and a hat both of tanned leather, and riding a nag so tall and skinny and docile everybody roared with laughter—and had applied for the position vacated by the unwillingness of the man who had served the widowed patrona to serve her new husband. Considering the disdainful attitude toward him on the part of qualified men in the neighborhood, Señor Bundschuh must have regarded the newcomer as a godsend. Miguel had, from the beginning, employed a keen sense of propriety in introducing the photographer to the manifold duties of a patrón. He also had taught Don Adolfo the use of the whip, and how not to use it. Miguel's industry had deserved praise most of the time. But praise was likely to falter in front of the great satisfaction his own vanity seemed to give him; he had the bearing of someone who has proved his worth to himself and can forego proving it to others. Little had ever become known of Miguel's life story. Whatever his age was, it sat lightly on him. His crisp hair, though receding by now, had barely greyed in the years. He was a miser, and it was bruited about that he had money hidden away in his hut, which no one was allowed to enter. He was never seen in church. On Saturday nights he would ride to town, and treat himself to a glass or two of Chilean wine. He did not consort with women, and discouraged any forwardness.

And Diego? With all his eccentricities, the old stableman, a relic of the days of Bundschuh's predecessor, was about the most reliable man on the hacienda. If nothing else, his devotion to Juana should prevent him from engaging in gossip harmful to the place.

"It's not that I don't want to be helpful," Bundschuh said after a long period of silence, puffing out his cheeks in a kind of adolescent embarrassment. "I just feel that you're making conditions, and it isn't up to you to do so." He cast a blank look at Ehinger who came out from behind the red portiere.

Nonchalantly, Ehinger raised his brows in a mute query, and as M. Philibert, glancing from his companion to Bundschuh and back again, uttered a sigh of exasperation, the young man said, "Is it that hard to kill a man—a sick man?"

"Surely you know I do not want to kill him," Bundschuh objected with restraint. The flurry of sympathy he had just felt for Philibert was gone. And so was the image of a dead man's body athwart a burro—that far-fetched poignant snatch of remembrance which, for a torturing while, had impaired the control of his reflections. Ah, these criminals here knew how to work havoc with his nerves! His cigarette had gone out, but its end still dangled between thumb and index finger, slightly shaking.

"Herr Bundschuh will give the whole business another good thought," he heard Philibert suggest. "He is aware of his responsibilities. Roy, after all, is his ward."

"Yes, come to think of it, you're Roy's guardian, ha, ha!"

Bundschuh sat bolt upright. He raised his right arm and kept it aloft for a while, as though someone had said that he was drunk and

he volunteered to prove he was not. "I shall not debase myself to the
level of your jokes. No. I warn you. I gave my orders. If you are as
clever as you pretend to be, you'll comply with them. Burro or no
burro."

"Palaver over, patrón?"

"Palaver over," Philibert answered Ehinger, since Bundschuh added
no other word.

His short arms lay in front of him on the polished top of the table.
He eyed his reddened, perspiring hands with a distaste meant for his
weakness in front of the two men, who filed out, deaf to the hiss of
protest behind them.

His only comfort in that hour was that Juana appeared to have lost
her interest in his guests. Upon his return from Ulloa, she seemed to
have taken for granted at once that Philibert had failed in Huacho.
And Bundschuh had again postponed the talk with her which had
been on his mind during his ride. The less said the better. The less
said to the girl about any affair, the better.

Measured by non-Latin standards, Juana's days were monotonous.
A hacienda is not a woman's business. But neither did Juana really
rule over the household of her stepfather. She spent the mornings
supervising the work done by a couple of rather incompetent servant
girls, and only seldom entered the cookhouse. At times, she went to
see some of the Indio women, and Bundschuh did not mind it. The
main occupation of her afternoons was her horses.

Her schedule had hardly altered with the years. Except for her
charitable attitude toward the helpers' women, her way of life had not
changed since her homecoming from the boarding school in Majamarca.
Señor Bundschuh kept telling himself she ought to get married. But
she had few acquaintances in Murcia. Her mother, a native of the
East, had not joined in the social activities of the upper crust of the
town; and Bundschuh's own aloof habits had not improved her relations with Murcia people. Besides the *cura,* some storekeepers and one
of the local seamstresses were about the only persons Juana spoke to
on her visits to town. One of the more constructive thoughts which,
among many depressing ones, had struck Bundschuh, after learning
of Requesens' elevation, was the idea of offering his stepdaughter as
a kind of lady's companion to the yanqui-born wife of Don Lorenzo.
Considering their different stations in life—as in a spurt of equalitarian
sentiment for Requesens he had neglected to do—that was a downright

foolhardy notion, and nothing would come of it, he knew.

Nothing ever came of well-laid plans. Life had its own wilful growth. To expect it to meet a man's plans was like trying to compel parallels to meet in the finite. "Parallels meet in infinity. . . ." Bundschuh smiled wryly: the memory of this axiom had come to him from very far-off. It had come to him from his service days in the Kaiser's Navy.

X

ROY WAS SLEEPING under the effect of the drug which Ehinger, before sunrise, had forced on him. In his sleep the sick man had clutched the poncho right up to his chin. His legs were bare. One of his knees was bent, the foot propped up against the mattress. The sinews standing out from the hollow of the bent-up knee vibrated under the skin in a hardly perceptible quiver, their edges thin as the blade of a knife. For a long minute this small pulsating muscle of the bent-up knee was, to Ehinger, the only symptom of life in the benumbed body. He did not look into Roy's face.

Standing at the threshold, he had placed his foot to keep the door open a few inches. With his fingers he covered its rusty upper hinge to stifle its noise. Against his raised palm he felt the intermittent pull of the draught, which was stirring the half-loosened screen in front of the window. Ehinger was waiting for a sound to issue from Roy's throat. It was eleven o'clock in the morning, and the reverend father from Casaquiara would be here after the midday meal. Philibert, "disgusted with nursing," had left for a walk.

Ehinger's eyes wandered sidewise and down to Roy's face. A fat fly with opalescent wings had alighted on his scrubby chin. His mouth twitched, and his fists opened and closed and opened again in a feeble attempt to chase away the insect. The sun, high up in the sky, touched the foot of the bed, and the shaft of glaring light seemed to deepen the shadows about it.

This would be the kind of hour, Ehinger reflected—this would be an hour indeed for the iterative voice of the priest to search the mind of the sick man. Bending ever deeper down over him to call him back from his narcotic slumber, the monk would patiently bide his time to reach the sensorium of his victim. He would stand at the bedside, towering over the head of the sinner, the crucifix in his outstretched hand, the censer beside him. . . . Ehinger, reared in the Lutheran faith, harbored exaggerated concepts about the power and cunning of Catholic clerics. They were supposed to keep the secret of the confessional; but surely Roy could no longer distinguish between confession and mere talk, and the priest would trick him into talking. Philibert seemed to think little of this danger. But, then, Philibert—had he really been a general in the old days?—had his room in the rear of the house, and to mute the groans of the sick man had even put up a matting on his door. *He* did not hear Roy's delirious utterances which ascended from a recollection so abundant in images that Ehinger, forced to listen to them, had sometimes at night felt like getting up, grabbing the coarse blanket, and muffling Roy's soliloquies till they subsided in an impotent rattle.

Ehinger fingered the earthen vial in his pocket. Its glaze felt smooth and cool. A handy shape it had. . . . It was shortly after their arrival at the hacienda, and one was exchanging civilities still, that Bundschuh had told them of the North American collector who, some years previously, had offered him a substantial sum for "these pieces of pottery." Pointing out the varishaped receptacles on the shelf—some of them, crudely sealed, were "sure to contain poison still"—he had proceeded to explain that Indians on the level of archers and hunters were as a rule not acquainted with the art of pottery, and "hence the great offer." Ehinger recalled with a sneer Bundschuh's pride in his "museum"—the miniature idols, the cords and woolens, the bright-colored featherwork and the patterned leather, and the bows and arrows and axes. Legally, "all those treasures" belonged to his stepdaughter, Bundschuh had added that night, and Ehinger remembered that he had leaned down to Philibert's ear and had murmured, "Her dowry, no doubt." Funny, wasn't it?

Ehinger's glance, as though absorbed by his recollection, must have been going astray for some time. For when Roy's eyes met his own now—the eyes alone out of his immobile face had shifted in Ehinger's direction—it seemed to him that they had opened several seconds before, and been resting on him. As if caught, he wiped off his grin, and hurriedly shut the door.

No, he would rather not speak to Roy at this moment. With the drug lifting its spell, his mind might begin to clear up again before it submerged once more in the pit of pain. Ehinger had come to abhor the meandering ways of Roy's twilight thinking. At times what he said made no sense at all; at others there was in his words a minute conciseness.

Then, the old days were still in Roy's mind. He would report on "today's rat-catcher's record" to someone not present, obscenely lower his voice and with snickers and winkings describe the "job" he had done "according to orders." Such detailed reporting had never been done in the reality of the old days. This departure from custom, together with the stiff, crude German he used in addressing the specters appeared to flow from a long-suppressed lust to mock them. And that mockery seemed to include Roy's own business in the old days, thus scoffing at death itself and the devil.

There was no way of talking to Philibert about that abomination. He was "not curious." His guess was that a cancerous condition was eating at Roy's brain. It was one of the symptoms of lunacy, he volunteered, that images of no perceptibly greater importance than others remained on the surface of the consciousness, "as grains no bigger than others sometimes stay on this side of a sieve no matter how hard you shake it." But, so he also said, who knew whether the state in which "poor dear Roy" was living had not its own yardstick of importance . . . and broke out in a laugh, gloating over the vexed expression of his companion. Indeed, no help would be forthcoming from Philibert. He, Ehinger, had to attend to his chore by himself.

There was no sound behind the deal planks of the sickroom. Midday stillness reigned over the hacienda. The clatter of a solitary horse could be heard in the distance, nearing and withdrawing again. It was a very warm day. The simmering heat lingered upon the windowless hallway. Ehinger rotated the poison-flask in his hand. Its colors shone in the shadow.

The liquid was said to take from six to eight hours to destroy a man. That knowledge, too, Ehinger owed to Bundschuh. The hypodermic out of Roy's kit was at hand. He would die, then, on the road to Casaquiara, or shortly after arriving at the monastery, and the fathers would bury the "Belgian adventurer who had come to the Republic to make his fortune." Ehinger could have called what he set about doing a mercy killing. The term was not foreign to him. Yet the sobriety into which he had argued himself did not allow of such fancy notions.

He crossed from the hall to Philibert's quarters, closing the door behind him. He took some papers from the stack near Philibert's trestle bed, and stepped into the small niche adjoining the room. He knelt down in front of the brazier and started to rekindle the charcoal.

A burro outside was braying. Ehinger stopped, and listened to make sure no one was near the building.

When he and Philibert left the casa yesterday after their talk with Bundschuh, that man Miguel had stood near the gate glaring at them with open hatred. Perhaps the overseer feared what he thought were to be his competitors sooner or later—agricultural experts, ha, ha. . . .

But this joke afforded Ehinger no amusement. Now, he picked up a piece of corrugated iron to fan the fire still only glimmering up from the embers. At last the flames leaped up. Ehinger put the kettle on. He got up from his knees, and went back to the hallway on tiptoe.

It sounded as if Roy were muttering something, in French.

"Want anything?" Ehinger asked, opening the door. Peering over to Roy, he saw that he had not moved. He did not seem to suffer. "One is going to give you a nice little shot," Ehinger said, approaching the cot. "Do you hear me? A nice little injection. So you won't have any of those bad headaches today."

"Hein?"

"Now, now, now, no need for getting upset," Ehinger said, slowly clicking his tongue. He had not planned to inform Roy at once of his intention. Nor was Roy likely to grasp what he said. But inarticulately Ehinger felt that, once pronounced, his words would fix in himself his perhaps still wavering aim. He gazed down at the horizontal man . . . and for a second or two he was aware, as he always had been in front of prostrate people, of the limitless power man, if he so wills, has over man.

Eyes wide open, Roy appeared not to see him. "Ebenauer . . ." he suddenly called with accentuated clarity.

"Yes, it's me," Ehinger whispered. "Ebenauer, the old comrade of Roubiliac—"

"Présent!" Roy cried out, jerking his shoulder on the pillow.

"You'll be all right again, my good old Roubiliac. We two aren't made for being sick, eh?"

"I wouldn't be sick, if those damned doctors—"

"Yes, yes, doctors are no good."

"Operating on me, those fools!"

Ehinger repeated that doctors were no good.

"Stupid experiments . . ."

"Yes, stupid, Roubiliac."

Roy licked his lips. "Doctors want to see what makes me tick, what? Take off brain-pan—"

"Now be sensible, Roubiliac. You are much, much better."

"Naturally, I am better," Roy declared with conviction. "I was not sick, to begin with. Only those experiments, you know. Twenty men, sir, for experiments, sir. What makes man tick? Can you find it out, sir? I bet you can. I bet." The smirk which distorted Roy's face, as he lowered his lids in a travesty of reassurance, suggested a ham actor playing a villain's part.

Ehinger held his breath to keep off the offensive odor. He had taken Roy's trousers up from a pile of clothing on the floor, and overcoming a spell of nausea, flattened the bent-up knee of the sick man. With a gentle shove he lifted his legs. There was a corpse-like heaviness in the emaciated body. Roy kept mumbling, but Ehinger did not answer the nonsense his lips produced. He put the soiled trousers on Roy, whose torso scarcely stirred.

Roy's fingers held fast to the poncho, as if the warmth of the stale air had not been reaching his lungs. "Injection . . . ," he said, his lips almost motionless.

"Yes. Sure. Sure, Roubiliac. A good, nice, soothing injection. A little shot." Ehinger bent down to pick up the striped blanket that Roy had suddenly released in a renewed spasm of pain. But he stopped his arm in mid-career with a derisive gesture, which fortified him immensely. Roy's mentioning the injection made him once more note the whimsical nature of his insanity: it closed his consciousness to a word when it struck his ears, and after minutes and minutes carried it to his brain. And that phenomenon irritated the murderer to the point of cold hatred.

Back in Philibert's room again, Ehinger opened the small oblong metal box containing the hypodermic, and dropped it into the boiling water. He was aware of the superfluousness of this effort. Still he went about the job with meticulous care. The picture of himself disinfecting the deadly instrument had seized his imagination at the very moment that he had stolen the vial, and had protected him ever since from visualizing the action which was to follow. Cautiously he scooped the hypodermic out of the kettle. Then he removed the kettle, and with a handful of dirt scraped from the earthen floor of the niche smothered the flames in the brazier. The embers gasped with a faint hiss.

He pulled the gay-colored flask out of his pocket. He pressed it hard down on the top of the small makeshift table against the wall, and cracked the neck, deadening the noise with a rag. He had calculated the stroke well. In his ignorance he had expected the liquid to exhale a malodorous smell, and he dared not breathe for a second or two. As the glass tube of the hypodermic sucked it up into its hollow, the poison looked greenish and slimy. "Now then," he repeated over and over again to drown the hoarse sounds which emanated from behind the partition. He wrapped the broken vial, and tucked it into his trouser pocket. "Now then!" he said lustily, entering the sickroom.

Roy had pulled himself up to a half-raised position squarely across the cot. He had not succeeded in reaching the edge of the bed with his knees. His calves and bare feet stuck out from the mattress horizontally. He was trembling all over.

"Now then, what *is* the matter, my boy?" Ehinger said, in spite of himself retaining the nursery tone. "*Alors, mon vieux,*" he added in his guttural French, "*promenade, eh?*"

The doomed man lifted his bloodshot, yellowish eyes. His expression was marked by a paroxysm of fury. "*En avant!*" he shouted amidst a blast of unintelligible words, "*en avant!* Why don't you open the shutters, you silly Dutch whore?" An impenetrable fog engulfed both his mind and his vision.

The murderer felt a faintness creep up from his arms through his every fibre, and pass off in a flush of perspiration. He wondered whether, chiming in with Roy's hallucinations, he should not tell him this was late at night, sleeping time.

But Roy no longer commanded a single rational thought. His frothing lips ejaculated lewd words like spittle, his voice now mounting to animal shrieks, now falling down to a child-like murmur.

With one single jump Ehinger was near him. Standing in front and over him, he pressed his left hand against the breast of the madman. His icy fingers registered the astounding strength of resistance. "Now then, now then," he repeated. His teeth were tightly set. He had relinquished any pretense to persuasion. No mercy was in his resolve. And suddenly he felt in his own body the excitement of his mounting desire to reach the releasing climax. . . . Afterwards he asked himself why he had not freed his right hand from the instrument, and grabbed the raving man with all ten of his fingers instead of lifting his own left knee and squeezing it against Roy's stomach. For that was what he did before, with a vicious dig, he jabbed the needle into the flesh.

The twinge quieted Roy instantly. He panted, his knees hunched up. His arms, fingers stiffly spread, were fluttering in a pathetic attempt to fend off the fiend sprung at him out of the darkness.

Ehinger withdrew from the wretched body. He could not recall where the hypodermic had struck. Roy's breathing was changing now to a calmer rhythm. The eyes in the waxen face closed.

Ehinger turned. He did not waste another glance at his old comrade. He went to fetch a piece of cloth from Roy's haversack. He wound it round the broken flask and the hypodermic, and put the bundle into his pocket. As he unbolted the entrance door, an edge of low laughter joined the crazy voice audible again from behind Roy's partition. A rectangle of sunlight invaded the hallway. Ehinger crossed the shimmering space, and walked out of the house.

A horse neighed.

Only when he took another step forward did Ehinger see the girl. She had halted at about thirty meters from the house on the pathway, and her mount was nibbling at the heavy leaves of a great tree. Juana's head was thrown back. She seemed to scan the sky in which a pair of big birds drew sleepy circles.

Ehinger was about to turn away, when suddenly he felt the bundle in his pocket get loose, and in the next breath he heard the crack of the flask on the ground. In wrestling with his victim he had, without noticing it, torn one leg of his trousers. He bent down to collect the vial's fragments, and then hastily went back into the house, into Philibert's room.

When he left the guest house half an hour later, the girl was no longer on the path.

Father Crisóstomo arrived in time. From behind the aloe hedge Ehinger and Philibert watched Bundschuh and the squat, black-browed, astoundingly vulgar-looking lay brother bundle Roy, nearly lifeless, up to the burro, and disappear with the cargo among the foliage.

"Keep still, will you?" M. Philibert said, annoyed by Ehinger's continuous snickers. "It's an honest catch-as-catch-can with a Christian soul."

Ehinger stopped his muffled laughs. Neither of them moved for a long time. For the hundredth time the girl came back to Ehinger's mind. It was not likely that she had recognized the source of the thud on the gravel. But she must have heard it. She had lowered her head and shifted it in an oddly delayed, almost fearful motion. And lifting his eyes while he collected the pieces of the vial, he had believed that he could see, across the intervening space, her face turn stony with embarrassment and consternation.

XI

Juana had noticed the disappearance of the vial from the "museum" at once, and had been tempted to point out to Bundschuh the empty space on the shelf. But what she divined choked her voice each time she opened her mouth. From the beginning she was aware of Ehinger's intent. She knew that the bedridden man in the guest house—she had never talked to him, and possessed only a hazy recollection of his constricted face—was desperately sick, perhaps approaching his last extremity. Stories about men killing a friend to spare him the ultimate agony were not entirely unknown to her.

There is, in those parts, a song, a *triste* about such a stouthearted fellow. Tears roll down his cheeks as he stands over his comrade struck, in the rubber forest, by a poisoned arrow. And suddenly the desperate man feels the knife astir in his sash. And the blade starts to talk. "Many a foe have I put to sleep," whispers the knife, and then entreatingly argues with its master that by killing his friend he would in reality get the better of Death, "the great foe of all." And whenever a singer reached the last stanza of that song ("And he raised the friend's head and slashed his throat, while his own lips were moving in prayer. . . ."), he would evoke a loud twang from his guitar before putting his flattened palm across the strings to deaden their tones.

Now a song is a song, and life, as Juana knew, is a different matter. Yet whenever in the hours following the theft of the poison flask she thought of Ehinger and his likely purpose—and how little else did she think of!—the face of the *triste's* hero invaded her imagination. This face bore Ehinger's features. The shadow of great sufferings lay over them—but also their light: the power of a man who, cast out by the unthinking world, had arrived at his own law, and faced sin with no man-made code between it and himself.

Before the three foreigners came to the hacienda, her stepfather had told Juana of their respective Swiss and French and Belgian passports, of Colonel Requesens' acquaintance with them, and that it was about time some new men were "put to work on the old place." A little later he had dropped a word about their "military training," their "soldierly discipline" both of which should make them "easy people to have around." And since, somewhat later again, he had warned Juana to talk about them as little as was "advisable," her surmises had come fairly close to the truth, as she saw it. Beaten Army men from abroad, fugitives, refugees shunned and whispered about! Had not her own father been a soldier himself overseas once? Had not her mother told her how, after his country's defeat, he had come to this hemisphere in search of a new world? Yet had there not been, in the "museum," such objects as a cross-shaped medal of iron, a spiked helmet, and an officer's sword—objects long removed, to be sure, but still reminding her that her father had not been ashamed of the war he had fought and the defeat he had suffered?

Curtly and without any sign of extraordinary emotion, Bundschuh had informed Juana of his impending journey to Casaquiara and his "humanitarian project." For twenty-four hours she was alone. Once she was on the verge of going to the guest house to ask Ehinger a blunt question. But she could not picture herself talking to him about crime or sin, or about lawless daring and a superhuman mercy that may look like sin to heedless judges.

Upon his return, the past night, Bundschuh had said little about the padre's reaction to his "project." This morning, however, he had seen to it that Juana's favorite horse was saddled before the hour Father Crisóstomo was to arrive. This was the only subterfuge he employed to keep her away from the casa and the road.

She had understood Don Adolfo. She did not mind complying with his wish. She had meant to take her habitual ride over the grassy land eastwards. But she had made an aimless detour. And suddenly she had found herself on the pathway to the guest house. . . .

After she had watched Ehinger step out of the building—and he, as she noted, had seen her—Juana rode back again, as if resuming her routine must help her regain authority over her senses. Under her fingers she felt the playful, affectionate pull of her mount. There was no need for watching the road. She knew every inch of it. It had been her father's favorite ride. She believed she still recalled the gleam in his eyes, when, riding by his side on her first pony, she would catch a glimpse of his fair-bearded profile.

In truth, that memory was alive in Juana only through the accounts of her mother. Bewilderment and an echo of old disapproval had been in her mother's voice whenever she told Juana about those rides and about her husband's inscrutable passion for the untouched land. The woman who subsequently, out of attachment to this place, had stooped to marry a photographer of rather questionable antecedents had never grasped the core of that passion. Nor, until this day, had his daughter understood this enchantment—the infatuation of Northern man with boundless, mute space. She had never attempted to reason it out; and it was not reasoning which now gave her the sense of that fascination.

For many a day and night she had struggled against the remembrance of Ehinger marching into the nothingness of the untilled land. It had happened weeks before he stole the poison. His whiskered chin thrust forward as if listening, he marched straight ahead, and did not turn his head when she rode by him. Did he, or did he not, resemble her father? Should not Diego, her father's man, have been the first to notice any such likeness? But Diego, cantering beside her, had jerked his head in the opposite direction, pretending he must loosen the sombrero cord round his chin. He had refused to see the obvious; perhaps he had thwarted her query to warn her that a man of his modest station had better not be asked about such a one. . . .

All that came back to Juana now. The mental image she held of her father was about as faded as the small sepia-colored photograph of him in the "museum." But faded as it was, it had—weeks ago—relieved her of a great dread. It had persuaded her that what seduced her attention was a mere freak of nature. Now, in this hour, that counterfeit of a revered image assumed authenticity! All her life Juana had been wont to connect whatever was daring and noble with the memory of her father. What she assumed the young foreign soldier in the guest house had done seemed to establish a link between him and her father far beyond all physical likeness. . . . It was an altogether perturbing experience. Her father and the hero of the *triste* and Ehinger threatened to dissolve into one picture, and it was shining brighter with every second her mind beheld it. Juana was not unaware of the childish fancy behind it. Yet its very waywardness endeared it to her. She was ready to hold fast to whatever suited the strange emotion which, late enough, had entered her life.

She was riding in an easy gallop. The level country was behind her. Before her rose a cluster of cuca bushes. Her mare fell into a trot again. Berries came down in little showers, as the horse brushed against the straight branches. At one bend she saw a group of children raking leaves. The luster of their naked bodies was lost in the verdure when she came nearer.

Suddenly it occurred to Juana that the "museum" was hers by right. The earthen flask with the poison, then, was hers! Was it not as if she had given it herself to Ehinger as a present? Would she not have given it to him, had he asked her?

She did not know how much time had gone by when she dismounted in front of the stable. Diego, busying himself with his charges in their boxes, was silent. He did not look at Juana, while he unsaddled her horse, and kept patting its neck until she left.

No sound was to be heard as she walked along the road to the casa. She could not see the guest house from anywhere on this road, hidden as it was by rank vegetation.

She entered the casa from the rear. No midday meal was prepared. The living room had not been done. Apparently Bundschuh had sent the servant girls away.

A high-wheeled motorcar stood on the road. From the front window Juana saw, above the wall, only the folded canvas top of the car and Father Crisóstomo's profile. He stared toward the gate. He did not seem to notice her. Even when she threw open the casement, his great head did not move. Why had he not gone to the guest house? Or had he already been there, and discovered what had happened? . . . Juana stood holding her breath.

So slowly did Father Crisóstomo rise from his seat, she realized that he had only when he stretched to his full height. His eyes still bypassed the casa. He turned his head toward the gate and the grounds beyond it. After a short while he began to wave his arms, their increasingly vehement motion spreading the wide sleeves of his habit. "Take him down," he cried out, "take him down. . . ." Who was the padre shouting at? . . . Juana heard the wild screeches issuing from somewhere behind and to the right of the casa. She had heard them earlier, to be sure, but had thought them to be the yells of an excited old monkey. Now she was sensing the truth. She rushed over to the side window and drew back the curtain.

On the overgrown pathway, Bundschuh had come out from the foliage. . . . And while the inhuman savage shrieks assaulted the girl's ears, she discerned among the dark leaves the reins at which Don Adolfo was pulling, and with them, the big yellow teeth of the burro and—a split second later—the whole of its head. The sick man was sprawled across the animal's back, his arms furiously beating its flanks and its neck. . . . It was an obscene spectacle. But what struck Juana with horror and an unfathomable feeling of complicity was her realization that Roy was alive . . . no, was half-dead, in the throes of ferocious pains.

Bundschuh's exertions had brought the unwilling mount a few steps forward. He seemed to be halting to take a breath. But at this moment, the rebellious spirit of the pitiful rider transferred itself, in a flash, to the burro: with a braying which drowned the shouts, hoarsened now, of the sick man, the animal planted its forelegs against the ground, and then, kicking and tossing its head like a blooded stallion, threw its human burden into the air. Juana saw a pair of arms catch the falling figure: a squat man in monk's clothing—tripping over his cassock, he had stumbled into her field of vision—held Roy in his arms, preparing to push him back onto the burro, that all of a sudden stood meekly.

In fact, had it not been for this sturdy Indian lay brother—he had marched all the while at the tail end of the sorry troop—the whole of Bundschuh's plan might well have come to naught. The man must now have heard Father Crisóstomo's reiterated command. He gripped the human wreck, lifted it with the support of his stomach, as one lifts an unwieldy bundle, and carried it off, taking large strides, toward the gate.

"The doing of your stepfather, señorita," a voice said, and Juana did not glance behind her, for it was immaterial whether it was Ehinger who talked, or the image of him in her mind. "Yes," he went on with a short laugh, "this is Señor Bundschuh's doing."

"How did you come to the house?"

"Through the bush. There is a way. A man can make himself a way."

The insolence of his speech, tense and breathless at once, stoked a flame in the girl.

"Surely you do not think, señorita, that I wanted to miss this. To miss a good view of what Bundschuh is doing."

"He has his reasons," she said, half against her will. The animal's braying had died down, as had the shrieks of the sick man.

"Loyal to him, are you not, señorita?" the young foreign soldier said in his awkwardly correct Spanish. "Reasons! Bundschuh knows that no one will call him to account. If a man knows no one will call him to account, that is reason enough for doing what he wants to be done. Wants to be done, I say . . ."

The lay brother carrying Roy was approaching the gate, Bundschuh with the burro behind him. The scarlet poncho that had served as a saddle had slid down in the struggle, and caught by a thorn bush, was softly swaying in the wind which had sprung up. Juana forced herself to stare at this fluttering speck of color. She stared at it with wide-open eyes, fixedly.

"Did you understand me, señorita? Do you understand your step-father? You should. You should for your own sake."

Outside, a layer of mist descended from a suddenly overcast sky. Slowly the girl turned round. "What did you do with it?" she asked in a strained whisper. "What did you do with the flask you took away from in there? What did you do with it?"

Ehinger's eyes did not recoil. This was the question he had expected. This was the matter that had driven him here.

"So you know?" he countered, calmly. "What I did with it? Just that. It takes time, though."

They both cocked their heads toward the front window: the car had started, and they watched in silence as Father Crisóstomo drove off in the direction of the gate.

"It takes time . . ." she echoed in an uncertain tone, which abruptly rose to an outcry, "but you—you should not be here!"

"Is it so dangerous that I am here? Good. Your stepfather will come. Maybe he will bring the priest here, if they decide not to drive on at once. For a glass of brandy, maybe. Now if the priest is with him, the patrón will be nice, I think. 'This, reverend, is my new agricultural expert, a man from faraway Switzerland,' he will say, boil as he may with rage. If he is alone, he will be far less polite, to be sure. I can take it."

"Go away," she said. "You can leave, can you not? Go away."

Her solicitous, pressing tone stiffened Ehinger's determination. He must carry out on the spot the grand idea which had come to him while he was lying hidden in front of the guest house listening to the admonishments of Philibert to keep still. . . . He returned the girl's beseeching gaze with a smile of sadness.

The reflection of the fog before the windows made his face appear sallow and weary. "You must go away," she repeated, tonelessly.

"Yes, I killed him," said he. "Your stepfather arranged for it. He wanted to torture him, kill him piecemeal. This I have prevented."

"Why do you blame him? Why do you blame anyone? Why do you blame yourself? You knew he must die. That's why you did it. I know it. I knew it all along. . . . Please . . . please go."

"You knew—what? That Bundschuh is a great one? A very great one in leaving to others . . . to other men, or mere circumstances, to do what he wants done? Others have to finish Bundschuh's jobs. See? He wanted to do away with Roy—"

"Why? Why should he have wished for his death? Why for his?"

"Why? One after another."

"Why should he want—?"

"He hates us, does he not? And with no one to call a man to account, hate is reason enough for killing a man. Bah! One after another . . . So he begins with Roy. The thin edge. Men of Bundschuh's kind always begin at the thin edge. Do you think he didn't know about my taking the poison? I snatched it under his very nose! He enlisted my mercy." He leaned forward, his chin with the beard thrust out toward her.

She had not moved.

"Enlisted my mercy . . . Just as he has enlisted something else at other times. A snake, for instance, a poisonous serpent. There were certain advantages to be gained for Señor Bundschuh if the señora died, no? Your mother. She had certain claims to this place, no? Your mother. She was bitten by a snake. Did he call the doctor from Murcia? No. Everybody knows that your mother died because Bundschuh did not call the doctor. A good, a very good man told me so. No one can call Bundschuh to account for the death of the patrona. At the worst, señorita, it was culpable negligence, see?"

Inarticulate sounds of protest came from Juana's lips while he spoke. She could not summon the strength to form words, to interrupt him with a shout and tell him to his face that this was a lie, a wicked aspersion and lie. . . . His final word said, he stalked out of the back door, unseeing, passionate righteousness in the last forceful gesture of his hands, triumph in his gait.

XII

THE NEWS OF Roy's death on the road to Casaquiara annoyed Requesens, to say the least. Bundschuh had had no right to ship off the Belgian, whatever his reasons had been! And the reasons he made so much of in his letter only went to prove that the man was highly unnerved.

His message had come to Don Lorenzo's hand at two o'clock in the afternoon, shortly before he was to join the Cabinet meeting called by Dr. Zapeta for the express purpose of reaching a decision on the airplane purchase. The delaying tactics of Don Lorenzo in the matter were exhausted, and now his job was to foil the project as such, and kill it in the teeth of his own grandiose promises to the Army.

This, however, was an unsolvable problem, and he would have failed under any conditions. But on leaving the meeting, Requesens felt sure that it had been mainly the letter from Murcia which kept him from deploying, as he had sworn to himself he would, his whole cunning. As it was, he must have shown very little of it, for the congratulations of his colleagues, as they stepped out of the Palace with him, sounded sincere and even envious.

He declined to enter either of the two limousines waiting for the Cabinet members on the walled-in driveway—short as the distance is between Palace and Government House, Ministers in Huacho do not walk in a group to and from meetings—and declared he would take off the rest of the day, tacitly pretending he wished to be left alone with the thought of his success. As soon as the cars were driven away, he walked off in the direction of the Club Nacional.

Crossing the lobby, a place impervious to the sunshine outside, he noticed that the Club was almost deserted. He did not turn his head in passing the wide-open door of the dining room. In one of its corners a party of belated lunchers were enjoying themselves. From upstairs the click of colliding billiard balls could be heard at intervals.

A waiter followed His Excellency into the reading room, and when Requesens gave him a blank nod, he drew out one chair after another, his eyes fixed on the distinguished Member who halted at the large oval center table.

"The usual," he said over his shoulder, while he began to leaf through the newspapers without bending down. From where he stood he could not see the men in the dining room. He did not recognize their voices. Nor did he care to find out who they were.

His thoughts were with Bundschuh again. Perhaps Don Adolfo ought to be informed that his fears were highly exaggerated by now. In the past two weeks, pleasant doubts had dawned on Lorenzo as to the gravity of what might happen, should the strangers' presence in the country, or even his association with them, be discovered. There had been certain signs that not all men of authority were overly eager still to play the game of the late war's Allies. But how could he convey this impression to Bundschuh without encouraging him to follow his own volition even more freely? Tomorrow another flush of hysteria might prompt the man to send M. Philibert to Huacho. A stern, a very stern letter to Don Adolfo was called for. . . . "Over there," Requesens said brusquely to the waiter who was entering with the drink, and tossed his chin in the unmistakable direction of the one armchair which the man had failed to draw out.

No one ever sat in this armchair, a huge dark green velvet affair with winged arms and a high, erect back. While the other seats in the room were arranged around tables, or stood in pairs or by threes in the panelled embrasures of the French windows, that one chair was turned with its front to the wall. It was set apart conspicuously. Beneath the varicolored rows of books, an oil lamp was placed nearby on a shelf, its brass foot, patterned porcelain shade and chimney polished and shining, as if the ancient contraption still waited to be allowed to shed its light on the historic occupant of the green armchair.

That man had been a great reader indeed. Perhaps he had often merely sat there, a book in his lap, to avoid a certain recurrent discussion. His fellow members loved to warn him that his British-imported ideas would not do in the country, that the Army would not stand for "parliamentary innovations," and that a firm hand still was needed in the Republic. Afterwards some contended on their honor they had prophesied his fate to the dot. "But he was deaf to reason," such surviving co-members would say with compassion even now, forty-odd years after the tragic occurrence. "Here we were standing," they would say, each pointing out a different spot, "here we were, see, waiting for the attendant to report that our coachmen were ready—for it was late, and a nasty night it was, too—here, then, we were standing, sleepy and tired most of us, shall I say . . ." And being old men, and past excusing their inactivity at the fateful instant, they would freely confess to their perfect stupor that night when they heard the sudden uproar in the lobby and saw the assassins rush in headlong. "And next thing, we saw two of them (they all wore mufti) fire at the Senator. He had no time to open his mouth, or to pull himself out of his armchair. And thus," the old fogies concluded, if a junior member were listening to them, "the so-called New Year's Revolt started. The rug had to be changed afterwards. Miraculously, the green velvet of the chair showed no spots. He fell forward. Right here, you might say, the Thirty-fourth Amendment was born—which, when all is said and done, turned out to be all to the good. . . ." For although the membership list of the Club included, as it had at the time of the murder, several Senators, the historical necessity of that Amendment, which greatly restricted what was left of the Senate's power, was generally acknowledged in these rooms. Why, then, the armchair was held in such awe remained a matter of conjecture. But no one had ever found fault with the sentimental tradition.

Therefore it took the waiter some time to recover from his shock at Don Lorenzo's daring. Not before he had been called back to his duty did he put the tray on the shelf. "Anything else, Your Excellency?" he asked, filling the glass. "Is Your Excellency comfortable?"

While he slowly drained his glass, Requesens gave an affirmative sound. The loud syncopated laughter in the dining room had given way to a string of snickers. The caballeros were telling each other dirty stories, no doubt.

If it had been Philibert and not Roy, Don Lorenzo reflected, yes, if Philibert had died on the road to Casaquiara, or on any other road, for that matter . . . in that case he would be more lenient toward Bundschuh, would he not? The bond between Philibert and Mauricio Hojeda was visible to no one, not even to themselves. Nevertheless it existed, and a thousand contingencies could be pictured which might bring it to their mutual knowledge—

A new volley of laughter emanated from the dining room. "My friend, my shrewd friend!" said a thick voice, soaring above the common hilarity. Then the voice lowered again to a titter. The men seemed to be on their way to the reading room. Obviously the rug had swallowed their clatter when they rose from the table. "Don't tell me you haven't figured it out for yourselves," the thick voice, coming closer, continued. "Don't tell me you don't know what's up." Requesens was not able to place the voice. There were scores of his fellow members he did not know. According to Don Esteban, the Club had been rather broadminded of late in its admissions.

It had indeed—as Lorenzo, in a flush of antipathy, had occasion to realize at this moment. For the voice which answered the thick one belonged to a wealthy Huacho upstart of Bolivian birth, whose dogged bids at the auction of the General's effects, some weeks ago, had made him odious to Requesens. In a humorously plaintive tone this merchant said, "You know, sometimes we Huacho people are the last to get a piece of news—about the way the cuckold learns last of the pastime of his señora."

"And what *is* the version peddled in Majamarca?" a third voice cut short a new series of laughs.

"Version? Now listen, señores, I was talking of something conjectural, a guess admittedly based on hearsay and rumor. . . ." The party seemed to linger near the doorway.

A cigar was lit: Requesens distinguished, across the entire length of the room, the scratch of the match and after a pause the smacking first puffs of the smoker. "All right, Don Gregorio, as you like, as you say. We won't press you. We won't pump you. We are just the poorer for it." It was the merchant again who had spoken.

"Come on, Don Gregorio, my friend, and let's have a cognac," the other said. "Where the devil is that ass of a waiter?"

"Now really, do not bother," the man from Majamarca objected, "don't ring. Really, I couldn't stand one more drop." It seemed that an amiable contest was developing among the three men, with much shoulder patting and insincere protestations, while the Majamarcano argued that he must hurry along.

"Don't let me catch you doing business with someone else in Huacho, Don Gregorio," the merchant warned with vulgar good humor, "and since you won't find *me* in my office now, what's your hurry?"

"Come on, Don Gregorio, be a good fellow. A single cognac, no? In the Parisian fashion . . ."

"Here," the merchant said. A chair was pulled out: its brief grating on the parquet disclosed that the company intended to settle down at the window nearest the dining room.

"But no drink!" the guest insisted, "and not more than five minutes. No drink. Five minutes. Believe me, I *have* to be off. And I didn't say I had to be off on account of business, did I? Maybe there are some other things to attend to . . . in the Parisian fashion."

In the ensuing guffaws one could discern the zeal of the two Huachaneros to prove their appreciation of the provincial. They must have seated him between them. Their own voices were muffled now by the drapery on both sides of the recess.

"Your word of honor, then?" the stranger asked. "Your word of honor that you won't ask me where the story comes from? It comes from a good guesser—that much I may tell you. No questions asked about the rest—is it a deal?"

His words reached Lorenzo very distinctly. The man from Majamarca had now dropped most of his Eastern accent.

The merchant said something about Madame Ninon's establishment, and the Majamarcano acknowledged the information by a sort of extended grunt.

Then he said, "You both were talking about the Palace. Don't fool yourselves, señores, the Palace was not carried by surprise. The hands of the old blackbird were *not* forced. No one cowed him. Take my word for it, he was not afraid of the Fafreras junta, the so-called junta." He halted for a split second. "For Dr. Zapeta *was* the Fafreras junta. He had it all fixed with Fafreras. Or Fafreras with him. Do you actually believe, caballeros," he went on with what must have been a gesture dooming the others' loud gasps of incredulity, "that Dr. Zapeta would have acted as he did, if he hadn't wanted things to go as they finally went? Do you think he wouldn't have at least tried to reach the Majamarca garrison if he hadn't wanted that ridiculous committee of youngsters to have its way? It is said that the barracks here were alerted. Were they? By whom? But suppose they were—this I have on first-hand authority: the Palace did not so much as put a 'phone call through to Majamarca. Two infantry regiments, plus six batteries fully equipped, are not a force to be sneezed at." He slapped his leg. "There you are."

"There we are—where?"

"Now take it the other way round. How about it? Prior to the day that Fafreras went to the Palace, no one in his right mind would ever have thought Leandro Fafreras capable of so much as lifting a finger, let alone exerting himself, to put someone else into the saddle. He did precisely that. Which can only mean he must have relied on some kind of agreement for the future, some promise worth swallowing his pride for."

"He is not that clever!" the third man exclaimed. "A mestizo!"

"Wouldn't be so sure," the Boliviano said. "He is quite clever, this mestizo."

"Believe me, there must have been an agreement."

"As to what?"

"Yes, as to what! No one but marvels why Dr. Zapeta took it upon himself to baffle the public by the appointment, challenge opinion abroad, and saddle himself with Don Lorenzo. . . ."

Requesens had realized before this that the men were talking about him, and with a morbid foretaste had waited for the inevitable. But for all that, his name, pronounced, came to him like a vicious arrow.

"Can't you guess?" the gossipmonger proceeded, hushing his voice. "No? I can. What he wants is to get rid of the erstwhile Victor of Murcia. And before his own term is up, too. Get it? He wants Don Lorenzo to become impossible before he can make a bid for the Palace."

"You don't mean it, Don Gregorio! He would never dare."

"Don Lorenzo? Why not? Don't forget he had some fine schooling abroad in getting at things beyond a man's natural reach. So Dr. Zapeta wants him to fall into some trap. You'll admit it isn't hard to make a man of his stripe fall into traps?"

"But does anyone in Majamarca assume Dr. Zapeta will run for a second term, to begin with?"

"That's just it," the stranger answered the merchant zestfully, "that's just it. Move one: Don Lorenzo falls into said trap, and commits some folly. Move two: Dr. Zapeta steps in. Soft-spoken, cultured Dr. Zapeta steps in with Fafreras' help or—agreement or no agreement—without it. Emergency powers are nothing new in the case of some incident, some attack on the security of the Republic—"

"And foreseeing such a development," the third gentleman broke in, ". . . foreseeing it, he goes out of his way to deliver the Army to Requesens? It makes no sense."

"Eh?"

"I said, he's delivered the Army to Requesens!"

"Has he?" the man from Majamarca retorted. He waited an impressive time before continuing. "The Army . . . the officers' corps consists of men, of ambitious men, of men with thoughts in their own heads. And then, emergency powers, my friends, though maintained by the Army, may affect the Army itself. And then, emergency powers have a notorious tendency to survive the emergency, eh?"

"Or in other words," the merchant took over, "knowing that the elections will go against him and his whole coalition nonsense, the President . . ."

"Yes," said the man into the awe-stricken stillness. It sounded as if he himself had been suddenly muted by the audacity of his story. When he began to talk again, he resumed his tentative language, throwing in for good measure an alcoholic stammer. "Just wanted to tell you . . . Since you insisted, señores . . . All guesswork, naturally. Maybe I am wrong. But food for thought it is, no?" He got up. "And now I simply must be off, friends. Coming my way?"

And all at once they were out of the reading room. Lorenzo heard them asking questions and answering them themselves, the three of them talking at the same time. He heard their affected amusement ring against the wainscoting of the lobby, and the attendant wishing a good day to the gentlemen, and their polite wrangle to give each other preference at the exit. Upstairs the billiard players had resumed their slow game.

Slowly Requesens leaned forward to fill his glass. His back hurt. He took a long draught. As he replaced the glass, he noticed the clear print left on it by his fingers.

"Your Excellency . . . I didn't know Your Excellency was still here," said the waiter who had entered through the papered door leading to the scullery.

"Had a nap?" asked Don Lorenzo.

The wizened saffron-colored face of the old man remained serious. "I did take a little rest, if you'll pardon my saying so, Your Excellency. May I bring you some more? Or anything else? Does Your Excellency feel all right?" He had come closer, and Requesens tapped his arm lightly.

"Hm? Oh, of course. Thanks. Now, don't look at me that way. I know. I forgot. I shouldn't have sat in this chair. I know. They used to kill people in it. Those were incredible days, no?"

"Yes, Your Excellency. Now that Your Excellency is good enough to remind me of it . . ." He ceased, silenced by the laugh which came from the Minister.

"You won't give me away, will you?" Requesens asked, a travestied plea in his voice. "As it is, I've been punished already for sitting in this chair. Had a sort of snooze myself. And what a nightmare I had!" He rose, stretched his legs, and tried to release the tightness of his collar.

The waiter mumbled a word of regret.

"Oh, it's all right now, quite all right," Don Lorenzo said, and began to walk toward the door. For a second he stopped to cast a look at the embrasure where the three men had been conversing. "There's one good thing," he added on his way out, "I am not superstitious. And also it isn't so easy to kill me. Not me."

"Not Your Excellency . . ." echoed the waiter. Don Lorenzo had never treated him with such familiarity. And why did he leave at this hour?

The waiter was a slow-thinking man. In the course of the afternoon the peculiar behavior of the Minister evoked in him a train of thought entirely disconnected from the history of the green armchair. As it happened, Don Lorenzo's former batman, Ramón, was a cousin, or second cousin, of the old man's wife (and probably at one time also her lover), and in the roundabout manner not uncommon with dull-witted people he now came to think again of the business he had with the cripple Ramón.

He did not object to his wife's design to get Ramón to draw a will in her, his "only relative's," favor. He merely disliked the errand as such. He foresaw the abuse which Ramón would heap on him, as he had on some previous occasions, and the open relish with which he would savor a report of his "beloved cousin's" persistence in the "family matter" and her continuous nagging.

To imagine the inconveniences of married life, as of all intimate contacts with women, alleviated Ramón's own discomfort. He had been a dashing blade in his day, his body lithe as a willow. His associations with women had been nearly uncounted wherever he went with his master. In Paris, a moneyed lady jilted by Don Lorenzo had found much solace with the half-breed pueblo-Adonis. Her liberal gifts had made him a man of some means. Returning from abroad with his master, he was about to ask for his discharge, when, egged on by one of his women, he took it into his head to gain an Army commission. He joined the Expedition against El Seringuero; and though his untrained conduct made him the laughingstock of his platoon, his resolve to acquire distinction did not falter. One day he appeared at headquarters and implored

Requesens to help him to a last-minute chance, for the little war was as good as over at that time. In a burst of good humor the colonel bestowed a sergeancy on Ramón, and made him assistant executioner. Some people used to say that the great misfortune which befell Ramón shortly thereafter was caused by the part he took in El Seringuero's hanging. Actually the emasculation he suffered was the act of a jealous husband or lover in Murcia.

The changes that came over the castrated man defied the notions of science. A kind of venomous manliness replaced the effeminacy which a surfeit of women had bred in the handsome half-caste. Perhaps his experiences as a hangman had tapped a hidden vein in him. The acquired refinement of his speech yielded to an ever-ready obscenity. Accidents, or any violence, in the vicinity of the tumble-down house he had purchased were known to attract him with promptitude; equally known was his disinclination to succor those in distress. The one human being Ramón excluded from his misanthropy was his former master; and surely the fact that Requesens had got him an invalid's pension, as if he had been mutilated in combat, could not alone account for these feelings. There was, behind his devoted love of Don Lorenzo, an unwholesome expectation.

This, then, was the fellow to whose house the waiter from the Club Nacional repaired on the following morning. He was unable to hide the objective of his visit, and thus exposed himself to the usual vituperations. The eunuch was tinkering about in his courtyard, and only after a while bade his caller sit down. He was, so he said with studied negligence, on the eve of taking his leave of Huacho.

Where to?

"*Aie,* friend . . . away."

For how long?

Ramón eyed a cardboard box extricated from a pile of rubbish. He shrugged.

On business?

Yes, on business.

The waiter decided to conceal the news from his wife: she would chide him for not pushing their own affair with Ramón any farther before the latter's departure. He sat uneasily on his camp stool. He asked himself whether he should try to humor Ramón by reporting on the curious conduct of His Excellency the day before. But the intimacy Don Lorenzo had shown him had left its stamp on his mind, and he did not feel like "giving Don Lorenzo away" even to Ramón. He tried to think of something else which might break the uneasy silence between them, but meanwhile Ramón had begun to talk himself.

He had straightened and was weighing the cardboard box in his arms. Ah, he was still worth his money, he said with animation. His dear cousin had better get it into her head that he had no time for fooling around with women. She'd find plenty of other men still. There were millions, literally millions of men in the Republic who could lie with women (here he used at least four different words in succession, a crescendo of filthy disdain), but how many men were there in the Republic fit for the business *he* was about to set out for? How many, eh? A dozen? Three? Two? No, just one. He, Ramón.

XIII

Don Lorenzo had gone straight home from the Club. He had found Priscilla having tea with Dr. Zapeta's niece, Margarita Partridge. They had met the young widow—Major Partridge, R.A.F., had been killed in North Africa in '42—at the Day-of-Independence reception at the Palace a short week earlier.

Lorenzo had been pleased to meet her. He had known her late father, Señor de Gracián, one of the few native gentlemen ever to be elected to the board of the Majamarca-Huacho Railroad. His daughter had come into all his money.

As it turned out when Lorenzo joined the ladies upstairs, Mrs. Partridge had come to call on Priscilla for her advice: she was planning to buy one of the vacant mansions in the neighborhood of the Casa Requesens, and wished to profit from her experience there in matters of redecoration. What good luck, she remarked, to have Don Lorenzo himself on the spot to advise her! As could be seen, he was doing well by his own place—and at a reasonable price, Doña Margarita assumed.

Lorenzo smiled at his wife. He had told her that, upon his elevation, he had been presented with a "nice sum of money" by Don Esteban. Now he seemed to apologize to Priscilla for answering the visitor's question by informing her with a blank face that "all those bills" were mailed to his uncle directly. "It is his property, after all. . . ." Under no circumstances would he have been willing to discuss with someone in the confidence of the Palace the costs of the redecoration of the building.

"You are all right, aren't you?" asked Priscilla, when he declined the cup of tea she was offering him.

He said he was perfectly all right. Priscilla had given no sign of surprise at his coming at this unusual hour. Her pose of silent compliance, the expression of patience on her face, told him that she divined his urge to talk to her . . . to argue with himself in her presence. He resented her sagacity, and presently convinced himself that nothing but fatigue had made him return to the Casa.

He was still waiting for an afterthought to rise from the cauldron of his reflections, if not an argument strong enough to discredit what he had overheard at the Club—fantasy, as he spasmodically tried to impress on himself, born in the mind of a provincial huckster! He was talking to Margarita Partridge, complimenting her at length on her decision to take up residence in this part of the town.

The young woman apparently did not mind such conventional niceties. In returning them, she did not in any way allude to Don Lorenzo's own recent homecoming. Most of the time she looked at Doña Priscilla. Only once did Lorenzo prick up his ears. Speaking of the painters' scaffolding outside the walls, Señora Partridge laughingly referred to the "barricading" of the Casa. But in the next second she inquired what color the painters would put on.

Lorenzo said it would be an ivory shade, and that, Don Esteban consenting, some of the stucco would also go. He sighed comically to indicate the paradoxical situation which forced a man to take care of such minor affairs at a moment when so much weighty business had descended upon his shoulders. Then he stood up, and left, after having kissed Priscilla's forehead.

He thought of walking up the street, having a look at the property little Margarita Gracián intended to buy, and perhaps strolling along the grass path continuing beyond the end of the pavement. Instead, he found himself walking downhill.

He turned into one of the lanes at his right.

Two soldiers came out of a public house, and saluted his braid. It occurred to him that pictures of him should be much more on display than they were. Children were playing in the gutter. A dead rat lay in the middle of the alley. Someone closed his shutters. A friar stood in a doorway, listening to an unseen man who whispered to him hoarsely from a door kept ajar by a naked foot.

The superficial gratifications swaying him throughout the past weeks had not fully destroyed Lorenzo's wonderment at the proud course his career had taken. The firmness with which he had in public faced the great change and its aftermath had not been sincere. He had been longing all the time for some additional confirmation, for the kind of assurance that nothing short of his own detached reasoning can give to a man. But every time that he set out to solve the miracle of the Fafreras junta, his soul had seemed to have recourse to a lofty contempt of facts. Was the talk overheard at the Club that product of reason and logic he himself had never arrived at? Assuredly it was not. . . . But suppose, he proceeded, that a man walks through the night, and an isolated lightning flash makes him see, or only assume he sees, an abyss in his road. Would he question what he believes he has seen?

Lorenzo took another turn. Already he heard the traffic noise of the Plaza. He wished he were in mufti, and could enter the little café to his left, or sit down at the one rickety table put out on the cobbles. Three girls, all leaning out of one window, were giggling after him. A drunk, his back against the wooden fence of a vacant lot, hunched up his legs at the sound of his footsteps and stretched them out again flat as Don Lorenzo came close, forcing him to step over them.

Why not make common cause with Fafreras? Why not convince him that success of the dictatorial aspirations of the Palace would not benefit him by a long shot? He could tell the one-time sergeant a couple of highly instructive stories about men who to their own undoing had trusted budding dictators in the days of their rise. And if persuasion should fail, might Fafreras not be placated by cajoleries, nominated—through a surprise move in open Cabinet meeting—to an ambassadorial post, or . . . or simply bribed?

This was the first time that Requesens had ever considered putting to use his foreign funds. The idea did not shock him. It even appeared to exert a certain fascination, and thrust upon him the image of the man who originally had handled, or owned, those funds, and who, unafraid of ridicule, still claimed them.

Lorenzo stopped short. He had caught sight of the white-helmeted policeman on the Plaza. Absurdly high up on his green-white-blue platform, he gesticulated with visible relish. If he, Don Lorenzo Requesens, were to cross the square now—diagonally, let it be assumed —the fellow would halt all traffic with an imperative tooting, and snap to attention. He would, of course, do likewise for Colonel Leandro Fafreras. He might even do so for any major or captain.

Don Lorenzo lighted the cigar which he had taken out quite a while earlier from his leather case. His eyes on a garish lottery poster, he reflected that nothing was wrong with the renown of the officers' corps. Nor, for that matter, had the tongue-wagging company at the Club actually found fault with its power. But how about his own renown in the officers' corps? A legend, Loyarte was saying. But a legend must have a meaning. It must contain a message for those who cherished it. They waited. They fed on such hope as the saga of his extraordinary career seemed to proffer. The Night-in-the-Palace group? How far was it his clique, how far that of Fafreras? There was, to be sure, Loyarte, a man with a smoldering sense of enterprise, and apparently free from high-flown ideas. But he was rather preoccupied with personal affairs. According to his own confession, he was desperately in love with some young lady out East, whose family did not approve of his wooing. An aura of self-pity was about him. Lorenzo needed a man of a greater stature at this juncture. Boldness was needed.

A cruising cab drew up at the curb. Don Lorenzo turned, and stepped into the car. "To Carjavel Airfield!" The driver did not seem to recognize his passenger.

Lorenzo closed his eyes. It had leaped to his mind that the one thing he had not contemplated since leaving the Club Nacional was how to avoid the "trap" by mere caution. That discovery frightened him—as though two Lorenzos existed, one who was wont to calculate his every step, and another who was in the throes of unbridled emotions. Even his detractors were said to admire the sang-froid he had shown in 1941. "How wise of you, Don Lorenzo," one of the younger colonels had ventured to tell him that night at the Casa Ninon, "not to have lashed out in those days, or allowed yourself to teach an old-fashioned lesson to that mud-slinging nobody!"

That mud-slinging nobody! Why had he not opened his mouth ever since that poor joke about the General's mantle? True, he had been busy in other directions. For a fortnight incidents which resembled slow-down strikes, a nuisance hitherto unknown in the Republic, had troubled Huacho workshops; and at the same time the irregularity of public services had increased considerably. No demands had been raised anywhere, nor had criticism surpassed its customary scope among street-corner grumblers. Although the "post-war discontent" of the laboring class was treated by El Huérfano's sheet merely in obscure, truncated comments, and he had not been on the stump in person, no one questioned that he was behind the unrest. He *had* been busy. But as a rule *La Semana* was multifarious. Why was it silent about him, Lorenzo?

Why had the Minister of Interior not objected to the recent release by Huacho Broadcasting Station of information on El Huérfano's movements? Supercilious as the tone of this news was, it was not altogether derisive. "The leader of the People's Party has gone East." What of it? Since when had that starveling been a leader? Did no one remember that "leader's" effrontery toward the man who was the General's successor in office? Don Lorenzo had planned to ask his colleague about that outrage.

"To the gate, señor colonel?"

"No. Stop. Stop here."

The foreign flag floated limply beside the Republic's colors atop the big hangar. It had been turned over to the great air line even before the end of the war. The General had been hasty. Had there been money involved? At any rate, a conflict was sure to arise now: the new craft would have to be housed—and where else than at Carjavel Airfield?—and it would be disgraceful to have them kept under canvas, with the foreign machines in the sheds.

The driver, having been paid, seemed hesitant to drive away. Would the señor colonel want to be driven back? Or was his own car waiting for him inside the gate?

The Minister turned his back on the inquisitive man. He pretended to look at the expanse of uncultivated fields adjacent to the airdrome. Ever since the drunkard in that small lane almost tripped him up with his lolling long legs, he had known where he was heading. When the taxi behind him rumbled off at last, Don Lorenzo started walking back in the direction of the town. After a few minutes another taxicab overtook him. He hailed it, and gave the driver Ramón's address. This was the sort of decision he had come to trust: reasoning catching up with the voice of his heart.

The man in Murcia was much too valuable to be left to himself and the weakling Bundschuh. Ramón must bring him here.

XIV

THROUGHOUT THE VARYING moods of that stroll and his two cab rides —and even while he gave Ramón his instructions—Lorenzo could not shake off an increasing feeling of resentment toward Priscilla.

He was not unaware by any means of the mountain of deceit he had piled up between her and himself over the years. Whenever he discussed some of his business with her, or in front of her, his instinct would counsel him to allude vaguely to one piece of the truth or another. Thus he had always been in a position to come home, smile at his wife, or merely smile down at his crossed legs in her presence, and begin, "Remember, Pris, that affair we heard about the other night?" or, "Some time ago I told you about a new acquaintance of mine. . . ." This was, for instance, the manner in which, in a short talk years ago in Berlin, he had mentioned the name which was Philibert's then, calling him "one of the coming men in this madhouse." It goes without saying that he had never breathed a word about his dealings with M. Philibert, or—before it or after—ever referred to the latter's arrival in the Republic.

But now Lorenzo had come to feel that this self-imposed secrecy was also a burden. He disliked the thought of augmenting this load. The prospect of having to conceal his experience at the Club from Priscilla gave him a sensation of being left really alone in a hostile world . . . and only the prospect of Priscilla telling him, directly he should hint at the story of Fafreras' intrigue, that she had warned him from the first, checked his dread of that impending forlornness.

It was toward the end of his interview with Ramón that certain recent remarks of hers came to Lorenzo's mind which tallied with that unpleasant picture. Ever since the Day-of-Independence reception Priscilla seemed to have delighted in bringing Fafreras' name to his attention. She would say that the colonel's appearance was far less picturesque than she had been taught to assume, or his skin far lighter, or she would express her wonderment that he had come all the way to Huacho for the sole purpose of attending the Presidential party.

While Ramón was staring in grave expectation at his silent master, a fleeting suspicion returned to Lorenzo: this very afternoon he had had the impression that, had the Gracián girl not been present, Priscilla would again have come back to the Day-of-Independence fête and the sight of Colonel Fafreras.

For once Don Lorenzo was right in reading the mind of his wife. But Fafreras had been so much in her thoughts in the past week, Lorenzo would have been right at almost any hour in his assumption. Yet it was true that Mrs. Partridge's call had reminded Priscilla of Fafreras in a still stronger fashion. It had been an unexpected visit.

To be sure, the President's handsome niece had taken an instantaneous liking to her at the party. Or so it had looked. At any rate she had been responsible for Priscilla's failure to prolong her conversation with the wife of the American Chargé d'Affaires. For though Doña Margarita had barely spoken a few words with Priscilla in the first hour of the festivity, she came up to her after a time, and with a humorously conspiratorial stealth extricated her from the cluster of "Government ladies" that occupied the circular center sofa of the great sala.

Hadn't all the Day-of-Independence oratory tired Señora Requesens? And wasn't she weary of all that refined formality? And yet these people were fond of deriding British punctilio!

Priscilla was at a loss to respond to that onrush of light intimacy. Slipping her very soft, small hand into Priscilla's arm, Mrs. Partridge steered her through the crowd, and took her to a small adjoining salon, incessantly talking. But no sooner had she, there, with a low laughter addressed Priscilla as "a congenial soul," than she allowed someone, or something, in the ballroom to divert her attention again; and in the next minute she had left Doña Priscilla standing in the middle of the salon, waving back at her with a radiant smile.

Except for the upholstered benches lining the four walls, the high-ceilinged room had no furniture. It was precariously lit by two heavily shaded electric lamps hanging above an empty picture frame. In front of the aperture connecting the salon with the ballroom, there stood a big potted palm, whose leaves swayed slightly in the draft which entered through the wide-open balcony door. From where she had been left, Priscilla had a fairly unobstructed view of the sala. The thought that she was not likely to be seen pleased her. After a short while she discerned Lorenzo's dress uniform. He kept himself close to one of the allegorical statues adorning the corners of the great room and, standing very erect, appeared to be listening to the thick-set gentleman previously pointed out to her as the Senator from Majamarca. But soon the two men were lost to Priscilla: a troupe of guitarists in garish costumes marched toward the farther end of the ballroom, where with much agitation a kind of stage was about to be cleared. Making up her mind not to join the bustle right away, or perhaps to wait for the President's niece to return, Priscilla approached one of the upholstered benches. But a smell of mothballs made her withdraw, and she walked up to the balcony.

She recognized Fafreras directly she stepped out. He stood in the left corner of the narrow platform, both hands propped against the short stretch of its iron railing. He made a sidelong bow. As he straightened, the row of medals on his tunic emitted a thinly tinkling sound. At the same moment the guitarists started their performance in loud unison. Since the colonel had not been introduced to Doña Priscilla, she expected him to introduce himself, as is the custom at big social affairs. Later, it seemed curious to her that she had not for a moment thought of turning her steps; as it was, she acknowledged Fafreras' salutation with a distinct nod.

"I hope I do not intrude on the solitude of the señora," he said.

She said it was she who was intruding.

But it was she, he remonstrated gallantly, who was trying to find some solitude here. As for himself, he had had his share of it.

She crossed over to the other side of the balcony, and he slowly turned to face her, finally releasing the rail. "It is of no use, señora. One is in it—so one is in it. That goes for parties and most other occasions."

"I didn't expect to find so many people," she said. She wondered whether he knew who she was.

"Perhaps the señora did not know what gregarious people we are," he said, half answering her unspoken question.

"Oh, this is a great day for Huacho, is it not?"

"It is," he replied with automatic assurance. "A gregarious nation, yes. And yet how many lonely men!" He held a lighted cigar between his fingers, but he did not put it to his lips.

H

"That is a melancholy thought," she suggested after a pause, opening her fan, a beautiful thing of lace and ebony that once had belonged to Lorenzo's mother. "Do such thoughts always come to you in a festive assemblage?"

He seemed to look up from his cigar, and though Priscilla could hardly see his face across the breadth of the balcony, she felt a wave of kindliness coming from him. "Not always. But sometimes such assemblages do make me think of our loneliness. Sometimes I also think of the millions, the many millions who have lived in our country —for if you take all the centuries past, they must have numbered many millions—and then I am chilled by the idea that each single one of those many millions was in truth occupied only with himself. I admit," he added in a kind of impatient regret, "that *is* a melancholy thought. History . . . our history is a melancholy record."

"May I disagree with you, colonel?"

"On our history?"

"Good Lord, no. You would not expect me to know much about it, would you? I beg to disagree with what you said about men in general. For what you think has been true for this country over the centuries would not be less true for other places. We all love at times to glory in the callousness of our race. It gives us . . . well, it may give us a kind of independence. But many people," she said in a changed key, "do think and worry about others."

It was not likely that he had seen her brooding expression (this was the one moment which she would recall with embarrassment). "Man is complicated," he declared after a silence. His naturally firm voice lacked comfort. He drew a deep breath. "Ah, worry about others! Yes, take the previous occupants of this building. . . . The señora does not know? This building once belonged to the Holy Office. No one would say that the reverend fathers did not worry about others. Oh no. Their conscience, I dare say, embraced all men, believers and infidels alike. But what did they know of the infidels? They thought they were occupying themselves with the souls of the infidels, and yet they were occupied only with their own true belief. . . . But that, I grant, was a special case." Again his tone, as indeed his choice of subject which Priscilla felt eluded his intellectual grasp, revealed his uneasy mood.

She was bewildered, and merely raised her shoulders to indicate that she had no opinion in the matter. "But lonely?" she asked, a little helplessly. "Do you think those reverend fathers were lonely?"

"They fought loneliness their own special way," he replied. "Ah, the señora would be surprised to learn where loneliness can drive people here. Of a certain family it is told that when they recited the Ave María, they addressed her as 'Mother of God, our lady and dear relative.' They regarded no mortal worthy of their kinship. How lonely they must have been, and how callous in their hearts! That family is extinct now," he remarked upon her short laugh. For the fraction of a second it looked as though he were to join in her amusement, but he continued, "And the awkward custom did not recur, to be sure. It too is extinct."

"And so are those days once and for all, I suppose."

"Who knows?" he countered with the stock phrase of the country. He tossed his cigar over the railing.

A man down below—probably one of the soldiers of the guard posted at the rear entrance of the building—having picked up the discarded cigar from the gravel, shouted a throaty *gracias, señor!* Only the gleam of the waxing moon illuminated the lawn and the flower beds. The windows of the Palace were shuttered throughout. A couple of brightly uniformed constables patrolled close to the high wall of the park, the heads of their horses bent low. The shouts of the people's fiesta were far off.

Priscilla turned her face back to the colonel, who was twirling his great mustache. It ran in her mind that his seemingly aimless talk and its romantic cynicism reminded her of the Lorenzo of their early days in Paris. She said, "This is one of the things I do not understand hereabouts. Everybody in the Republic complains about the unextinguishable past, and everybody is as proud of it as the next man."

"The señora is a keen observer," he said eagerly. "Our native ladies have never thought it worth their while to observe the state of their country. I confess that has been our fault all along, and century-old habits are not uprooted overnight. You, señora, are of a happier breed in that respect, I presume. Giving rein to your observation, you might be tempted to give good advice."

She exchanged a stare with him. She realized that he was not on this balcony by chance. More than his words, it was the aura of falsehood about them which matured in her the conviction that the colonel had lain in wait for her, and that Margarita Partridge had maneuvered her into the salon for his sake. "You flatter me," she said as lightly as she could.

"I don't think I do," he muttered. "Did the señora also observe how many sad-eyed people could be found in our gatherings?"

"Good Lord, sad-eyed guests! That sort can be found at parties anywhere in the world."

He was unruffled by her renewed reference to the world outside the Republic. "What makes a person sad while he is with others may be a thought he cannot bring himself to think. He feels there is a thought, a notion, a feasible concept. . . ."

"How can anyone know that 'there is' a thought without at the same time bringing himself to think it? No, no, colonel, such theories may fascinate a philosophical man like yourself, a man who is trying to secure for himself some solitude where he may find it least, but surely not the crowd at a fête—"

"I am not talking about crowds, señora. Pray forgive me for interrupting."

The sound of the string instruments, growing powerful and even wild now, seemed to provoke her. She folded her fan, muffling the click of its frame in her cupped palm, and said, "It is only fair to tell you that I am the wife of Colonel Requesens."

"I know, señora," he said gently.

She was unable to see whether his reply was accompanied by a bow or some apologetic wave of his hands. He had withdrawn to the wall and its deep shadow. 'What a theatrical side-room conversation!' she thought. Yet she came back, "And what would such thoughts be a man 'cannot bring himself to think'?"

"Simple thoughts, mostly."

"Such as?"

He was immobile, and said nothing.

"The love of one's neighbor? The love of one's country?"

"Most men take the latter for granted in themselves," he said with a sententiousness which signalled that he wished to ignore her irony, "and as for the former, most men take for granted that it cannot exist."

"You *are* a philosopher."

"An old soldier, señora."

"Man is complicated, colonel."

He stepped out of the shadow. It was odd that his shoulders should look as if weighed down in spite of the broad metal strips on them, which caught the lights as he passed by the door, advancing in her direction. "We were talking about the lonely men in the Republic," he said.

She decided that this could not be happening. If Fafreras were anxious to enlist Lorenzo's support for whatever it was, he would not have picked as an intermediary the niece of Dr. Zapeta! She reached for the railing behind her.

He stood close to her. "Some day those lonely men are not unlikely to overreach themselves. What yardstick do lonely men have save the echo of their own voice? Occupied with themselves only . . ."

"Men are not easily changed," Priscilla said.

"True. Men used to loneliness do not easily open their hearts to a host of friends, or even a small group of them. Such a group, together with their proven friendship, may drive them even deeper into loneliness. What a man lonely by nature is really in need of," he said, "is *one* friend, *one* great friend. . . . Do you care for a refreshment, señora?"

She tossed her head toward the salon. "As a matter of fact, I do."

Fafreras mumbled something about champagne, while he turned to leave with exaggerated zeal.

She opened her purse to take out her compact. But its mirror was blunted by the darkness. It occurred to her that it was much darker than she had thought it was, so clearly did she still see the face of Fafreras before her. She stepped back into the room. The guitarists had ceased their playing, and the buzz of the voices in the sala grew very loud. Perhaps the President had withdrawn to his private quarters. Priscilla had put her fan on one of the benches, and as she turned to take it up again, she saw Lorenzo emerge from behind the palm. "Here I am, Lorenzo," she called out in a low voice, and went to meet him halfway. She took his arm, and when he asked her, she said she had been feeling tired, and wanted some rest.

"And did you find some?"

"No, not really," she answered, "or not at all."

Lorenzo made a remark that caused him to laugh. He was winding their way through the throng. An orchestra had replaced the guitarists on the platform, and the young people started dancing. She said she wanted to go home, and he stopped a footman and sent him to the cloakroom for his plumed hat. "You know," he observed with another laugh, "there is something sad about three hundred men of importance. Each of them seems far less important. And I do not exclude myself. . . ."

Priscilla had found little peace in the hours left of that night. And the following night had been equally restless. There was no escaping the fact that she had offended Fafreras. She imagined the big man returning to the balcony, the glass with spilling champagne daintily in his awkward grasp, flushed with ardor and expectation, and finding her gone. More than almost anything men in the Republic hate being made fools of; surely Fafreras had defied that risk bravely by engaging her in a naïvely precious conversation, and zigzagging up to his offer of closer friendship—or some league—with Lorenzo. She could not question that he knew she had understood him perfectly well. But could he not assume that someone had come to fetch her, taking her back to the sala? She wished he would entertain no such idea. She almost hoped he would stand on protocol and, gravely hurt, avoid future contacts. For now it was crystal clear to her that she had left the balcony with the resolve to withdraw from the unbidden mission Fafreras was anxious to entrust her with. She wanted no part in the farce enacted by the caballeros of the Republic!

Still she kept pondering the likely goal of the "friendship" which Fafreras appeared to solicit. Did he expect some special reward for the rôle he had played in the junta? Had he played it for some ulterior reason, one which Lorenzo did not wish to perceive? Or did Fafreras aim at a new political scheme? And where—this was Priscilla's recurrent question to herself—did Margarita Partridge enter the picture?

After two days Priscilla had made up her mind that no damage could come to her husband by remaining unaware of the veiled offer. He would not remain unaware of it, nor the offer remain veiled, if Fafreras' desire to reach his friendship should be pressing enough to outweigh his reluctance to lay his cards on the table. In no case could her refusal to act as a go-between be held against Lorenzo.

Half against her will she yet probed the righteousness of her decision. But her hints at the impression she had gained of Fafreras met with no response from Lorenzo. The only reaction she drew from him was a casual word to the effect that he was sorry he had not introduced "the señor sergeant" to her. "Though you wouldn't have been amused . . ." he said. "Believe me, Don Leandro would have perorated endlessly on his own achievements." Lorenzo's superciliousness served to prove to his wife that the business touched on by the colonel must be very far-fetched.

She was, then, willing to shelve the whole episode, when Mrs. Partridge's unannounced visit threw her into new doubts. To be sure, afternoon calls are habitual with the ladies of Huacho during the social season. However, Doña Priscilla had politely made it known to some of them at the reception that the Casa Requesens was not prepared as yet for entertaining, what with all sorts of workmen about the scaffolded building. Thus, when Mrs. Partridge appeared, she armed herself against guile in case the young woman should try to continue the "negotiation" where Fafreras perforce had broken off. But Margarita did not utter one word about Fafreras. And when Priscilla, partly from curiosity, but also vexed by what she believed was subtle cunning, made a sally herself, and reported that she had run into the "mustachioed colonel" upon her desertion in that "dreary salon," Mrs. Partridge merely asked her to pardon her poor manners, was deaf to Fafreras' name, and presently talked again about the old mansion up the hill.

In the light of that failure, Priscilla's determination to abstain from any action was vindicated. She felt doubly so when Lorenzo, the next morning, showed a venturesome, energetic humor. He admitted to it, his forehead furrowed with the import of the hour, by pointing out to her a notice in *La Libertad* that informed its readers of the impending Government purchase of "a respectable number of modern airplanes." It was a move, to quote the newspaper, which would be hailed as a new symptom of the vigor and the youthful spirit of the Republic, and of the men fate had put at her helm.

XV

As COULD HAVE been expected, El Huérfano dissented from the great acclaim said to welcome the airplane purchase. Why, so asked *La Semana,* should the Republic rearm at the moment when world peace was restored, and the apparatus for its maintenance under construction? Did the Government propose to start a war of their own? If so, against whom, and where, and what for? And so on in the usual nagging vein. Hardly worth much attention! But within twenty-four hours rumors went round that a group of citizens beyond the suspicion of sympathizing with El Huérfano—businessmen, freighters, exporters —were equally unenthusiastic about the reform of the Air Corps; and since these men were known to be in the tow of certain foreign legations, their rumored objection rang with the echo of a voice stronger than their own.

Thus Requesens would have been justified in bringing the matter up for reconsideration at a Cabinet meeting. He could have backed out of it on mere technical grounds with little trouble or shame, and have freed himself from the specter of Mauricio Hojeda. As for the officers' corps, he should have been able, after the project had come to naught, to blame it on the Palace, and at the same time on the notorious decay of the junta's spirit. Such tactics might even have rallied the young caballeros closer about him again.

However, he cast that idea out of his mind. He decided to pursue the road which, originally, had not been of his choosing. Was he gripped by a lust to face all his foes at one and the same time? Had El Huérfano challenged his spite? Both may have been the case. But what really drove him on was an inarticulate morbid notion—the nebulous idea that the knavery of a Philibert asked for more than mere patchwork on his part. His impending interview with that man bred and trained in every conceivable trickery and intrigue imbued him with a feverish determination.

The ink was not dry yet on the letter asking the foreign Chamber of Commerce to advise the airplane factory of Huacho's interest in the proposed deal, when Don Lorenzo summoned a local contractor, and ordered blueprints for five modern hangars to be erected at Carjavel.

His A.D.C. was present at this conference, and when the contractor had gone, visibly a little doubtful as to the promised payments, Requesens informed Loyarte that he would put himself at the helm of the training program, the new pilots' school—never mind the name. Never mind the unusual self-assignment, he added to himself, or the technical qualifications outsiders might say he lacked.

And what plans had His Excellency regarding the pilots themselves? Who would be eligible for the new Air Corps? The young man, who stood in front of Requesens' desk, did not close his lips fully as he fell silent, and that expression of expectancy, together with the slightly receding chin, impaired the mark of intelligence on his handsome face.

"Ah, that, my friend . . ." Don Lorenzo replied, opening his hands, and took his eyes away from his aide. Conversing with the Senator from Majamarca at the Day-of-Independence reception he had learned that the girl Loyarte was in love with was no other than the Senator's daughter, apparently a well-educated young lady. The Senator had made much of her schooling abroad before inquiring after His Excellency's opinion about "the young blade" and the chances of his career. "That, my friend," His Excellency now said, "is a problem which will need some brainwork."

"May I suggest to Your Excellency . . ."

Don Lorenzo nodded with an absent-mindedness which Loyarte could not but interpret as a rebuke. Actually, Lorenzo had only become conscious of the shadowy nature of his present business. Not only the distribution of the new jobs incumbent upon him, but the new Air Corps as such had begun to seem far away and ghost-like to him. For if that accursed Majamarcano at the Club had not merely gossiped, another man would soon reap the fruit of the whole project, and he, Lorenzo Requesens, would be left standing on quicksand.

"Perhaps this is premature," the lieutenant was saying, "but since Your Excellency has honored me with your confidence . . ."

"I told you to go ahead, didn't I?" Don Lorenzo said. He looked out into the evening rapidly enveloping the Plaza. This was the fourth day since Ramón's departure.

Loyarte relaxed his posture. Many tacticians held, he began, that an efficient air force was the backbone of an army in more than one respect. . . .

How had Ramón reached the hacienda from the Ulloa station? Had Bundschuh had the decency to drive him and Philibert back to the depot? Damn that affair between the stepdaughter of Bundschuh and Philibert's youthful companion! In his last letter Don Adolfo had made it plain that he "could not and would not stand for this abomination." Perhaps he did not dare leave the two alone, and would make some imprudent arrangement for getting Ramón and his charge to Ulloa. Another of those instances where sex threatened to encroach on affairs of the first order.

"Your Excellency may be reluctant to give preference to the Night-of-the-Palace group. It might look like reward, like compensation. . . ."

It was one of the newly discovered merits of Loyarte, Requesens meditated while he listened to his pleasant voice, that *he* did not allow sex to interfere with greater issues. His "desperate love" had turned out not to be blind: the dowry of his beloved was no mean prize. The Senator's cattle and tanneries, his steamships plying the River downstream from Majamarca, his timber tracts in the hinterland of Ollaytaytombo, the brewery, not to speak of his real estate and his presidency of the Banco Oriental, constituted the only fortune in the country which Lorenzo had ever heard mentioned abroad.

Loyarte broke off. In the end he had talked with an emphasis out of tune, to Requesens' ears, with the triviality of his idea. The plan to create, in organizing the new air force, another, a larger, more active junta had long occurred to Lorenzo. It had begun to outweigh in his thoughts the risks of the airplane purchase. But his irrational trust in the forthcoming counsel of Philibert now superseded that plan's fascination. Yes, Philibert would know how a man could build up an élite guard *and* make sure it was to remain in his own hands!

The lights in the Palacio Municipal had gone on one after another. Requesens kept his face still turned toward the window. If the two men should have missed this morning's train, the primitive schedule of the Northern Railway would delay them for another two days. . . .

"It will please you to hear," he suddenly said, his gaze returning to Loyarte, "that the Senator from Majamarca seems to be interested in a certain lieutenant, and not entirely averse to his hopes." He made his swivel chair face the lieutenant. "Eh? So you see . . . if I were you, I would worry less about affairs of state. Not that your remarks were wasted on me. But things need their time. Do not talk too much about them. About the Senator, *or* about the Air Corps commissions."

Loyarte flushed crimson. "I do not talk about either," he said.

"Good. That is a wise course to steer," the Minister declared. After a pause he asked Loyarte to dismiss the orderly in the anteroom.

"I am very grateful. Whenever Your Excellency needs me . . ."

Requesens heard Loyarte tell the orderly that he no longer was wanted, and then a lorry rolled across the Plaza and drowned the footsteps of the two men withdrawing outside. Requesens listened to the rumbling sounds dying away. He pulled out his pocket knife and began to sharpen a pencil lifted from the small onyx tray on his desk. . . . The Senator from Majamarca! It would not do to attribute his influence to his wealth alone. Don Esteban called him "the walking conscience of the right people." It had come as a great shock to the old gentleman that, two years or so before, this Walking Conscience declined an invitation to his estate. How could it be that this same Walking Conscience bounded toward Lorenzo at the Day-of-Independence reception, put one arm round his shoulder, patted his back, and, with scores of curious in hailing distance, said, "We never met, Don Lorenzo. But people of our kind know who each other is just the same"? What had caused the Senator to change his views about the man he had refused to meet on a purely social plane? The Senator was not known for bowing to mere outward success or glamor. He had been a great friend of the General; yet he had opposed him fiercely on occasions.

Surely the Senator had not approached him with so much kindness for the sake of Loyarte's career. . . . While the pen knife cut deeper into the soft wood of the pencil, Lorenzo recalled that the malice overheard at the Club stemmed from Majamarca. Could the Senator be in the plot being hatched against him? Was he the one to set the trap? . . . The drunken Majamarcano at the Club was not likely to have his story complete. His conjectures about Dr. Zapeta were fantastic. Dr. Zapeta was not the sort of man who would embark on a strong-arm venture.

But what did he, Lorenzo, know about Dr. Zapeta really? While he was doing the spadework for the promised Army reforms, that silver-tongued rascal might well—

The pencil slipped from his hand. The telephone on his desk had rung. He reached for it, but did not touch the receiver. At the other end of the line the receiver was put down after that one ring. And then it rang again, twice this time, and then there was quiet. It was the signal agreed on with Ramón. Philibert had arrived in town.

Everything had gone smoothly on Ramón's trip. Bundschuh had brought the two men back to Ulloa himself. He seemed to have had some personal errand in the neighborhood of Ulloa, or on the road, which he wanted to take care of on his return trip—

"Never mind old Bundschuh," Don Lorenzo interrupted Ramón. "Did *he* ask you any questions?"

Ramón shook his head. They stood outside the elongated rectangle of frail light thrust down from the upper floor onto the flagstones of Ramón's courtyard. "He is a *nice* man, señor colonel," said the eunuch.

"Yes, yes, a gentleman of European culture," Requesens muttered aloofly. He was not ready to go upstairs yet. In fact, he had—to his own bewilderment—been far from impatient to come here. Upon leaving Government House he had asked the taxicab driver to take him to the Casa Ninon; and getting out of the car there, he had not been irritated in the least when he had to wait for almost half an hour for another hack to turn up. He had had plenty of time. He had plenty of it now.

The idea had struck him like a bolt while he changed into civilian clothing. The simplicity of his scheme had so startled him at that moment that he had stopped in mid-air while slipping one leg into his trousers, and been nearly thrown off balance. A minute later he wondered whether it had not been the crumpled copy of El Huérfano's sheet sticking out of the wastepaper basket which had guided his thoughts. In truth, that idea had lain, as it were, all the time on the surface, and only common cowardice had prevented him from picking it up. . . .

El Huérfano must be killed. Dead, he was sure to incite his followers to a pitch of fury. They would cry murder, would riot, engage in violence and savage crime . . . and then the Army—he, Lorenzo Requesens—would be called on to squelch the disturbance. And this would be the moment to make known to the Palace *his* pleasure, to trap the trappers! Gone were the days when young Lorenzo, having vanquished El Seringuero, could be shipped overseas in a hurry. This time he would turn against the bandits high up after having rescued the country from the banditry of the lowly. The road to glorious imaginings was wide open before him. Their gaining reality hinged on so little a thing as the life of El Huérfano! His detestation of him was to be the handmaiden of greater causes.

"Yes, our guest *is* a nice man," Lorenzo repeated, glancing at Ramón with the blank benevolence which a sudden great resolve often instills into wavering men. How simple life was! He derided the hazy, fanciful expectations with which he had looked forward to the arrival of Philibert. "Too bad," he added, "that we have to keep him to ourselves, Ramón, eh?"

Ramón's falsetto echoed that last, mysterious statement of his master. As Don Lorenzo turned away from him, he squatted down on a bundle of straw piled up against the low parapet of the basin. From there he could keep an eye on the lighted window and the man's shadow continuously flickering across it. He felt happy. The señor colonel would not fail him, whatever it was he might be preparing for.

Lorenzo returned these feelings. Before he opened the door upstairs, he gave an affectionate thought to his faithful man sitting below in the dark in his rumpled cotton suit, a symbol of the confidence of the millions he had set out to conquer.

M. Philibert faced the door. In the middle of the room there stood two candles held by empty beer bottles. An iron bed, which had not been here previously, occupied the farthest corner. The dismantled Venetian blinds were propped against it.

"Good evening," Requesens said.

"Here I am," said Philibert, as he walked back to the bed to sit down, leaving the wicker chair to his caller. He cupped his chin in both hands.

"You must be tired."

"A hasty journey," Philibert acknowledged, barely moving his lips.

"My man would not have rushed you so much—"

"Trains. Know all about them." M. Philibert's outer appearance was still as neat as ever. It was hard to imagine how he managed at the hacienda to keep spotless the one suit he seemed to possess.

Requesens said, "I was sorry to learn about the death of your comrade." He waited in vain for a reaction.

"Here I am," said the other again with coolness.

"Here you are. You see, friend? I told you your time might come sooner than we both thought it would. Naturally, when we talked last, I did not know I would be in a position to shorten the waiting period."

"Right. Haven't congratulated you yet," Philibert remarked. He sat higher back on the cot, leaving his legs dangling. A thin cloud of dust rose from the poncho spread over the bedding.

Lorenzo looked straight ahead. He proceeded with some effort, "So it goes. Yes, so it goes. Life is full of turns. As for you now . . . You may not know that in this country the Minister of War can commission whomever he wants as an officer in the Army. If he so wants, he can, for instance, give a commission to a civilian, to an untrained man. Or, for that matter, to any soldier of any foreign army. For some years the late General himself had an Irishman as his A.D.C."

M. Philibert lifted his head a little. "I take it you wish to go even farther back in history. Or was selling Army commissions a custom still alive during the General's time in your country? For you want me to buy a commission, don't you? Why do you hesitate? Go ahead and tell me that a captaincy—or is it to be a colonelcy?—is a bargain at the price of five hundred and eleven thousand dollars."

"You are on the wrong track," Don Lorenzo answered with sonorous dignity. "I have something entirely different on my mind. Actually, you will even be able to retrieve a part of that sum."

"A part! Another part, five hundred thousand, I guess, being charged against the captaincy."

"Still wrong," Lorenzo said. He could not help admiring his own restraint. "The Army commission—which, by the way, belongs to a more distant future, if only a somewhat more distant one, I hope— that commission has nothing to do with the cash transaction I have been considering for some time. Nor would I have touched on that subject now—"

"How big is the sum you have been 'considering,' colonel?"

"Quite big, quite handsome."

"And you're offering me a paying job in addition?"

"In due time."

"And my freedom?"

"Right away. That is, the amount of freedom any army officer has. An army officer is always under orders, isn't he?"

"What is the dirty work? Surely you do not doubt that I know it is rough work you wish to enlist me for."

Don Lorenzo tilted his chair backwards. "It *is* rough work," he confirmed, "but the risks will be small. With me behind you, they will be negligible."

"How negligible?"

"Still a stickler for words?"

Philibert stared at him moodily, saying nothing.

"And aren't you surprised?"

"At what?"

"At my readiness to return you to human society? At my arrangements for your comeback, a comeback both honorable and profitable?"

"History moves in leaps," said Philibert with a judicious air, and made some steps to and fro, almost circling the two candles on the floor. "Though, come to think of it, it doesn't in the present instance. Hence, I suppose, my total lack of surprise. For isn't what you are about to suggest entirely in the line of my past history, at least as you see it?"

"Your past history is a failure. What I am to suggest won't be."

M. Philibert's eyes did not release Requesens, while he came close up to him. "Who is it you wish to do in?" he asked.

"El Huérfano," Lorenzo said.

"Why?"

Don Lorenzo replied first with a shrug. He felt relaxed: it came to his mind that the course events would take upon El Huérfano's death, the short stretch of disorder he counted on, would in some way or another release him from all his promises to Philibert. "Why?" he repeated at last. "What do you expect me to tell you? If El Huérfano's liquidation were a measure to be dependent on cool and thorough reasoning, it would be up to the courts, and not to me and you."

"You misunderstood my curiosity, colonel. I am not asking for judicial explanations. That would be absurd in the light of my past history. I am asking a simple question. Why do you want him done in?"

"He is in my way. Old accounts must be settled."

"They only must, if he is still in your way," muttered Philibert, stepping back. His shadow shrank on the wall.

"Aren't you interested in my price?"

"I am above all interested in the guarantees which you offer. You wish to hire me for a liquidation. Not that I said I would do it. Anyway, you wish to hire me. You offer some of the money which is not yours—"

"It isn't yours either, don't forget that."

"—some of that money, plus some sort of job, and a reasonable amount of freedom. Now what are your guarantees? Against the police and the courts on the one hand, against El Huérfano's partisans . . ."

Watching the slyly challenging gesture with which M. Philibert seemed to complete his unfinished sentence, Lorenzo was fascinated by the quick perception of the man who paused but a moment.

"And what, on the other hand, are the guarantees you propose against possible future changes in your own ordre de bataille, colonel?"

"Ordre de bataille? Settling old accounts with a bothersome nobody hardly requires anything worth that expression."

"I do not believe in the urgency of those old accounts. At least I don't believe in them as the main reason for the measure you want to hire me for. Even if you brought in your honor—the sense of honor (remember?) for which you were said to have a passion—I would refuse to believe you. I've come to think you are not the type to make sacrifices for your sense of honor. You don't do things for the fun of it. You don't do things without ulterior reasons. And I, I do not do things, no matter how much they may be in my line, whose ulterior reasons I don't understand."

"I told you the fellow is in my way."

"What *is* your way, Requesens?"

Don Lorenzo uncrossed his legs slowly. He got up and walked to the window. He did not see Ramón's figure in the dark. Beyond the low wall of his courtyard purple specks dotted the night, the glowing embers in the braziers of the neighbors preparing their late meal.

"I've had a great deal of leisure at Señor Bundschuh's," Philibert continued. "Some other man in my shoes might have used it to ponder the past. I did not. And as my present was rather empty, shall we say, I could not help giving some thought to your affairs, Requesens. I've asked myself what you were up to. I asked myself why a man with your funds (to call them yours for the sake of the argument) should have been eager to join the game once more. War Minister of the Republic! His Excellency! I take it the chief attraction of that office used to be the commissions a man handing out Army contracts can secure for himself. Now you couldn't possibly be interested in such trifles. War Minister of the Republic! Good God, you used to live in the world, Requesens. Pushing around a handful of ragged sepoys can hardly hold much attraction for you!"

Don Lorenzo had turned around earlier. "A minute ago I was about to compliment you on your cleverness," he said. Philibert sat on the chair. "I realize it would have been a mistake. Don't you see that the littleness of one's world does not make it less one's world? This is my country. It has been the country of the Requesens for more than two hundred years. This land was a great and glorious empire when your own country—oh, Mother of God, where was your country then! History moves in leaps, I agree. This country is on the eve of a reawakening. Its sense of independence is surging up. It needs only new courage. It must find again the sense of its destiny—"

"And a man who may lead it to fulfilling that destiny, eh?"

"Nothing of the kind. What I wanted to point out to you, my clever man, was only that to be the Minister of War of the Republic is by no means so puny a calling. It is worth a man's exertions."

"And so is the Presidency, I presume."

A great silence fell.

"Ambition, Requesens, is a deceptive thing. In its throes a man is prone to accept any motive—"

"Enough of that silliness!"

M. Philibert fumbled at his belt. "I am not in your service yet," he said in a matter-of-fact tone. "I am far from admiring your patriotic mettle, Requesens. Of course I am also far from admiring, or finding fault with, the lust for power in you—as your enemies might call it some day. I still have not made up my mind whether you are not primarily dreaming of some more wealth—wealth to be squeezed out of your own country, for a change. But then," he said, and straightened, "combinations of motives are possible."

Requesens was leaning against the window sill. "Unlike yourself," he said, "I've had very little leisure of late, and could not occupy myself with speculations, or abandon myself to pipedreams. You are not conversant with democratic institutions. How could you be? If you were, you would know that, in a democratic country, every man, at least every man of good birth, dreams of himself at times as the occupant of the Palace. I do not pretend to exclude myself from that dream."

Philibert shifted his reddened eyes. "Colonel Requesens . . ." he finally said, not unkindly.

This was familiar ground to Don Lorenzo up to a point: it was almost like talking to Priscilla. But here in front of him was not the familiar and familiarly critical recipient of the wisdom, the valor, and the morality, of which he would boast—at different times or at one and the same time—in front of his wife. This stranger had confronted him squarely with his aspirations. He had made him realize that they antedated his frightening experience at the Club and his anxiety, ever since, to find some means of foiling the plot.

"As I said," M. Philibert went on, "complex motives are not out of the question. It would be wise to consider complex means to achieve what you have at heart."

"To do away with El Huérfano," Don Lorenzo said surlily, "that's what I have at heart."

"Granted. But pray tell me, how is his removal to smooth your way from there on? How is it to further your ends?"

"His disappearance is an end in itself."

"Do you think he is so bitterly loathed by and large, regarded as so great a menace, that by admitting your part in his removal—*post festum,* of course, and if all goes well—you will emerge as a hero?"

"He *is* a menace."

"To whom?"

"*You* ask this question? You? Yesterday he inflicted pinpricks on decent men and spread scandal. Today he stirs up the laborers in the workshops, takes exception to Army reforms. Tomorrow he'll reach out for more. Must I go into details? Since when do *you* people think so leniently about fellows of El Huérfano's persuasion?"

Again Philibert pronounced Don Lorenzo's name with an inflection of rebuke. "You say he will be a real menace tomorrow. To whom, to whom?"

"To law and order. To the right people."

"Are the right people right for your purpose? Wasn't it the right people who wronged you some years ago?"

"You needn't urge me to settle accounts with *them*. Don't worry, I will."

"So will El Huérfano. . . . Don't you see that he is your ally, Requesens?"

Lorenzo did not start. The very enormity of the statement seemed to deprive it of an immediate effect.

"You are playing about with your Army, your officers," M. Philibert proceeded with deliberate calm, "or do they play about with you? I wouldn't know. Reforms, a modern air force . . . Something else still? Don't you see that there is another army to be had? Have the masses never entered your imagination? Law and order! Why not stop fawning on a monster which shackles your ambitions, and unleash another that may give you the great, the real chance? Or are you afraid of the morals of the right people? A good spell of savagery will obliterate their importance, believe me. This is 1945. You can no longer play the game according to the rules of your Eighties."

"What do you know about our Eighties!"

"Next to nothing. But you can hardly deny that I know a lot about the times we happen to be talking about."

"Not as far as this country is concerned. You do not understand it. I seem to recall that I told you so, some weeks ago, in this room. Like all exiles, you're judging your country of exile by the standards of the country you left behind. You may be quite sincere in this. Perhaps you are sorry that you and your friends did not band together with your own Huérfanos in good time—you see, I happen to know something about *your* Thirties—and fascinated by the thought of that failure, you now want to force your advice on me. It's easy to give advice, unbidden advice, mind you, and leave the great risks to others."

"Leave the risks to others? Why, I am prepared to take the greatest of all risks myself. In fact," Philibert said and pointed a forefinger at his breast, "that's where I come in. You see, I may be willing to talk to him myself. To El Huérfano. If it should not work, you can disavow me, call me a madman, swear you've never seen me, and get Bundschuh, together with the Murcia alcalde, to do likewise. If it should work—"

"But that is madness!"

"All the better as far as your own risks are concerned. In case it shouldn't work, you'll easily get an alienist to testify to my madness. He will be agreeable to the wishful diagnosis of so exalted a personage."

"Your jokes are in bad taste. When I declare that what you suggest is sheer madness—"

"According to the rules of 1880 it probably is. Maybe even according to yesterday's rules."

"Yesterday's rules are those of today in the Republic."

"No," Philibert said and rose again. "Little as I know of the history of the Republic, Requesens, I do not think that her ambitious colonels—

yesterday, or at any time before yesterday—hired foreign outcasts to do their shooting."

"Why don't you just say you don't have the courage to take over a rough job?"

"Courage! Any country fair tightrope walker has courage. And even the courage needed for eliminating human beings is far less rare in men than schoolteachers think. At any rate I do not suppose that anyone can call me averse to eliminating human beings. For a worthwhile purpose, that is."

"Such as collecting bank notes and jewelry in the ghettos of Poland in '39!" Requesens burst out.

M. Philibert balanced on his heels. "Such as collecting bank notes and jewelry in the cleaned-up ghettos of Poland."

"And how about getting back a parcel of those bills? Wouldn't that be a worthwhile purpose, too?"

"I shall come to that presently."

"Bah, you're just a coward!"

Philibert let a moment pass before he replied, "I would prove I am not —wouldn't I?—by going to see El Huérfano by myself. . . . One moment, colonel," he said, and stooped to shorten the candlewicks with a rapid snatch, "you are about to inquire after my price. Well, then, if I should succeed, I'll take care of my interests myself in the new setup." He smiled up at the open-mouthed face of his interlocutor. "You see, I am laying my cards on the table."

XVI

EL HUÉRFANO WAS rumored to be staying at Ollaytaytombo, an ancient settlement of three or four thousand people, "and of no greater import than its railroad station." Halfway between the capital and Majamarca, it handles some westbound traffic in timber. Requesens denied that El Huérfano had gone there to canvass the lumbermen. His contention was that the fellow meant to mold the laborers of the Eastern estates to his will, but alert to the fierce resistance he might encounter, was planning some inconspicuous trips to the plains from Ollaytaytombo.

It was fairly late in the afternoon when M. Philibert arrived at that station. He had had a compartment to himself, which had sheltered him from intrusions. He even had found some sleep.

M. Philibert put down the small strapped valise with which Ramón had replaced his knapsack. Still standing close to the train, he lighted a cigar behind cupped hands, and took stock of the place from under his brow. The station building, a low, whitewashed structure, was about a hundred meters to his left. Farther off in the same direction the signalman's cabin peeped out from the foliage of young trees. The turntable beneath the engine shed, overgrown with weeds, seemed out of use. M. Philibert strained his eyes to discern a uniform among the crowd of natives milling about the macadamized platform. Their clothing was of livelier colors than the garments Murcia folk wore. The station master rushed by him, waving a small stiff flag. His was the only uniform in sight. M. Philibert grasped his suitcase.

Except for the stamp which should have attested his entering the Republic, his French passport was flawless; and Requesens had assured him smilingly that the affection for all things French in the country would protect that document from overzealous investigation.

At first he had been annoyed that Bundschuh had handed over the passport to Philibert. And M. Philibert did not tell him that he had wheedled it from Bundschuh by threatening to ignore the call to Huacho. To Bundschuh this *was* a threat. He was eager to have Philibert leave, and present in person his, Bundschuh's, grievances to Requesens. They had outgrown mere discomfort. He would call Ehinger all sorts of names in his absence, and complain that "the red-whiskered devil" had bewitched the girl. "You don't believe there is such a thing as witchcraft," he said to Philibert, tossing up his short arms in exasperation, "and you are free to invent your own word for what is going on under my nose. Do you know that the girl has hardly talked to me ever since Roy was sent off? You maintain that she doesn't associate with Ehinger. But you can't watch him all the time, can you? Oh, good Lord . . ."

Once in Don Lorenzo's presence, Philibert had been oblivious of those petty worries of Bundschuh. As the interview turned toward serious business, he even savored the recollection of Ehinger's presumed pastime at the hacienda. Fornication was about the only thing which at times superseded a man's ambition. Left alone to his pleasure, Ehinger was less likely to grudge his senior companion this outing. "Ehinger? Don't give it a thought," he had replied to Requesens' query. "I'll write him I took sick. I have that underling in the palm of my hand. He doesn't know *this* much about my affairs."

He had overstressed his contempt of his young companion—though not his indifference toward him, and his conviction that they had parted ways for good and that loyalty without a common target was like wine seeping out from a leaking bag. At this moment he did not suppress a flash of satisfaction: Ehinger would stand agape, could he watch him strolling through this crowd of peóns, a free man, a man with a job to do, a man with a mission.

There was an acid smell about these humans, a wretched lot notwithstanding the bright dyes of their tatters. Unlike the knots of loud-voiced people at the Huacho depot, they appeared to expect nothing from anyone. The women made no attempt to offer the trifle of salable stuff in their baskets. Once Philibert was nearly knocked over by the quick turn of a half-naked adolescent who, with some others, was busy throwing stones at the row of scavenger birds, black, red-necked creatures that perched on the station's roof. A well-fed friar stood on its threshold, hands folded before him, and cast an indifferent glance at the arrivals. Philibert noticed that there was no need to enter the building: the platform was, without fence or hedge, abutting on a dirt road.

Of the settlement nothing was to be seen. No conveyance was present. Two saddled burros grazed on the opposite side of the track. The bird-like shouts of the children, now behind Philibert, riddled the gurgling sound of the water crane. The murmurs of the grownups rose and fell. Only after a while did he see a young woman standing, near a curbstone far to the left, beside her diminutive donkey. Her profile, strong and earnest, was set against the glow of the hour.

Philibert crossed over to the woman. "Ollaytaytombo?" he asked, raising his arm toward the sunset.

No, motioned the woman.

"Where?"

She thrust her chin east.

He decided to ask no more. It was preferable to get ahead of the natives who evidently were waiting for the train's departure—a daily habit, as could be assumed. Also, other passengers had alighted from the train along with Philibert, and though they had lost themselves among the rabble at once, he told himself that some of them might well be competitors for the handful of habitable rooms the town was likely to boast.

Directly he stalked off, deep oxcart ruts hindered his strides. To his left thick undergrowth lined the road, viciously encroaching upon his path. Timber stacks obtruded upon his view at the right. After two hundred paces the log piles seemed to recede, following a gradual bend of the rails and giving way to matted verdure. At the same time the dried-up ruts ceased, and the level roadway grew more narrow. A range of hills, indistinguishable from the banks of clouds, loomed very far-off in the north. M. Philibert was assailed by a feeling of being hemmed in, not accounted for by the wide monotony of the landscape.

He threw away the cigar, and spat. "If this isn't the maddest excursion I've ever been on . . ." he heard himself say. Nor was he sure these were the first words he had uttered. 'Watch me, colonel,' he grimly addressed Requesens in his mind, 'I could give you a register of undertakings each more hazardous than opening a deal with a muddleheaded soapbox orator. Are you still worried about my Spanish? I told you it had improved. Moreover, it has its advantages, as it is. I can always maintain I erred. Didn't I also explain to you that as a foreigner, as the kind of tourist, writer, or newspaperman, I might pose to be I can talk to him in a way you yourself never could? El Huérfano can shrug off, and in good humor too, whatever I say as a foreigner's fancy. And the foreigner may return, his job not accomplished, to be sure, but no harm done. . . .'

Whatever was to come out of the venture, to have forced his counsel on Requesens was a victory. They had not arrived at their agreement lightly. Philibert's lack of anxiety to have his reward fixed seemed to worry Don Lorenzo. And as if to vex him still more, Philibert had advanced a "collateral proviso" so extraordinary he still felt a shudder of self-admiration in calling it back to his memory.

They had been discussing the "old funds" (to use Don Lorenzo's expression) perhaps for the tenth time that night, and Philibert had said that what he had in mind under the circumstances was their use for a good cause. Don Lorenzo wanted to know what he meant by "a good cause." What he was going to tell him, Philibert answered, was likely to sound unreasonable to the colonel. To put it bluntly, he was wondering what course Don Lorenzo might pursue in his future foreign policies.

Don Lorenzo waited. He was standing before Philibert, the wasting candles behind him, and though his face eluded their light, the sudden gleam in his eyes did not escape M. Philibert.

"There is a minor point I'd like to take up at this moment," he proceeded in a changed tone. "It is not altogether independent from the future conduct of foreign affairs. Many good men, compatriots of mine, are in foreign countries. They look for refuge. . . ."

The idea had entered Philibert's brain on the spur of the moment, and its unselfishness, its purity had moved him deeply. Afterwards its luster grew dull. The sight of the country on his journey imbued him with a personal pride which displaced his simple patriotic emotions. The awareness that he was about to stage singlehanded a coup d'état in this strangest of lands had no room for limited notions. Its very vastness exhaled readiness, solicited rape. Sleeping their century-long siesta, the twilit forests and jungles, the puny patches of millet and corn, the borderless steppes, and the unmined ranges, urged on the traveller their waiting bounty.

At one particular turn on the way to Ollaytaytombo the railroad track affords a view of the River. It so happened that M. Phillibert, starting up from his revery, saw the waters where they break forth from between the thrust-out boulders of the descending plateau. Issuing from the spinning foam, the stream hurries on there to calmer currents. It is a beautiful sight. But the avidity with which Philibert took it in, while the shriek of the engine rent the great stillness, was not meant for the land-scape's marvels. His thoughts at that moment soared high above his impending mission. They showed him his calling in well-nigh conquista-dorial proportions.

But that moment had passed with the view of the River. As the countryside coming toward him flattened and emptied, he had experi-enced all the doubts of a man vanquished and wasted.

Now, as he strode along, he felt them again. The station, the railroad seemed miles away—Huacho, Requesens, far as the moon. The quiet preyed on him. To rebuff it, he summoned the past to his mind. But the past lay dead and deserted, overcast by the shadows of failure and sense-less exertion.

Suddenly the road was at its end. It was as though the blade of a gigantic knife had cut it off. M. Philibert gave vent to a string of pro-fanities. Had the Indian wench at the station misinformed him? He was about to sit down on his valise when he noticed, hidden by the tall grass, the abrupt rectangular turn of the roadway to the left. Advancing a few more steps, he found himself at a junction. He craned his neck to the right to discover whether that was the more likely direction. Thus he failed to see the two men coming out of the side path on their mules before one of them, coming to a halt, accosted him.

"Going our way, friend?" he asked in what Philibert thought to be a less corrupted language than would have befitted the man's appearance. He was a fat-jowled mestizo, rather tall. His legs nearly touched the ground.

"Ollaytaytombo," Philibert said ill-humoredly.

The half-breed gave a yank on the bridle. "It is sad we cannot take the señor with us," he said, patting the flank of his mount, as it sidestepped. "It is two more leguas. On business, señor?"

"Travelling. Travelling the country."

The man seemed tempted to call out to his companion, who had gone on. But then he let his hand drop. "May the Virgin protect you. This is good country." He gave the rein to his mule without any further look at M. Philibert, and the animal fell into a fidgety trot. Philibert could not see whether the two men began to talk to each other once they were side by side again. A cloud of dust enveloped them soon, and soon that cloud, too, was lost in the changeless horizon.

He resumed his march. He had not eaten much during the day. He considered opening his valise to have a sip from the pint bottle of brandy which he had bought at one of the stops. But having tasted it before, he knew that the aguardiente did not agree with him. Weird dreams, he remembered, had visited him on the train ride.

The sun was very low. The farther he marched, the farther away the foothills appeared in the north. He heard no birds, and saw none overhead. Were there no monkeys here out East? Or was it true that they had a way of withdrawing from a region prowled by a panther? Perhaps the country was infested with beasts. Had not the slit eyes of the mestizo smiled with malevolence as he called it "good country"? Philibert began to chide Requesens in his mind: why had he not informed him in more detail about his journey? He had admitted that he had never been in Ollaytaytombo himself. He had talked about the ruins of a great temple nearby. For the rest, he had said, it probably was an Indian place such as a hundred others in the Republic, and had—of a sudden!—made light of the police surveillance in "such places." Later, he had asked him to postpone his departure for a couple of days: he would find out more about Ollaytaytombo, its people, its public houses. M. Philibert had objected to any postponement; he still recalled his apprehension lest Requesens find another intermediary, or go to Ollaytaytombo himself on some pretext. He had felt the keenest possible relief when Requesens was ready to equip him with cash on the spot—indubitably the sum originally earmarked for hiring him as El Huérfano's assassin.

He reached for the money bag which he carried, fastened round his neck, under the shirt. Again, as he had done several times earlier, he changed the valise from one hand to the other. Oddly enough, he felt less thirsty now. Suddenly he saw the outline of the town's belfry. It rose serene against the fading blue, only to vanish from his sight the next minute, like a conjurer's trick. His expectancy mounted with every foot of the ground he put behind him. Now he perceived the belfry again and, after another hundred steps, the first pink-painted thatched shack. An inexplicable sense of security seized him.

Women loitered on darkening thresholds. The men in flapping white shirts squatted in front of their dwellings against the adobe walls, barely lifting their heads under their tilted-down straw hats. A smell of stale grease came to meet him. He decided to accost one of the men.

"You made good time, señor," said the tall fat-jowled mestizo, darting out of a half-open door. "Recognize me, yes? The señor looks for a good place to stay overnight, yes?"

"Some kind of supper and a bed will do," M. Philibert answered, smothering the expression of surprise on his face. He walked on.

The mestizo joined him. He chuckled appreciatively. "The señor knows he cannot ask for much in Ollaytaytombo. A supper, a bed. I shall guide the señor. Night comes. I shall carry the valise. What would our señora say, our darling señora, if I'd come with a distinguished guest who has to haul his own luggage!" He snatched the suitcase from Philibert's hand. "A poor town, but not forgetful of manners," he added with stilted courtesy. "It was bad enough I could not offer the señor a seat on my mule. We discussed the situation, I and my cousin. That was my cousin, señor. . . . He said that one of us should have dismounted, and should have offered his animal to the señor. The road is hard on men not from our country. Sometimes they come to visit the ruins. But as a rule the caballeros forewarn the alcalde, and he has mounts prepared for them at the station."

"Yes, I know. I could have done so myself, my friend. I was impatient."

"Men not from this country are often impatient," the mestizo conceded. They had turned a corner, and now passed the wide-open door of a cantina, which emitted a medley of voices. A man came forward, greeting the mestizo with a little shout, but, stepping backwards, disappeared again. Dusk began to descend. "Politicos," the guide said in a tone of pity.

"Politicos everywhere nowadays, eh?" Philibert ventured.

"The señor would not be interested in their provincial talk."

Philibert did not look at his cicerone. By now the low huts had yielded to two-storied stone houses on either side, and fewer people stood on the street. Here and there an early light shone through the shutters. "I have travelled much," he said on a sudden impulse.

"But our roads are poor. I would not know about roads round Huacho. But some people who come from there say that our roads are bad. Some other things are better here. A man is happy wherever he is, or is not happy at all. . . . I am glad the señor agrees," the half-breed added quickly, though Philibert was at a loss to reply to this unexpected epigram.

He reflected on the recompense he should offer to the man. Quite evidently he had lain in wait for him, and would get a coin, or a drink, from the tavern keeper. He walked ahead now, elbowing through the groups of unshod peasants who clogged the approach to the town square; they all turned their heads away as though refusing to be disturbed by a

stranger's appearance. Actually, they were gazing fixedly at the preten-
tious four-storey building which, as Philibert noticed, blocked the vista
of the belfry. A meeting of some kind was evidently going on.

The guide led M. Philibert along the arcade to the right, past the
croups of some nags tethered in front of an empty plank booth, giving,
perhaps by way of a joke, a wide berth to their switching tails. From
time to time he looked behind him, or jerked his thumb, as if to point
out, in the fading light, the sights of the city. All the while he kept his
brisk pace, and barely waited for Philibert to catch up with him before
he whisked into a lane whose arched entrance was almost indistinguishable from the ornamented façade of the house at the corner. "Coming,
señor?" he shouted over his shoulder.

At the same time there was an abrupt clamor on the plaza, and Philibert believed he saw the peasants cross it diagonally in a surging movement. Certainly there was shouting. But since night approached rapidly
now, and his eyes were intent on keeping in view the man with his
valise, he could not turn to look at the commotion. Also the shouts
abated abruptly.

"Market day today?" he asked as soon as he was abreast with the
mestizo.

"You made good time, señor," the man called out, pushing open a
door.

Advancing into complete darkness, Philibert would have stumbled
over the two stone steps leading down to the taproom, had his guide not
caught him by the elbow.

"Señora! Honorable señora!" he called. "Ah, not here. Busy. I shall
make some light." He brushed against Philibert, who presently saw him
climb onto the bar, strike a match, and light the kerosene lamp which
hung from the raw ceiling. High up on the wall there was a large picture of the General, yellowed and fly-specked.

Philibert moved the suitcase near the door. "And now, friend—" he
began.

"And now, señor, some aguardiente!"

Philibert walked over to one of the three round wooden tables in the
room. As soon as he was seated, he bent down to scratch his legs which
were covered with insect bites. He was a little angry with himself for
having followed the man as a matter of course: perhaps there was a
better place somewhere in the town, and also a less deserted one. It
would be difficult to get news here about the whereabouts of El Huér-

fano. "I wish I could have a glass of beer," he said with an ill-concealed sigh of annoyance.

"Hey, señora!" the man, having climbed down from the counter, shouted upwards, facing the small door, left ajar, in the rear. "Where are you, señora? Won't you come down? Darling señora! You'd better not confuse this caballero with those coca-chewing churls in the plaza, with that riffraff imposing on our town with not a single centavo between them. Actually," he said, lowering his voice in an affected tremolo, "I wrong her. Our darling señora knows a distinguished guest when she sees one. Of course, she would not be the person to tell a yanqui from a Russian or an Englishman."

"Of course not."

"Not that it makes any difference. This is not Huacho. Politicos in Huacho have their predilections for some foreigners and their dislikes for others, I have been told."

"Have you ever been in Huacho?"

"Señora, do you hear me?" the mestizo resumed his stentorian chant, while he winked at Philibert. "A customer is starving down here and he's close to dying of thirst. Coming from our great capital, as he is—or is the señor not coming from Huacho?" he interrupted himself. "He is, he is," he yelled up, his eyes uplifted, so that only their whites could be seen. "Now really, honorable señora—"

A tempest of words issuing from the dark staircase silenced the man and wiped the facetious smile from his face. "You, you, you and your like!" the woman cried out, appearing on the landing. Her voluminous skirts swaying about her thin hips, she strode up to the half-breed who withdrew toward the bar. Her surprisingly Caucasian-looking features beneath the wealth of plaited oily hair expressed utter disapproval.

Philibert was at a loss to grasp the vernacular of her tirade. Since she had given no sign of noticing him, her harangue probably did not concern itself with his presence or the demands it might make on her establishment. The mestizo did not attempt to throw in so much as a word. Biting his thick lips, he gazed down at his sandals. Only once did he raise his hands with a shrug which involved his whole body, and thereupon the high-pitched voice of the women lowered, and Philibert discovered an unmistakable pleading in her intonation. He got up to put an end to the passionate discourse. But the woman turned her back on him, shifting away. His hapless cicerone seemed equally unwilling to accept a third party's interference. For the man had started talking at last. Persuasion rang in his words; they sounded as if weighed out, deliberately retarded at times, and wildly burst forth at others, pitting themselves against the woman's dissenting silence. Then the "darling señora" took over again.

While M. Philibert returned to the table, still staring at them, he thought to himself that there was no falsehood in their preoccupation. They were oblivious of him. The scene was in accord with the impressions forced on him in the half hour past. The pastel-colored diminutive dwellings at the settlement's outskirts, the garrulous naïveté of his guide beneath its veneer of sophistication, the open-mouthed torpidity first and then the voluble shouts of the bare-footed mob on the square, the uncertain light, suggesting a net thin as a spider's web thrown over the city, and the instantaneous nightfall—all that had something dreamlike and remote about it, and something innocent and even childish. Indeed, here he was at the closest quarters with a half-civilized pack—clay in the hands of the rabble-rousing Huérfano if he so chose tomorrow; here "M. Philibert" was with no white man in hailing distance, no wires in sight to attest to the ordinary means of civilized communication. Yet he felt secure, and even moved by the patronizing sympathy of a Gulliver lost in the quaint preserve of pygmies. He was unknown here. For the first time since leaving Europe he brushed shoulders only with people who did not know what manner of man he was. For the first time in many long months he was safe from being recognized by anyone aware of his antecedents. A perception of freedom dawned on him, of a release from that bondage into which the blind pursuit of one road thrusts a man. Within this unknowing world, freedom was his for the asking. . . .

Sudden quiet called him back from his musing. About to answer another argument of the mestizo, the woman thought better of it. She stepped behind the bar, took a bottle from the shelf on the wall, and put it on the counter noisily, leaving it to the mestizo to fetch two glasses.

Laughing feebly, the mestizo followed her with a long, worried look as she came out from behind the bar, crossed the room, skirts swinging to and fro, and went out on the street. The contours of her torso and head remained visible through the opalescent pane of the door, slightly trembling in the light of a lantern which seemed to have been lit near the entrance outside. For a time, the man stood as if struck dumb. "Did the señor say a supper and a bed?" he began at last, collecting his thoughts. "*Aie,* our señora will feed the señor. She will feed you a big,

big piece of her roasted guinea pig, be sure of that."

"Now, friend, this is very good of you," M. Philibert said, watching the man, who had come up to the table with bottle and glasses to pour the brandy, "but I feel the señora is not in favor—"

"Not in favor!" the mestizo exclaimed with a guffaw, and dropped down on the chair next to Philibert. "Nothing *but* in favor she is! I swear to the Mother of God, señor, she is in favor of you. Hospitality," he went on under his breath, still shaken by what looked like forced amusement, "is a poor expression for her feelings for you. A bed? See her standing out there? She may be trying to get you something into that bed, too! She is broadminded. This town of Ollaytaytombo is very broadminded, and will not begrudge a little pleasure to a visitor of distinction. Small breasts, good vigorous legs . . . The señor is not an Englishman, no, to object to a little pleasure after an arduous journey? . . . Are you not comfortable, señor?"

The expression of Philibert's face and his posture must have given away his lack of ease. He felt the revolver in his pocket rub against his belt and press into his flesh whenever he moved; he wished Requesens, or Ramón, had given him a shoulder holster for carrying the weapon they had handed to him. "You will be my guest for that roast," he said, after he had pushed the revolver deeper down in his belt.

The mestizo filled both glasses again.

Philibert gave a reassuring smile. Outside, in the distance, windows were slammed shut, a door was banged. A woman giggled somewhere. "Will you take me to the ruins tomorrow?" Philibert asked after a pause. "We Frenchmen have always felt much interest in the past of the Republic."

"I may be busy tomorrow," the man replied.

"Of course I will pay you well," Philibert said, draining his tumbler a second time. The aguardiente tasted less harsh.

"Thank you very much, señor. Ruins. Naturally I shall take you there if I am not busy. It's customary for travellers to go to the ruins. But I always say ruins should not be the only attraction for a traveller coming all this way. Where exactly did the señor come from?"

Philibert covered his glass with his flattened hand. "Huacho."

"Another drink? After dinner maybe? Now I shall remind the señora of her duties," the half-breed mumbled with a wry smile, but he only moved to bring his chair still closer to Philibert's. "It is suppertime, no? It really is past it."

"It is, friend," Philibert said. Since the man showed no intention of getting up, he shook his head, and reached out for the bottle, helping himself to the drink he had just rejected. "Really, you'd better ask her now about supper. And as for tomorrow, well, if you *should* be busy, I still consider myself in your debt. I shall pay you. I shall pay you for guiding me here."

"The señor is angry?"

M. Philibert had drunk another long draught. He *was* angry. He felt that this inexplicable shell about him must be pierced. His quickened pulse urged him to hasten his business. If this should not prove to be a good place to start his investigations, he must leave and go to another tavern. "And also I shall pay you," he went on with labored bonhomie, "if you take me to one of those meetings."

"Meetings, señor?"

"Why, didn't you yourself say that there were many out-of-towners in Ollaytaytombo? Didn't you say it was market day?"

"Market day?"

"Or not. At any rate I heard people talk on the train about those meetings," Philibert insisted.

The mestizo lifted the bottle and held it obliquely up against the light of the lamp. "You have a pistol, señor," he said, turning back to Philibert. "Why do you have a pistol? Do Frenchmen always carry a pistol?"

"An old habit of mine," Philibert said negligently. "You saw me on the roadway all by myself, did you not? Now a pistol may come in handy against a panther, let us say."

The man nodded in what seemed to be agreement.

"That is why I carry a pistol," Philibert continued, and pressed down his chin in a throaty laugh. "Ah, here is the señora!"

The tavern keeper had entered the room again. She closed the door with a loud bang which was followed by a brief rattling noise, walked past the two men with swinging skirts, and looked into the face of the stranger, her lips drawn.

M. Philibert greeted her with arms spread.

"The señor will enjoy a roast," the half-breed called out.

"It is always better to talk over a good meal, señora, you know that," Philibert said in a jocular manner, "and as it happens, I and my friend here have to talk things over." The experiences of a whole lifetime should have told him he was on the wrong path. They did warn him.

But in the same breath a kind of wild defiance swept him. He leaned forward on his elbows which rested on the top of the table; and while the woman, probably walking toward the staircase—her sandaled feet did not betray her—vanished in the shadow, he said in a cordial whisper, "Ah, women! . . . Now tell me, friend, have you ever been at one of those meetings yourself? Have you ever seen that fellow? I mean to say that new politico, that orator, or popular leader?"

"El Huérfano, señor?"

"Yes, that is the nickname, I think."

"We shall talk about him over the meal, as you suggested," said the man in a hushed tone that emulated Philibert's own. "Will the señor permit me to make a suggestion?"

"Go ahead, my friend!"

The mestizo detached his right hand from the bottle. "It would be a good thing for the señor to give his pistol to our señora for safe-keeping."

"It's safe enough, it is perfectly safe with me."

"Hand it over, no?"

Philibert took his arms from the table.

"Do not move, señor," the half-breed said without changing the volume of his voice.

"My friend," Philibert pronounced with effort, "I am a French citizen."

"No?" asked the man.

"It would be very unwise of you—"

"Do not move!"

"I want to show you my passport. You can read, eh? Or maybe you can't. Why, if the alcalde wants to see my passport—fine. Take me to him. And if you think," he said with a cheerful toss of his head which scarcely hid his panic, "that El Huérfano should have a say in the matter, that is, if he is really as powerful hereabouts as I heard people say, and if you know where to find him—"

"Who sent the señor?" the man broke in, getting to his feet. At the same time he reached, in a rapid move, across Philibert's shoulders to clasp the back of his chair, violently yanking at it and bringing it about to face him. "Who sent the señor from abroad to spy on El Huérfano, if no worse? Eh, who?" Towering over him, he pressed his hand against Philibert's chest.

Being thus held down with increasing force, M. Philibert could

K

still have kicked the testicles of the insolent half-breed with his knees —he must have recalled that device of keeping at bay an aggressor. But he was as if paralyzed. A stabbing pain in the bladder, never felt before, lamed his thighs.

"Who? who? who?" he heard the attacker shout, and in the following second he was jerked off the chair, and the mestizo hurled him upon the earthen floor, kneeling on his stomach and grabbing his hands. Philibert twisted his head to escape the foul breath pouring down on him. Dirt entered his mouth. He retched. He distinctly saw, enormously magnified, the toppled chair raised above him. Then he was lost in a blackness which blunted his agony.

XVII

An intermittent, mercurial brushing against his hand was the first sensation he became aware of again. Automatically, he tried to fend off whatever it was that touched him, but an edged obstacle cut into the flesh of his wrists. He managed to open his eyes a little and, though a leaden heaviness behind his temples dulled his vision, he saw the small hunchbacked lizard that had played about his dangling hands scuttle away. He let his tongue run over his palate. Water dripped down his face.

He discovered that he was propped against the wall in a half-sitting posture: the rough grain of the bricks was chafing his back. He saw legs—an unsteady frieze of legs in white and in dark clothing. Then hands emerged from the rippling shadows—some fleshy and hanging down limply like cuts of meat from a butcher's hook, others with doubled fists, and still others with thumbs stuck into belts. His eyes shut again.

There were four men. They leaned against the bar. A piece of cardboard had been put round the kerosene lamp. In the two hours since Philibert was beaten into unconsciousness by the mestizo, the latter had been joined by a pair of robust Indians of the type who had been in the market place at nightfall, and, somewhat later, by a small, stooping man in crumpled European clothes, whose ill-shaven, sickly, bespectacled face looked out from under a soiled grey homburg.

"Try it once more," this man said, overcoming a spasm of stammering.

The mestizo nodded, and one of the Indios advanced toward the vessel with water which stood close to Philibert's feet, and took a rag out of it to exchange it for the one on the captive's forehead.

"We can take off the shackles, no?" asked the mestizo.

"No," the other said.

"He is helpless. He no longer has his pistol."

"You do not know his sort."

After dropping the cloth into the water, the Indian returned to the other three on tiptoe. Someone rattled at the entrance door, and one could hear the señora shouting from an upstairs window that the cantina was closed for the night.

"You do not know his sort," the white man repeated.

"I took care of him, no?"

"Yes. I think it was good to take care of him. You were fortunate. But the thing to do would have been to notify me first, and not take him on by yourself."

"I followed El Huérfano's orders. He ordered me to take care of the man right after we met him on the road."

"You know how El Huérfano underrates personal danger. You should have notified *me*. If *I* had not got hold of El Huérfano before he spoke to the crowd—"

"If you had not got hold of him, our visitor would still be where he is, and in his present condition, too," the mestizo remonstrated, profiting by another stuttering spell of the white man.

"He just moved, did he not?"

"He will sonner or later," declared the half-breed, "sooner or later he must come to. He is not really hurt. He had five glasses of aguardiente, or even six of them."

"Another mistake on your part."

"Mistake . . ." echoed the mestizo several times in an undertone before he said, "He can do no harm, and this is the decisive thing. I cannot conceive what harm he could do. This is why I say we should unbind him. One day he will return to his people. Why should he be made to call us brutes?"

The white man gave no reply save a loud contemptuous grunt. It was the first sound which clearly reached M. Philibert. While he tried desperately to open his burning eyes, the previous exchange of words had merely skirted his senses. He made an attempt to feel the cord of his money bag with his chin. With his lower lip he moistened the skin under his nose: a scab of clotted blood seemed to have collected there. Prudently he shifted his legs. Another cutting cramp in his bladder evoked a deep moan from his throat. He strained his nerves to gain a firm concept of his surroundings. He managed to recall his fall, his nausea . . . but these things came to his mind as one remembers an accident he was caught in through no one's fault. The touch of the money bag's cord beneath his shirt afforded some satisfaction. He had not been robbed. He leaned his head back against the wall. He shook off the compress which had slid down over his nose and mouth. "Water," he said.

"Drink," said the stranger, whose white face Philibert now discerned, A cup was held up to his lips. "Drink, and let us have a talk."

Philibert gulped the stale water.

"I warned you, señor."

"You warned me, ah, did you?" Philibert mouthed over the brim of the earthen bowl. He had recognized the one who had struck him down. But though he kept his gaze fastened on the mestizo, he still could not remember what had preceded his vicious assault. At last his lips formed the word "pistol." The presence of a white man should have comforted him. It did not. "Who are you?" he asked, taking his lips from the cup.

"I shall introduce myself in due time," the stranger said haltingly. He had taken a step toward Philibert. "Some more water? A drop of aguardiente?"

Philibert shook his head. It still ached furiously. But the pain in his urinary tract had not recurred in the past minute or so. He noted that his legs were shackled, too; a rope bound his ankles.

"Who are you?" the white man said clearly. "Now try to think, will you? What is your name?"

"Passport . . . You've got my passport."

"We have."

"So you have my name."

"You must talk, señor," the mestizo said. "What is your name?"

"Philibert."

"What business do you have with El Huérfano?"

"No business. I have no business with anyone here in this country. I was not careful with that brandy. We talked, no? We talked about all sorts of matters. We were alone, were we not? We were talking about my pistol. I did not know it was illegal to carry a pistol in . . ." For the life of him he could not think of the name of the place.

"You must tell us what it is that makes you so curious about El Huérfano, señor. This man here is a friend. He is a great friend of El Huérfano."

"Take away these things," Philibert said, raising his manacled hands a little.

None of the four men reacted. The two peasants kept themselves near the door, standing bolt upright, the fingers of their crossed arms holding their shoulders.

"Take them away?" the white man repeated. "Not before you tell us why you wanted to see him with an Army pistol in your pocket."

Philibert argued with much clarity now. He understood that his tormentors suspected him of an attempt on El Huérfano's life. It was the height of ironic misunderstanding! For a second he felt like laughing out loud, but the gravity of his condition whittled away its involuntary humor. He told himself that the suspicion of these men must have other motives than his imprudent talk. Yet he might have been spared his predicament, had he not allowed his tongue to get ahead of his brains . . . had he not allowed this dolt to intoxicate him! Was he no longer the man he used to be? Had he lost his superiority over men so quickly? Or had he never been above ordinary men, and had merely been made to feel so by his banding together with others in a wolf pack? Shreds of such self-accusing speculations flashed through his head, while he looked at the twitching face of the white man who started talking again.

"You see," he was saying, "you do not happen to be the first."

"What first?" Philibert protested in a brusque tone that hardly fitted his situation. So Requesens had lied to him! So he had previously sent someone here, or to some other place where El Huérfano happened to stay, with the order to do him in; that man had failed, and now he had dispatched *him* on the all but hopeless errand. . . . He turned his head. He could no longer bear the expressionless leer of the white man.

"The monsieur does not choose to answer our queries. I am afraid civil language will not do with him. . . . You want to be free of those things, did you say? Monsieur, it is up to you."

"I told you—"

"You told us nothing," the white man interrupted the prisoner, "nothing at all." He snapped his fingers, and one of the two Indios came forward, extending his arms as if to remove Philibert's shackles —probably the impeded and also slightly exotic speech of the stranger had confused him—but a shout halted him in mid-stride.

The calm with which the white man, still scowling at the peasant, extricated a large silver case from the pocket of his tight-fitting jacket and lit a cigarette infuriated Philibert. "Why do you stop him?" he growled, ceasing from his attempt to move his legs. "Ask your friend over there. *Him* I told everything last night . . . tonight. Make him repeat what I said word by word. I told him truthfully I was a tourist. . . ." A new twinge cramped his bladder. He tried to hunch up, while streamlets of sweat ran over his body.

"There *are* tourists who come to Ollaytaytombo," the mestizo suggested, "but he did not look like one to me. And when I found out that he carried a pistol . . . Also his luggage does not look like that of a tourist. No books, no papers, no big glasses. That I found out only afterwards, of course." He lifted his shoulders. "But there *are* tourists, that much I will say. They come to see the ruins three leguas outside of the town. That much I will say."

The white man had pulled himself up a chair, and sat down, straddling it, legs wide apart. He took off his hat, and threw it behind him on the table. He was completely bald. His cigarette glued to the lower lip, he stared down at the prisoner.

A kind of firmer reasoning seized Philibert's mind. He began to doubt his surmise that Requesens had sent someone else to El Huérfano before, or rather, sent him to do away with the fellow: surely these henchmen of his would refer with a more explicit resentment to any such incident. Well, then, if he was not exactly a tourist, he yet had meant no harm, had he? Presently his plight appeared to him in the light of innocence betrayed. He felt some of his old confidence returning, while he said disdainfully, "It is a disgrace. An abominable disgrace. And to think that your country is called a civilized one in the world outside." But under the unwinking gaze of the white man above him, his indignation faltered. "How can a tourist prove . . ." he muttered, "how can he prove that he is a tourist?"

"He can be made to tell the truth."

"You both will be sorry!" Philibert cried out, suddenly. "Take me to El Huérfano. Take me to him the way I am, to your own great shame! Let these men carry me to him, wherever he may be. Let me talk to him, and you will soon realize the extent of your folly."

"Take you to him?" the mestizo countered. "First, he is to leave Ollaytaytombo in a few hours—" An imperative gesture of the other silenced him.

"A few hours!" Philibert vociferated. "I'll need but a few minutes!"

"And if unshackled and given your toy," said the white man, "maybe less than that, no?" He blew the smoke of his cigarette straight into Philibert's face. "I am telling you, this is a dangerous customer. We had a very similar experience in my own country some months ago. I told El Huérfano about it. It was not a Frenchman who came to meddle in the affairs of our *partido*, but a foreigner it was, a European. He too had all sorts of little whatnots in his luggage, to be used in case we would not listen to reason. To his kind of reason. We got rid of that one in no time. A good riddance . . . a good riddance." He was no longer observing Philibert. Looking at the mestizo, he had (perhaps to steady his speech) rested his chin against his left shoulder, and at the same time dropped his right arm over the back of the chair.

M. Philibert watched the short fingers that held the cigarette come closer and closer to his neck and cheek. He twisted his trunk, and raised his fettered hands in a futile motion of self-protection. He all but expected the burning cigarette to touch his flesh at any moment. In his imagination he already smelled the stench of his blistering flesh. Incredible as it may sound, this was the first time in this trying hour that a memory of similar inquiries and their brutal proceedings, which he had ordered and witnessed himself, dented his consciousness. . . .

"In short," the stammerer continued, "I for one know the species. I know these emissaries from the brethren overseas who don't know *that* much—" he took a last, long puff at his cigarette, and threw its end, still aglow, on the floor—"not *that* much about realities in our republics. Hey, you! Emissary! Or shall we say commissar?"

"Leave him alone," the mestizo said. "This is not our way. We want to question him in an orderly fashion."

"Orderly? These comrades are made of durable stuff. They are not easily bent or broken. Under certain circumstances they are said to prefer being broken to going home and having to report their failure. Am I right, commissar?"

His face averted, M. Philibert had kept his eyes fixed on the last gleam of the cigarette, which now vanished in the dust of the floor. He said feebly, "I do not know what you are discussing, señor. The whole thing is a ghastly mistake."

The mestizo took a sip from a glass which he replaced behind him on the counter before he stepped up to his friend. "*I* will question him," he announced. "The señor came to see El Huérfano, yes? Why? Who sent the señor?"

"The señor! Did you not ask these questions a score of times? Go ahead. Waste your breath on him. Waste your breath on a killer."

"Granted he is a killer," Philibert heard the half-breed reply, while he himself could not take his eyes from the white man, who rubbed the nails of one hand against the palm of the other, "he is a poor killer now, thanks to my interference."

"And how about the men behind him? How about our meddlesome brethren overseas?"

The mestizo bowed with a smile. "Friend, we have known—I mean to say, we have known before you came—that certain men abroad wish for the elimination of El Huérfano from our party. It is as you said. I do not know why El Huérfano is not to their taste. *He* does. I do not. Do you? I doubt it. El Huérfano is a great one for listening. Why should he not listen to you? But did he tell you anything? Did he tell you *why* the comrades abroad seem no longer to be in full sympathy with him? No, he did not. Why should he?"

Philibert gaped at the change that had come over the man, and at the determination with which, ignoring the other's snorts of protest, he continued,

"And do you not think you have been hasty in your conclusions? You were very eager to convince El Huérfano that this Frenchman was sent here by none other than our brethren overseas. But did you convince El Huérfano? You did not convince me. Others may have dispatched this Frenchman, be he a killer or not. There are many people in the Republic itself who wish El Huérfano evil. Take the aristocrats in Huacho. Take the merchants. Take the Army."

"Would they dispatch a *foreigner* to do evil to El Huérfano, a fellow as conspicuous as this sorry parcel?" the white man objected with the nearest approach to condescension the impediment in his speech permitted him to assume. He lifted his leg to point at the captive, who had succeeded in heaving himself by little jerks into a more erect posture.

His guide of some hours ago—that confounded mongrel who had so brilliantly played a simpleton's rôle!—looked before him, impressed by the argument of his interlocutor. "That is true," he mumbled after a long silence. "Maybe they would not dispatch a Frenchman. Maybe they would not."

M. Philibert had been quick to grasp the inter-party strife that obviously beset El Huérfano's faction, also the change of heart of his

political patrons abroad. If ever an entering wedge had proffered itself
to a schemer, here it was! "Once more, señores!" he pronounced, "I
urge you once more to take me to your leader."

"What for?"

"Isn't that plain? Neither of you will set me free. El Huérfano
will."

"It is impossible, señor."

"You don't know how much you'll regret this!"

"Threats, eh?" said the white man between his teeth, and leaned
from behind the back of his chair to dig a vicious fingertip into Philibert's upper arm. Then he examined his shackles.

Philibert turned his bloodshot eyes to the mestizo. Compared to
the other's repulsively narrowed features, his face seemed benign and
not free from some compassion.

But his eyes were fastened on the man whose greater insight evidently
had cowed him into admiration. "Do you think it wise to leave him
here till our return?" he asked, almost meekly.

"Who would stay with him?"

"My wife."

His wife! So the "darling señora" was the wife of the treacherous
rogue!

"How about the ruins?" the white man said in an attitude of perfect
serenity. "Any way of keeping him there?"

"Yes."

"Here . . . no, it would not be wise to keep him here for days—"

"Or weeks . . ."

"—unless you close the place, which again would set tongues in
motion."

"So you suggest the ruins?"

"Could our two friends take him there before daybreak?"

The mestizo nodded. And presently warming up to the proposal,
he began to describe a certain stone hut which stood among the ruins
of the ancient temple.

They were talking across Philibert's hunched-up body, insensitive
to whatever he said to dissuade them from their plan. Fate, he cried
out to himself, could not be so obtuse as to allow a pair of blockheads
to deal this blow to his hopes. "Don't you see I am a sick man?" he
finally asked, his voice falling. "Don't you see that, you two? Look
at my condition. Look at it. Don't you see I've come to this pass through

no fault of mine? I am innocent. Your brandy, the pistol . . . I was rash, I admit. And now this error, this ludicrous misunderstanding. I swear, I swear El Huérfano would clear it up in no time. I am sick, very sick. Can't you see it? Aren't you human beings, you two? Aren't you . . . ?" His Spanish deserted him. In starting this performance, he had decided coolly to impress his misery upon them, appeal to their pity. But the deliberate display of suffering and despair was carrying him away. He was honestly moved by the magnitude of his misfortune. Before his very eyes the greatest of chances slipped from his hand! Tears rolled down his cheeks.

The half-breed walked over to the bar, and climbed onto the counter.

"Give him one more look," said the white man between his teeth. "It's worth it, friend. You do not often behold a weeping commissar."

The mestizo waited one more second. Then he extinguished what was left of the flame.

XVIII

The note M. Philibert had mailed to Bundschuh before his journey to Ollaytaytombo had not deluded the recipient. Not for a moment had he believed in the "attack of fever" Philibert wrote would delay his return "for maybe some weeks." Nor was he astonished when, a fortnight later, he received a letter from Requesens lacking all the cordiality of their previous communications. He did not doubt that the two men in Huacho had entered into league against him. But neither that alliance nor its aim, enigmatic to him, made him panicky. He saw them both in the light of the fatalism which step by step was entering his heart. Starting out with some belated strictures on "what was done to the Belgian," Requesens' letter strongly advised Senor Bundschuh to keep an eye on Ehinger, and "stand for no nonsense nor engage in any." This was the response to his pleas to free him from the red-whiskered devil! How naïve he had been to make Philibert their mouthpiece.

However, his feelings were beyond the bitterness of a man ill rewarded for his services. Much had happened since M. Philibert's hurried departure with Ramón, and the fact that none of it would be likely to arouse the interest of Don Lorenzo strengthened the detachment with which Bundschuh began to think of him.

Bundschuh's apprehensions had come true. His stepdaughter met Ehinger regularly. According to the grave warnings of the old stableman, Diego, they met at various hours in the afternoon, preferably near the cuca grove. Now he, Diego, understood why the señorita no longer cared for his company on her rides . . . . In the ambiguous foreknowledge of dread, Bundschuh had known of these trysts even before the old fellow had come to see him one morning, professing the "double-edged pangs" of his conscience. Never would he have dreamed, he went on to declare in his fancy parlance, of informing on the señorita, the apple of his eye! But the patron, not being born into criollo life, might not be aware that "even here in the Northwest" people were bound to look askance at such freedom. Even if the young man were "one of their own, a caballero of the true breeding," such secret meetings would be an eyesore to them! When Diego dared to say that the late patrona would "turn in her grave," could she learn of the goings-on ("and maybe she can, patrón") Bundschuh had curtly dismissed the stableman.

For days afterwards all parental warnings died on his tongue. Juana had not shaken off the ties of her habits. She would sit down at the dinner table, bring up the worries of this or that Indio woman, and ask Bundschuh for advice, or some help. Punctually she related to him the news of Huacho Broadcasting Station. One night the name of Requesens slipped into her account. Did Don Adolfo know that the Minister was building up a large air force? And did this mean another war?

No, Don Adolfo did not think so. Behind her attempt to convey to him the excitement the radio speaker had shown on that occasion, Bundschuh sensed Juana's desire to probe his own sentiments toward Requesens. "An air force?" he said. "He will do it. He always accomplishes what he sets out to do."

"How long have you known him?"

He said he had known him for a long time.

"Did you know him before you came to own this place?"

Señor Bundschuh forked a morsel of meat, and contemplated it before putting it to his mouth. It was not likely that Juana knew of the great good fortune which had helped him to the hacienda and of Requesens' help in that matter. But she could not be ignorant of his dislike of being reminded of his photographer's days. There was nothing unusual in that aversion. Pride in inherited landed property is common to all social layers in the Republic. Did she wish to humiliate him? Her new experiences, the "shameful freedom" of which Diego had mumbled, might well evoke such caprices in a young woman. . . . Then, while he took an ample draught of his beer, it occurred to him that perhaps Ehinger planned to approach Requesens, and had told the girl that he did. "Requesens," he said at last, "is a whimsical man. A friendship today, an air force tomorrow. A person has to know his own place in dealing with him. It is not important whether a person wants to deal with him. What counts is his own wish. You cannot push him." He stopped. He had not looked at the girl. His mind was gripped again by the question of how far she already had gone in her surrender to the man in the guest house.

"When you knew him first, and later, came to this place—"

"Yes," he broke in, "that's when I learned my lesson."

She watched him fold his napkin.

"It is a cool night," said Bundschuh, starting from his unhappy reflections. "Will you accompany me on a stroll? We could walk over to the stables. It would not be bad to go there once in a while when Diego expects no one. He is getting very old."

It was an unusual proposal, but Juana said she would go with him. The night was cool. There *are* such spells in the Northwest in June. The moon was invisible.

"Won't Diego be offended?" she asked, as they stepped out of the casa. "We sneak up on him, or so it looks."

He carried a flashlight, but the shimmer of the lamp inside the house, breaking through the shutters, guided them.

"Perhaps there will be a commercial air line to Murcia sooner or later," he said after some steps, "and that will make a world of difference for the hacienda. I could revive your late father's banana groves. . . ." He talked on, in an inconsequential manner. It was as if what he must say to Juana could not be exposed to the faint gleam which still was about them. She walked by his side in a sure-footed gait. As he fell silent, and no answer came from her, he recalled the small Juanita of the days of his curious courtship. He well remembered her initial inquisitiveness which had implied a kind of ready confidence embarrassing to him . . . embarrassing to him in somewhat the same way a burglar might feel if a blind man, misjudging the business at hand, volunteers to hold the ladder. It had been an awkward sensation, he remembered, and it seemed to have blighted the intimacy of those first encounters. He had never been able to regain it, and never again had it been offered to him. . . . "You pay too much heed to old Diego," he said. He could see her profile quite well now. He did not succeed in imagining, within these contours, the wide-eyed pale face of the small Juanita he had known. She had worn her hair in two braids down her back.

"He is a good man with horses," she said, indifferently, at last.

"He is a good and loyal man. Yes, that he is. He is not dumb by any means either. What he says makes sense. Yes, that it does. But he can hardly amuse you as your only companion, can he? It is bad," he continued with more assurance, "it is bad. You have so little change here,

Juanita. I too am an aging man. You don't have any friends in the neighborhood. No one is to blame for it. It happened that way. There are no girls your age in the neighborhood. Town people are a different lot again. I know it. I've been thinking of it for a long time. I thought of a change of skies. No?" Her apparent interest in Requesens had reminded Bundschuh of his foolhardy project of some weeks ago to try to place her in the household of Don Lorenzo's wife. He waited for Juana's reply. But again there was none. "You could go to Majamarca."

"Majamarca?"

"Yes, visit with one or another of your schoolmates. You exchange letters with them, no? New Year's letters? You would not impose on them, I know. Also you would not come empty-handed. You could bring presents. I would buy some nice presents in Ulloa." Again he glanced, across the narrow stretch of darkness, expectantly at the contours of her face. But only the barrage of innumerable frogs from the banks of the irrigation ditches reached his ears. He was conscious of his incompetence in this discussion. How wrong had his wife been in assuming that he would be a good guardian for the girl.

In his limited way he had come to love his wife. To yield to her judgment had been a proof of this affection. Slightly disturbed, he had begun to search for such proofs in himself, as if he had wondered whether his nature was capable still of sincere feeling. Thus he had no doubt come under her thumb. In the end—in that terrible hour when the age-old distrust of modern science (which is not confined to the Indian natives of the Republic, for the symbiosis of two cultures works both ways) cracked the crust of her enlightened education—Adolfo had not had the power to contradict her pleas to let her die "in peace" and without the "unholy, senseless tricks of the drunken quack"; and when the *cura* she had asked for finally came, it had been too late for both doctor and priest. He had failed his wife in her last hour. Was love less strong than hatred? He had not failed in his greatest hatred. . . .

"Change of skies?" Juana was saying.

"It would be not unheard of. Young ladies travel nowadays even in this country, do they not? It will do you good, Juanita. It will be good." He had made up his mind that he should not fail his wife this time. Nothing should rob him of the resolution this hour seemed to bestow upon him. As if inadvertently, he lit his electric torch. Juana had gotten ahead of him and halted on a low mound. But the beam of his torch caught only her skirt, and Don Adolfo did not raise the flashlight.

"Is it because of him?" she asked distinctly.

He watched the trembling ringlet of the light of his torch on the ground. "Yes, Juanita," he said at last in a subdued voice, "it is because of him. You do not realize what sort of man he is. One day you will." Instinctively he turned his head in the direction of the guest house. He saw nothing of it. "And Juanita . . ." he continued, "your mother, she would not have liked it."

"I am grown up," she declared after a while. Her tone seemed intent on rejecting his last words as being in bad taste. Never before had she talked to him in this fashion.

"Do not run away from it. One day I will tell you what sort of man he is. Yes, I took him in. Yes, this is true. I was indebted to Requesens. He asked me to take them in. You know that. Men such as the colonel have acquaintances everywhere. In all countries, and among all sorts of men. It's his affair. It is none of my business. It is none of our business. But though it is none of our business, we may, we must stay away from it. We must stay away from him. It is no good to get involved, Juanita. Not with this kind of man."

"I suppose sometimes you can't help it," she said.

"No, sometimes you can't," he admitted. He turned off his flashlight. "Sometimes you can't help getting involved in business you had indeed better have stayed away from. But remorse . . . any remorse, Juanita, implies the regret that no one warned you. Warned you against yourself."

"Did I commit a crime?" she said challengingly, "Or am I about to commit one? You talk about remorse. I was told that it follows only a crime, or . . . culpable negligence." Her eyes had become accustomed to the night by now. She believed she could see how he twisted his face, as he continued,

"Remorse—the mere notion of it—has a far-off ring for those who've never experienced it. To tell them what it is like is like asking a blind man to touch the shadow on a wall and get the feel of the body that casts it." He stroked his forehead, fingering his tweed cap, before he said, "But why do I talk to you about remorse? There is another thing, Juanita, something much closer to you. Not morality. My God, no. In fact, you'd be entitled to laugh at me as a self-styled champion of criollo morality. And it is not the memory of your mother alone—though I do not remind you of her lightly. Nor, for that matter, myself, Juanita . . . There is something else," he repeated after a pause in which the girl thought he must hear the wild throbbing of her heart. "There is danger. Immediate danger. I do not know what he promised you. I do not ask. Men always promise, and many of their promises are not kept. But this time it is different. He is not like other men. His life has not been as the lives of other men. I did not conceal it from you, did I? One day you must realize it. Perhaps he will tell you . . . brag about his life. Men do. Even such men. Some do. It is a way of silencing remorse. . . . Suppose you break off your friendship then, and he won't like it. He may have told you too much by that time, bragged too much. . . ." His voice sank down to an intense whisper. "He has poison, Juanita."

She gave a short cry and, as she stepped down from the small mound to walk up to him, she seemed to sway under the impact of sudden emotion.

"Do you remember those small glazed flasks in the museum?" he asked with a new courage. "Today I hate myself for having told them— him and Philibert—that some of those flasks still contained poison. Arrow poison, curare. He stole one of the flasks. Listen. Do not be impatient, please. Listen. He stole it. He. Not Philibert. I swear it. I can. I recall the day, the hour in which he stole it. He has hidden it. I went to the guest house one afternoon. For I know—oh, Juanita, I can't help knowing that it is in the afternoons . . . I went there. I searched the whole house. . . ."

Her laughter struck him in the face. After a moment of complete bafflement he grasped that this was not the echo of the poignant irony with which every great disillusionment confronts a person, nor a spasm of unnerved laughter such as a shock often entails. This was a laugh of open relief, of amusement, of license, and cynicism.

"Is this your great secret, Don Adolfo?" she exclaimed, her throat still choked. "Is this why you took me out into the dark? Did you really feel your great secret would not stand the light? Or is it something else, Don Adolfo?" She pitied him for his benighted suspicion. But at the same time she despised him for his clumsy attempt to ward off what to him might have the aspect of another act of culpable negligence. She wanted to insist, make him talk of himself, of his own remorse. But his duplicity overwhelmed her. Without uttering another sound, she passed by him, careful not to brush against his arm stretched out in a helpless gesture.

Once he called out her name. But already she was lost to the night, and after a short time the crunching sounds of her feet on the gravel revealed

L

that she had reached the back of the casa. He would not have been astounded if she had taken the path to the guest house.

They had covered about a third of the distance to the stable on their walk. To go back to the casa seemed impossible to Bundschuh. He feared he would pursue Juana into her bedroom, resume his warnings, perhaps lose his temper. . . . But as he stepped out now, the weak cone of the light of his torch before him, he noticed that his great indignation gave way to a state of amazement. How could this be? How could this charitable, soft-spoken, docile girl have changed overnight into a cynic? How could the affection that only yesterday had tied her to the memory of her parents, an almost sickly attachment, if not a cult, have released her from its bondage? The discovery of a new happiness? The discovery of her own life? But all that had come to her almost as a parody, as it were, and even the wild beauty of the horrible man—clenching his hands, Bundschuh acknowledged it and evaluated its attraction—could not corrupt her so completely!

Like a quivering star, a small light shone toward Bundschuh. One of the lanterns was burning in the stable. He walked more slowly. A feeling grew in him that reasoning could not explain the change in the girl. Not his reasoning. Like Ehinger's love, his own reasoning was a spurious fragment.

Thoughts of this extraordinary kind had crossed Bundschuh's mind a good many times since the arrival of his guests. Whenever he assessed the risks of his situation, its material dangers, these thoughts had underhandedly entered his humors. Had they not been responsible for his desire to see Crisóstomo? Three times he postponed the meeting, as if ashamed. For no sooner had the wish to talk to the padre taken possession of him than his material worries altered the objective of his plan. And when he finally did go to Casaquiara, and stayed there from Vespers to early Mass, no time had been left for anything but enlisting the help of the reverend father for the sick man. Father Crisóstomo had seemed to approve of the matter-of-fact way in which his visitor presented his request.

Smooth speech was foreign to the priest. His Herculean build, still erect, his resounding voice, his plain language that often seemed to belie his calling, his candid weakness for rich food—his whole person had always inspired Don Adolfo with wondering comfort. Father Crisóstomo had the habit of closing his eyes when he listened, and dilating them wide while he talked. His lined great face, darkened by age, the sun and fevers, never gave away his thoughts.

Although Bundschuh had seen him on the streets of Murcia on earlier occasions, and also met him once at a fair, he had come to know the padre only in 1930, on the day El Seringuero was launched into eternity. Afterwards he learned that the *cura,* alarmed by the restive mood of his parish, had applied for Crisóstomo's assistance; and Don Adolfo was grateful to the little *cura.* For without Crisóstomo's presence the mob might well have done him bodily damage as, discharging his promise to Don Lorenzo, he took the photographs of the hanged brigand.

"Called by an angel," as he would contend when the danger was over, Father Crisóstomo had rushed to the scene of the incipient riot. Bundschuh, his trembling hands on the tripod, saw him storm through the cordon of the irresolute soldiers, shouting at him from afar, "Go on, you bonehead! Haven't you learned your trade? Go on and have done with it. And you," he thundered to the left and the right at the open-mouthed assemblage that receded before his enormous strides, "into church with you all! Down on your knees, and pray for his soul. He has done murder, your El Seringuero. He has sown hatred. Hatred was in his soul. You whine and clamor he has loved you, loved the lowly. How can any man love whose soul is blackened by hatred, hatred strong enough to slay men? Fools! Into the church with you all. Go on. Get going!" Waving his arms furiously, Father Crisóstomo had meanwhile come close to the gallows. Bundschuh's camera clicked . . . and one of his pictures was to show the monk with his right arm extended toward the dangling Seringuero, his great face lit up by the zeal of his exhortation.

Colonel Requesens had confiscated that ambiguous photo, together with its negative, and Father Crisóstomo was never to see it. Nor had Bundschuh ever alluded to it. After his marriage he would invite the padre to the hacienda each time he was known to be in Murcia. Sometimes he had come, and had heartily partaken of a meal. On none of these visits had he preached to Don Adolfo, urged him to practice his faith, or reminded him of the subtler aspects of human existence.

In this present hour it seemed to him that Crisóstomo had, all that time, merely been saving his strength. He had given him assistance the other day, lent him a hand, so to speak, with no strings attached. He had posed as a man of good will pure and simple. . . . In truth, he lay in ambush for him! He had hoped such an hour would come. He had been waiting for just such a predicament to present itself to Don Adolfo as the logical outgrowth of his stay in the Northwest. . . .

Outgrowth! Logical! Nonsense. Naturally, this could not have happened to him, had he not come to Murcia. But surely it did not have to happen to him only because he had gone to the Northwest twenty-seven years ago, anxious to go as far away as he could from Huacho.

Throughout these twenty-seven years Bundschuh had never experienced the kind of thought that may move a man with homicide on his conscience to paint to himself the unlived years of his victim in all their hypothetical wealth. At times he even had felt, as strongly as on the day it happened, the hatred for the man he had slain; and then it would seem to him that such power, that the durability of his hatred, justified what he had done. It justified it better than any circumstantial defense.

. . . Had Adolf Bundschuh, erstwhile seaman in the Kaiser's navy, been really surprised when, on a warm July day in 1918, he met the man in Huacho? Had he not toyed with the image of this meeting ever since he heard that stray German sailors were supposed to be hiding out in the Republic?

And then he literally ran into the man on the Plaza. He was lolling against one of the bill-covered columns of the arcade near the Palacio Municipal, unmistakable despite the linen jacket he wore and the naval cap stripped of its imperial insignia. His aquiline profile was set off against the ochre paper of the posters. A ray of the sun retrieved him from the twilight of the arcature, and his shape first produced the impression of a wax figure on exhibit in the lighted niche of a stage. As Bundschuh approached the apparition, the man waved his hand, which held a short pipe, in a lazy salute. "Hello," he said through set teeth, "hello, deserter!"

In the years which followed this encounter, Bundschuh had frequently tried to persuade himself that their old enmity might have melted away under this foreign sun, had the man greeted him in a different fashion—and that, without the bond of their ancient hatred, things in the end would have taken a different course in spite of all. But his true insight told Adolf Bundschuh that, had his old acquaintance embraced him and kissed him on both cheeks, he would still have wished him no good.

He had disliked him throughout their common service years in the Navy. He was a bow-legged dark fellow with deep, shining eyes. There was something outlandish about him. He took his being disliked for granted. His own attitude toward Bundschuh had none of the dogged, stark passion that animated the latter. Candid rancor seemed not to be in the man's nature, which rather had recourse to a sober, ironic, sly reaction to facts.

They both were enlisted men, stationed in Kiel, and later sailing on one of the Kaiser's new cruisers. Adolf Bundschuh was not a good mariner. Neither was the other, but his assignment to the galley won him a petty officer's rating after a time. One day Bundschuh fell sick. He accused the petty officer of having poisoned the food, and his charge found credence among the crew. Growing bolder, he would contend that the presence of the "black-haired, black-hearted bastard" was sure to bring bad luck to the vessel. That loose talk came to the notice of the captain, who punished Bundschuh severely. From that day on he did not question that all his adversities aboard the cruiser sprang from the malevolence of the petty officer. A mulatto woman who carried on with both men in an East African port at last lent a motive to Bundschuh's irrational aversion. After a rough affray between them, the captain demoted the petty officer. Thereupon Bundschuh's scorn knew no bounds. The other reciprocated in kind: he derided *"Dummschuh"* and his brainless accusations, his superstitious belief in demonic powers. . . . The end of the cruise had found their antagonism in an uneasy stalemate. In Egypt, Bundschuh had sometimes found himself savoring the fact that life had put a world between himself and the odious shipmate.

Now he was here in Huacho. Together with some other men from a raider sunk by a British submarine, he had drifted for weeks on a raft. He had been interned on shore, had escaped, and had sneaked across the two borders, drawn to Huacho—very much like Bundschuh himself a year earlier—by the rumored indifference toward men of his ilk in the Republic. He had contracted malaria on his trek.

Except for his good health, Bundschuh was worse off than the new arrival. He had failed in his professional pursuits. Exploiting the anti-German feeling whipped up in Huacho at last, the two local photographers, Italian immigrants, had thwarted his attempts to set up shop. He was reduced to doing menial work for the boarding house where he had run into debt, and whose owner, a slovenly, toothless woman, meant to starve him into marrying her. But for all that, Bundschuh had withstood the temptation of selling, or pawning, his photographer's equipment. It was his only agent of hope.

Perhaps it was to discourage his one-time shipmate from staying on in Huacho that Bundschuh, in that first hour, revealed to him his plight in "this rat-hole of a capital, so called." But the man only laughed at its backwardness. They both laughed. Their common contempt made them feel good. They repaired to a cantina.

Adolf Bundschuh did not inquire on the strength of what reports back home the other had called him a deserter. Also, the newcomer did not repeat the slur, and even listened, if impassively only, to Bundschuh's account of his having been "shanghaied" to this hemisphere in 1914. Not with one word did either of them touch on their past dissension— not even by such allusions as grown-up schoolmates would use in re-calling past playground scuffles. Nor did the two men discuss the effect which the four war years had had upon all the brave sailors they had known in peacetime.

Notwithstanding his weakened body, the new arrival directed his mind right away toward the future. He had some money—not much— and suggested that they "go into business." His plan was to buy some wares which as a rule were not for sale in the town's markets, and to peddle that stuff in the remoter neighborhoods of the city. As he told Bundschuh, he had on his trek occasionally supported himself in that fashion.

His sense of enterprise impressed Bundschuh. He was flattered by the man's references to his command of the language and his knowledge of local customs. He did not stop to consider that these qualifications were hardly reason enough for offering a partnership to a man in his own beggared condition.

The scheme came into being; and soon the two Germans could be seen, each with a pack on his back, going from door to door in the north-western suburbs and inveigling gullible women into buying a length of garish cloth, foreign-made shoes, or a rhinestone. (These were the days when modern tanneries were established in Huacho, which brought, poor as the wages were, a certain unwonted prosperity to some house-holds.) Bundschuh's landlady fumed at his truancy. But after less than a month he was able to repay her a substantial part of his debts, and with the help of his partner was moving into the latter's quarters. The vulgar ruses and threats which he employed to make the lovesick woman release Bundschuh, together with his possessions, should have given warning. But step by step a definite admiration—not to speak of a measure of half-willing gratitude—had replaced in Bundschuh's heart all older feelings.

Another month passed before his resourceful friend proposed to "double the profits": he would try his luck by himself in the Old City while friend Bundschuh was to continue on their old beat. In reality, the newcomer had taken a liking to one of the least reputable Old City taverns. He had grown fond of its regulars' card games and dice, the brandy there was to his taste, and the light women frequenting the place gave the coup de grâce to his initial disdain of life in "this capital, so called."

Though Bundschuh could no longer doubt that he now was earning alone what money they both were spending, he restrained himself from calling the disloyal partner to account. But business went down rapidly. The local hawkers, who had always canvassed the pueblos beyond the city limits, got wind of the profits the foreigners made among urban workers, and began to infringe on Bundschuh's route. More than once he had to return from it without a single centavo, only to be berated violently by his slothful partner. They began to quarrel. Soon they quarrelled each night.

And one night Bundschuh's costly equipment was gone. Roused from a drunken slumber, his partner made no bones about the "transaction." Yes, he had pawned camera, tripod, and all, with a nearby broker. And why shouldn't he? Were they not business associates? Was it not incumbent on either of them to raise capital? And anyway, had he not rescued Bundschuh from the clutches of the mercenary old hag? And did friend Bundschuh not see how sick his old comrade-in-arms was? Common decency ought to make him extend his help to a sick man.

Bundschuh replied reasonably at first. He proposed to renounce his share in all future earnings. What earnings? the other wanted to know, cynically. Bundschuh kept pleading. He must have his photographer's equipment. His whole future life depended on it. Here, or in Egypt, where he might go back some day. Egypt? Why not return to the good old country? the other inquired, why not? Ha, ha, ha . . . The old hatred surged up in Bundschuh—magnified by the thought that he was the dupe of a man who had been casting evil spells upon him ever since their paths crossed for the first time.

It was the intoxicated state of his adversary—he had also taken to chewing coca leaves—which gave Bundschuh his chance in the fight that ensued. It lasted a bare three minutes. Bundschuh easily grabbed the wallet from the beaten man. An hour later, his precious equipment was in Bundschuh's hands again—while the pawnbroker had gotten most of what was left of the money, plus the wares that remained from the peddlers' business, which thus came to an end.

Bundschuh did not go back to his lodgings. He took his equipment to a deserted hovel near Carjavel Station, where he happened to have spent a night on a previous occasion. He buried the wooden box containing the camera beneath the earthen floor.

In the early morning, his partner came. He did not bother to argue, or to tell him how he had detected his refuge. He started threatening the moment he entered the hut. He declared he would give himself up to the authorities and inform on Bundschuh; they both would of course be interned as enemy aliens, and shipped back to Germany after the war, ha, ha, ha. . . . Bundschuh tried to appease the unnerved man, whose feverish eyes roamed the place in search of the treasure. Bundschuh admitted he had acted arbitrarily. He would look for work, any kind of work. He would make up whatever damage the other figured he had suffered. The other scoffed at this promise. He was sick. He needed money on the spot. Bundschuh had better hurry: this was Saturday, and the pawnbroker would close his shop early. A maudlin tone crept into the man's threats and admonitions. It could be seen he was reluctant to fight, and that his own reluctance embittered him greatly.

He left in the midst of another outburst of sardonic "promises." But he did not withdraw from the vicinity of the hut. Whenever Bundschuh stepped out, the bow-legged shape was in his field of vision, sauntering along the railroad track, or standing atop the elevated loading ramp of the station, or talking to some of the workmen in the yard. By nightfall, however, he had disappeared.

The most sensible course for Bundschuh to take would have been to leave Huacho that very night. But in those days the trains of the Northern Railway were running but once a week in either direction.

Bundschuh got himself some food in the railroad workers' canteen and gulped three glasses of brandy. Then he walked back to his hut. He sat down on its stone step. It was a very dark night. He came to the conclusion that leaving Huacho would do him no good. His shipmate had followed him across half the globe, drawn to him by the magnetism of their mutual hate—a bond as forceful as the ties of the greatest of loves. Now, with a claim on him into the bargain, the enemy would pursue him wherever he went. . . . Bundschuh did not accept this fanciful prospect without protest. He realized there was no reason in it. But after what must have been hours of brooding, he surrendered his common sense to his anguished hatred, as others may surrender their intelligence to an overmastering affection.

For all that, the notion of killing a human being with his hands made Adolf Bundschuh shudder. No murderous passion was in him. He did not crave vengeance. He wanted his freedom back, his peace of mind. He found himself wishing for some miracle that would remove his persecutor. He painted to himself all the contingencies which might accomplish such a miracle. He told himself that a penniless foreigner such as his persecutor, a German, an ill-natured drunkard beset by the singleness of his concern, arrogant, and contemptuous of his present surroundings—Bundschuh told himself that such a character was bound to run into trouble at his hangout. This was the hope which drew Adolf Bundschuh to the tavern in the Old City.

What guided his hand when he stabbed the wretch in the back amid the free-for-all which happened to be in progress in front of the cantina, as Bundschuh approached it, was something that seemed to have broken loose from the man Bundschuh.

His old shipmate went down with a rattling moan. Bundschuh elbowed out of the drunken mêlée, and managed to toss his switch-blade knife into a barrel standing under an archway. Finding his retreat blocked by a new influx of wild-shouting drunks rolling down the precariously oil-lit lane, he took cover under the collapsed tarpaulin of a fruit cart upset in the shifting waves of the brawl. He lay there for a long time, and barely breathed, or dared scratch his itching head, lest one of the melons separate from its pile and betray him. He heard the yelling and the screams of pain of the scufflers, the thuds of their blows, and the crashes of splintering jugs and bottles, but he had no conception of the battle's distance from him. At last he perceived a hole in the canvas. At this moment a great hush fell over the fighters, and they unlocked their bodies. Bundschuh, being (as he now saw) a mere fifty steps away from the scene, already thought himself to be detected, when the sight of the suddenly sobered men freezing into a semi-circle—and turning their backs on his hide-out—revealed to him that they had discovered the corpse. One of them lifted a lantern over it, and then put it down carefully on the cobbles; and hardly more than three seconds later the whole mob had decamped, running, limping, and sneaking, past the tarpaulin under which he cowered, staring at the twin swinging doors of the cantina, which intermittently caught the light.

As the two constables arrived, shouting pompous commands at no one and brandishing their sabers in a display of law and order, the dead man lay deserted. His remains reposed in a puddle of blood and spilled liquor. His eyes, illuminated by the lantern left beside them, seemed to gaze at the windows slammed shut before the disaster and instantly darkened. There was much palavering on the part of the constables, and they also dragged the publican and some other men out of doors, and maltreated them. Finally they got hold of a burro somewhere, and heaved the body athwart its high-pommelled saddle. Then they led the animal and its load up the slanting lane. The last Bundschuh saw of his departed shipmate were his arms dangling almost to the ground. As he slipped out from beneath the canvas, some vermin which had nested in the overripe fruit had begun to crawl under his shirt. It was to produce a nasty rash on his skin, which plagued him long after taking his leave from Huacho.

He had never learned how the case was closed there.

. . . Don Adolfo, somewhat out of breath, halted his steps. The stable door was closed, the large wooden bolt put up. Yet the light still shone inside. It shone brightly. The horses stamped the ground in their stall. Their chains could be heard rattling against the boards of the manger. Water was dropping somewhere. Before turning, Adolfo listened for a long time to its tapping sounds.

XIX

JUANA STOPPED TALKING. She was astonished at the reserve with which she had given her report. She had let four days lapse before telling Ehinger of the nocturnal discourse with her stepfather; and now, all she had told him in effect was that Bundschuh wanted her to leave.

"The joke of it is that you will leave," Ehinger suggested with a flat laugh. "If we play our cards right, you will." He sat on a blackened tree stump, shoulders stooped, and gazed down at the space between his knees. A multiple file of red ants was issuing from the rotten timber beneath him, and bustling off toward the straits formed by his boots.

Juana was standing in front of him. Her tall figure was set off against the declining sun. Farther off, her pony grazed in the shade of a cluster of shrivelled papaya bushes. The blue poncho under its English saddle instilled an odd color into the monotonous hues of the uncultivated, grass-specked expanse.

Looking up at the girl, Ehinger tried to smile reassuringly. The seriousness of her eyes disconcerted him, and he was angry that it did. This was no time for permitting her flighty ideas to distract him from his goal.

"To leave . . . " said the girl, "to go away . . . To go away and never to find out the truth!"

"A whole neighborhood cannot be wrong," he answered. "How would *I* have come to know of the incident, of the shocking, the tragic incident . . . yes, how would I have come to know about it, if everybody hereabouts had not long known what really happened that night six years ago?" He spoke with that precise, even intonation he had long realized impressed the girl more than any display of emotion and force. He picked up a twig and began to crumble it between his long fingers.

Naturally, he had never stopped to figure how much reality there

might be in the dated rumor about the circumstances of the death of
Juana's mother. It had been imparted to him as hearsay by the lorry
driver Jacinto, the only man at the hacienda who, from the beginning,
would exchange a friendly word or two with the stranger (and later, far
more). Jacinto's story had served Ehinger well. It had been the lever and
agent to bring the girl to him; and having decided that it must do more
for him now, Ehinger seemed to detect an increasing reality in the
apparently shopworn gossip. By now it had to him more reality than the
unwitnessed minute-to-minute truth of Señora Bundschuh's last hour.
. . . He was glancing down again at the caravan of the busy insects.
Juana's shadow lay across his feet.

She still did not move in the least. "There is something else I have
thought of," she said, "another explanation, another way to account for
what happened that night."

He gave a noncommittal gesture.

"When I came home from school for the funeral, I did ask why the
medico had not been called. I did. I asked Diego—"

"Why didn't you ask Bundschuh himself?"

She remained silent for a while. Then, in a subdued tone, she proceeded, "It happened to her on a walk. Not very far from here. She
liked walks. It was very long before they found her. Three hours, Diego
said. And so did Miguel. The leg was terribly swollen already. Could it
not be," she asked intently, "that my stepfather knew it would be futile
to call the medico? Worse than futile? Diego reminded me of a boy
whose leg the doctor amputated some years earlier after he had been
bitten, and who died just the same. The Murcia medico is not a good
physician. Could it not be that my stepfather knew that it was too late?
That he took it upon himself to spare her greater suffering? It could be,
could it not?"

A dawning resolution warned Ehinger against reacting to Juana's—
perhaps unintentional—allusion to the death of Roy, or rather to the
legend she had spun round it. But neither was he willing to give away
his informant. The friendship he had struck up with Jacinto had remained unseen by anyone, and had to remain so. . . . Playfully, he was
tossing the bits of his twig into the path of the ants. Everything *could* be,
he at last said. Still there were things a person knew deep down in his
heart without building elaborate theories. Why, to repeat this very
pertinent question, should she have made her inquiries to old Diego,
and not to Bundschuh? The answer was plain, no?

"I swear there was no suspicion in my mind, then," she declared. "Not then, or ever since, until you spoke to me."

"In your mind, in your mind—that may well be. But deep down you felt the truth. And so did everybody else at the hacienda. I sometimes wonder whether you white people do not underrate your own Indios."

"They have their peculiar ways of looking at things past," she said. "Truth as we understand it matters little to them."

"How do we understand truth? Truth . . . Properly speaking, truth is only what happens to me now, now, in this fraction of a second. Or what I am doing now, in this very moment. See here . . . I am crushing these ants under my foot. Watch me, watch my foot. . . . Now wait, wait for another minute only. . . . See?" He smiled. "Do you see these other ants? They are busy removing the dead. Look at them, look. The dead will be gone in no time. Now . . . who killed them? What killed them? I? This boot? Or some earthquake, or landslide? To them, a catastrophe killed them, a natural catastrophe. Even if you could ask them, the truth you'd get at would not satisfy you."

"And if I asked you?"

"If you asked *him,* that is?" he retorted with a measure of triumph. "You don't think you could make him confess, or do you? Oh yes, men can be made to confess. To 'confess'!" A grim sort of amused pensiveness shook him for a moment before with a changed, sobered, and disapproving inflection he pronounced, "This can't go on, *Mädel.* You cannot keep running after a phantom. You can't spend your life trying to disentangle the past. You must decide. You must make up your mind on the strength of your feelings. I take it you've never had to make up your mind about anything. Sheltered life, eh? This time—"

With an unexpectedness that silenced him, she opened the top button of her bodice. "Here they are," she said, handing him a small rectangular flattened bag of dark oilcloth.

"The maps!"

Her calm seemed to belie the dreamy tension which had held its sway over her throughout their talk. "They may be obsolete," she remarked, "though these were good and reliable maps when they were new. That much I know. My father was a real scientist."

"He must have been. By all accounts." Ehinger untied the cord of the bag. She had mentioned the maps only yesterday, and upon his instantaneous request promised to furnish them. He felt greatly gratified at this proof of her obedience and collaboration. He tucked one of the stiff-backed maps under his armpit, and spread the other out on his knees, crouching over it, his chin low on his chest.

Juana saw nothing of his face save the reddish beard which, at an acute angle, stuck out from under the brim of his helmet. She repeated that her father had been a trained scientist. He had had new ideas about wild rubber. In his days the trade had long declined, not least on account of the ghastly things said to have happened in the forest. Although those atrocities already belonged to the past in her father's time, their memory may have contributed to his giving up the planned expedition. Her mother used to make a point of that whenever she was talking about his "rubber ideas." Eastern people never thought rubber tapping to be a respectable man's occupation.

Ehinger unfolded the second map on top of the first one. Of a sudden the cicadas in the papaya trees started to trill through the stillness which had followed Juana's words. When Ehinger lifted his head in the direction of the bushes resounding with the symphonic song of the little creatures, his face bore an expression of avidity and enthusiasm.

It was as though he had been trying to find in a mirage the picture conjured up by the old maps on his knees, and those other pictures, more distinct and based on calculation, which Jacinto had been evoking in him. The lorry driver had brought great news from one of his recent rides to Ulloa.

It was not a fantastic tale. During the closing months of the late war, a North American business company had undertaken a new exploitation of the upper Otomayo valley. They had encountered great difficulties in recruiting labor: their "tenderfoot methods" had failed to lure the savages from the impenetrable woodland into which their tribes withdrew a generation ago. Still the gringos had begun to import machinery, building material, rails, rolling stock, canned provisions—only to abandon all of it, together with their project, almost on the day the war in Europe was over.

Jacinto's report was deficient in detail. Its coherence was faulty. But he swore that those entrepreneurs had left behind a handful of caretakers, agents, so it was bruited about in the public houses, equally willing to watch over the costly equipment till doomsday, or to sell it for a song, as likely as not for their own profit. That was Jacinto's story. It was evident that he had not passed it on without selfish reasons. He had shown himself to be a man superficially conversant with the ways of the white world. Whatever he fancied Ehinger to be, he seemed to take the rapacity of his race for granted. Apparently the severe warning of Miguel, the overseer, never to accost the patrón's guests, or to answer them if accosted himself, had bred in him the notion that some business deal was in progress at the hacienda; and Philibert's hasty departure had added the idea of some conflict which had brought that deal to naught, leaving Ehinger stranded and ready for new adventures. Despite the double barrier of tongues between them—Jacinto depended to some extent on the local lingo—Ehinger had been quick to grasp his fantasies. Some kind of perturbing personal experience appeared to make the man anxious to get away from this place. From the outset Ehinger was convinced of Jacinto's desire to throw in his lot with "the señor from Europe." Upon the scantiest encouragement he had intimated that he was prepared to appropriate one of Bundschuh's two lorries. . . .

The tuneless melody in the trees came to a dead stop, but Ehinger still stared at them. The girl had moved away from him. She, he was reflecting, must get the money from Bundschuh. The money he would need for the enterprise. Bundschuh must be persuaded to make amends to Juana, to give her the legacy she had been cheated out of, or just give her money somehow. Title and method did not matter. They did not matter to him, and would not matter to Bundschuh. They must not matter to the girl.

He heard her call the pony. Alarmed by some lizard or snake, the animal had run off a few meters, trailing the reins. Now it stood whinnying loudly, and meekly tolerated the approach of its mistress.

There was an element of provocation in her self-assured movements, as she took up the reins, looped them on the saddle, and tightened the surcingle. Was there not something akin to this tranquility of her body hidden underneath the stubborn naïveté with which she fought her dilemma? Her worry about "the truth" was hateful to him. It seemed to be guided by an irrational trust in a power beyond Ehinger's ken; and the fact that he could not grasp the nature of that trust, nor conceive of its power, irritated him to the point of fury. The irony of life, making him dependent on the pious vagaries of a young woman! He had taken uncounted women in his life, and the very lives of them all had been dependent on him.

Juana was walking the pony back to the bushes. She tethered it, and then patted its flank and stroked the cropped mane. A smile lingered on her lips when she returned to the man, who had stood up.

She was almost his own height. "Good maps," he said, with forced indifference, "modern enough. But it isn't maps we'll need most. You know that, no?" He passed his moist hand over his mustache, and pretending to talk to himself, growled something about money against his fingers. As he withdrew them from his mouth, his plaintive mutterings barely concealed a rising choler. Yes, why delude themselves? The powers that be had turned him into a penniless refugee. His companion, Philibert, the great gentleman, had left him in the lurch, bent on using for his own ends the assistance which that high-placed personage in Huacho, their common protector, had offered them both.

Could he not apply to this protector himself?

Hardly. He was sure Philibert had by now prejudiced that gentleman thoroughly against his companion. Such was the cruel might of defeat, of expatriation and persecution, of penury, it made an honorable soldier a traitor to his comrade-in-arms.

"You might still hear from Philibert," Juana said, and as he merely groaned, she added that he also might hear from home.

The two maps lay on the stump behind him, stirring slightly. He turned, picked them up, folded them, and put them back into the oil-cloth bag, which all the while, its cord slung round his wrist, he had been dangling in a slow rhythm. "Home? Hyenas. Hyenas prowling among ruins, corpses, and rats. My home has no longer any voice. How could I hear from it?" Indeed, he continued grimly, the powers that be had done a complete job, and only now did he realize how complete it was. Did she not see how those accursed powers mocked his inventiveness and the new lease on life he was striving for? Did she not see that?

She nodded.

"They mock our love . . . my love," he said in a marked afterthought. "Here, take them, take the maps, put them back wherever you took them from, my good girl. We will not need them."

"But we will! If you think it *is* the right plan, we *will* go ahead with it. We will. I am no child. No matter how much you ridicule my sheltered life, I know that men have ambitions. I know it from my father. You must not be left to your inactivity. I know it. We will go ahead with this plan of yours. But can't we wait?"

"Till the rains come?"

"The rains . . ." she echoed dejectedly.

A wide motion of his arms emphasized the deadlock their planning had arrived at. Ehinger's drawn face did not betray his disappointment. Yet he dreaded procrastination. Bundschuh's inertia was uncanny. Some of these days the reticent Don Adolfo would start fighting in full earnest the man he could not but blame for his stepdaughter's defection and what, in these parts, was sure to be regarded as license. What weapons had *he* to fight Bundschuh? The threat to tell others, the capataz perhaps, who Bundschuh's guest really was? Bundschuh would merely sneer at so hollow a menace. It had crossed Ehinger's mind that he might suggest a bargain to Don Adolfo. What he knew of his antecedents—not least from the cordial talks, in the first weeks, with the "one-time German sailor"—inspired Ehinger with no awe. So he had thought of offering Bundschuh a kind of agreement whereby he would pledge himself to leave the girl alone against the promise of money. But Bundschuh—torn between his apprehensions about the girl, the petty puritanism of an upstart, and his rather mysterious allegiance to Requesens (had it never occurred to him that he might cow the great one into condonement, if not connivance?)—Bundschuh was most unlikely even to listen to that proposal. Nor was Ehinger too certain that he himself would abide by his pledge. The girl's was the first voice that had spoken to him in human terms since that other life of his had come to an abrupt end.

She was saying that she must go now.

"Good-bye, then, *Mädel*," he agreed with a show of melancholy exasperation. "It *is* a good plan, but nothing will come of it. . . . Can anything, for that matter, come of my love? Look at me. I can give nothing to the girl I love. Nothing except for these bare hands—"

She put her hand up to his lips.

"Yes, these bare hands and the will to use them! Ah, this will has not been broken yet by the hatred of the whole world. Not yet."

"What can *I* do? Please tell me what I can do."

He was thinking feverishly. Juana had hurt Bundschuh gravely. Ehinger was ignorant of how far exactly she had gone. But she had offended his conceit, no doubt. Outright demands on her part would enrage Bundschuh, and there was no way of guessing how his wrath might discharge its energies. Nor any way of preparing against them. To egg on the girl was a desperate undertaking. But any risk was preferable to delay. So he said, "Why are you so reluctant to ask him for the money we need? He owes it to you. You know he does, and so does he. He must make restitution. He must give you your heritage. There must be a heritage. And whether you ask for it today or in a year from tomorrow makes no difference, does it?"

M

"There isn't much money at the hacienda," she replied after a pause, "not at this time of the year."

"He must have some funds at any time of the year."

"Some he has," she admitted, avoiding his eyes.

Ehinger had extended his arms, but let them drop. "Yes, *Mädel,* you may wonder. You may well ask whether I mightn't advance this suggestion even if I didn't love you at all. You would be in your right to ask such a question."

No such thought had entered the mind of Juana. After remaining thunderstruck for a moment, she chased away the shadow of that aspersion, presented to her, half ironically only, in a vein of self-accusation. Nothing was left to him but his hands? What was left to *her?* Had not events already robbed her of her home? Even if she decided to remain, there could be no return to the complacency she had taken for peace. "But don't you see that your suggestion . . ." she began, only to conclude with a rapid gasp. "I want to leave myself. I must."

"Why not go to Majamarca on a visit with your school friends?"

"Please do not talk that way," she said. "I know that horrible things have happened to you, things of which people here have no conception. You cannot be like other men. I know that. You've been so much alone. You've come to doubt everything, everyone. . . . Do not doubt me."

He stood rigid, his eyes agleam with the last ray of the sun. There was still some space between them. Then he drew her to him.

His words came to her amid caresses—German words of endearment which summoned faint childhood memories to her confused thoughts. "Give me some time," she stammered, "only some. . . . I cannot . . . I cannot ask for restitution. That I cannot. But I'll get us money. Somehow I know I will."

His fingers were ruffling her hair. Like someone listening to the breath of a dying person, he strained his ears to grasp her whispers. His fingertips wandered over the finely textured skin behind her ear lobes, along her jugular vein.

"Do not think I listen to him. . . . Whatever he says is as nothing. Aren't his clumsy warnings . . . aren't they only the voices of his guilt? His horrible guilt? How could I listen to what they say? He can't even imagine love. . . . Our love is loathsome to him. . . . He has no love. No, he hasn't. . . . But I cannot . . . I cannot ask him for anything . . ."

Over her head, which had fallen on his shoulder, Ehinger gazed at the sapphirine horizon. He kept telling himself that he must make her his mistress. He had told himself so on several similarly propitious occasions, and many a time in her absence. Something had always tried to bias him against his urge. To yield to it would only be sound tactics. Still those warnings were not to be stifled. It was sorcery. He must undo it instantly. Now. Now and here. He drew her still closer to him. Darkness would be over them in no time, he told himself, while, unmoved, he felt the salty flavor of her tears on his lips.

XX

BEFORE LEAVING HUACHO for his constituency, the Senator from Majamarca had asked Lieutenant Loyarte to his pied-à-terre. He had been frank with the young man. No, he was not in favor of his courtship, or—not to discourage unduly what he presumed was sincere love—he was not in favor of it yet, not at this moment. Conditions were not settled in the country, its aspect of domestic peace notwithstanding; and who but Army men were the first to bear the brunt of great political changes?

Great political changes?

Possible changes . . . Surely Don León had not forgotten that the seven-year term of Dr. Zapeta was to come to an end a year hence. Everybody, to be sure, was looking forward to his re-election and a prolongation of the coalition Cabinet. But developments were subject to contingencies and even hazards in a democracy. Don León was *so* young—

Twenty-seven, Loyarte threw in.

Too young, that was, to recall all those excellent junior officers who in times not so remote were driven out of the country by unexpected political changes. Even the General, of blessed memory, had not always rescued such scapegoats. They were left to the embittered idleness which is the lot of the exiled soldier. No, the Senator did not wish such a lot for his daughter, and could Don León blame him for it?

So the Senator *was* expecting violent changes?

"Who talks of violence, lieutenant? And mind you, I said *unexpected* changes. Here again your great youth may hamper your judgment, Don León. Your entire adult life has been lived under abnormal circumstances. The present party truce has smothered the free play of democracy as we have developed it in the Republic over a long and frequently painful stretch of decades. The unexpected belongs to that free play. It belongs to our liberty."

Unexpected changes indeed! Loyarte was not so young as to be ignorant of the methods the Conservatives, the Senator's party, employed in elections. It was a venerable joke that upon its compulsion thousands of citizens would leave their graves to betake themselves to the polls. However, the fashion in which the Senator conducted this "man-to-man talk" did not admit of jocular remonstrances. Loyarte had been prepared for an interrogation about the sorry state of his finances, or a rebuke for the correspondence he carried on with his beloved María much against custom. Instead, he was made to listen to obscure warnings.

Afterwards, the lieutenant blamed his wish to impress the ardor of his love on María's father for his failure to grasp the pith of his warnings. Had he cautioned him against his attachment to Requesens? It would be absurd: Requesens could only profit from a defeat of Dr. Zapeta. And as for himself, León—had his junta not met Dr. Zapeta with defiance? How could an "unexpected" change in the Palace adversely affect the erstwhile junta? The Senator had also intimated that the new commander of the garrison of Majamarca was not precisely a man after the heart of the *gente decente* out East. To that Loyarte should have pointed out that Fafreras' connection with the original junta had loosened considerably of late, and that none of its members today would support the colonel blindly. As it was, he had taken only small heed of the Senator's dispraise of Fafreras, so eager had he been to hear his talk return to plans for María's future.

He had returned to them. Unctuously he had mentioned once more the prudence which befitted a young man "contemplating matrimony even in a more distant future," and wound up his lecture by saying he would be pleased to see Don León again on his next sojourn in the capital.

For some days, Loyarte considered informing Requesens of his curious experience with the man he had begun to regard as his future father-in-law (for with all the bewilderment left in his wake, the Senator had raised the young man's hopes). But the reticence of Requesens in discussing the Air Corps commissions, his condescending, if fatherly, way of blocking access to his ulterior plans, advised the lieutenant against rash action. Moreover, the humor with which Requesens had two or three times referred to the entanglement of Loyarte's heart went against his grain. It aggravated a malaise gnawing at him since the fateful days of May—the unease of the gambler lest his gains be denied such recognition as is reaped by mere toil or genius.

As a matter of fact, it was his gaming instinct which, back in '41, had drawn Loyarte toward the fallen star of Requesens.

He had left the Military College in Majamarca in the summer of 1940, already in debt, and burdened by the romantic expectations of the adolescent girl he had fallen in love with. He came from an impoverished family, had not been a brilliant student, and was aware that nothing short of extraordinary daring would further his career. Humdrum Army life and the complete lull in domestic politics put him in the position of a gambler who finds himself in a place where cards and roulette wheels are unknown. True, he was not alone in this mood: the business-like measures of the General "to meet all possible emergencies of the world situation" (to quote one of his spiritless pronunciamentos) brought many a more level-headed officer to the brink of despair. But none of them, save Loyarte, had stood up for Requesens.

It had been a noble thing to do. But behind it was more. Loyarte coolly took stock of the inalienable assets of the outlawed man: his distinguished ancestry, his shamefully obliterated victory in the Northwest, his knowledge of foreign countries, and the great power of body and soul which must have helped him overcome the adversities of his start. The long odds against which Loyarte staked his future on Requesens at the very nadir of the latter's fortunes seemed like senseless bravura; and, to the lieutenant's good luck, his superiors considered it as such. But when all was said and done, it had been a very risky gamble.

Once a player has put his money in the pot, patience becomes the prime ingredient of his success. Don León had, alas, not always remembered that rule at the gaming table. But he had recalled it regularly when, in the years of Requesens' absence, he sat down to the dreary business of writing letters to him. It became less and less dreary with the waxing discontent in the officers' corps. And ever more often Loyarte could tell himself that the wild card on which he had wagered was to come up sooner or later.

Yet it was not he who had infused Requesens' name into the discontentment. There was, apart from the magnetism of a name wrapped in enigma and martyrdom, a highly rational element in the attraction it exerted. Requesens was free as no other man was from those logrolling friendships which, as the General got on in years, prejudiced his loyalty to the Army. If, then, the Army should one day look for a leader with no bonds other than its own, Don Lorenzo might meet the requirements to perfection. In short, one wondered pretty generally in Army circles whether he would be willing to forget their disloyalty toward him in exchange for the blanket of oblivion they were willing to spread over the scandal of '41.

Loyarte chose an obscure way of appraising the man out East of the betterment of his chances. He continued to write about "the Requesens legend," and would frequently hint that it was no one but he who kept it alive. He reckoned on his fellow officers' disinclination to speak out loud what they spoke in whispers. He dreamed of himself as the kingmaker of the coming Minister of War, or, more accurately, as being able to convince Don Lorenzo one day of his kingmaker's work.

He kept silent on the occasion of the Night-in-the-Palace, trembling lest one of the others pronounce Requesens' name, and thanking the Virgin for the presence of Colonel Fafreras which, at this stage of events, was sealing all lips.

So far so good for a gambler. Yet in the end Loyarte missed the right moment to emerge as the spokesman of Don Lorenzo, and act, bidden or not, as the junta's spokesman to him. It was Fafreras, not he, who gave the malcontents the signal to band together in earnest, despite the agreement arrived at at the Palace. Fafreras, not he, invited Requesens to join the meeting at the Casa Ninon; Loyarte did not learn of its actual purpose before, in the reflection of a hundred mirrors there, he beheld his own consternation.

He had not really lost out. (Perhaps his chatter on the road from the caucus that night—an hour previous he had received a letter from his beloved mentioning some well-born young partisans of El Huérfano in Majamarca—had silenced what doubts Don Lorenzo may have entertained as to his watchfulness and perception.) Still, when the new Minister made him his A.D.C., Loyarte had had to accept the honor as a downright present. And sometimes he still felt that he was being treated as the recipient of a gift.

Withal, he honestly admired Don Lorenzo. He assumed that his recurrent aloof brooding and even his spells of highhandedness were dictated by the musings of a subtle, deep, far-roving mind. As he gradually shook off the effects of the oratory of his future father-in-law, he could not but contrast unfavorably such voluble haziness with Don Lorenzo's reserve. So after about a fortnight he formed the resolution to let his superior at least know that the Senator had not much love for Colonel Fafreras.

But at the very moment that Loyarte girded himself to pass on the news to Requesens, he was made to realize that the latter seemed to have cautioned himself against too close a friendship with Fafreras.

Twenty-seven of the fifty airplanes, Loyarte was told by Don Lorenzo, were ready abroad to take off. He, Requesens, had insisted that all the machines must be flown to Huacho. He had persuaded the Cabinet how wasteful it would be to start a training program here and another one at Majamarca. "Wasteful and senseless in more than one sense," he now said, moving his head into the light of his desk lamp, and permitting his aide to note an abortive twinkle. Nor, he went on, had he wanted even to hear of foreign instructors, and the President had agreed that the Army would, to put it mildly, not savor another such intrusion. Finally he had taken up with Dr. Zapeta the matter of "the foreign occupation of Carjavel Airfield," suggesting that the thorny problem be solved by the Army. "And this, lieutenant, is where you come in," he added. "This is where you come in—Captain Loyarte. I want you to supervise the work on my hangars."

The first thing Loyarte thought of upon hearing these words was to utter in a low, probing tone the name of the lieutenant colonel who nominally was still in command of the so-called Air Corps of the Republic. Only after Requesens replied that that officer, worn out as he was by disillusionment, was hardly the man to deal with the changed situation, did Loyarte thank His Excellency for the great proof of the trust he had in his loyalty.

"Why do you say 'loyalty,' my friend?" the Minister countered good-humoredly. "Don't you think it is your abilities I count on first and foremost?"

"I cannot pledge abilities other than God has given me, Your Excellency. He alone knows whether my abilities are great enough to repay this debt of gratitude. But my fidelity I can pledge without reservations."

Don Lorenzo made a whistling sound with his lips, like a man suffering from great heat. "Fidelity is a dangerous word, captain. Loyalty is a dangerous thing. It is quite different from other beautiful emotions. Quite. Take love. Love can stop, vanish in indifference, in an annulment of love, as it were. Not so loyalty. If it stops, it is at once treason."

The new captain squared his shoulders. He struggled against an impulse to unburden himself completely to Don Lorenzo and repeat to him all of the Senator's opaque talk. But it seemed so distant, so immaterial, when balanced against the solemnity of this moment.

Also His Excellency did not appear to expect an answer. It was late in the evening, and half an hour previously Don Lorenzo had said he felt tired. "Not long ago," he remarked while he was unlocking one of the bottom drawers of his desk, "someone tried to tell me how greatly this country has changed since the 1880's. I suppose what he had in mind were the beliefs of the Eighties—heroism, fidelity, mettle, fearlessness. Do these beliefs no longer exist? Must the use of our greater knowledge necessarily destroy those ancient virtues? I doubt it." Talking slowly, he had lifted a notebook from the drawer. He put it before him on the desk, eyeing it with an expression of reluctance. His thoughts were with Philibert. ("Playing about with your officers, Requesens? Or are they playing about with you?")

He was convinced by now that Philibert had come to grief. It had been agreed that he would send his messages to Ramón from wherever he should be. When no message came within ten days, Don Lorenzo had gone to see his colleague at the Ministry of the Interior, feigning an interest in "news from small Eastern townships," one of which "might be picked as a new garrison." He had been allowed to scan what there existed of recent police reports, and read that El Huérfano had decamped from Ollaytaytombo, his final destination being "the near neighborhood of Majamarca." But the search in these files for Philibert's name, or any indication of his presence in the East, had been in vain. Lorenzo could not bring himself to consider that Philibert had deserted his mission, or was trying to leave the country; his obvious fervor, his admitted hope to retrieve some of the money, had been too great, too sincere! Don Lorenzo was convinced that Philibert was dead. Although his death threw open the vista of an uncontested enjoyment of "the old funds," Requesens did not gloat over it. Philibert's disappearance was like the undissolved chord of a tune which, in variations, had been with him for half a lifetime.

Loyarte did not make the tiniest movement.

Don Lorenzo raised his eyes, but failed to focus them on the new captain. His mind had swung back to the days shared with the man who had to call himself François Philibert in the end—to their initial mutual distrust, the testing, groping, slow-growing loyalty of common business, and to the services rendered by himself to the mad cause, whose last vestige now vanished in the trackless wilds of his own country. . . . "Well, señor captain?" he said, absently.

"Your Excellency was talking about the ancient virtues in the Republic," Loyarte ventured.

"Was I? Did I say I refused to believe they had changed?"

"That's what Your Excellency said. And with me, if Your Excellency will permit me to say so, that concept indeed has not changed since . . . ever since that day in '41. . . ." He lowered his voice to the shade of a confidential snicker. "That day . . . when there was some talk of teaching El Huérfano an old-fashioned lesson."

Requesens was rubbing his nose. He still did not look at his A.D.C., and there was no saying whether he had accepted the little memento in good grace. "I haven't failed you, have I?" he remarked. "Now . . . here now starts another era, captain. But mind you, times of success may put a greater strain on a man's loyalty than seemingly hopeless circumstances. Take self-sacrifice, heroic self-sacrifice, or take the thrill of great risks, or the grim satisfaction and the challenge of being outnumbered. Times of success offer no similar satisfactions. They may weaken a man's character, undermine his strength, and the Almighty knows that there is nothing harder for a man to regain than his inner strength. . . ." As though that observation had caught a last glimpse of his friend Philibert in Lorenzo's mind, he realized with a pang how much he would have preferred the subtle scheme of the dispossessed man to the wanton, clumsy affront his present undertaking was likely to effect. But no alternative was visible. "These . . ." he said, benevolently hushing a renewed outburst on the score of the great fidelity of his aide, and opened the notebook with a click, "these are some of the caballeros I shall be glad to accept as trainees in my pilots' school. Sit down, captain, sit down. Got a pencil? All right . . ."

Exhilaration swelled up in Loyarte at the sounds which followed those unassuming words. The names Don Lorenzo read belonged, to the last man, to participants in the Night-in-the-Palace! His suggestion had fallen on fertile ground, after all. This was his own plan, and here it was put into practice. This was more than the captaincy that had been bestowed upon him. Different though it was from the king-maker's glory Loyarte had coveted for so long, this was the prize crowning his patient gamble.

"My beloved María [he wrote some hours later], You will be pleased to learn that as of tonight your León is a captain. Without relinquishing my duties as Don Lorenzo's aide-de-camp, I am to be in charge of one of his most important construction projects. I may safely predict that this assignment will give me authority far disproportionate to both my new rank and my age. Now even your father must cast aside his prejudices. He must realize that what shapes a man's destiny are not always the forces above and the hazards to which those powers may expose him. For the first time, my beloved, I can say that your confidence has not been wasted on someone unworthy of it.

"I am writing this in the stillness of one of those heavenly nights Huacho is ofttimes graced with in the last days of July. As I look up from this sheet of paper, I can see the outline of the Cathedral against the sky, in which the stars have begun to pale. But the light of the moon still touches the glazed tiles of the façade. I think I'll miss this view very much when I move, as I shall, into more spacious quarters. In how many hours of incertitude, discouragement, and exasperation, have I not glanced over to the ancient *campanario,* waiting for the deep, melodious tones of its bells to comfort me! I almost feel ungrateful in deserting those proven friends. But life is a process of growing, and no one can grow without outgrowing something.

"There is one thing, and only one thing, however, which man never outgrows, for this 'thing'—Love—grows with him, and in fact makes for his growth. Never, my beloved, would I have reached this gratifying moment without the support of your love. And never would this moment have come into being without the affection and love I have felt for Don Lorenzo, and which could not fail to appeal to his heart, longing, as I have detected it to be, for human warmth beneath its crust of poise.

"Ever since I was a child I've heard people discuss 'what the Republic needs most.' Don't you think, my María, that what she needs most is Love? I know this is an hour of exaltation. I am not ashamed of it. Not ashamed of admitting that the love I feel for Don Lorenzo has given a new ring to my patriotism, as my love for you has always given guidance to my ambition. I have heard it said that ambition is nothing but part of one's self-love. But is self-love itself not the ambition to become worthy of the fellow-feeling of those to whom one is drawn? . . ."

XXI

"No, WE REALLY aren't *old* friends," Margarita Partridge answered Priscilla's question. "I think my father knew Don Lorenzo. I was a mere babe when he went abroad. But in 1930 . . ."

Doña Priscilla took her lips away from the straw through which she was sipping the milky maté.

"If you'll promise not to make fun of me—"

Priscilla brought up a hand, smiling.

"—I'll admit to you that as a schoolgirl I was smitten with his pictures. For a short while his pictures were to be seen everywhere in the days of the Expedition."

"They were? I didn't know that. He never told me. Frankly, I don't think I ever did justice to the Expedition. 1930 was not a happy time for me. I had family troubles. We married at Christmas '29, and I already had family troubles then. So 1930 was not a happy time for me," Priscilla observed again, casting a fixed smile over the tense expression which she feared was on her face.

"Are your parents still living?" Margarita inquired.

"My mother is," Priscilla answered. "As I said, I had no concept of what Lorenzo accomplished in 1930. A bandit! It sounded almost like a policeman's job to me. Only when his uncle spoke about the job Lorenzo had done did I understand it. And at that time Lorenzo himself no longer cared to talk about it. He seems to dislike the memory of Murcia."

"He has all the reason in the world to dislike it," Doña Margarita affirmed with that tone of authority which sometimes rose from her volatile manner of speech. "Murcia *was* an accomplishment, and never in the history of the Republic has a man been rewarded more poorly for one."

Lorenzo's praises sung by the young woman embarrassed Priscilla. A couple of minutes earlier she had been put out by the unabashed vehemence with which Margarita had touched on "the new unpleasantness" Lorenzo was up against.

"But I am not free from bias in recalling 1930," she went on now.

"Because of those pictures?"

"Not merely because of them," said Margarita, adopting the inoffensive irony in Priscilla's voice herself, "or rather, because of them, too. You see, I suffered for Don Lorenzo in 1930."

"You did—what?"

The young woman sat deeper down in her upholstered chair. For a second dimples appeared in her face. "I suppose I must tell you the whole story. What happened was this. We girls formed two regular parties in those weeks. Those who imagined Don Lorenzo as rescuing distressed damsels most of his time in the Northwest, on the one hand, and those who'd think of the bandit he was fighting as a new Robin Hood, on the other. . . . So one morning, we—I mean the Requesens faction—rose very early and sneaked out of our homes (God alone knows how we did it). Each of us had brought some flowers along, and after we'd met, we all went around to decorate Don Lorenzo's pictures wherever we saw one. Now you swore you wouldn't make fun of me!" Mrs. Partridge added quickly, halting the flow of her open-vowelled English.

"Has he ever known about this demonstration, or about the schoolgirls' Requesens party?" Priscilla asked. She could not help visualizing the chubby face that must have been little Margarita's, gazing with her large jet-black eyes at the likeness of a youthful Lorenzo.

"Certainly not," Margarita Partridge exclaimed, "and that was an additional punishment. Punishment came to us on the day after our exploit. At least it came to me. My parents blamed the 'modern' school for my undignified behavior. And next thing I knew my darling old nursery maid was replaced by an English governess, and each morning a teacher would come to the casa, an eternally snivelling old fellow. So I suffered for Don Lorenzo, didn't I? But all that," she continued, without returning her visitor's conventional little grin, "doesn't really answer your question, Doña Priscilla . . . your unspoken question. You did wonder, didn't you, why I should be so interested in Don Lorenzo's welfare? I'm sorry," she said, and tilted the plate with French pastry which stood on the massive table between them. "I mean,

I had no right to peep into your mind."

Priscilla helped herself to one of the diminutive iced cakes. She flicked off a crumb that had fallen on her lap, while her eyes wandered over the forbidding furniture of the room. "Everybody has *that* right, my dear," she said, "and not everybody is as candid about it as you are."

Margarita, who followed her glances, remarked that "this dreadful stuff" was an involuntary legacy to the Palace from the wife of one of her uncle's remote predecessors "who had to leave in great haste," and at once began to recount some of the history of that hapless *presidente* "who was far from being a blameless caballero." She spoke with a polite indifference which indicated her preparedness to drop the subject at any minute.

The large drawing room where the two ladies were conversing was situated on the third floor. It was part of the temporary lodgings which Dr. Zepeta's niece hoped to exchange as early as New Year in favor of the mansion she had bought. An aspect of useless ostentation emanated from the dated surroundings. The three heavily draped casements afforded only a hampered communication with the cloudless afternoon outside. Despite the verbose lightness to which Mrs. Partridge reverted increasingly as she proceeded with her story, Priscilla was oppressed by a sense of being hemmed in, if not cornered. When the young woman fell silent, ending her tale on a note of seriousness, she said after a pause, "If I were really wondering about your interest in my husband's welfare, as you put it, please be assured I did so in a spirit of appreciation. He hasn't . . ." She took another sip of her maté. "We haven't been spoiled in Huacho, after all."

"No, he hasn't been spoiled," the other assented immediately. "In the beginning, though . . . His appointment must have come as a pleasant surprise to him. Surprises of that sort are quite unusual in the Republic. As a rule a man's nomination to a high office comes as the last step on a long and tortuous road brimful with intrigues, briberies, and open struggle. In that respect, Don Lorenzo's appointment will go down as a noble exception in our history. But naturally this new unpleasantness he is up against . . ."

"It *is* an unpleasantness," Priscilla said evasively, "but I think the very absurdity of El Huérfano's insinuation has put his mind at ease by now."

"He hadn't thought that El Huérfano would leave him alone entirely after his taking office, had he?"

Priscilla frowned at the rug. El Huérfano's 1941 campaign against her husband was a subject never mentioned in her presence, nor, for all she knew, in Lorenzo's. "This attack came as a shock to him," she replied with the outspokenness of her impatience. "Why, only ten days ago he showed me that sheet, *you* know, and declared that something must have happened to El Huérfano on his travels, for *he*'d never allow such utter drivel to get into print. (It was an article about currency, our currency, or some such abstruse matter.) And then, a week later, that savage piece! Not that it is any less drivel. Or do *you* think this Huérfano will convince anyone that . . . ?"

"That the new planes are put into service to intimidate the masses, the 'downtrodden masses'? No!"

"So you've read it," Priscilla said, as if to herself. *La Semana* had done more than level that insensate accusation at Lorenzo; it had called him, among other names, "the notorious adventurer of our Berlin legation."

"Has Don Lorenzo ever thought of taking the bull by the horns?" Mrs. Partridge asked, pursing her small mouth.

"I can't tell you, my dear," Priscilla replied, shaking her head. "You've lived in a foreign country yourself. You know how hard it is to understand affairs you're not supposed to understand much about to begin with. You know how very hard it is to assert oneself."

"You are not the only one, Doña Priscilla."

"That's what I just implied."

"That's not quite what I meant, Doña Priscilla," said Margarita, staring meaningfully at her caller. "You are not the only one to be puzzled, to be put out . . . yes, to be put out by Don Lorenzo's reserve. Most of the time my uncle seems to be in the same boat."

"Is this a message from him?" Priscilla asked under her breath.

"Heavens, no! But . . ."

Priscilla replaced the gourd-like vessel from which she had drunk the maté on the silver tray on the table.

"But if it ever occurred to my uncle that I'm not just the little Gracián girl who fell in love with a dashing Britisher only to come back, four years later, as his widow, and not yet quite grown up . . . if that ever *should* occur to my uncle, this *might* be the sort of message he'd entrust to me in the present situation."

"You've grown up all right, Doña Margarita," said Priscilla, her voice still very low, "but you're still very young. A message delivered, a message passed on—do you think it is a message heeded at once? . . . Four years? You must have been very happy in those four years."

"Major Partridge was a fine man."

"He must have been. . . . Would you like to tell me more about him some day?" Priscilla murmured, as though this token of dutiful sympathy could undo the humiliating pity she realized the young woman felt for her at this moment.

But apparently Major Partridge's widow would not yield to any such soft evasion. She unfolded her legs which had been tucked up on her seat, and bending forward, crossed her arms on her knees. "May I be candid once more? May I? . . . You see, as it happens, we both don't care very much about Huacho politics—you because you weren't born here, and I, I suppose, because I was. Don't think I am itching to try my hands in politics. But this thing, this fellow, this Huérfano, goes beyond Huacho politics. It goes beyond politics anywhere. Life is too short and too beautiful to have it smashed to pieces by the Huérfanos."

The increasing gravity of the young woman's tone readied Priscilla for a reply, but the other went on,

"The President is Don Lorenzo's *friend*. Little as I know, I know that much. I also know that bygones are bygones with him. Don Lorenzo's conflict with this fellow, this scum . . . that conflict, if we stoop to call it that, must not necessarily remain his alone."

"Is this . . ." Priscilla asked, steadying her voice by breathing out first, ". . . would this be the message if you had got one? Was this what you wanted Colonel Fafreras to tell me? That night, here, downstairs?"

"Colonel Fafreras?"

"When you took me to the rear salon where he was waiting for me on the balcony—"

A peal of laughter cut her off. "*I* wanting him to tell *you* anything? To tell anyone anything? But I loathe him! That's why I left you so abruptly when I saw him. I just didn't want him to rub his mustache against the back of my hand, and assure me how much I'd grown up." Margarita got up, and walked rapidly away from the table, evidently looking for a cigarette; she noisily opened one silver, or tortoise-shell, box after another on the sideboard crammed with knickknacks. "My father used to receive him occasionally (God knows what for), and one day I chanced into the library while *he* was there all by himself, and he took me on his knees and . . . well, I assure you that his grunting delight in patting my *derrière* wasn't purely paternal, my dear. . . . Good heavens, I seem to be wallowing in silly childhood memories this afternoon!" she said before she came back to Priscilla, her round face still flushed with irritation. "But such an experience sticks in one's mind, doesn't it? No, I wouldn't have *anything* to do with that half-breed upstart under *any* conditions. How on earth did the idea ever get into your mind? Did he talk to you about El Huérfano? about my uncle? about myself?"

"No," said Priscilla in a level voice, "no. Not one word." She was trying to persuade herself that there was a world of difference between the intriguing and the coquetry of Margarita and her own craft in staying away from her web. Of course, wealthy Margarita Gracián had no taste for El Huérfano. No one had. But no one overrated the possible effects of the muddy gossip he set afloat. What really actuated Margarita to meddle in men's affairs was, in Priscilla's judgment, her pride in having escaped the cloistered ignorance which used to be women's lot in the Republic.

Later in the day, another thought came to Priscilla—and this notion was to remain with her throughout all the interminable deliberations, the excitements, the anguish, and the catastrophes, on this day still in store for her. It was to remain with her as a whispering voice, as it were, which now would challenge her indignation and sharpen her reasoning, now slacken it, sooth her conscience, and promise to manumit her from the bond of a disenchanted love. Perhaps Lorenzo had, once more, caught the fancy of little Margarita! Perhaps she had gotten wind of the lack of intimacy in his married life. The Casa had six servants now, not counting Ramón, and surely each of them eavesdropped and tattled day in and day out. Perhaps the President's niece played with the idea of winning the idol of her adolescence as a lover, or even for good. Divorce is looked upon as a scandalous step in the Republic; but Priscilla wondered whether her being a stranger might not buffer such a blow to public opinion. Perhaps Margarita counted on that, too. Yes, perhaps she wanted to obligate Lorenzo to herself first of all.

The discourse of the two ladies had not ended with the outburst about Fafreras. Encouraged by Priscilla's seemingly livelier response, Margarita had urged her to use all her influence with her husband, and advocated a rapprochement with the Palace, "the natural thing in the face of *that* danger." The young woman had not recoiled from ponderous platitudes in warming up to her proposal. She had spoken of Lorenzo's "destiny," and its "fulfilment," and of the rôle fate meant him to play "on the stage of history." Though the young woman had herself laughed at those words in the same breath, their resemblance to the manner of speech which Lorenzo at times still employed could not fail to catch his wife's attention.

As it was, a new sobriety seemed to reign over him these days. A bare two weeks after the event, he began to look back with a sort of composure at the effrontery of El Huérfano. Did Priscilla not see herself that the fellow had become desperate, realizing he had appealed in vain to the baser instincts of the public? This time, he had not even managed to arouse the curiosity of the *gente decente* and their malice. No one at the Club had so much as alluded to the incident. There was no indication that it had made the slightest dent on his popularity with the Army. The People's Party was no longer a topic of interest. All through the month of July, Huacho Broadcasting Station had not wasted a word on El Huérfano's itinerary out East. In short, before worrying any further about the ridiculous contretemps, why not recall the attitude of *La Libertad* which had never, except for some dignified minor asides, taken cognizance of the dwarf?

Lorenzo was favorably inclined toward the great newspaper. It stood wholeheartedly behind the reform of the air force, and yet had not given any publicity to the origin of the new machines. It had reported on the construction planned at Carjavel, and—an appeasing hint in the direction of those timid merchants and their hangers-on who were afraid of antagonizing certain foreign legations—had contended that in the long run the economy of the country would profit as much from the novel development as it was hoped would its armed forces. For two days news from the Pacific theater of war occupied the front page of *La Libertad*. On August the ninth, however, it gave prominence again to national affairs, and among them, announced the forthcoming cornerstone ceremony of the Pilots' School.

Paradoxically, the approach of this festivity seemed to disquiet Lorenzo anew. He could be seen shaking his head without the slightest provocation, or opening his hands, palms upwards, while he looked at nothing, his lips closed. He was reviving the junta, that much Priscilla did realize, but she had no concept of the objective of that reorganization. She saw him defy custom by receiving the new Air Corps officers one by one, and at many a late hour she heard, from her bedroom, his rasping voice holding forth downstairs in the sala.

One night, crossing the upper-floor corridor, she again heard it, this time rising from the patio to the window at the rear end of the passage. Since she knew that Captain Loyarte, who had been with her husband, had left the Casa a good while earlier, she stepped up to the opened casement to see who the late visitor was.

A fortnight ago, electric bulbs had been installed on the walls of the patio. They all were ablaze now, but the profusion of creeping vines dimmed them. The bright colors of the tiles, cleansed from weeds at last, were overcast by the greenish light thus produced. Lorenzo was alone. He stood facing the house, his feet wide apart, before the bronze goddess put outdoors recently, addressing the statue with an ardor which intermittently broke through his low voice. After a minute he stepped aside, as if he had been expecting the goddess to step down from her pedestal to confront him at close quarters. One of the lights now illumined his face fully. It occurred to Priscilla that his physique had changed in the last weeks: chin and neck had thinned, his nose had lost some of its vulgar fleshiness, and a tinge of frailty deepened the shadows on his temples. Priscilla withdrew from the window. But not before another hour did she hear his steps in the corridor.

She did not see him the following day. Her semblance of sympathy toward Mrs. Partridge's entreaties notwithstanding, Doña Priscilla believed she had made up her mind to stay clear of her intrigue; and the fact that this was the second time she had been asked to influence her husband's conduct only seemed to fortify that determination. How could she possibly influence Lorenzo?

The specter of his "Berlin adventures" had in all these years not left her—and with it, the endless procession of her attempts to unravel the truth from Lorenzo's words and from hearsay. Something in her had always anticipated the futility of those attempts, and stifled her warnings. Had it been only her experience? Had it not also been the awareness of her own rectitude? And had that awareness not tarnished her irreproachability? Had this preconception of her own decency not made her a party to Lorenzo's evasion?

At night, silence hovered over the dinner table. Several times she felt tempted to inquire after the reasons for Lorenzo's distraction, but the image of him standing in front of the effigy of the goddess was embarrassing to her. She was struck by the mien of utter blankness with which he put to his mouth one blindly forked morsel after another in rapid succession. Contrary to her habit, she issued unnecessary orders to the two servant girls.

"Shall we go to the sala?" Lorenzo said behind the smoke of his cigar, interrupting another volley of instructions she was giving to one of the maids. "I won't have any callers tonight."

She rose instantly. "Oh . . . and congratulations."

"Congratulations?"

"Dr. Zapeta will be at your ceremony, won't he?"

"And you?" he asked over his shoulder. He stood in the doorway. "Will you honor the Air Corps with your presence? There will be a reception after the ceremony, buffet, champagne, and all that. A tent will be set up."

"I'll ask Mrs. Partridge whether she'll be there," she replied. She was still in the dining room.

"What do you need her for?" came his belated comment.

She saw him sitting beneath the portrait of his father, a foreign newspaper on his lap. Six tapestried armchairs had replaced the bamboo settee and the old chairs in that corner. The crystal chandelier had yielded to four bald white half-globes screwed to the ceiling.

Priscilla took a seat opposite her husband at the other end of the wide hexagon formed by the armchairs. Its floor space was covered by one of the late General's costly Oriental rugs. She held an unopened book in her hand and slowly, her glance fixed on Lorenzo, she lowered her chin to prop it against the small volume.

"Odd," said Lorenzo, taking out his glasses, "it *is* odd that you seem to make your appearance the day after tomorrow dependent on the Gracián girl."

"I like her."

"Yes. Nice woman. And clever, too, I suppose." His face behind the spectacles mirrored nothing of the lights. "Her father was a very clever man. Whichever party was in the saddle, he rode the crest of the waves. As far as money went, that is. He had no ambition. Imagine a man with his money, and never any ambition! Clever? Perhaps."

"Lorenzo . . ." she said into these indifferent words of his, "Lorenzo, don't you think it means something that he'll take part in your ceremony?"

"Dr. Zapeta? Why should he not?"

"Your Pilots' School wasn't exactly his idea."

"No."

"Lorenzo . . . coming from me, this might surprise you . . ." She felt her indecision as a real physical weight.

"What, Pris?"

"Lorenzo, did you ever consider working more closely with him?"

He turned a page of the newspaper. "What makes you think that the Minister of War does not work closely with the President in this country? The close collaboration of the two is an old tradition—though in the General's days it rather used to be the other way round. It was the President who worked closely with the Minister of War. But there," he said, and pushed his glasses far up on his forehead, "was a man he feared.

She bowed her head. "He is your friend, Lorenzo. I feel he is. He went out of his way to show *me* his friendship at the Day-of-Independence fête."

"You are a very attractive woman."

"I am your wife."

"Don't forget that the Chargé d'Affaires of your native country was there."

"No, no, Lorenzo, that wasn't it. Lorenzo . . . he shares your feeling toward that fellow."

"My feelings toward 'that fellow' are subject to changes. At a certain time I couldn't help wondering whether this Huérfano might not offer the prospect of a more reliable friendship than all the well-born señores in the Republic put together. Now, now, don't look at me that way, Pris. That was pure speculation, pure speculation. . . ."

"I know nothing of 'all the well-born señores'—"

"You know something about some of them."

"I know what you tell me."

He began to fold his paper meticulously, running the nails of index finger and thumb along its creases.

"We all must overcome some resentment at times, don't you think so, Lorenzo?"

"Resentment? Every last one of my moves, these days, is dictated by reasoning, Pris."

"I don't ask you what your moves actually are," she said with the merest indication of a sigh.

"At any rate, I am not worrying about El Huérfano, these days."

"Don't you want to stop him?"

"Business before pleasure."

"Dr. Zapeta—"

"—shares my feelings toward El Huérfano. Supposedly."

"He means well. This much I know."

"How?"

"*I* mean well, Lorenzo," she said.

Lorenzo let a minute of bewildered reflection pass before he said, not without feeling, "You are choosing a peculiar moment to say so, Priscilla."

"Did I have to say so explicitly? I have always meant well."

"Overcoming resentment, no doubt," he muttered.

"Perhaps I had to at times."

"Was it difficult?" he asked with a frivolous note.

"As long as I had hope, it wasn't. See here, Lorenzo, I don't mean to rake up our whole lives—"

"Go on. Go on. As long as you had hope . . ."

She put down her book. "I loved you a great deal."

"Except for that resentment, eh?" He seemed to regret the retort: the prodding note which he added had an almost teasing inflection. Still he said, "You loved the sinner and hated his sins. It's an old formula, Pris, and has never done much good to the sinner."

"I was talking about Dr. Zapeta."

"As long as we are on the subject, we may just as well talk about those old sins of mine that serve Dr. Zapeta so well."

"Bygones are bygones with him."

"Not quite. He may not take those bygones very seriously. But he enjoys their existence just the same. What else could he play up against me with equal ease? There is always 'public opinion abroad' to be played up against me, no? Do you know what actually prompted him so graciously to consent to my appointment? He wanted a War Minister he could keep in line. And what can compete with old sins as a means of keeping a man in line? My record was my main asset to the Palace. This record so stained in the eyes of democratic virtue. Oh yes," he went on, "he would not be disinclined to tell me pompously how much he detests El Huérfano, and that his party ought to be outlawed, and that he must take the matter up with the House of Deputies as soon as it reconvenes—"

"That would be a good idea, would it not?"

"I repeat I am not interested in El Huérfano. Not these days. After all, a man can't do everything at the same time." He threw up his arms. "Don't you realize that Dr. Zapeta is rather fond of the venomous mementos El Huérfano sends me? They keep me in line. Or so Dr. Zapeta thinks."

"Aren't you seeing ghosts?"

"Isn't it customary for sinners to see them?"

"Must you use that word? You know you don't believe it."

"I begin to feel its solace. It covers so much. It covers a man's errors and his negligence and his miscalculations—yes, above all, his miscalculations—the one unpardonable sin for a man in my shoes, and come to think of it, the one unpardonable sin for any man of action, of ambition. Of ambition for his country as well as for himself. To speak of sins, of past miscalculations that is, gives me some assurance that I am seeing the light at last—"

"What *are* you interested in, Lorenzo?" she interrupted him.

"I *am* seeing the light, believe me. For a while I calculated that Dr. Zapeta was scheming to put me out of office, was setting some sort of trap—"

"Why? Why?"

"He didn't put me into office, did he? And not everybody overcomes resentments. Still I miscalculated. What he really works at is to ensnarl me, reduce me to his henchman. Forty-seven isn't so far off, and it would be nice for him to have the Army watch over his re-election. He feels that my star with the Army is rising. So let's do some favors to good Lorenzo in time. . . . It is clear as daylight," he exclaimed, "and the Gracián girl could have saved her advice. . . . Sorry, Pris. I hope you didn't think I would not guess who was behind your sudden solicitude, and who, in turn, was behind hers."

"I should have known you'd only scorn me," said Priscilla. "Experience should have taught me that I cannot help you. I saw you were troubled, Lorenzo, greatly troubled. So I went ahead and . . . all right, then, so I passed on what looked like sound advice under the circumstances."

"What circumstances?" he threw in. She and her Margarita and Margarita's uncle would be surprised to learn how propitious circumstances were for him. He would talk to the President all right. As it happened, he would indeed, and pretty soon, too. But it wouldn't be about El Huérfano.

"Propitious circumstances? Propitious for what?"

"For clearing the air once and for all. I'll talk to him, don't worry."

"You will talk to him? About what?"

Lorenzo uncrossed his legs. Then he said, "There is one thing men talk about. No matter what they pretend to discuss, that's the thing they talk about. And this being so, it may well be the one thing worth any talk. *Is it you or I?* That is the one thing men talk about."

A long silence followed. Priscilla's eyes did not leave Lorenzo, whose solemnity was gone when he continued,

"I didn't scare you, did I? You need not be scared in the least. No foolhardy nonsense is on my mind. These are not the romantic 1880's. Nowadays such affairs are settled with the right word in the right place."

No, she said, she was not scared. Did he want her to know more about this right word in the right place?

When Lorenzo had sat down, he had deposited his half-smoked cigar in the ash-stand. He relit it.

"You rehearsed this right word last night, didn't you?" she asked after a pause.

He puffed on his long cigar.

"But after what I told you . . . but now, Lorenzo, now there's no longer any reason. You say: 'Is it you or I?—is it Dr. Zapeta or you? But what is there, after what I've told you now, what *is* there to fight about between you two? What is there for you to fight for?"

"Pris, let me tell you this. There's been a great to-do these past years about what this or that nation, or this or that man, was fighting for. Now let me tell you this. Only he who attacks fights *for* something. Only the attacker does. The other fellow is merely fighting for survival. And I've had enough of spending my energies in fighting for survival. That's what I've done ever since I was made an orphan. I'd rather be the attacker for once. The aggressor . . ."

"The aggressor?"

"It's an appalling term, I know. It is these days. I picked it deliberately. You are my wife. You must know where I am heading. You are free to inform your new friend where I am heading—"

She got up hastily, and said it was very late.

He came to her bedroom half an hour later. Had she misunderstood him? He had been hasty. He had not meant it the way it sounded. Actually, he was very appreciative of the interest she took in his complex situation. Also one day some opportunity would arise, he was sure, to tell the Gracián girl that he had appreciated her advice, too. His present plan did not call for the head of her uncle—good God, no!—and thus she, Pris, and Dr. Zapeta's niece might still be on the best of terms a year from this day. And first of all he hoped he hadn't frightened her.

"I told you you didn't."

"I am sorry, Pris."

"You were frank."

"I am sorry about some of the things I said tonight. I didn't intend to hurt you. Nor to imply that you haven't been a good sport. We've gone through so much. . . . Eh? . . . But I haven't been the worst of husbands, after all. . . . I wish we could forget. Forget some of our failures."

The bed lamp kindled tiny sparks on the polished brass of the Dutch chandelier. "Lorenzo," she said, "there's something I've been wanting to tell you for the past two days—since peace, as the radio announced, was in sight in the Pacific, too. Travel restrictions will be removed in the States. I have been thinking of a trip, of a visit with my mother. A trip, yes."

"For how long?"

No answer came.

"I do not blame you," he said with ready melancholy. "You need a rest. You've had none with me. I have no rest. This office is not simply the glamorous comeback we thought it would be. It's less. It's more. It puts a great strain on me. On you, too. Naturally. So, a vacation . . ."

"Not a vacation," she said.

"I know, I know. Of course you'll have family matters to attend to—"

"Oh, Lorenzo!"

He looked as if he wanted to come up to her. But then he remained in the middle of the room, one foot put forward on the patterned straw mat.

She stared at the brass over his head. She felt that one word on her part accepting his regret would bring to a standstill the inexorable flow of their estrangement. But she also felt that, in an altogether crazy mental contortion, he expected her to say that she too had a share in their failure. And how could she, how could anyone, feel guilty before his hundredfold guilt?

XXII

THE CANVAS WIND-SLEEVE atop the observation tower floated lazily in the tepid breeze of the forenoon. Huge gonfalons displayed their colors round the sites of the air sheds "under construction." The old hangar and the administration building stood without adornment. Captain Loyarte had solved the delicate problem on his own initiative: in return for the promise not to raise the Republic's flag on the structures not hers, the manager of the foreign air line had agreed not to mar with its streamers the national spirit of this day. Shortly before sunrise, however, four poles had been erected close to the hangar, and Loyarte had had hoisted on them the green-white-blue cloth with the three-headed serpent.

The lieutenant colonel who nominally was in command of the Air Corps had not appreciated that procedure to Loyarte's full content. The two señores had been talking little to each other this morning; already on the day before, some uncertainty as to their respective authority had shaken the self-assurance of the new captain and destroyed much of the delight he felt in his duties.

He was pacing an unfinished landing strip strewn with discarded steel matting. North of the administration building, the triple rows of the new planes were deployed in converging diagonals at both sides of the one usable runway.

The craft had been flown to Huacho from the southeastern sister republic by civilian airmen. Before returning home after a short week, these foreigners had given the necessary instructions to the old pilots of the air force, wartime-trained men. The newly appointed trainees had hardly been more than lookers-on. Yet Loyarte had already glimpsed in them some of the notorious arrogance of technical experts—eager as these gentlemen, on the other hand, were to listen to his political information. At any rate he had decided to stay away from the machines and their crews altogether on this morning. He did not wish to stand idly among them. The señores, he reflected, would learn how to respect him. . . .

Now and then, as he strode along, he threw a glance in the direction of the grandstand near the gate; and each time a shadow fell on his small face. At almost regular intervals, he adjusted the light blue aide's sash he wore across shoulder and chest.

It was ten o'clock. In less than half an hour the sky would be furrowed with planes, the President's flag would go up at the gate, the band would intone the anthem, and Don Lorenzo would deliver his three-minute speech—"a speech right to the point," as he had predicted—and Dr. Zapeta would answer with one of his mellow addresses and go through the motions of mortaring the selected brick into the cornerstone, and then the bishop would give his benediction. It would all be replete with great dignity and import. The captain could visualize it all. Yet he found himself deriving only small pleasure from it.

He had spent a restless night in one of the emergency cubicles of the administration building. The ambivalent foretaste of the trick he was to play on the foreign air line had kept him awake most of the time, together with a curious letter from his María. To top his unease, he had now discovered that the major who happened to be in charge of the infantry detachment was a man to whom he owed a gambling debt. When, earlier, he approached the tent put up between the gate and the flower-bedecked cornerstone block, that officer, coming into his sight, had at once grinned at him, lifting his hand from the wrist and rubbing one finger against another in an insolent little gesture, which others, too, must have noticed.

But quite apart from that untoward coincidence, the presence of the major's detachment—an entire company of the Sixteenth—puzzled Loyarte. He had not been told, nor, to his knowledge, had the lieutenant colonel, that infantry would turn out in force; and he could not but ask himself whether Don Lorenzo had not had some ulterior motive in ordering him to stay at Carjavel continuously "for the last two days prior to the event." And this wonderment had turned almost to shock, as the obnoxious major, shelving their personal business, mumbled something about "security measures." What measures? Were the mounted police and the honor guard drawn from the ranks of the Air Corps not sufficient guarantors of safety and order? Was Requesens withholding something from him?

The information His Excellency had apportioned to his aide permitted the latter a good glimpse of what was afoot. Requesens' intentions were as simple as they were daring. His request for a concentration of the fifty new planes in Huacho was still in abeyance. He flattered himself that this day's performance, this show of new strength at his disposal, must tip the scale in favor of his demand for an "undivided air force."

Now, even counting on the pusillanimity of Dr. Zapeta, that demand —not unknown to the new Air Corps señores, thanks to Loyarte— amounted to a gamble on the part of Requesens. Considering the fact that the old aviators would pilot the machines at this parade, this gamble relied on a bluff. Both should have attracted the gaming instinct of Loyarte. Was it María's perturbing missive that impaired that attraction? Was it the remembrance of the nebulous utterances of her father?

Lost in his brooding, Loyarte had passed the point of his regular face-about on the unfinished runway, and again come into calling distance of the tent. The clatter of glassware and cutlery was already emanating from behind the canvas. He had meant to keep an eye on the social part of the arrangements himself, but the presence of the infantry officers lolling about in the shadow of the striped marquee dissuaded him from attending to that unmanly business. The major stood, his short legs crossed, amid the small gilded chairs, and placidly drew on his cigar. His men were getting ready to line the road of entry. The slovenly fashion in which they rallied surprised Loyarte as little as did the spiritless commands of their non-coms.

The day had grown very warm under the sultry sky. The captain took off his cap, which was rather large for his head, and smoothed his hair with the scented handkerchief which he liked to carry tucked into the sleeve of his tunic. Spectators began to trickle in from the road. It seemed that some of the infantry men had been detailed to shepherd them to the lot roped off about two hundred meters away from the scene of the forthcoming ceremony. There was something solicitous about the guidance given to these people—middle-class folk in drab attire, as Loyarte noted in another flash of astonishment. The police were walking their richly caparisoned horses at a conspicuous distance from them. "Security measures indeed!" muttered the captain, replacing his headgear at the right angle. He swung round on his heels. He remonstrated in his mind against the uncalled-for secretiveness of Requesens. But his censure did not exceed a sulky reproach, such as a lover may voice toward his beloved, assuring her of his unchanged affection in the face of incomprehensible conduct.

The mood that sentimental thought entailed thrust María's letter upon the perception of Loyarte again. So inexorably did it rise to his mental eye that he only belatedly marveled at the view of two of the old planes taking off—another item on the program no one had told him about!

His first reaction to the letter had been one of sheer mortification. How greatly had he misjudged the girl! True, she had at one time written about some young Majamarcanos, students and artists, rumored to be taking an interest in El Huérfano. But that information had born the stamp of light and humorous gossip. Not for the life of him would he ever have imagined that María herself might indulge such an indecorous hobby—if hobby, or pastime, it was! To mix with the scum of the outskirts and by-streets, with river longshoremen, brewery hands, shiftless peóns who had drifted to the city, street-corner loafers, questionable females perhaps—to mix with them for the sake of listening to this Huérfano! It was beyond belief. Yet this was what María had done, and not only once. This was the "extraordinary experience" she had gone to great length in describing. Tacitly riding roughshod over the exultation of his own letter, she seemed to oppose her enthusiasm about the "paramount issue of these days" to the pride her León took in his advancement, his intercourse with her father, and his new proximity to Requesens.

Loyarte had not known that El Huérfano was stumping in Majamarca. Requesens had not mentioned his name for some time. And with his recent outrage aiming at the very existence of the Air Corps, his name had become taboo among its young officers. Had El Huérfano taken up in Majamarca the subject dealt with so impudently by *La Semana*? Had María been listening to vituperations against the man she knew her León to depend on? It was unimaginable. Unless he wanted to presume a frightful hypocrisy in the girl, it was, as a matter of fact, unlikely. There was not one sentence in her letter that could allude to El Huérfano's polemics against Don Lorenzo. Her account of the outdoor rally she had attended—who had escorted her there?—was conditioned merely by the ready warmth of an inflammable soul. Surely she had no truck herself with the "awakened sense of social justice" and those "new forces" that an "undersized, sickly-looking Indio" was said to have gathered. Surely his "moving language" had merely appealed to her charitable, romantic disposition, not to her judgment. Surely those "ragged unshod laborers whose faces lit up at the sound of his voice" were not any closer to María's heart than the obscure notion her mind held of their mode of living; and the "brotherhood of those without even a shirt" was an empty phrase from the pen of a young lady whose chests overflowed with silken garments! Had a taste for the adventurous—not improbable in the María whose hazy daydreams about León's future had not so long ago fired his own imagination—led her to this morbid preoccupation with the brave new world to be thrown into the laps of the shirt-less? Or was she revolting against the snug, cushioned tyranny of her father by flaunting her disregard for everything he stood for? And if so, did that rebellious spirit not prove that she was impatient of the procrastination the Senator imposed on their union? Loyarte tasted some self-possession again at that thought.

He formed a practical resolve: whatever might be at the root of María's florid report from Majamarca, it was to be of service to him. He would bring certain matters winnowed from it to the consideration of Don Lorenzo: the incredible liberty granted out East to El Huérfano's tirades, the effect both those tirades and the spectacle of that liberty must have on Majamarcanos (people less accustomed than Huachaneros to political vociferations), and finally the news that "a foreigner, a white man, perhaps a trained insurrectionist" was travelling with the self-styled leader.

Loyarte hoped that to have formed this decision would make him feel hardened against sentimentality. His pace had slackened. Yellow dust hung over the new machines. It betokened the last-minute activities of their crews. Excited commands reached his ears whenever the two old planes, flying slowly at low altitude, repaired to a more distant segment of the airdrome. Was this another "security measure"? Such, he moaned to himself, was an A.D.C.'s lot; two days away from his master's presence made him an ignoramus.

The honor guard marched by, and Loyarte saluted the standard held aloft at its head. A gust of loyal attachment to this world of his swelled his breast as he stood at attention. A group of young officers in unzippered flight jackets passed by, riding a towing tractor, and hurled their laughs at him across the field. "*Aie,* where have you kept yourself, Don León?" one of them shouted through the horn formed by his hands. "Beautiful day, friend, eh?"

"Beautiful day . . ." Loyarte returned, waving his arms. At this moment a man in overalls came running toward him to report that His Excellency's car had left Government House. Loyarte hurried back toward the gate.

The tuning-up trombones had fallen silent. Sprays of voices from in front of the tent as well as the sounds of martial shouts from its rear indicated the first important arrivals. Already a knot of colonels surrounded the reviewing stand. The uniforms of at least three foreign attachés, holding themselves a little apart, were thrown into profile against the bunting that covered the structure. Without stopping, Loyarte shaded his eyes to discern the rows of onlookers behind the ropes. But a solid block of infantry regimentals obstructed his vision. Under the marquee a respectable number of ladies had already taken their seats on the dainty gilt chairs. The continual fluttering of their gaily-colored fans seemed to mingle with the slower tempo of the shimmering heat outside the shaded space. The entry road was aswarm with vehicles. . . . It *was* a beautiful day, León Loyarte said to himself, his bearings restored completely, and he did love Requesens, and did love the foolish girl in Majamarca. Ah, she ought to see him, at this moment, stepping up to the gate all by himself, as if singled out by the bugle which signalled the approach of His Excellency, his friend, his confidant, his protector!

According to the program, His Excellency should have reviewed the new machines on the ground immediately, with his aide beside him in his car. But he had the conveyance halted at the gate, left it, and dispatched Loyarte back to order the crews to stand at ease and inform the lieutenant colonel that the President would review them himself after the demonstration.

What caused Requesens to change the schedule of the parade (and also to forgo the company of his A.D.C. for another short while) was his disinclination to look into the faces of the young caballeros and read in them their hunger for early glory.

He too had not found much sleep in the night, and what there was of it had followed the agonies of twenty-four hours of self-search.

Uncounted times in these twenty-four hours he had scrutinized Priscilla's reasons for urging advice on him first, "meaning well," and then tossing in his face the news of her planned desertion. He had come to the conclusion that their talk had been a sort of test to her, an ordeal called upon to decide her future actions. Had there not been some irony in her comment on his "frankness"? Had she not expected him, in that hour, to give her at last a picture of the full complexity of his situation?

She had asked for too much. How could he have told her of the money abroad, of Mauricio Hojeda, of the Bundschuh hacienda, and of the incredible man who had vanished in Ollaytaytombo? How could he have stripped his soul down to nakedness without at the same time wrecking his dignity, his self-esteem, the image he held of his honor? Even if she had forewarned him of her intention, he could not have done it. He could not do it now. His confession might prompt her, as his silence threatened to do, to make good her threat and leave him. And by now Lorenzo realized that to lose her would be an unbearable blow. His love, this consciousness of his love—this one noble thing in his life—was contingent upon her companionship, upon her presence, no matter how cruelly chilling it might be at times.

At dinner he had pleaded with her again to "honor the Air Corps" on the next morning. But their meal had been broken off prematurely by the lieutenant colonel, who had stayed for two hours to discuss the technical details of the parade.

As Don Lorenzo, amid a bevy of staff officers, passed by the tent, bowing to the ladies, he recalled the crude superstition to which he had decided around midnight to have recourse. If Priscilla appeared on the morrow, he would follow her advice, be civil to Dr. Zapeta and even show him some deference. But if she remained absent, he would cross the Rubicon and demand from Dr. Zapeta that he make known, on the spot, his resolution in regard to the undivided air force. Lorenzo stopped short on the landing before he ascended the three red-carpeted steps to the platform. Once more he glanced at the tent. Priscilla was not there.

But as it was, his will to submit his line of conduct to the self-imposed lottery had been greatly weakened by the events of the small hours of the morning. Their strain was telling on him. His ruddy complexion was overcast by greyness. In fact, his compressed lips, the spasmodic working of his cheek muscles, and his vacant gaze, might have given away his true frame of mind to the reporter of Huacho's great newspaper who the following morning was to speak about the Minister's "visible awareness of the increasing responsibilities of his office."

Don Lorenzo motioned his entourage to the front of the stand. He shook hands with some of the gentlemen, hugged them for a second (as is the custom), and gave the appearance of responding to their congratulations. The officers kept a passage open for him, but he ignored it, and remained in the rear of the platform, his hands clutching a railing, insensitive to the flowers they crushed in their grip. He turned his head to the left. His eyes only gradually took in the scene: the pylons and flags and banners, the concrete of the runway, the sandy wide stretches, and farther off, the clouded mass of his machines and the men he divined in the distance. Then he overcame a last hesitation and threw head and shoulders to the right. The multitude of the spectators taxed the space allotted to them. And another sizable stream was still filing in. . . .

Indeed, the handbill, a copy of which the zealous Ramón had brought to the Casa shortly after midnight, his face glossy with the foretaste of trouble, had not managed to keep the public away from the fête. Here they were, and in force too, the "working people, the starving serfs of the exploiters," those nonentities who had been incited to demonstrate *"at least"* by their absence against the "extension of the government's bombing facilities" allegedly designed to "imperil the remnants of civil liberties in the Republic." Here they were, curious, docile, and burning with their innate desire to cheer their betters!

Unlike his aide, Don Lorenzo did not deign to notice the preponderance of city folk among the spectators. Yet it was he who, some hours earlier, had induced the Minister of the Interior to give the day off to all Government clerks and have them transported to Carjavel.

Nor was that the only favor which his colleague, Basilio Gonzales, upon receiving him unannounced at 3 a.m. at his residence, had rendered to Requesens. He had pledged himself without batting an eyelash to nip in the bud any disturbance which might result from the "bizarre leaflet." He had summoned the Chief of Police out of his bed, and ordered him to take into custody a number of men whose names (to the astonishment of Requesens) he read from a list evidently compiled for an emergency of this kind. He informed Requesens, moreover, that in his opinion "the puerile last-minute attempt to stir disorder" had not originated with El Huérfano himself. The authorities in Majamarca had the fellow well in hand, so accurate reports had it, and it was nowise necessary to suggest extraordinary measures out there, and make a mountain of a molehill.

Suggest? Since when had the Ministry of the Interior been wont to "suggest"? And what did it mean to state that the Majamarca authorities "had the fellow in hand"? Had he been out of hand ever? And if he had, why had Don Basilio given no proper account of the situation? The last Cabinet meeting—nothing except economic matters had been on its agenda—had offered ample opportunity to apprise him, Requesens, of what was brewing in the East, if anything was!

Don Lorenzo had put none of these queries to the placid man who had looked at him with sympathy, one hand lost in the wide-open silken robe and the wooly growth on his chest, the other crumbling the handbill of the People's Party with contemptuous carelessness. Time had been pressing. Consulting another notebook he extricated from his papers, Señor Gonzales had proceeded to discuss with his visitor as a matter of course which of the regiments to send to Carjavel "for additional safety, or rather, for your own peace of mind, Don Lorenzo. . . ." Though a Liberal, the Minister of the Interior was a reliable colleague. He was known for never gainsaying other Departments. He also enjoyed much popularity, not least on account of his splendid reform work within the police corps of Huacho.

The two mounted squads which approached at this moment bore witness to that success. The riders spread out in a canter, and their chargers came to a split-second halt, forming a wide semi-circle about the grandstand.

Close to the gate the honor guard stood as if rooted. A flurry of agitation rippled the assemblage as the band moved into position, its brass sparkling in the sunlight.

Requesens relaxed. Loyarte was back, standing respectfully at his elbow, and he ordered him to put down the name of the infantry major for a citation. That man had done well by his duties.

"His duties, Your Excellency?" echoed the A.D.C., but he received no enlightenment. For His Excellency had to step down to welcome the bishop.

Meanwhile the planes had rolled off in three tightly disciplined waves, and the roar of their motors distracted everybody's attention from the touching scene of Don Lorenzo's bowing over the ring of His Grace. Everyone craned his neck upwards, and those who were still on their way from the gate stopped to watch the machines pierce the ground haze. Only the Minister of the Interior disengaged himself from the Cabinet group which had arrived, and passing the bishop with a free-thinker's cool nod, proceeded to heave his enormous weight onto the rostrum.

Being a very old man, the bishop preferred to wait for the Chief Executive near the cornerstone. Lorenzo, waving for a chair, was in a quandary: he had pictured himself receiving Dr. Zepeta in the stand, towering over all heads. So he asked for the indulgence of His Grace, and with firm strides returned to the platform.

The three silvery phalanxes were overhead now, raising their altitude in graceful circles. The colors of the Republic shimmered on their wings. Loud admiring gasps were audible all about Don Lorenzo. He also heard his aide bid the guests clear some space for the President's party.

Lorenzo was just about to order Loyarte down to the bishop, when he felt someone pull at his sleeve—lightly first, then more strongly, almost commandingly. His Excellency disengaged his rapt stare from the spectacle in the sky, shifted his head, lowered it, and saw the flushed face of Ramón. The eunuch must have climbed the elevation from one of the sides, eluding the eyes of the police. Torn-off leafage of a garland and even some crimson petals stuck to his jacket.

"Señor colonel," he whispered with a voice that broke with excitement, "it came this morning, señor colonel, this morning. . . ." In an imbecile stealthy manner the index finger of his right hand tapped uninterruptedly against something in the cupped palm of his left.

Lorenzo, his face going dead white, snatched the envelope from Ramón. His chin made a furious motion to chase away the man, as he tore open the letter. And while, nearly deadened by the roar of the down-sweeping planes, the band struck up the anthem ("Oh ancient land of heroes/Oh blessed soil of trust . . ."), and the President's pennant rose in two jerks, and the bugle signals rent the public's vivas, and while Dr. Zapeta alighted from his limousine, his niece at one side, Doña Priscilla at the other, Don Lorenzo—unable to move—looked down at the sheets he held at his hip and recognized the handwriting of Philibert.

To read on the spot what this revenant had to report was out of the question. But his mere being alive reopened the prospect of getting the better of Dr. Zapeta by other means than forcing his hand in public. . . . Lorenzo saluted. He would postpone his demand for the undivided air force. He would not humiliate the President, he said to himself, while he desperately tried to catch the eyes of Priscilla.

XXIII

RAMÓN WAS WAITING at Government House for his master's return from Carjavel. He was aware that he had overstepped his zeal by delivering the letter at so inopportune a moment. It was by way of apology, then, that he approached Don Lorenzo as soon as he saw him dismiss his A.D.C. on the upper landing of the great staircase, and reported that the "thick envelope" had been brought to his house that morning by a man in the uniform of the Majamarca-Huacho Railroad who was unwilling to disclose where or how or by whom he had been charged with this errand.

No word of praise or reproof came from His Excellency. He sent the eunuch away with a scowl about as forbidding as the gesture that two hours earlier had made Ramón withdraw from the grandstand in so great a hurry.

Not until Don Lorenzo sat down at his desk did he take out the letter again. Several times in the course of the fête he had tried to gain a second glimpse of the missive's contents. But whenever he reached for the sheets, crumpled by now in his pocket, he had felt someone's eyes upon him, or heard someone's voice accosting him with another outburst of congratulations. And on his ride from Carjavel to Government House, Loyarte had not stopped talking, watching him all the time with almost improper inquisitiveness.

Philibert's letter was very long, that much Lorenzo had noted in his one glance. Its first line—the only one he made out in that one unnerving second, with the President's party coming closer and closer—had looked like good news . . . and re-reading this first line now, it occurred to Lorenzo that the optimism it must have evoked in him had mellowed greatly the speech with which he had greeted Dr. Zapeta.

It was a deceptive first line.

"I was right! [Philibert, omitting any salutation, wrote in German] I was a thousandfold right! But perhaps you have told yourself this much by now, and it is no longer news to you that Col. F. has taken our little friend under his wing. You had not much respect for the one-time mestizo sergeant, I recall, and spoke slightingly about his intellectual faculties. Still he was smart enough to do what *I* advised *you* to do! They have become partners! I only can guess what F. is up to eventually. I do not think you will like it. If you had not insisted on billeting me with Don Adolfo and keeping me there, I could have been with you and could have advised you in time, and our little friend would be *your* partner now and not that of F.! As it was, I came too late. I was right, but I came too late. But I *was* right!

"Small solace in my present condition! I am not free. I am being detained at a place which I figure lies about 15 km northwest of the railroad track and about half a day's journey (on foot) straight east of O. Here I am being detained by a gang of railroad thieves, or rather, by the old monkey who works as their fence. This man has also occasional dealings with convicts escaped from the penitentiary which lies midway between O. and his place. I am not sure he does not work hand in glove with the prison warden in cases where ransom can be gotten. It is in the hope of getting ransom that he takes care of this letter. Naturally he knows that I am a foreigner. He asks for 30,000. You must send this sum in two sealed envelopes, one of them to be given to the engineer of the freight train leaving Huacho each Monday morning, and the other to the engineer of the regular Thursday noon train. Each of these envelopes is to contain the halves of the bills.

"All this is likely to sound crazy to you. As it is, never before in history has a man been put in a similarly ironic position.

"On the very evening of my arrival in O. I ran into some of the closest collaborators of our little friend. A month earlier that encounter would have been highly beneficial to our undertaking. Or at least I would have had a chance of going ahead with our plan before his deal with F. had materialized. I must have sensed the importance of avoiding delay. I was hasty. That haste got me into trouble. It was too late. I had no opportunity to talk to him. I got involved in a ridiculous argument, and was bodily attacked. The henchmen of our little friend were convinced I had come to kill him. Imagine!

"Imagine furthermore that they fancied I was a trigger man sent after him by Moscow! Here is a piece of information that will come in handy to you, no matter what course events might take. There *is* a link between your P.P. and the Comintern. Remember how you dismissed my suggestion to that effect, as we talked over the situation? Asked about the origin of the funds at the P.P.'s disposal, and how they managed to meet the printers' bills, you, instead of facing the obvious, pretended to suspect 'some wealthy young provincial crackpots'! Nonsense. There is, or was, a link between our little friend and the Comintern. How close it was, or is, I do not know.

"Before I learned of his alliance with Col. F., I did not grasp what made his henchmen so panicky. Now I understand it. The deal with F. is a full-fledged defection from the party line. Though I wonder what made them think that Moscow knows already of the apostasy of our little friend, I can easily see that their bad conscience drove them crazy with fear.

"I am taking a desperate chance in writing you all this. I am not so foolish as to underrate the dangers to which I expose myself by committing all this to paper. I am doing it for your sake. Nor is this the only sacrifice I have been making for your sake, as you will realize presently.

"The attack whose victim I was took place in a tavern owned by a mestizo (one of the collaborators of our friend mentioned above). There I was tortured. From there I was, on the same night, taken to a hut close to one of the walls of the temple ruins. An eerie place. A place swarming with buzzards, nauseating rodents, and insects lashing out at me day and night. I was ill, very ill. My guard consisted of two peasants who scarcely ever talked to me. I suppose they were sworn to secrecy. My captors wished to keep my presence there, as the whole incident and my very existence, unknown to anyone. They were afraid lest rumors about a conflict between our friend and his supporters abroad (which they imagined would spring up as soon as my presence was talked about) would have an undesirable effect on some of their partisans. As I was to learn, their reaction to the deal with F. is not unanimous!

"Perhaps you know more about the present state of the P.P. than I do at this writing. The thieves who detain me are either too indolent to keep themselves informed on politics, or else do not want to discuss them with me. Still I heard through them that a great number of 'fourth-class passengers' recently have been travelling east. There seems to exist a racket that gets people without railroad tickets on trains, and those stowaways they call 'fourth-class passengers.' Be that as it may, what I found out about the P.P. I did through the wife of the above-mentioned tavern keeper. Leaving O., together with his boss, on the same night that I was assaulted, this mestizo forbade her to come to the ruins. But he has little power over her. She is a remarkable woman.

"She would come at night, and as my condition grew worse, stay on for hours, brewing concoctions and feeding me, and massaging my legs, and at one time she even applied leeches to me. I think I owe her my recovery. But she did not cure me out of goodness.

"She too did not doubt that I had orders to purge the P.P. of its leader. I could not dissuade her from that notion. She was deaf to my protests, and kept saying that she understood the nature of my denials, and appreciated my loyalty toward the men who had entrusted me with this difficult task. She disagrees violently with the present policies of our little friend, even though her husband is one of his lieutenants!

"Now I am coming to the craziest part of my story. One night—I was fairly well by that time—she brought a small barrel of brandy along as a treat for my guards. The two fellows had grown devoted to her, body and soul, in the weeks of my illness; they must have feared I would die on their hands, leaving them with a responsibility which seemed to scare the wits out of them. So they suspected nothing and enjoyed the brandy. It did not take long before they were both snoring. Then the woman offered me her help in making my getaway.

"I shan't describe the following hours in detail [Philibert went on]. Suffice it to say that the woman, anxious to have me avoid the town, led me first uphill through the underbrush and over deforested, stump-studded slopes, and then down a timber slide fallen to rot—that is, northeast first, and then southeast and east. It was a six hours' march. No mean exertion for a man who had nearly forgotten how to use his limbs!

"We rested on the bank of a lagoon formed by a tributary of the River (as I was to discover later). The woman fed me out of the basket which she had carried on her back, and I also took some drops from her brandy bottle, much as I hate this vile stuff. I must say I felt pretty good despite my fatigue. I felt even better when the woman started explaining to me how I was to reach the track of the railroad, or better, the station where she advised me I should board the train. Since my money was gone (together with my passport), she gave me some of her own, enough to take me to Majamarca, as she pointed out. And before I could ask her why she thought I was anxious to get to that town, she said, 'That is where *he* is. That is where he has gone to make a compact with one of the colonels. A powerful colonel. The commander of the garrison there.

It will not be hard to find the traitor. He has become bold. The colonel protects him, surreptitiously still, for their pact is not known yet. They say he is talking right on the streets. You will find him. You will succeed in getting close to him. When he talks, they are all in raptures, so you can get up to him. I hope you will still have the six cartridges then. Do not waste any on the road. Perhaps you will need all six. Do not miss.' And with that—I do not propose to depict the fanaticism which animated her whole being at that moment—she handed me the pistol.

"A joke, is it not? A joke on you! Now you may see with what manner of folk you shared the hatred that blinded you against the simple realities of the situation. A joke on me? Maybe.

"I need not tell you that I feigned full co-operation, though I was afraid she might (now that I was her ally!) ask questions about the men, or the organization, that she supposed had sent me on my errand. But the pitch of her hatred was such as to exclude ordinary curiosity.

"There was a path eastwards and on it we set out after sunrise. We met several fishermen, and the woman talked to them in her unintelligible lingo, and they voluntarily gave her directions. Marching on, we now lost sight of the lagoon, now drew closer to it, until we reached the stream. Soon we came to a grass rope bridge. There we parted in great friendship—she, convinced she had saved the purity of the P.P., I, thinking only of my impending return to you. True, running afoul of insurmountable obstacles on my self-chosen mission, I had failed. Yet I would furnish you with news of the highest importance!

"Fate decided differently. The woman was careless. She overrated the stamina left to me. She gave me only spotty information about the road on the other bank of the stream. She said nothing about the penitentiary I was to pass by.

"What happened to me in front of this accursed place was this. I was deathly tired, footsore, hungry, groggy. I took the penitentiary for a convent or such like (in fact, it *is* an ancient Jesuit mission building), and was already staggering up to the entrance, when I saw the sentinels on their watch tower. Don't ask me how it came about that I did not see them from afar. I didn't, and this may account for my sudden fright. Now I could have entered the place just the same. Looking back, I realize that the cause for my alarm, for my wish to get away, was my consideration for you! I knew I was weakened. I knew they could make me talk in there. Talk about what, you may well ask. It was I who had been wronged, I who had a claim on the justice of this country! But where does a man end, in fact, where does he *begin,* when he is made to talk within the walls of a prison? All this, I admit, did not come to me through cool reflection.

"I am not ashamed to tell you that I ran, yes, ran away from the sight of the penitentiary. I sneaked along the wall first and then round a crooked corner, and then I began literally to run, insensitive to the demands of my aching body. Perhaps it *was* an attack of madness. But before being amused at it, my friend, *you* try to stand up to what I had to among your savage compatriots. Ah, there is no use going back to that fateful moment again and again. All my life I have taken for granted a vein of irrationality in men, and counted on it. But I never expected to live to feel it burst in myself!

"I collapsed. When I came to, the old monkey was standing over me—I mean the hunchbacked rogue whose broad face I've been seeing day in, day out ever since. He said I was not the first to come his way. Smudged and dirt-covered, as I was, hollow-cheeked, my wrists still showing the traces of manacles (for my guards at the ruins had put them on every night), tottering like a drunk as he raised me by my armpits—what else could he take me for, a couple of miles away from the prison building, but an escaped convict? The color of my skin and my speech puzzled him at first, but soon both only served to stiffen his resolution to hold me for ransom.

"No one in these parts can conceive of a foreign white man without funds, or at least without wealthy friends at his beck and call. His convictions on that point are so deep-rooted that he hesitated for weeks to let me write this letter, paradoxical as this may sound, considering his objective. But finally I managed to give him the impression that I would be left on his hands, a useless mouth to feed.

"I do not think that any other man in my shoes would have withstood, in the course of all the ordeals, the temptation to involve *you,* whether in the hope of extricating himself from a horrid situation, or out of sheer malice. I did withstand this temptation even in the worst of my fevers, and I am withstanding it still. But do not count too much on my endurance. It may reach its saturation point. I may find myself compelled to act, come what may, to act irrespective of wider consequences!

"We shall have to change our grand strategy, of course [the missive closed with baffling abruptness]. I trust I shall hear from you without delay."

Mechanically Don Lorenzo folded Philibert's letter, and put it into the inner pocket of his tunic. He had unbuttoned it as soon as he closed the door of his office behind him. The afternoon had grown extremely warm. Unseeing, he thumbed through this morning's still unopened mail. He was about to take off his glasses and to get up, when a small greenish envelope caught his attention.

At least one letter came in every day marked, as was this one, "Personal," or "To be opened by His Excellency only." It would contain an anonymous denunciation, or, written by a schoolmaster or village alcalde, the plea of a family for the release of its son from service. Don Lorenzo's interest in this sort of correspondence was small; in having it put before him regularly, he had merely given expression to the new, "basically democratic" spirit of the Ministry of War. Most assuredly this thin greenish envelope did not arouse the slightest curiosity in him at this moment. Yet he unsealed it, as if to prove to himself that the shocking news from the East had not thrown him off balance completely.

A single sheet remained in his hand. Great, sweeping lines opened the communication, but the clarity of the hand decreased toward the ending. The signature "Fr. Crisóstomo, O.S.I.D." was put down in strong majuscules again. Requesens had to read the message twice. This is what he read:

"Your Excellency,

"I cannot presume that you still recall the padre from Casaquiara who came to Murcia in the last crucial days of your Expedition. Fifteen years must be too crowded a time for someone like Your Excellency to remember so inconsequential a meeting. May I say that I on my part have thought innumerable times of Your Excellency in these fifteen years. But may I at the same time say that I would try to reach your attention today, even if my memory had retained nothing of the harassing hours which brought us together in this very place.

"Passing through it, I was laid up by an attack of my illness two days ago. Last night Adolfo Bundschuh came to see me. He had come to see me at our Monastery some months ago, and upon his call I travelled to his hacienda. I understand that my business there is not unknown to Your Excellency. This I learned last night.

"Your Excellency, can you not remove from his place the man who so greatly troubles Bundschuh? It is not my will to interfere in your affairs. Who am I to judge of your decisions? I merely beg you to remove this man. I cannot properly walk, and the fever has so weakened me that I cannot think of pleading with this foreign man who [the rest of this line was illegible] The *cura* here is to take me to Casaquiara, probably tomorrow. I am almost certain that my superior will be willing to offer our hospitality to Bundschuh's guest and have him stay with us until such time as you can make up your mind in peace, or take council with the gentlemen who apparently have put that burden on you. Supposing it to be the Will of the Creator to have this man find his way to us before he is turned over to Justice and [again some words were illegible] But scant as my knowledge is, I pray to our Lord that He may move you to heed my plea, and let this man be taken away from Bundschuh's place forthwith. That done, the hour will come in which you can reach a resolve without the pressure of outward events."

XXIV

IT WAS STIFLING hot at the hacienda. Bundschuh had stepped out of the casa any number of times this afternoon, determined to cross the road and take the path to the recently cleared field; at noontime, Miguel had advised him that Jacinto would be there with the new disc harrow and the tractor. But each time Bundschuh came close to the gate, he had stopped and returned to the house to dip his head into a basin of cold water.

Now he was sitting at the table of his living room. He had emptied a bottle of beer. His forearms lay on the top of the table. He looked out through the side window. Clouds had collected in the west.

'I know why I didn't go over there, and waited till it was too late,' he said to himself time and again. 'I meant to ask that scoundrel of a Jacinto, and sternly too, what he was doing in the cantina the other day at four o'clock in the afternoon. I meant to. But I am afraid of him. Why? . . . I don't think he saw me in Murcia. But even if he did—or even if he, or anyone else, knew what I was doing in Murcia that day— what is there to be afraid of?'

There was nothing to be afraid of, and in fact he should not think of scolding Jacinto either. He should be grateful to him. For it had been the sight of Jacinto's lorry parked in plain daylight in front of one of the taverns which had made him stop his car and get out; and without leaving his car he surely would not have talked to the *cura* on the sidewalk. Most likely he would not have learned that Father Crisóstomo was in Murcia, sick, laid up at the rectory, "a victim at last of that strenuous annual tour through the border pueblos he feels he cannot forgo," as the *cura* had observed, "a victim of his saintly devotion to service. . . ."

Without that chance encounter, Don Adolfo would have been unaware still that Father Crisóstomo had been absent from Casaquiara when his message arrived there—that note in which he had asked to be received "in a matter of grave importance."

The sad news about the padre had called forth in Bundschuh, first of all, a sensation of relief. It lifted from him the suspicion that Father Crisóstomo had been avoiding another meeting on account of the trouble the moribund Belgian must have caused him.

As Bundschuh, ushered in by the hesitant *cura,* entered the room where they had put Father Crisóstomo, he was greeted graciously. The padre lay on his back, a linen sheet shrouding his powerful frame, a compress on his forehead. He did not complain, but admitted to his great fatigue. He was glad his good brother, the *cura,* would get him home tomorrow. He was homesick, having left the monastery a long time ago. "Think of it," he added, suddenly tossing his head on the pillow, "I left there long ago—the day after your Belgian was given a Christian burial, may God have mercy on his soul."

The compress had slid down from the father's head, and Bundschuh extended his hand to replace it.

"Ah, don't thank me," Father Crisóstomo interrupted Bundschuh's murmured thanks with some of his habitual gruffness. "You won't believe this, Don Adolfo, he thanked me himself. . . ." His voice faltered, but he kept mumbling about "the Belgian," as if he had assumed that to learn about the last hours of that wretch was the objective of Bundschuh's visit.

Not this had been on Bundschuh's mind when he begged the *cura* to take him to Father Crisóstomo! And now, while the padre's unintelligible words brushed against his ear, he recalled with great clarity what had guided his pen in writing the note to Casaquiara. He felt again that hour's fervent desire to cut off, through Crisóstomo's help, the sombre memories risen to life. True, he also remembered his bewilderment at picturing himself on his knees in the narrow stall, breathing its close, incensed air, with the latticed opening before him, through which he would whisper away his ancient sin. No doubt, he even had smiled at that fantasy, as a man may deride his witless other self in a dream. But this self-ridicule had not fully destroyed the promise held out by the dreamed-of procedure.

Was the priest unaware of his longing? After a while he began to talk more intelligibly again. "A poor soul your Belgian friend was, Don

Adolfo. His mind was deranged. Yet deranged as it was, it knew of contrition."

Perhaps this was an invitation extended to Bundschuh—the first glimmer of the hoped-for release. At once moved and puzzled, Bundschuh remained quiet, staring into space, until the padre, in a changed tone, asked,

"It was hard on you to have him around, no? Him and the others . . ."

Bundschuh heard the query. Father Crisóstomo's head reposed deeper now on the cushion. It came to Bundschuh that once before the priest had extricated him from a deadly impasse. Less than five hundred steps from this room he had saved his life imperiled then—fifteen years ago —by a selfish whim of Requesens! The thought of applying for the padre's assistance against the great trouble sent him by Requesens this time presented itself to Bundschuh on the spur of the moment . . . and upon another sound of encouragement from Father Crisóstomo's lips, Don Adolfo began to talk, and told him as much as he knew himself about the deceased Belgian and about M. Philibert and about the horrible man still at the hacienda.

It was a hurried and almost breathless report, and no sooner had it come to its end than the *cura* knocked on the door. The doctor was with him, and darting a hostile glance at Bundschuh, warned the patient against "carrying on conversations." The ailing priest, swallowing with difficulty, had said nothing more than that he would send word to Don Adolfo from Casaquiara, and had made a feeble motion of regret and farewell.

So Bundschuh knew nothing of the letter which he had written to Requesens. The only expectation he entertained upon leaving the rectory was that Crisóstomo might appeal to Juana, writing her, or might come himself again, talk to the girl and perhaps also challenge Ehinger in person. But eleven days had run their course, and nothing had been heard from the monastery. And with each day's passing Bundschuh realized with a mounting sense of poignancy that once more he had traded the longing for peace in himself for a hope, dwindling by now, of expedient help.

A prolonged crash of thunder broke the train of Don Adolfo's meditation. Streaks of lightning had been flashing over the sky for some time.

Expediency! Expediency was needed, was it not? If those loathsome thoughts should keep obsessing him, he would make a fool of himself in no time. Avoiding a Jacinto! It was ludicrous. No, it was dangerous, highly dangerous. Men more experienced than a señor Bundschuh were known to have gone on the rocks once they had become the laughing stock of their Indios.

What did his Indios know of the monstrous troubles eating away at his heart? Nor would they care if they did. Did they not already grin at the scandalous carryings-on of the señorita? Did they not already mock the patrón's reluctance to put things straight, and evict, whip in hand, the cynical parasite in the guest house?

He had infected the girl with his unbounded cynicism. She no longer took pains to conceal her daily meetings with the man. She barely concealed the nature of their relation. An expression of matured knowledge would come on her face whenever Bundschuh began speaking to her. Yet she would engage in their usual talks during the evening meal with no visible embarrassment. Of late, she had even asked questions about the state of his affairs—with a peculiar note, to be sure, which seemed to signal some solicitude lest his present worries harm his business. But while such misgivings, to his mind, were proof of the girl's remorse, yet she went out of her way to show him her lack of respect on other occasions. She had more than once remained in her room at dinner time without explanation, and when he came upstairs, she had not even answered his raps.

Don Adolfo took out his tobacco pouch. Thinking of the girl, he should have felt very angry. But an unaccountable sadness seemed to dwarf his resentment.

Suddenly the rain came down. Its first cataract came down so abruptly, it blinded both windows and darkened the room within a second. Bundschuh did not move when the door swung open. He merely stopped rolling his cigarette, while an oblique glance went to the capataz who stood in the doorway.

His shirt—he wore no jacket—was drenched. He took off the dripping leather hat and dashed it against his leg. "You are all right, patrón, no?" he asked, raising his voice over the howling of the wind.

"Why shouldn't I be all right?" said Don Adolfo. Across his hands cupped about the cigarette he was lighting, he contemplated the puddle of water at Miguel's feet.

The capataz gave another push to the door behind him. He had to labor against the storm outside. One thunderclap followed another now.

Bundschuh said indifferently, "Naturally I am all right. I had paper work to attend to. I did not feel like going out in this heat. And, then, that paper work . . ." What a strong man his overseer appeared, it crossed his mind. "Why do you stand there? Sit down."

"I must go, patrón."

"You cannot go now, can you?"

"I must go to the stables."

"Why?"

"Diego."

Bundschuh gave no reaction. He wondered where Juana had taken shelter in this storm.

"Patrón, he has gone. Diego has gone."

"Where?"

"I wish I had been told last night, patrón. But the stable boy did not inform me until an hour ago."

"Where has the old fool gone?"

"Gone never to return, patrón. That was the message the stable boy gave me."

"Never to return?"

"He's taken the piebald with him."

"The piebald was no longer much of a horse, was he?"

"Patrón . . ." Miguel said with open astonishment. "The old fellow has stolen the horse—"

"Why did he leave? . . . You don't know? No farewell message from the old fool, no?" The overseer's silence gave Bundschuh a kind of moral support. He was about to tell the man he should not waste another thought on the loss of the worthless nag—nor on the reawakened sense of adventure that must have driven the old stableman away—when Miguel, stepping nearer to the table and leaning forward, said,

"The señorita, patrón. She's stopped coming to the stable. The patrón knows that, no? The patrón also knows that the afternoon rides with the señorita were about all Diego cared for. Her horses were all he cared for. Wouldn't even look at the burros next door—"

"Good riddance," Bundschuh cut him off. "You will find a better man, I am certain of that." He was sure that the man was squinting toward the staircase—as if he did not know, the hypocrite, that Juana was not here. He must have seen her any number of times go off on her afternoon walk and take the direction of the guest house.

The rain had stopped. The sudden stillness—for the wind, too, had ceased—made doubly loud the gurgling of the water in the drain pipes. Some light was returning to the room.

"A drop of brandy, capataz?"

"Thank you, patrón," said Miguel, "but I must go now. The stables must look a mess. Yes, I will find a good man for the horses. The patrón will not miss Diego. And the señorita—"

Against his will Bundschuh threw up his arms. A moment before he had half turned in his chair, as though he intended to fetch the bottle of aguardiente from the sideboard. Now he only stared at the capataz, who instinctively straightened.

"Something might happen to him," he said in a low voice.

"Who cares what happens to the ancient crackpot on his journeys?"

"To the other man, patrón . . . Something might well happen to him. All sorts of things may happen to an inexperienced man, a foreigner. Outdoors, say. An accident, say . . ."

Don Adolfo brought his elbow back onto the top of the table. He stiffened his heavy lower lip and blew the smoke upwards in rings. He observed them travelling past his overseer who stood, unmoving, close to the table. His wide hairy nostrils, his sunken cheeks, his bony shoulders, and the immense forehead, gave to the ageless negroid face an aspect of great fierceness. "No," Bundschuh muttered, as the man slowly turned. "No. No, Miguel."

XXV

"... As THIS STATION put it an hour ago," said the firm female voice on the radio, winding up the speech Bundschuh had been listening to —mechanically first, and then with mounting perplexity—"the problem of the ruling caballeros is not the suppression of the laboring masses. Their problem, the long-range problem, is the elevation of the masses, their elevation from a misery so abject the privileged have never dared look at it, a despair so great and unrelieved that it knows of no alternative to apathy other than revolt. The problem is the awakening of the masses to a new sense of responsibility, to a new love of the Republic. Love, not arms will conquer them. Have the ruling caballeros ever stopped to consider— Have the Deputies of our so-called Chamber, those shadowy men who convene for a bare two months each year, have our corrupt Senators, those spokesmen of privilege . . ." Dissonant whistlings rushed into the oration, their shrieks skimmed by stray bars of the anthem. Bundschuh silenced the witches' Sabbath issuing from the small box.

He had turned its dial, when night fell, thoughtlessly, perhaps only to rest his eyes on the glimmer of the battery-fed lamp of the radio. He sat in the dark. The brief savage thunderstorm had burned out the dynamo. He should have asked one of the servant girls to bring candles. But they both had left to find out what damage the cloudburst had done to their families' huts. They had barely put the patrón's meal on the table.

He had not touched it. He could have gotten himself a candle when, following an inexplicable impulse, he went upstairs to Juana's bedroom. But he remained where he was, perched on the girl's bed.

He knew where she was. She had been there before. Regularly, perhaps. Though Bundschuh had no proof of it, it would have been absurd to doubt it. But, except for one day (when she declared she had been "delayed at the stable"), she had always returned to the casa in time for the evening meal. Had she met with an accident in the storm? Or was she afraid "something might happen" to her lover? Had Miguel been threatening him on his own initiative?

The strain which these unanswered questions put on Don Adolfo had kept him from immediately grasping the message emanating from the radio. As the speaker announced "The Voice of the People," he had vaguely presumed that this excited performance originated somewhere across the border. But the names he had heard through the threefold screen of his brooding, his indifference toward public affairs, and his incredulous wonderment at a woman talking politics, had enlightened him after a time. By now he was certain that this broadcast either echoed or spelled political unrest.

His first mental response was one of malicious joy at the effect the disturbances might have on Requesens. Served him right. His unspeakable callousness toward the plight he had brought on him was to be avenged after all! Not once did Bundschuh consider that this very unrest—brewing, as was to be assumed, for some time past—may have hindered the Minister's movements in his, Don Adolfo's, behalf, so fascinated was he by the notion that this was the pay-off for Lorenzo Requesens. It came to every man in the end!

He turned on the radio again. The howling cacophony had overwhelmed the Voice of the People. Huacho Broadcasting Station announced that it would send music. But only a series of whispers and rustlings followed this announcement.

Then these noises too were gone. After a while, Don Adolfo believed he was hearing a repeated knocking. But holding his lowered head between his hands, as he did, and thus covering his ears, he did not distinguish from where the sounds came. But they continued. Don Adolfo freed his ears. The front door was opened and banged shut. And almost at the same time the trembling shimmer of a beam from an electric torch fell through the partially opened door of Juana's bedroom.

"Are you here, patrón?" came the subdued voice of the capataz from down below.

Stepping out of the room and onto the stairs, Bundschuh saw the man, or rather, the light of his torch which played about as though Miguel were searching for the patrón in one corner after another.

For a second, Bundschuh's irritation at these antics displaced his real concerns. Still on the staircase, he asked Miguel sharply what brought him here again at this time of night. "Speak up. . . . Speak up," he cried in sudden alarm. "What has happened to her?"

"Jacinto . . ."

"What about him?" asked Bundschuh. "Why hasn't he repaired the dynamo yet?"

The overseer came over to meet him on the landing. "Patrón, did *you* order him to bring out the truck?"

"Why? Can't he repair the dynamo himself?"

"That I don't know. Patrón . . ." Miguel shouted to get the better of the blaring tune which of a sudden poured from the radio upstairs. "Something suspicious . . . something suspicious is going on."

"Stop talking in riddles," Bundschuh shouted back. "What happened to the señorita?"

"I do not know anything about her, patrón. . . . I think Jacinto does not want to repair the dynamo."

"So he has taken the truck to get help in town. That is all right, no? What's suspicious about that?"

The capataz shook his head. "He has not gone to town. I do not think he intends to. Not for that purpose, at any rate. The truck is parked on the road—"

"Facing toward Murcia?"

"Facing toward Murcia, lights off. Five or six hundred feet from where the wall ends."

"Is he there?"

"I don't think so. . . ." Upstairs, a sweet contralto had burgeoned out of the loud strumming, and its *piano* permitted Miguel to report gravely, "Patrón, they have declared martial law in Ulloa. A peddler stopped at my place while I was changing clothes. I couldn't turn him away, drenched to the skin as he was. He brought the news. Martial law. But he also says it is not a normal revolt, for the Army is staying in the barracks. He says the People's Party is stirring up trouble."

"You don't mean to say," Bundschuh retorted, "that Jacinto has anything to do with that, eh? Or do you think he belongs to that party, so called? Do any of our men?"

"An hour ago I'd have sworn that none of them even knew such a party existed. But one is bound to look at it differently when the thing is brought right to one's door step. It is not impossible, at least not unthinkable, that some of the seasonal labor have picked up one or another of the stories about this Huérfano."

"And Jacinto?"

"There's been something suspicious about him for weeks. For months. He's barely been feeding his children. He's been staying away much longer than he ought to whenever I send him to Ulloa. And there is one more thing," Miguel insisted. "Please listen to this. Patrón, he has been speaking with *him!*"

"I forbade everybody—"

"So did I, patrón. But what could I do? We need a mechanic. I couldn't dismiss Jacinto. . . . Can you imagine that he is conniving with *him?* And could *he* (I know nothing about men like him) . . . could *he* have some dealings with this People's Party?"

Bundschuh gave a short laugh. He brushed aside the flashlight which the gesturing hands of the capataz fluttered in front of his stomach.

"There are rumors about foreigners working with this Huérfano. Now *he* is a foreigner. A *suizo* . . . Is a *suizo* an *alemán,* patrón?"

"A *suizo* is a man from Switzerland."

"A Nazi, patrón?"

The word, though slurred over, assailed Don Adolfo with a sardonic sense of inevitability; but for all that, it came with a shattering sense of alarm. He no longer felt like gloating over the likely tribulations of Requesens. He realized—there was a kind of nostalgia in this common-sense reflection—that these tribulations sounded the death knell to any chance that Requesens might help him should the authorities start real trouble about the Nazi he sheltered. Minor authorities loved to work their blind revenge on innocent people in times of restiveness. "Nonsense," he replied calmly at last, "who put that nonsense into your head?"

"I thought myself it was nonsense, patrón," the overseer said, and all but sighed with relief.

"And you think that Jacinto—"

"We must find him!" the capataz, emboldened, hastened to interrupt, "first we must find him—"

"At this time of the night?"

"We must find out what he intends to do with the truck. The truck . . . it may be gone by tomorrow morning. It will be gone, I am sure, patrón, unless we get hold of Jacinto in time."

"How about the others? Any sign of restlessness?"

"No. Everybody's asleep after the storm."

"Got your revolver?"

Miguel tapped the weapon in his pocket several times.

"I'll get one myself. Or a rifle."

Immediately Miguel turned the light of his torch toward the alcove, whose portiere Bundschuh jerked to the side.

"Stupid, I . . ." he snorted. He located a candle on the bottom shelf. He lighted it, let some wax from it drop onto one of the upper boards, and fastened the candle among a row of pottery.

Miguel remained standing close to the table. He saw the patrón lean over the large wooden box which occupied the right corner of the "museum," and heard him push the key into the lock. So he was carrying the key in his pocket even at night! His stoicism was pretense. Perhaps he knew a great deal more than he admitted about the situation at the guest house. The overseer watched Don Adolfo intently. He had knelt down. The back of his bald head glistened in the light of the candle. Now he reached for it, toppling a vessel on the shelf . . . and almost in the same breath an outcry so ferocious issued from the alcove that Miguel instinctively took a step backwards.

"Robbed . . ." Bundschuh cried hoarsely, "two rifles stolen! Two. Money stolen. The money . . ."

"Patrón, patrón . . ." Miguel managed to say, while he was collecting his thoughts. Unbidden, he freed Bundschuh's hand from the burning candle. "But doesn't the patrón keep the money in the desk in his bedroom?"

"And what about it? What about it if I kept some in that trunk, too? Not much, of course not. Don't glare at me. Do something. We must do something. . . . But how did she . . . ?" His voice subsided like a broken wave. "Eh? Money? . . . I am not talking about money, am I? No. The rifles . . . Ammunition . . ."

"So they *are* in cahoots," said Miguel with a note of satisfaction, only to fall quiet as Bundschuh, his face still reddened with emotion, ordered him to take away the stinking candle.

Though he had been robbed, robbed in his own house, in his sleep probably, he was no object to stare at!

"There are four rifles left, no?" suggested Miguel from the sideboard where he was putting the candle into the neck of a bottle. "We must find Jacinto first. I think I know how to talk to him. In cahoots, then, they—"

"Stop your stupidity. Who is 'in cahoots'?"

Miguel, though interrupted, did not cease to talk. Diego, he said, Diego had always foreseen that nothing good would come of it.

"Of what?"

"So he left . . ." the capataz spluttered, "Diego, I mean, left."

"So he did, didn't he?" Bundschuh said, while he was releasing the safety-catch of his revolver, which he had taken out of its holster hanging on the wall. "Put out that light."

A long, deep-sounding *adiós!* at this moment, concluded the sentimental song habitual as a good-night performance with Huacho Broadcasting Station. Don Adolfo made a move as though to go upstairs once more, but he already stood on the outer threshold.

Outside, the two men were greeted by the concerted booming of the frogs. Thousands of them had come out of the reeds of the irrigation ditches to rejoice in the aftermath of the five-minute deluge.

Miguel said no further word. Somewhat against his will, he admired Don Adolfo's determination. For weeks he had seen him neglect his work, disrupt his routine for the sake of idle reflection. Now he was in such haste that he had left his cap behind.

After they had covered about a hundred meters, the lorry rose before their eyes. It stood in the middle of the level road, its tarpaulin top looming against the strip of the overcast sky visible between the outline of the tall grass on both sides.

"The patrón should have taken the rifles."

Don Adolfo gave vent to a sound of contempt.

"Or maybe not," Miguel said.

There was no reply. Originally, Bundschuh had put scant stock in Miguel's assertion that the acquaintanceship of Jacinto and Ehinger signalled a community of political spirits. Only after the discovery in the alcove had it occurred to him that, except for the woman he had just listened to on the radio, the one person to mention El Huérfano in his presence of late had been Juana! He could not recall in what connection she had done so: had she thrown in that name in talking, as she sometimes did, about the "natural discontent" of the Indios? At any rate, it dawned on him that Juana herself might be the link in the unnatural league his overseer maintained had brought the two disparate men together; and that notion had translated itself into an image of himself confronting the partisan threesome, loaded rifle in hand. . . . This image, and not (as he now, in a pretended afterthought, said to Miguel) "common sense," had been responsible for his decision to take the revolver out of its holster hanging on the wall, and leave the rifles behind.

The girl had behaved abominably. She had robbed him. Cynically robbed him. And though nothing short of magic could possibly have imparted to her his secret, Bundschuh felt in an unreasoning fashion as though her cynicism had sprung from some knowledge she had of his ancient sin. Yet he would beseech, not menace her. It would make no difference whether she was Ehinger's mistress, his comrade in the revolutionary venture, or both.

Thus he had resolved. But walking along now on the edge of the roadway, from time to time halted by a sign from Miguel who was marching ahead, he began to question the cleverness of his course. Why not let Ehinger go? Why not let him run to his doom in the turmoil of civil strife? No matter how that conflict was to develop, Bundschuh could not conceive of any other outcome than the total defeat of the amateur rebels (politicos inexperienced enough to make a woman their radio speaker!). The vanquished would be dealt with summarily; and that summary procedure would blur their identity, obliterate their individual antecedents. Bundschuh saw, in his imagination, Ehinger lined up in a row of ragged manacled rogues, standing beaten and battered before the Army tribunal—a listless court, chary of questions and aflame with zest to send their prey to the gallows. Here was the "accident" which Miguel had suggested this afternoon, and here it was brought about through none of his, Bundschuh's doing! . . . But while he was still beholding that fantasy, Juana appeared to his mental eye again—she, too, lined up with the vanquished and doomed, delivered to the rope by his own negligence, by his weakness, his pride. . . . She had behaved abominably. Yet he must rescue her.

The two men stood in the deep shadows of the grass, which swayed into their faces. Save for the stiffening northwest wind, nothing but the rattling of the tarpaulin was to be heard. Miguel beckoned the patrón to stay behind, and hunching his shoulderblades and crouching down low, he covered the remaining distance to the lorry alone. After an endless couple of minutes, Bundschuh saw the tremulous gleam of his flashlight.

"Clothes," Miguel said after another while, "clothes. One . . . two . . . three. Three saddles."

"Whose clothes?" asked Bundschuh who had now come up to the lorry. But before Miguel could reply he grabbed the man's arm and extinguished his torch.

Less than a hundred meters away Jacinto had come out on the road. A beam of moonlight, which happened to pierce the clouds, made him distinguishable in the dark. He must have used one of the well-nigh indiscernible trails the Indios cut through the thicket to shorten their way. He carried a medium-sized bundle on his head. He put it down by the roadside before he walked off in the direction of the casa.

"He came from the guest house," whispered Miguel. "He can only have come from the guest house."

"Where do you think he's going?" Bundschuh inquired. His hand, still on Miguel's arm, felt, through the slippery leather of his jacket, the shrug in the taut muscles of the capataz.

"I must talk to him, patron."

"Are we to run after him?" Don Adolfo burst out under his breath. "Why not call him?"

"Seems he's making for his hut," Miguel said in the faintest of voices. "He has no rifle, has he?"

The horizon blackened. The silhouette of Jacinto's figure threatened to merge with the gloom. "No," Bundschuh said, "he has no rifle."

"I must talk to him."

"To him . . ." Bundschuh repeated scornfully, "what does _he_ know?"

"It would be good to catch him when he is with his children."

Don Adolfo thought, 'I should have confided in this man long ago. An astute man. A man anxious to serve me. Perhaps out of vanity. Still. I should have confided in this man who knows that today is to-day, and a thousand years back is a thousand years back. Instead I've fooled around with that priest, relying on his hocus-pocus. Pah, he doesn't even want to be bothered with my insane self-accusations, though setting a Christian soul free from such deviltry _should_ be his business. Father Crisóstomo, my eye! Here, here was my man. A man down-to-earth . . .'

"Patrón," Miguel said in his hushed tone, "let me talk to him alone. These folk have superstitions—"

"Not Jacinto! A mechanic!"

There was no longer any need for straining their vision. New gravel had been strewn along the brick wall some weeks previously on ac-

count of the heavy dust, and Jacinto's footfalls revealed that he had
passed the gate, and would in fact take the path to his hut.

Miguel came to a standstill in front of the gate. He pointed down at
the gravel to indicate it would be wise to wait a while. "I must talk to
him alone," he declared after a pause in which Jacinto had been disap-
pearing from their view. There was a new firmness to his master's
ears in the capataz' voice. "A man has to be familiar with those superstitions, very familiar, to hold them up to another man."

It ran in Bundschuh's mind that the gate should really not stand
open.

"In a way I cannot describe, patrón . . ."

"Eh?"

"In a way I cannot describe, a man must believe in those superstitions himself to hold them up to another man. No offense meant,
patrón, but with you present, I wouldn't . . . no, I don't think I *would*
be able to believe in them, not even in that way I cannot describe."
Miguel's posture denoted a nervous fretfulness. He appeared almost
determined to block the road to Don Adolfo, who felt like asking why,
if that was the way the capataz wanted it, he had come to fetch him,
to begin with. But he only said that he would wait for him, then.

"Where, patrón?"

"In there. On the path. The left path. The path to the guest house."
He hesitated for the barest shadow of a moment before he walked
through the gate, while a gust carried away Miguel's clipped words behind him.

XXVI

THE EMBERS IN the brazier had burned down. In front of it, the two rifles were propped up crosswise against the walls of the small recess, as if to bar any further communication between it and the room once inhabited by Philibert. To the left of the niche, Juana sat on a chair by the plank wall, her feet resting on a valise, on whose mold-stained leather some discolored, frayed labels still attested to the wide and well-planned travels of her late father. The oil-lamp on the make-shift table at her elbow illumined one side of her face. She gazed through the opened door.

Beyond it, in the semi-lit hallway, she could see the outline of the man's shoulders and back and his outstretched right arm. He leaned his hand against the door, closed now, of the cubicle where Roy had once lived and suffered. Ehinger had been standing in this manner, his feet crossed, for a long time. He had ceased to talk.

Juana felt relieved that he no longer exposed his shaven face to the light. When, in the afternoon, he had first emerged from the niche with this "new-old face" (as he jokingly called it), while she lay on the bed, above her the drumming of the rain, the sickly whiteness of his cheeks and jaws—contrasting, mask-like, with the swarthy nose, forehead and temples—had perplexed her as much as the hideous bluish scar running from one ear down to the deep cleavage of his chin. The estranging effect of this sight had persisted throughout their talk. It had overwhelmed the note of sincerity in his utterances.

To Ehinger the past hours had taken a course very different from his blueprint. And the surprising, the shocking thing about it was that this change had been of his own doing. He was still convinced that, had he told the girl she must stay behind, she would not have raged, would not have attempted to obstruct his departure, or afterwards have

236

betrayed to anyone his joint enterprise with Jacinto.

For the first time since Philibert's departure from the hacienda, Ehinger was led to imagine the reaction of the older man to what he was about to do. Probably Philibert would make a fuss about the rumored revolt; he would say that Murcia, a town tainted with the memories of brigandage and unrest, was in times like these bound to attract the watchfulness of whoever the men maintaining order would be—and that he, Ehinger, was therefore wise to elude their attention and hasten his flight. References to the miserably small funds at his disposal would only elicit sneers from Philibert, who had always shown the loftiest disdain of money. Though possibly doubtful as to the prospective business at the frontier, Philibert would approve the chosen destination, an out-of-this-world place if ever there was one. He would furthermore counsel him to keep Jacinto well in hand, and to increase his severity with every new service the Indio rendered. He would wish him good luck, and remind him to keep his mouth shut. But, next, he would tell him that the girl was an intolerable burden upon his venture, and that her participation in the journey was a grave error and likely to cause its eventual failure. He would scoff at Ehinger's assurance that he could dispose of his mistress at any time and in any place, should expediency demand it. This was the time and place, Philibert would maintain. He would call his relation to Juana many mocking, insulting names. . . .

Yet it had no name—unless it was a burning awareness in Ehinger of the power he had over the girl. He had accepted her dependency upon him as a matter of course once his version of her mother's death had succeeded in alienating her filial attachment. Her subsequent total obedience was the self-evident upshot of their intimacy; power over the women of his choice had never astonished Ehinger. But the consciousness of his power over this one woman had grown beyond its natural range. It was frightening to reflect that this feeling alone seemed to keep at bay his dread of loneliness and irrevocable defeat, and that, while thus evoking in him a faint echo of his former grandeur, Juana's nearness and her love appeared to protect him, like a charm, against the vicious aftergrowth of that past.

"What time?" he asked without turning.

Juana raised her wrist to the lamp. "Half past eleven."

"On the dot?"

"Almost . . . I wish we were off."

"We will be. At twelve-fifteen. You heard Jacinto yourself. You heard him say that the capataz was a late bird. I'm not so sure Jacinto did well taking out the truck. . . . But then he could not have driven it across the whole place later without waking people. Anyway, we will be off soon. Stop worrying."

Her lips moved inaudibly. Yes, they would be off. He had been right in his prediction. In all his predictions. He had foretold that Bundschuh would not come. Yellow fear restrained him. Fear—and then again, hope. The hope that the course of events might rid him of her! Had she not admitted, albeit reluctantly, that Bundschuh must be aware by now of her claims?

Yes, her lover had been right in that prediction. Yet how little did he know of Don Adolfo. She for one felt that neither hope nor fear kept him from coming. His guilt did—that guilt which no claim, however strong, could balance. . . .

She could have sworn she had been pondering this thought at the moment when Bundschuh opened the door. It had been latched. But when Jacinto had gone, Ehinger must have forgotten to push the bolt again, after listening long into the night and the wind.

Bundschuh did not storm into the hallway. He slipped in sidewise, slamming the door with his foot. He looked crumpled and soiled. As he advanced to her lover, whom Juana saw recoil, she noted that her stepfather's lip twitched in a tic she had never before seen. "What is going on here?" he asked into a dead calm.

"Take it easy, Bundschuh, will you?" Ehinger said. He stood rigid again, towering over the intruder. "You may talk to her yourself. She is of age."

Bundschuh walked past the man who ironically offered him precedence, opening his hands. "What's going on here, Juana?"

"What you see speaks for itself, doesn't it?" Ehinger remarked drily.

"Answer, Juanita. It's you I am asking."

"We are leaving."

"With my man Jacinto? And hitching yourself to some disreputable gang?"

"Your man Jacinto is going to take us to Ulloa, Bundschuh, that's all," Ehinger replied in her stead. He was slouching up to the niche, both hands in his pockets. "That is all. Don't worry about that truck. You are worrying, aren't you, that we are taking it with us as a dowry?"

Only now, with the light touching Ehinger fully, did Bundschuh notice his shaven face.

"And if I were you," Ehinger continued, plainly delighted by the speechlessness of his host, "I would not make a nuisance of myself, Bundschuh. Now listen. As far as we are concerned, you weren't here, did not come here, knew nothing. If you understand me right . . ."

"You, I am asking you, Juana . . ." Bundschuh began again. Yet apparently he was unable to take his glare off the hated man.

"We won't give you away. Even if we should run into bad luck, we won't, Bundschuh. I am not a vengeful man. And as for her, why, she is still devoted to you, believe it or not. So she won't give you away either. Word of honor. So you know nothing, and your great friend in Huacho can't blame you, and won't. Don't you think that is fair enough?"

Juana had risen. The glances Ehinger cast in her direction were lost on the girl.

"Man," he went on, "I am trying to tell you that this is as fine an opportunity as any to end our hapless relationship."

"And taking her with you—no!"

"I am going voluntarily," she declared. "I am leaving voluntarily."

"I knew beforehand you would say so. I knew you would. Now two things have gone to your head. Two. Love, love, so called . . . and now, that ridiculous revolt. It will be put down in no time. You haven't seen them squelch this sort of thing. I have. I have indeed. . . ." He jerked up his short arms and then, suddenly, let them dangle down in an exaggerated show of disjointedness, while, heedless of a foul-mouthed interjection from Ehinger, he inclined his head on his shoulder and put out his tongue. "That's how they handle revolutionists," he said hoarsely, snapping out of the horrid pantomime, "and it isn't a beautiful sight. Revolutions are for colonels, not for the rabble this adventurer here intends to make friends with. The colonels get out from under it all right. Not so the rabble. And surely not a foreign adventurer who tries to pose as one of them. Don't you see, Juana, that this adventurer here— Don't you see that this unrest . . . that any such unrest anywhere is about the last chance left to men of his kind—"

"I warned you not to make a nuisance of yourself, Bundschuh!"

"Why don't you tell him we've nothing to do with this revolt?" Juana said, turning her whole body.

But Ehinger hesitated. He winked at his mistress, signalling that it was not so bad to have her stepfather's suspicions go in the wrong direction. Still, when he noted that his subtlety was wasted, he thrust out his chin toward Bundschuh, and conceded that it was precisely as his Juanita was saying. Bundschuh didn't really think, did he, that men of his kind would band together with Indian riffraff, Communist rabble?

Bundschuh did not take up the challenge in Ehinger's words. He had intercepted the look of expectation and perhaps even trust animating Juana's face as she turned to the man.

She repeated that she was leaving of her own free will.

The three people stood close to each other. With Juana's stepping away from the lamp, its gleam was mirrored in the barrels of the rifles. "I know you're doing what you are of your free will," Don Adolfo said at last with a quiver in his growl, while his eyes did not relinquish the rifles. "No one could force you. No one could have forced you, not you, to take that key from my desk when I was asleep—for that's what you must have done—and rob that trunk, steal money . . . money, mind you, earmarked for those same peóns you're so much concerned about, money—"

"That'll do, Bundschuh!" Ehinger broke in.

"Will it? Will it, Juanita? Will you go on listening to him? I told you what kind of a man he is. God is my witness I did. You laughed in my face that night . . . that night when I told you about the poison he got hold of— Stay here!" he shouted, wheeling around, at Ehinger who sauntered back to the hallway, carrying the two rifles; he had snatched up both of them at once.

"I am staying here," came his even voice. "I only want to get those toys out of reach of my very excited friend, Don Adolfo."

"Put them down."

"I will. I will, Bundschuh."

For a moment Bundschuh was made speechless by the compliant inflection of Ehinger's voice. In talking to Juana with mounting emotion, he had clapped one hand on the other and laid both against his chest. He did not remove them now as he peered over his shoulder and saw Ehinger lean the rifles against the wall noiselessly and with the prudence one employs in handling weapons in the presence of children. "You think . . ." he went on, distractedly first, and his lower lip twitched still more, "Juana . . . you think I made a big fool of myself, eh? That night? Nothing has happened to you. So nothing will, no? But he *has* that poison. He has it."

Juana waved her hands, and she might have tried to say something, but Ehinger called to her from the shadow,

"Leave him alone, *Mädel*. You cannot argue with a lunatic, a jealous lunatic."

"I am speaking the truth, Juanita," Bundschuh proceeded, smiling thinly, "no matter what this adventurer may bring up to discredit me. This . . . this desperate adventurer . . ." he said, an involuntary secretiveness thickening his tone. "A desperado, that's what he is. You just heard him brag that his kind—his kind!—wouldn't band together with Indian riffraff, Communists. . . . Take it from me, girl, they'd band together with *anyone*. They'd throw themselves on the neck of the Devil himself, if he still wanted them. For there isn't a place on earth where they can find rest and peace. Not one spot on the whole face of the earth! Outcasts . . . Proscribed . . . Ah, I told you, I told you what manner of man this Ehinger is, so help me God!" He let go of Juana's bodice which he had grabbed in the passion of his speech.

Her eyes went out to the silent shape in the hallway, while Bundschuh, stammered, "You knew it all along. You must have. . . . Hanging onto your radio day in day out, you must have put two and two together. . . . Knew more than I. . . . You knew about those criminals sought for by the whole world. And then, I told you!"

He had, he had indeed, she said to herself. He had told her whatever had been called for. A sort of mental block had kept her from facing the obvious. To meet it in this instant—now that her mind was made up—was almost a release.

"Why so squeamish, Bundschuh?" said Ehinger, breaking his silence with a click of his tongue. "Nazi is the word. German. One and the same . . . But what would you know about Germanness, you, a man who deserted Germany in the first hour of her need!"

A consciousness of his insufficiency crept over Bundschuh, while the man came forward a little. It really looked as if he alone of the three were at liberty to roam the place.

"Mark this, *Mädel*," he said across Don Adolfo's head, "—a criminal, a criminal if ever there was one, a confessed Navy deserter calling a German soldier names. Mark it."

Juana had made a step in retreat toward the bed at the other side of the aperture. She stared at her lover: large purple spots speckled the strange nakedness of his face like a rash. Rocking on his heels, he went on to mutter incoherent abuse.

Why did the girl not open her mouth? Her fascination with the man seemed complete! It was evident to Bundschuh by now that not one trace of sympathy was left in her for him. Why should he have any sympathy for her? She was not his daughter. A quirk of fate had foisted her on him, palmed her off as a ward, a human being he was responsible for. But he was not! Let her go to meet her doom. Let her. She was not worth his forgiveness, his charity, his love. Why force it on her? To calm his own heart? His heart had always judged of someone's worth first. That had been its strength. Blind love, blind responsibility, warmth offered blindly—pah!

". . . a thief," Ehinger was mumbling, "a murderer . . . Roy's murderer and not only Roy's—"

"Stop it, stop it!" Juana, leaning far forward, cried out.

"What was he saying?" Bundschuh asked dazedly. "Pay no attention to what he is saying. I don't. For this, Juana, is only between us, between you and me. . . ."

Ehinger had fallen silent. Reflecting frantically, he considered it fortunate that she had cut him off. He certainly did not want to throw the old story in her stepfather's face, and provoke his protestations. In fact, there was no longer much need for browbeating him. He was taken care of all right. Standing close by the old valise like an ungainly bundle dropped there, he looked flaccid and shrunken, and had no longer the stamina to fend off the abuse levelled at him.

"I do not accuse you," Bundschuh now said. his face contorted by a curiously searching expression. "I should have been more outspoken maybe. Earlier . . . I was afraid something like this might happen. Ever since I drove Philibert home from Ulloa that night I've been afraid." His voice became very faint. "Maybe . . . maybe I was not afraid enough. Not enough . . . I let things go . . . In myself, too . . ."

A shade of pity was in Juana's words, as she asked, "Don't you see I *must* go with him, Don Adolfo?"

"In spite of everything you know?"

"—and have known all the time," Ehinger threw in with a guffaw, "as you yourself just pointed out, Bundschuh. Man, man . . . come to think of it, you could plead imbecility if you were tried for your crime. Deserter! Really!"

Bundschuh looked at him quickly. There was an animal celerity in the way he tossed his shoulders about.

Juana repeated that she must go with him, and that he, Don Adolfo, knew she must.

"Know? I? . . . No," he burst out, "no, you will not. You are of age. Still . . . No! I promised your mother— Ah, you wouldn't understand that, bewitched as you are, bewitched. . . ." The pale face of the girl set off against the magnifying shadows that seemed to be all over the place, the incessant, almost rhythmical snorting of the adversary behind him, and the turmoil in himself, deprived Don Adolfo of the remnants of self-control that until now had made him stand up with some composure to the indignity of the situation. " 'Must go with him! Must go with him . . .' You must not. And you won't. You are out of your mind. That mad beggars' revolt is a death trap. With that criminal . . . Poison . . . Whatever his destination, he is up to no good. His like is steeped too deep in crime. . . . 'Must go with him.' . . . No. No, I'm telling you. As long as there's a breath in me . . . I'd rather . . . by God, I'd rather kill this abomination—"

One brutal stroke knocked the revolver from Bundschuh's fist even before he could turn. Ehinger—perhaps to avoid Juana's eyes—had watched him with great alertness. Little as he had credited him with such intent only a minute ago, he had not been taken by surprise by Bundschuh's paroxysm of wrath; and he had not overlooked the surreptitious movement of his trembling hand to his pocket. As Bundschuh, with a howl, lunged at him now, he held him off with a ferocious kick, while he dexterously scooped the revolver from the floor. At the same time a sweep of his head held Juana to the spot where she stood, and silenced her horrified outcry. "So . . . so that's how you want to play this game?" he barked at the disarmed Bundschuh, pushing him back to the table step by step. "Put up your hands, killer! *Hände hoch! Hoch!*" His iron left arm pressed the panting man closer and closer to the table. How often had he seen Philibert sit here, engaged in some mysterious work with figures. The realization that none of Philibert's refined reasoning would interfere with the business at hand made Ehinger's temper soar with a sense of power regained and of limitless liberty. It intoxicated him. He roared at his cornered victim. He heard Juana's cries, and through the veil of his rage saw her bolt away from the bedstead. But not before the dogged counter-pressure Bundschuh opposed to his prodding hand ceased of a sudden did Ehinger, amazed, understand that she was berating not him, but Bundschuh.

"Why did you have to come here? Why? Why? You knew yourself that I would go away, and why . . ."

Ehinger slackened his extended arm, but his hand did not let go of Bundschuh. After a triumphant last look at his stricken face, he shifted his eyes to take in the figure standing in front of the recess, her forehead lit by the lamp.

Her voice broke with exasperation. "You knew I'd have never thought of it . . . of going away with *him,* if I could have borne it any longer to be here. . . . Here where the horrible thing happened, a thing so horrible and unimaginable . . . ! To stay here—no! Here? Under *your* roof, at *your* table? I can no longer bear to live here, haunted by the knowledge of what happened . . . by the memory of my own callous ignorance. . . . That's why I must go. Away, away . . . never to see you again . . ." A violent sobbing shook her. "Oh, how well I can see it now. . . . Whatever I may have thought made me cling to *him,* this is what really binds me. I know there's no return from where *he* will take me . . . no return from *him* . . . I know it. . . ."

"Why, you despicable little snake . . ." Ehinger pronounced tonelessly. He was appalled. True, he had laid this snare himself. His strategem had worked to perfection. Yet the more his stare dwelt on her misery in this endless second—she had covered her drooping head with both forearms, and seemed to sway on her feet—the more did his fury wax. Circumstances alone had driven her to him! The power he had fancied he had over her was not in him! A strategem . . . his strategem had worked both ways! Philibert would have known it all along. He would laugh at him now, laugh, laugh, laugh! . . . But one power was still his . . . and Ehinger tasted it before he raised the revolver.

With an exertion whose instantaneousness gave Bundschuh the force his muscles lacked, he wrenched himself from the claw on his chest, and made a leap to shield Juana. His scream was deadened by the first detonation. It must have been the second shot, following rapidly, which hit him. He had upset the lamp on the rickety board. He wondered why its flame burned so brightly.

XXVII

DESCENDING THE STAIRS from the upper floor, Father Crisóstomo steadied himself against the wall. His hands were shaking with the ague. The voices of the Indios in the front yard made the living room of the casa alive with whispers. The loud admonishments of the capataz failed to hush the murmurs. Threads of the midday sun fell through the drawn curtains.

The priest glanced at the repast laid out for him on the table, and then turned his big head in the direction of the servant girl who lingered on the threshold of the rear door, carrying a basin, a brass jug and white towels. He made a sign of negation, while his sunken eyes searched for the aged dwarfish creature that dodged behind the maid. He had not seen her in the early hours, but he knew who she was, and her presence filled him with an ambiguous comfort.

When, upon his arrival, the peóns forced on him what information they possessed, they had not concealed their pride in the local sorceress. She seemed to have been among the first to rush to the scene of the catastrophe. It was she who had had the unconscious señorita carried to the casa, brought her to, put her to bed, and dressed her wound, while the overseer seemed to have spent all that time interrogating the mechanic—the accomplice, as he insisted, of the fugitive killer. Probably her reputed calling made the old hag avoid the priest's sight. He stepped up to the table. But the slice of bread he cut himself from the loaf remained uneaten in his hand.

"Padre! Padrecito!" the people outside were calling. "Padrecito . . ."

Blinking against the light as he opened the front door, he saw Miguel standing in the shadow of one of the bitter-orange trees, the whip under his armpit, his mouth open in ominous alertness. "The señorita is out of danger, children," Father Crisóstomo said, drawing himself up,

"God will help. We must pray for her."

Although his vocal chords had gathered none of their old vigor, there ensued a resounding silence. It seemed to freeze, one by one, the restive peóns into immobile postures.

Father Crisóstomo beckoned the capataz closer. "Leave them alone," he said under his breath. "Why hasn't the medico come yet? I told you you could take my car."

Miguel contracted his shoulders. He began to look, across the crowd in the front yard, at the row of bronze faces visible above the wall, as if those men, occupying the running boards of the automobile, had kept him from following the padre's orders. "I've dispatched a man on horseback, father. A reliable man. I could not send Jacinto. No, that I could not. And there is no one on the hacienda to drive a car except for him and . . ." He held his tongue, perhaps not altogether displeased by its slip. "If *I* knew how to drive a car, I would not have been here when you came, father, because I would have gone after the murderer myself, in the patrón's car, no?"

"When did you dispatch that man?" the priest inquired, deaf to the shade of insolence in Miguel's tone.

"The moment you said so, father."

"So the señor medico is drunk again."

"Maybe not. He may be delayed. I also ordered the man to go to the alcalde."

"Naturally, naturally . . ." Father Crisóstomo had been nodding uninterruptedly at the Indios. Some of the women had come forward to kneel on the gravel. 'Oh Requesens,' he was thinking, 'I pleaded with you. I wanted you to prevent this thing. I wanted you to help me to prevent it. Have you now forced me to bring justice against yourself? . . . Oh you fearful man, why did you allow your evil conscience to make you so hesitant? Why did you not write your note earlier? If it had reached me only one day earlier, some hours earlier only, I could have prevented all this. Now I can no longer act "according to suggestion." And what can I "suggest" now? . . . Was it for the sake of justice that all this had to happen? Is justice rooted so deep in the order of things that love can never get ahead of it?'

Miguel's eyes had slowly wandered back to the padre's drawn face. "Work is to be done, father," he finally said, "and this cannot go on."

The priest touched his elbow, and at the same time, as if playfully, reached for the cord of the man's whip. "Perhaps if you'd start on some chore yourself, they'll follow suit, eh? I promise you to stay, capataz. I came here because our Lord commanded me to come," he went on, increasing the volume of his voice. "He sent me late. But does He not know best? He has commanded me to stay here. And stay I will, children," he barked, transforming his hands into fists, to shake them both high over his head.

A ripple of assent stirred the dark heads which the men had bared, and their mutterings died away.

"Come . . ."

Miguel followed Father Crisóstomo into the casa, but before shutting the door, threw another lingering glance at the peóns.

"Where is Jacinto?"

"Locked up in the storehouse. A rat belongs to rats."

Without sitting down at the table, the cleric started to carve the cold roasted chicken. "I do not think he is a rat," he observed with a pretense of nonchalance. He noted that the two women had gone.

"*He* stole the truck—"

"The jackass! . . ." Crisóstomo admitted, munching.

"Father, I still say this Jacinto knows something about the revolt. But this is not for me to decide. The alcalde will decide that. He will also know what to make of this mob. Still, you know their ways yourself, Father. *You* are not misled, *you* don't think they are here just because the patrón was killed—you know it's the revolt, don't you? Though they keep their mouths shut about it."

"Revolt! I told you, capataz, there is no sign of unrest in Ulloa. Trains are running. . . . They had their market yesterday. . . ." He had his teeth in the meat of a chicken leg. "And whatever rumors that peddler brought you last night, capataz, they have not declared martial law in Ulloa, and I wish you'd stop doubting my words. For all I know, it's one of those Huacho affairs. I even heard it's an Eastern affair. How should this Jacinto be involved in it? Or those poor ignorant folk out there?"

"I just do not believe in Jacinto's story," Miguel objected. "Who, father, would think of going to the rubber forest nowadays? Nobody. He says he and the *suizo* planned to go there—"

"The *suizo* is trying to get there right now, is he not?"

"How do we know? . . . *Suizo!*"

Father Crisóstomo flung the picked bone on the plate. "We may leave this too to the alcalde, as you were saying." He was looking for a napkin, and finding none, wiped his mouth on the back of his hand. "I'll go upstairs, friend. I gave the señorita a pill. Not a powerful one, though, and she may wake up any minute now. Yes, it will be good to leave all investigations to the alcalde. He must be here soon." During these words, whose belittling vein was further emphasized by the sounds his tongue produced in sucking at his teeth, the padre was slowly walking toward the staircase. "And no fantasies, eh? About revolts and such-like. We both know little about such-like, friend."

His ear noted the sound of Miguel's abrupt departure from the room, and then, the loud monosyllabic answers with which he countered the renewed volley of questions that met him. Virtuous man . . .. Virtuous men were not easy to deal with. Their virtue gave them an overmastering sense of importance . . . Only when he was in Juana's bedroom did Father Crisóstomo remember that he had not even asked the señor capataz whether decent care had been taken of the dead man in the guest house.

How many dead men had the priest not seen in the course of his calling! Yet he could not forget the face of the dead Don Adolfo. Disfigured by the trail of coagulating blood issuing from the corner of its compressed mouth, that face had worn so striking a look of triumph that its lifelessness seemed merely like an extension of the glow which lights up the countenance of a man after the fiercest of struggles. What had gone on in the soul of this little *alemán,* this ordinary, rather vulgar and often prevaricating man, this one-time village-fair photographer and mountebank, fortune hunter and apparent friend of Don Lorenzo Requesens? What had gone on in his soul in that one second that his body slid down under the stare of the victor?

When Father Crisóstomo, guided by the commotion of the peóns and their wildly sputtering torches, entered the guest house shortly before dawn, the body still lay, as Miguel swore it had for the last three hours, with its back against the short end of the trestle bed, its legs sprawling, and its head twisted into the mockery of a relaxed posture. Miguel also swore that the patrón had had a revolver. But it could not be found; and Don Adolfo's hands, unbent, gave evidence that he had had no chance to use his weapon, and that the killer had either taken it from him at an early stage of the fight, or else had removed it from one of the pockets of the dead body. Don Adolfo, then, must have realized that he was at the killer's mercy. He must have clearly discerned his own defeat. Why did the terror sure to have gripped him not reflect in his features? Or the frenzy and agony of desperate courage?

Father Crisostomo sat down on the stool close to Juana's bed, careful to avoid noise. She was still asleep. She had turned her head to the wall. Apparently the wound on her left upper arm did not hurt her. Its flesh had only been grazed by the bullet.

Strangely enough, the man who fired it had not seemed to occupy her mind when the padre first talked to her—or rather, listened to her confusion, while the sun was rising over the mist before the window. As words started to disengage themselves from her stupor, they had seemed to hurl senseless questions at him. The one thing the girl had stated distinctly was that her stepfather had known what had forced her into her plan.

Had she merely referred to the "plan," indicated by the packed valise in the man's lodgings, to accompany him on his flight? Or had she tried to refute an accusation of her complicity in the homicide? Had it been the outcome of a resolve of both to oppose ruthless force to any attempt of Bundschuh's to stand in their way? She had, to be sure, been shot herself. Had she been so by accident only? The capataz maintained that she had stolen, besides some money, two rifles from the casa. Had she . . . oh, good Lord, had she had a share in delivering her stepfather to the onslaught of her lover?

Throughout the years, Father Crisóstomo had never altered his habit of addressing Juana in the patronizing fashion of busy grownups hustling past adolescents. Vaguely he had known that she went to Mass in Murcia, if irregularly only. Her quiet ways had never aroused his sense of responsibility. Her sheltered existence had put her far beyond those needs to which a lifetime spent amongst the dispossessed, the benighted, and the disgruntled, had taught him to minister. Now, in the tortured welter of his conjectures, he reproached himself bitterly with that unconcern. Even now, amid his repentant knowledge, it stood like a shadow between him and the girl. Had his service to the misery of men's bodies dulled his perception of the inner need?

He leaned forward to pull the linen sheet more tightly about Juana. In withdrawing, his unsteady fingers brushed against her shoulders.

Her eyes still closed, she moved her head. But her left arm, impeded by the bandage, held down the end of her loosened hair on the pillow, so that it receded from the forehead.

To his dismay, Father Crisóstomo noticed that sweat was pouring down his neck, as he waited for her eyes to open. Tears hung on her lashes. "What were you asking?" he said upon her first, unintelligible

word, proceeding with great effort, "Do not be ashamed . . ." His
speech would not come out. He was struck by a beauty he had never
seen in her before. He wished he could take her head between his hands,
and urge her to sob out her troubles. But all he managed to do was to
make a short, encouraging, assuring move with his spread fingers, and
tell her that the Lord's mercy was infinite.

"Deliberately . . ." she mumbled, "he did it deliberately. . . ."

"But you?"

"Do you understand me, father? Deliberately . . . he jumped forward
deliberately . . . right in front of the revolver, father!"

"Don Adolfo?"

"He was aiming at me. Don Adolfo saw he was. He could not help
seeing it."

"Don Adolfo?"

"Why did he do it?"

"What else could he do?" the padre said blankly. "He no longer had
his gun, had he?"

"But I abused him!" she said, raising her voice. It was as though she
had only now become conscious of the agitated hum down below in the
front yard. "No, not abuse. I told him the truth . . . told him *why* I
must go. And instead of leaving me to what was to happen to me—oh, I
did abuse him!—he jumped forward, covered me with his body. . . ."

"What 'truth' are you talking about, child?" Chrysostom asked in a
soft, prudent tone.

She halted the flow of her tears. "About my mother."

"About your mother?"

"Oh, I know you cannot talk, padre. I know you are not allowed to
talk!"

"Why should I not be allowed to talk about your dear mother?"

"He confessed to you, didn't he? To *you*—and not to the *cura*. He'd
meet him all the time. You came only seldom. That's why he favored
you as his confessor. I have come to understand that. He confessed to
you! I know you can never admit, never say to a living soul that he was
guilty . . . that he could have saved her and did not."

In his exertion to prevent his face from showing even the merest
shadow of denial or affirmation, Father Crisóstomo ground his teeth.
Through the material of his cassock, he noted that his hands were shaking on his knees. From very far off, a memory trickled into his thoughts.

"And that is what I told him," Juana cried out, "told him a minute, no, a second before he did it . . . did this inexplicable thing!"

Someone, someone in Murcia—the doctor?—had once called the death of Señora Bundschuh "highly convenient for the would-be haciendado." . . . But only once . . . Bundschuh himself had never so much as mentioned the deceased, that was true, and when Father Crisóstomo did, he had never reacted. . . . Could it be? Could it? Was this the sin which had caused him to court his friendship, furtively looking at his cloth all the time? . . . Had Bundschuh not tried to show him his special devotion since the death of the woman? Never had such rich meals been prepared for him as long as she was alive. . . .

The girl spoke again. "I told him I couldn't stay with him . . . that I had to go somewhere I'd never return from. He *must* have understood me. He did not answer. . . . You, I know, you'll never admit he was guilty."

"We are all guilty," the priest said automatically.

There was a sudden quiet in front of the casa.

Father Crisóstomo said, "I could spare you what I shall say to you, Juana. But truth must prevail. Well, then, Juana. You told—unconsciously, I am sure—you told Don Adolfo an untruth. Be calm. Most likely he did not understand you." He was poignantly aware of the great risk he took in aggravating her remorse in this trying hour; he was aware of his heedless temerity in flatly giving the lie to the old story in the face of what he believed he perceived; and, his heart pounding, he recognized the questionable, the sinful use he made of his priesthood. But an unextinguishable radiance was coming to him from the image of the dead man's face. . . .

With a loud gasp Juana sat up. Her left hand, making a retarded gesture that appeared to grope for the cleric's support, freed her hair. As she nodded, it fell down all over her face and caught the light in a reddish glimmer.

"Padre, padre," called a voice from downstairs, "the señores have arrived, father!"

The priest got up. He got up lightly. "I'll go now to meet the señor medico, Juanita," he whispered. "Dear Juanita, the alcalde will not molest you." He waited for her to raise her head before he put two of his faintly trembling fingers, inside out, to his mouth and winked at her conspiratorially.

"Here they come!" Miguel shouted.

"Don't shout, man! . . . I am coming." All qualms were lifted from

Father Crisóstomo. He would not allow the alcalde to interrogate the girl outside of his presence. He would know how to keep him from asking too many questions about the killer. Her own shame would caution her. He himself would say nothing about the dead Belgian. He felt in himself the power to cow the virtuous capataz into silence.

The dead man would not be given away. He had paid for another, a greater sin than his conniving with the exalted gentleman in Huacho and sheltering his infamous foreign friends. He had redeemed the real error of his life—that sin which had made him clumsily try to win the friendship of a priest. He had gone no further. The unhappy coward . . . He had been afraid of repentance. Yet he had redeemed himself. Singlehanded. One among millions . . . What did the ridiculous world of the alcalde, of Don Lorenzo Requesens, what indeed did the fugitive and his punishment matter, if weighed against the miracle in the soul of this one man?

XXVIII

THE VOICE OF the People, to whose effusions Adolfo Bundschuh had been listening a few hours before he was to heed the voice in his own breast, was heard in Huacho for the first time on the twenty-first of August.

It came as a tremendous shock to the complacency of the *gente decente*. They had only derided the handbills distributed in the night of August tenth to eleventh, discounting the successful action of Requesens and Basilio Gonzales in foiling their effect; nor, on August twentieth, had the *gente decente* become alarmed about the "hunger demonstration" in front of Government House.

Throughout these ten days, Don Basilio, that valiant Liberal, had adhered to his conviction that no mountain ought to be made of a molehill. The functionaries of the People's Party taken in custody in the small hours of August eleventh had been released after twenty-four hours. And it was Don Basilio again who with an improvised jovial speech from one of the second-floor casements of Government House had dispersed the three or four hundred people assembled in the Plaza around noon of August twentieth.

"I, my friend," Requesens said two days later to his A.D.C., "I did not believe for a moment in the alleged spontaneity and the harmlessness of that demonstration. Not I!"

Seated on one of the opposite armchairs, Captain Loyarte echoed the indignant sound Don Lorenzo made as he wound up his survey of the events leading up to the present crisis. It had been a long day for them both, and the captain was still wondering why His Excellency had insisted on his company at the late hour of their return to the Casa. He could not bring himself to assume that he had done so only to brag about his sagacity.

The air in the shuttered sala was close. Outside the two sentries strode up and down, and their footfalls reverberated heavily against the thick boards left behind by the painters in front of the building.

"Do you know what my colleagues did while the mob was chanting under our windows?" Requesens asked. "They were congratulating the Finance Minister on his foresight!" True, he continued, this learned gentleman had warned the Cabinet early in June that the decree whereby the Republic abandoned the fixed exchange value of her currency—a measure promulgated and pressed by the Finance Minister himself—might result in a certain rise of the cost of living; and it was equally true that this was the hardship the demonstrators were complaining about in their chants and on their crude placards. "But no one except myself recalled at that stage the balderdash printed in El Huérfano's sheet some weeks ago. No one felt like recalling it. They refused to see the connection. Hunger, Don Basilio argued, needed no provocation. A humanitarian! The day after, they all saw the game. The Voice of the People enlightened the caballeros." He pronounced the name of the rebel station with the utmost disdain. He took the vessel with the maté from the low table by his side. "That vaudeville soldadera!" he mumbled before his pursed lips caught the straw.

Loyarte left his drink untouched. He lifted his eyes to the ceiling as if sharing his master's contemptuous feelings. He blinked into the one lighted globe overhead. How often had he craved an intimacy such as was offered him in this hour. Now it shamed him. Sooner or later, he told himself, someone was bound to discover that the "vaudeville soldadera" was his María. How would he, probably the one person in the capital to identify that voice at its first word, account for withholding this intelligence from Requesens? He said glumly, "It is unbelievable, Your Excellency . . ." and fell silent again, still staring upwards. María must have received his letter five or six days before. His pleas to her not to become the dupe of demagog had been of no avail. The scorn with which he had treated "utopian politics" had not impressed her in the least. She had thrown herself into the midst of it . . . and it no longer looked altogether utopian!

Across the fancy gourd from which he sipped the concoction, Don Lorenzo scrutinized his aide. The outwardly impassive reaction of the young captain made him reflect, as he had already done several times, that he was hardly the right person to send off on tomorrow's noon train with the second halves of the bank notes constituting the ransom for

Philibert. No, Loyarte was not the man to bribe, or force, the train's engineer into letting him meet the receiver of the envelopes.

The envelope that contained the first halves of the bills had been sent on its way the Monday following the arrival of Philibert's letter. But the subsequent Thursday—last week's Thursday—had gone by without Lorenzo's making up his mind whom to dispatch on the second, far more decisive mission. To pay Philibert's ransom was not enough. He must be got hold of himself.

The note of the officious friar from Murcia more vexed than terrified Don Lorenzo. First, Bundschuh's betrayal had incensed him (and mainly that feeling had caused the delay in his reply to Casaquiara). Now—though without further news as yet from the priest—Lorenzo rather enjoyed the certitude that this pious man had spirited the Nazi off to his monastery. There he was safe from detection; and the fathers themselves, Lorenzo was confident, could be dealt with later. Everything might be, would be different later. If things should work out the right way, even rumors about his guests in the country would later do him no great harm.

However, such suspicions would be disastrous at present. Thus Don Lorenzo was haunted by a fear that some of the partisans of the infamous Majamarca coalition—fairly numerous in the vicinity of Philibert's place of detention, as he had hinted in his letter—might, through some incident, get wind of the suspicious stranger's presence there and report it in Majamarca. And how about that incredible woman who had liberated Philibert from the ruins? She would be looking for him, perhaps. . . . The day ending so peacefully now—for all that could be heard and seen between these four walls, it was scarcely credible that it had started with the blasting release of the Fafreras manifesto by the Voice of the People—had infused a new vigor in Lorenzo's decision to have Philibert brought back to him. If need be, he would keep him right here in the Casa, chain him to the wall of its cellar and gag him. . . .

Loyarte had stopped contemplating the ceiling. He looked at Don Lorenzo with a spirited expression. He had stuck his thumb into his service belt. His knees were together, his feet parallel on the rug.

His Excellency put down the gourd which he had emptied amid his deliberations. Even if Loyarte happened to be a better man for the job than he was, he concluded to himself, he could not send him away. His services were wanted here, and very much so.

Meanwhile the captain had again been tormented by his conscience. He could not disclose to his master his agonizing conflict. He could not inform on the foolish girl in Majamarca. However, as if to extend a token of his unchanged allegiance he said, "May I remind Your Excellency of our ride from Carjavel on that beautiful day? Beautiful as it was, I tried to bring up a disturbing piece of news that had reached me from out East the evening before—"

"On pink stationery, no doubt, eh?" Don Lorenzo threw in with a benign smile, which cut the young man to the quick.

Yet he went on, "I tried to report that a foreigner was travelling with El Huérfano. Mightn't that man have had a hand in bringing the coalition about? Foreigners have such outlandish ideas."

"Outlandish ideas . . ." repeated Requesens between closed lips. His vacant face reflected, again, the forbidding abstraction which, on the ride from the air parade, had stifled the openheartedness of Loyarte. But suddenly extending his arm and pointing with a prodding, petulant finger, His Excellency remarked, "I for one alluded to some such weird idea in the first hour! I alluded to it while we still were talking, talking, talking, with the mob splitting our ears from down below, and the Palace calling up every other minute. Remember this for your record. Two days ahead of the 'manifesto' of Señor Fafreras, I for one declared that not only did the *tumulto* originate with El Huérfano, but the rabble rouser himself must have been emboldened by someone greater than he. But does prescience ever pay in this country?"

Loyarte shook his head in respectful compassion. He could have replied that his superior's perspicacity had failed to translate itself into timely action. Only after the rebel manifesto was in the open—only this forenoon, in fact—had he put a potential move of the Eastern Army forces on the agenda of his staff consultations. Until then he had concentrated on security measures in Huacho proper.

"Well, Don León," Don Lorenzo said after a while, halting the swinging of his crossed leg, "the past is past. It is the future that counts now."

"May I ask one question, Your Excellency?"

Requesens opened his hands.

"Is Fafreras honest, Your Excellency?"

"In his threats? I suppose so."

"I mean . . . If Your Excellency doesn't mind, what I meant to ask was whether he is honest in this coalition, in this deal. . . ."

"Honest toward El Huérfano, that is?" Lorenzo countered with a quizzical glance. "An easy question to answer, Don León. Suppose the señor succeeds in replacing me. Suppose he does. What would he do with his rabble following? Try to ram El Huérfano's crazy program down Dr. Zapeta's throat? Make El Huérfano a colonel, or something? Pooh! Of course he'd try to rid himself of the fellow. Which doesn't necessarily mean he could do it. So his success would not be the end of the crisis by a long shot. It would be the beginning of civil war. The frivolity!" he exclaimed, carried away by the prospect. "To ally with the scum, with the beast below (as our more outspoken ancestors used to call it)! Unleashing the monster to get one's chance! Ah, within this monstrous frivolity, Fafreras' honesty toward his little friend is a matter of minor import . . . and of complete indifference to the forces of law and order."

"There is one thing I still cannot understand," said the captain after a pause in which both men had cocked their heads in the direction of the patio. But what caught their attention was merely Ramón's short-winded voice raised in some argument with the two soldiers posted out there. "The beginning," Loyarte proceeded, "how it all began in May . . . no one would assert that our group would *not* have succeeded without Fafreras. In reality, he stepped in very much like the rooster in the fable who fancies it's his crowing that makes the sun rise. Yet he could have opposed us. It would have been heavier going if he had—Your Excellency won't take amiss my saying so."

Lorenzo gave a benevolent shrug of protest. His A.D.C.'s using the word "group" in lieu of "junta" had not escaped him.

"And besides opposing us," Loyarte went on, rather forgetful of formality, "he could have made his own bid. Except for Your Excellency, of course, Fafreras was the only colonel who was not considered totally subservient to the General. He *could* have made his own bid for the office, and tried to get it without . . . without the monstrous frivolity he is using now. That he didn't do so doesn't make sense unless . . ."

"Unless? . . ."

"Unless he is sincere in fighting for 'those without even a shirt,'" Loyarte said, a little out of breath.

"You will oblige me by staying clear of that silly phrase."

"I am sorry, Your Excellency. I just can't help asking myself—"

R

"Nonsense."

"But then . . . why . . . why does Your Excellency think Fafreras acted as he did in May?"

Don Lorenzo passed his hand over his brows. "I wish, by the Mother of God, Don León, I wish I could answer that question."

"He may think better of it yet," the captain hazarded with a changed tone which seemed to retract some of his audacity.

"If I were you, I would not give one single thought to what Señor Fafreras' answer will be tomorrow night. It is a forgone conclusion. Or can anyone conceive of the señor laying down his command, resigning, and appearing before a court martial in Huacho? Resigning! That means surrendering. Surrendering to whom, may I ask?"

"It would be different if Colonel Villaroel had gone to Majamarca," Loyarte observed, giving tongue to a view held by everyone in the capital. But everyone also realized that Villaroel—one of the late General's close collaborators, this gentleman had been fetched from virtual retirement this morning and "given" the Majamarca command—could not be sent there without an impressive contingent of troops; and the Government could not possibly think of diminishing the garrison of Huacho.

Requesens had only nodded at the captain's remark, who more and more felt the indulgence exercised toward him.

More and more he felt that Don Lorenzo did not wish to be left alone with his thoughts, and that this was the reason why he did not dismiss him. "The ultimatum . . ." he said, "it must be known by now to every last officer in Majamarca. Not all of them can be in favor of the ridiculous deal. I wonder how much truth there is in the announcement that they have gone over to him in a body."

"So do I, so do I. . . . But do not forget, friend, that the novelty of the deal is not unlikely to have stunned the señores. And stunned men are easily charmed."

"No one is charmed here. Here, the manifesto—"

"So called!"

"Here it made no impression. I can assure Your Excellency it didn't."

"No, it did not," said Requesens slowly, almost sleepily.

Loyarte believed he could read his thoughts. The loyal attitude of the Huacho garrison left no room for doubt. Yet it did not seem to give Requesens any overpowering satisfaction. The Palace worried him. The Fafreras pronunciamento had rung with admonishment rather than implacability toward the Palace. It had reminded the Chief Executive that not every movement intent upon bettering the lot of the masses must be damned "Communist"—though, naturally, a man "so steeped in foreign ideology as a Requesens" would brand it that. Would the "preconceived views" of a Requesens "be permitted to direct the policy of the Palace"? This was plain language. But could a Dr. Zapeta be imagined siding with the rebels? The captain, like probably many other men in the country, still shied away from weighing the pros and cons that must have battled in Dr. Zapeta's breast. The crisis had come too soon to find him cleansed of all resentment toward his War Minister. Surely the deference Requesens had shown the President at the Carjavel ceremony—the groping and all but fawning mellowness of his speech, so inexplicable to the new Air Corps men—had not undone, in Dr. Zapeta's memory, the Minister's brash intention in expanding this arm of the service. At any rate, a sense of coolheaded realism appeared to inspire the Palace. Don Lorenzo's plan, laid before the Chief Executive this forenoon, had been far from arousing his enthusiasm.

As it was, the success of that plan—a "mass sortie of the air force upon the first sign of hostilities on the part of Majamarca"—would not have been assured. Technical, or else pecuniary, difficulties had delayed the delivery of the twenty-three planes making up the balance of the Government's purchase. Also, the people abroad had failed to live up to some of the stipulations of the contract: only two out of the twenty-seven new machines were equipped for bombing, and merely token bomb loads had been delivered with them. Requesens made light of that disadvantage. The mere appearance of the squadrons in the sky over Majamarca was sure to work wonders! But such contentions could not deaden in the minds of his listeners—nor, probably, in his own—an additional factor calculated to dampen fervor. The program of the Pilots' School existed largely on paper. The training of its candidates had hardly begun. If the new craft were to be flown, the personnel of the old air force would have to fly them.

Loyarte did not question their sense of obedience. Ever since the commissioning of the young señores, the lieutenant colonel and his crews had been anxious to prove their own dependability. But Don Lorenzo had not given much credit to their eagerness. Their morale was not high. The situation was muddled. In a different way it was no less so among the new airmen—the airmen-to-be, properly speaking, the Night-in-the-Palace group, the erstwhile junta. The failure of the cornerstone fête to result in some sensational move of Requesens' had disillusioned the young señores. Whatever advantage each of them may have fancied would accrue from such a move, whatever prize crown their self-alleged efforts in Don Lorenzo's behalf, their disappointment now was as poignant as those hopes had been vague. If Don Lorenzo had not deigned to notice the strain in the ovation accorded him this afternoon at the airdrome, he, León Loyarte, had. Against his will, he had come to prefer the sobriety prevailing at the De la Torre barracks to the boisterousness at Carjavel.

"It has been a strenuous afternoon," Requesens now said. I hope you got yourself some sort of a meal after our return to Government House."

"I did, Your Excellency. Thank you."

Don Lorenzo motioned him over to the armchair next to his own. "You must be tired, Don León. I am. Still there's one more matter I'd like to discuss with you. Sit here."

The captain, who had got up, was startled by the suddenness with which Requesens, while still talking, looked over his shoulder. He seemed to have sensed the inaudible approach of the old housekeeper. She did not come out of the passage beyond the papered door. "No, we don't need anything, my dove," he said, "and you ought to be abed, really."

"I ought to, Don Lorenzo," came the goiterous voice from the gloom, "only it's hard to find rest. Soldiers . . . and Ramón's bickerings . . . and the señora upstairs walking up and down, up and down . . . and now here—"

"Come, come, Isabel, you don't mean to be inhospitable, do you?"

"On the contrary," protested the old woman, widening the crack of the door, "I came . . ."

Loyarte cast a swift glance up the staircase. A stretch of light issued from underneath the door to Doña Priscilla's rooms. But no sound had reached the sala. The housekeeper was exaggerating.

"I came," she persisted, "to ask you and the young señor—"

"I told you we needed nothing."

"Business should not keep the señores from taking care of themselves. He too, Don Julio too, had a great deal to attend to, no? Sat up night after night. But he would have a late meal served to himself and his guests. . . ."

"Quaint creature," Lorenzo suggested with a forced yawn, when Isabel, her grumblings dying away, had pulled the door shut behind her. "It *is* late, though. You'll be driving to Carjavel from here."

"To Carjavel, Your Excellency?" asked the captain.

"They all are there, are they not? I shall be at my office at eight o'clock. You will call up there at nine."

"From Carjavel."

"Yes. Our friends must be kept aware that they are on my mind at any hour."

"At any hour."

"Don't leave," Lorenzo said, as his aide was about to turn. But his gaze went past him to the vestibule door. "I understand, Don León, you've got debts. Eh?"

"The scoundrel!" Loyarte burst out. "Ah, I watched that scoundrel scraping and bowing to Your Excellency this afternoon at the barracks! I watched him! What tactlessness! To pick this day to inform on me! It *is* the major of the Sixteenth! *He—*"

"You shouldn't lose your temper, captain," Requesens cut him short with a show of disciplinarian harshness, though smiling the next moment. "People who are in debt are always surprised that everybody knows about it. Major of the Sixteenth, nothing! Everybody knows about your debts, friend . . . which won't be so good," he added more to himself, interrupting the young man's apologies.

Loyarte stood stiffly.

"How much is it?"

"Those were dreary years—"

"Is it that much?"

"Your Excellency, those were dreary years. I never wrote you how dreary they were, those years of waiting, of working in the dark. . . . Gambling was about the only pastime I had in those years. Others were having a good time with women, married women, or girls in and out of the Casa Ninon. I, as good as engaged to be married . . ."

Lorenzo cupped his hand over his eye sockets and the upper part of his nose. "Look here, Don León. If you cannot compute the amount at this instant, let me know by tomorrow how much it is. Don Esteban— now this is strictly between ourselves—has recently been quite open-handed. You may have guessed yourself that I owe all this to his generosity." He twisted his shoulders to illustrate the modern splendor supposedly descended upon the Casa through the generosity of his uncle. "I wish to get you out of those debts. I am sure the old gentleman will help us. I promise you he will. He is rather proud, you know, of his nephew's position. Perhaps I shouldn't take so much advantage of that. But as I said, I wish to get you out of that mess. Once this nuisance . . . this Fafreras nuisance is taken care of, we shall put Don Esteban's munificence to good use.

"And don't you believe it was only the dreariness of those years that got you into debt, Don León," he continued before Loyarte managed to get out a word. "There was something else to lure you to the gaming table. Your miserable pay. Now let me tell you this. Once this nuisance is taken care of, that problem too will be cleared up. Regulation of officers' pay—it has been talked about long enough, I daresay. It was not I who postponed action. Nor need I add that what is closest to my heart in this respect is the pay of the Air Corps officers. This too is a promise. I pledge my word."

While he spoke—with nonchalant cordiality first, then lifting his voice, and finally, as he withdrew his hand from his face, also raising his head and fixing a martial stare on his A.D.C.—the latter retreated a couple of paces, as if overawed by the immensity of the windfall. He was not. He discerned the bargain offered to him. But he also realized that Requesens was taking for granted the influence he, León, was supposed to exert. Perhaps he did! Perhaps his dormant power was greater than he knew. His pride all but stultified him for a moment. While some expressions of gratitude and expostulation were dropping from his mouth, he saw his benefactor cross the sala and unseeingly nod in his direction. An unabashed grin moved the corner of his mouth.

"Nine a.m.," he said distinctly, "and now, good-night, Don León. Dreary years, eh?"

"I thank you, Your Excellency. . . ."

Lorenzo, at the foot of the stairs, heard the jingling of the captain's spurs, the muffled bang of the two doors, and then the sentries' snapping to attention outside, and the curt uproar of the starting car. Loyarte drove away slowly.

Lorenzo peered at the fragment of light visible through the latticed woodwork of the banister. He had not seen Priscilla since late last night. He had been summoned to the Palace at seven in the morning; and though he had found time to call her on the telephone in the afternoon, he felt as if he had neglected something.

In fact, something like a new mutual consideration had entered their relationship. Three days after the festivity at Carjavel, she had told him

Margarita Partridge would come to pay her a visit; they would walk up the street to have a glimpse of the progress on her mansion. The appointed day, however, had been August twentieth, and the two ladies had thought it advisable to postpone their meeting. The Gracián girl had shown no sign of life since. "No, Lorenzo," Priscilla had answered his query this afternoon on the telephone, "no, there's no word. And I can't possibly call her myself, can I?" No, he had said, she could not. And then he had heard a sigh of disappointment at her end of the wire.

Lorenzo's right hand reposed on the big wooden knob of the banister. Mechanically he began to turn his fingers on it, and the knob started to follow their rotating motion, its loosened peg squeaking in the socket.

For how long had this knob been loose . . . ? One day, as a child, he had heaved it down, and started rolling it across the length of the sala, and had been spanked for the mischief. This was the one time his father had ever beaten him. Later, much later, Lorenzo understood that this had been the day Don Julio was to leave for the rubber frontier.

Some day he must tell Priscilla of this reminiscence. He would tell her of Father's departure . . . and of his homecoming . . . and of what later he had learned of the harassing circumstances of those days preceding Don Julio's passing. Some day, then, he would thus correct his old tale about the "martyr's death" of Don Julio. She would, she must, wait for the day to come when he would talk to her frankly, as he never had to a human soul! He wished he could offer her this sign of his regret in this hour. But he could not. Such an hour of sincerity might tempt him to divulge the whole range of his hidden worries, and with it, the one secret triumph that was his.

Señor Fafreras was instituting a novelty, was he? What of it? So was he! He was bribing his spokesman with the air force. A group—was it? Never mind, caballeros, it *was* a junta. Don Lorenzo was about to buy it! Who said that sorry parcel of a lieutenant colonel was not to be bought, together with some of his crews? . . . Never before had his secret financial power so elated Lorenzo.

At the core, his triumph was greater than his elation. The stroke which had made him the master of the German money had always appeared to him as a retribution for the blow dealt to his father. Sometimes he had even felt as a man may who has righted a wrong surpassing personal discomforts. It was ill-gotten money all right; and a squeamish man, a little man might not have been any too fond of having his mind dwell on its origin overseas. But in a defiantly morbid manner, the gory source of the treasure pleased Lorenzo: it seemed to offset the record of meddling British humanitarianism which, when all was said and done, had felled Don Julio.

With an accelerating turn Lorenzo's hand relinquished the wooden knob. Its peg gave a last squeak. He stepped up to the new electric switch near Don Julio's likeness. One globe after another lit up; then on another turn of the switch, they were all bathed in blackness.

In the patio Ramón was coughing.

Lorenzo decided to get up very early in the morning. He would be at Government House at seven, or even at six. He must keep abreast of news. Perhaps Fafreras would lose courage. Perhaps he would make some move ahead of the deadline. Perhaps he would bow to his, Lorenzo's, superior intelligence. Perhaps some sort of agreement could be worked out in the eleventh hour. Money was ready.

Walking away from the switch and past the armchairs, Lorenzo had lost his direction. He held his arms outstretched before him, and suddenly felt against their palms the varnished panels of the vestibule door.

He pressed the brass handle down. The moonlight creeping in illumined the oblong passage, and evoked a shimmer from the glass on the photographs on the wall. He went forward. The key of the big entrance door was not turned, its chain down. Cautiously he opened one wing of the door.

The sentries did not hear him. They stood somewhat to the left in the middle of the pavement, their rifles thrust out obliquely from their featureless shapes. Their long shadows folded at the foot of the opposite building, and rose upon its façade. The two men were engaged in a monosyllabic, oddly dignified whisper. Lorenzo did not step farther. The night air came up to him—the waiting, enigmatic mood of the town.

XXIX

WHILE LOYARTE, DRIVING at an uneven speed along the deserted streets, still painted to himself the lofty flourishes with which he would toss the money at his creditor's feet, he became keenly aware of the task that stood between himself and that pleasant vista. His mission with the señores at Carjavel was a clear one. But its basic simplicity made it a very hard one. To urge soldiers to obey future orders of their superior, at the same time dangling advantages before their eyes, presupposed a doubt whose merest shadow might well defeat the urger's purpose.

Upon Don León himself, Requesens' promise had had no such effect. Requesens had not looked like a man who feels the ground receding from under his feet. The trust he reposed in his aide did not emanate from despair. Yet it failed to work as a great challenge. The bargain he had offered to León seemed to diminish his own stature.

Or else it was León's stature that began to shrink in his own mind. The business proposition he was about to enter into, this *quid pro quo,* instilled a strange element into his devotion for Don Lorenzo—that love born from and carried by his enthusiasm for a great gamble. It was perfectly true that greased palms had not been foreign to the Army gentlemen of the romantic 1880's, nor to those who had lived before or came after; and these usages had encroached as little upon their self-respect and their recorded bearing as the rains or the mosquitoes had from time immemorial.

Still, the thought of those precedents made little difference to León's feelings. There had, up to this day, been no falsehood between himself and his María. In a hazy fashion his unhappy financial circumstances were known to her, and he was sure she would welcome his delivery from them. At the same time he would hate her to know about the munificence of Don Lorenzo's uncle. . . .

If any money had changed hands in El Huérfano's compact with

Fafreras—and some perhaps had, difficult though it was to imagine its sources—María certainly had no knowledge of it. Her idealism was naïve. It was without blemish. The line of his future conduct toward the girl was obscure to León. He was fairly confident that her father would know how to protect her after the collapse of the coalition out East; and within this vista—the one he forced himself to behold most of the time—he had visualized himself as dismissing María's actions as an idealistic folly, to be obliterated by them both. Now he began to fear that, compared to his business with Don Lorenzo, her unblemished idealism might look far less foolish even in its defeat.

He was angry. He told himself that reflections of that sort hardly measured up to the great earnestness of this night. His obligation was to go ahead, tackle his task. Nothing would compel him to accept Don Lorenzo's bribe, least of all a success in his undertaking . . . though no success seemed complete without proper reward.

It occurred to him that the officer he had decided to rouse from his sleep at Carjavel was a case in point. In the past three months this first lieutenant, originally of the cavalry, had made no little consequence of his "signal rôle" in Requesens' elevation to office. Together with "a snippet of a captain," he had been the bearer of the invitation extended to Don Lorenzo to join the gathering at the bordello; and he insisted that but for his own ardor, subtlety, and boldness, Requesens would have stayed aloof from the momentous meeting. It was improbable that this contention had come to the Minister's ears. He had put the first lieutenant on the roster of the new Air Corps simply because he belonged to the Night-in-the-Palace group. That appointment did not sate the lieutenant's ambition. He was an extremely handsome man, but his peculiar sexual habits had since cadet years exposed him to harmful gossip; and he responded to it by carrying, as the saying has it, a chip on his shoulder. Withal, his hurt pride—the pride in his alleged history-making exploit—did not interfere with his gratification about Don Lorenzo's progress. His embitterment had not deadened the voice of conceit that reminded him of his personal stake in the further success of the Minister he "had made" by volunteering to go to the Casa Requesens on that delicate, dangerous errand. León, though conscious of the natural jealousy of the lieutenant, meant to play on his hope for a belated reward. He would use him to gain an up-to-the-minute picture of the situation. Perhaps he would make him his confidant, or even his helper.

It was well past one o'clock when León drove through the gate of Carjavel Airfield. To his astonishment the administration building was ablaze with light.

The trick Loyarte had played on its foreign owners on the morning of August eleventh had been a triumph of daring. Instead of provoking a diplomatic incident, the foreign air line had three days later offered most of the building for the Republic's use. Erected in the spendthrift temper of the late war, the structure was far too spacious for the foreigners anyway; and most likely their Government, viewing with some alarm the Republic's sudden friendship with her ancient antagonist to the southeast (as evidenced by the airplane purchase), had asked them to do this favor to the Air Corps. This magnanimous action—looked at with suspicion in certain quarters—had enabled Requesens to provide the officers, old and new, with decent emergency quarters. Considering the present crisis, it had come at the right moment.

León parked his car near the hangar. As he approached the building, loud voices filled its ground-floor lounge—the new mess hall—reaching his ears through the closed but unshuttered windows.

León advanced along the front wall. He stopped behind the large drain pipe running down the side of one of the casements to peer, unseen from within, into the crowded hall. For a couple of seconds he had the sensation of being back in the mirror-tapestried upstairs-room of the Casa Ninon. Wherever he looked, that anticipation of great events, those pent-up anxieties and guarded passions, that self-assurance commingling with proud awareness of civic virtue, and that overweening sense of importance, again cast their hues on these faces. It was an altogether ghostly impression—so strong that his reason needed some prodding to convince him that a great many of the caballeros had not been among the guests of the ill-reputed villa that night. Nor did anyone preside over the assemblage the way Fafreras had over that other. León did not see the lieutenant colonel. Officers stood about in circles, listening to one another, visibly impatient to break in, talkers and hearers alike overtaken by intermittent fits of gesticulation. Others sat at tables with half-emptied liquor glasses or their maté gourds before them, and absently thumbed through the garish commercial booklets left behind by the foreigners. It was not a picture of violent arguments and clashing loyalties. In fact, León was struck by an aspect of aimless excitement.

He drew several paces away from the shining rectangles which the windows projected onto the narrow stretch of dust-covered green, and beckoned to one of the sentries. After making sure the man did not know or at least did not recognize him, he ordered the soldier to fetch the former cavalry lieutenant and tell him a friend was waiting outside.

When he had entered the confines of the airdrome, the twin searchlights of the observation tower had been immobile, their rigid beams almost vertical, losing themselves in the sky. Now they started moving. Their glare grazed the grounds, scooping from the blackness the gleaming wing of a plane, or its glittering cockpit, or the ungainly shape of some craft under canvas, or a huddle of soldiers asleep under their ponchos on the bare soil, who would lift an arm in defense against the shaft of brightness falling into their dreams.

"You, Loyarte? I thought so. . . ."

León had not seen the lieutenant come out of the building.

He strode up in his slightly rolling gait, his arms akimbo. "How are things, señor *ayudante?*" he asked.

"Where?" countered León.

The other blew some air from his lips, noisily.

"How are things in there?" León inquired after a brief pause. Against his will a tone of conspiratorial tension clouded his voice.

"Asking *me?*"

"Asking you," León answered with as much gravity as he was able to put into two words. He was determined to ignore the jibes of the poorly rewarded history-maker; he had been prepared for them.

The lieutenant said with affected poise that little had changed since this afternoon.

"Little? What exactly, then, has?"

"Group tension wearies men and at the same time stirs them."

León commented upon the shrewd observation of his friend, and almost immediately felt him relax under that flattery.

As the man continued to answer his queries with noncommittal brevity, employing less and less of the irony of his opening words, Loyarte came to feel that the spirit of the señores in the mess hall was better than he had feared. Had he not been yielding to the superstitious notion that his personal business with Requesens cast an ill spell on his enterprise? He began to walk, and the other joined him. They were about the same height.

"Shall we speak out what is on both our minds?" the lieutenant suggested after they had covered a stretch in silence. "Shall we? The paramount question is this: will the air force take off in case . . ." It was not certain that the low oath that interrupted, or followed, his sentence, was intended to leave it unfinished. In the decreasing light of the moon, neither of them had seen the pile of iron matting at the edge of the unfinished runway, and the lieutenant had run against it. He bent down to nurse his knee. "Well, then," he went on after answering negatively León's inquiry as to whether he had hurt himself, "well, to that, I can only reply that up to the moment I left them not one single man had as much as touched on that problem." He was wheeling round, and looked with surpirse at León who too had leaned down and was rubbing his legs.

"These damned mosquitoes!" he mumbled. "And what is all the excitement about over there, then?"

"Excitement? I do not suppose there's less of it in the barracks, or at Government House, or, for that matter, at the Palace. Of course, I wouldn't know. . . . Moreover," he said, dropping his sullenness, "a man should never peer through windows, Don León. He should be where the others are. Literally as well as figuratively speaking, ha, ha!"

León made an attempt to join him in his laugh. He was by no means amused, but realized that a show of assent was the price he paid for this comradeship. He drew the handkerchief from his sleeve to blow his nose. "I *am* where the others are, friend," he finally said. "How could it be otherwise?"

"A joke, Don León, it was a joke," the lieutenant said, striding out.

"Or did anyone ever doubt it?"

"Doubt what?"

"That I am where the others are?"

"Where are the others?" the handsome officer asked. "Except in there?"

"It was you—"

"Yes, it was I who said that no one so much as touched on the problem. And that is as far as you can trust my sense of observation."

León said nothing. He put his hands to his hips. Then, like a tuning fork, his voice pronounced the name of the lieutenant colonel.

"He has had an amazing comeback since the parade, hasn't he?"

"As a technician he has," León admitted.

The ensuing silence testified to the lieutenant's view that such prudent qualifications were out of place at this juncture.

"Is he there?"

"He is. Or was. He's held a staff meeting."

"A staff meeting?"

"Of a sort, I take it. Technical matters."

Don León thought to himself that foresight indeed did not pay in this country. Some days before, he had made bold to remind Requesens that none of the new airmen belonged to the staff as yet. His Excellency had merely remarked that, considering the "decrepitude" of the old air force, its so-called staff did not deserve bothering with. For all practical purposes *he* was the staff of the Air Corps.

The lieutenant came to a halt. Some of the lights in the building had gone out. No, he declared upon León's inquiry, no, he did not think it would be wise for the señor *ayudante* to "barge in on the remnants of the company in there" at this late hour. Those who had already turned in would misinterpret his reviving the discussion in their absence. Not that he for one was presuming Don León had any particular subject with which to revive the discussion. . . .

"I should think the señores might wish to talk to someone who's been with the Minister throughout this day."

The searchlights stood unmoving again in the sky. "The Minister has plenty of time," the erstwhile history-maker remarked. He moved a little forward and away from León. "Colonel Fafreras won't give any word before tomorrow night. He could, but he won't. Hasty decisions are not in his nature. Whatever errors a man gets himself into, they do not change his nature."

"Errors? A crime!"

"Quite so, quite so," the lieutenant concurred. "But crime or error, the Minister has plenty of time to meet either . . . to prepare for meeting either. Unless he really plans to strike first."

"He is patient," León said.

"His nature. I remember well how patient he was when I came to him on that forenoon. He *is* a patient man."

"Yet he may be forced to strike first."

The other lit a cigarette. He held the match between his fingers until it burned down. "That's known," he said.

Had he, or the rest of them here, gotten wind of the veto Dr. Zapeta opposed to Requesens' plan of "preventive action"? This, León admonished himself, was the moment to bring forth Don Lorenzo's promises, to extol his love of the Air Corps, to be outspoken to the extent of rudeness, as businessmen were supposed to be in talking over the give and take which was the core of all business. But there was no energy in León.

The man in front of him lifted his wrist watch close up to his eyes. "Two. Past two. As you know, everybody will be up at six, friend. So you too will have plenty of time, *ayudante*. For sounding our morale—"

"I've no such intentions."

"You oughtn't to have. Morale is good," he declared negligently.

Did he expect his loyalty to be accepted on the strength of its tacit self-evidence? Whatever his intent was, its effect was ambiguous. Was this effeminate man still at the mercy of his hurt pride—this self-styled kingmaker of Requesens? Or was he beyond that old dream? Was his ambiguity deliberate?

This talk, at any rate, was leading nowhere. Why, then, did he, León, stand here beside this fellow, without stirring a limb? Why did he not rush over to the building, storm into the assemblage, grab the flag from the wall, leap onto a table, threaten all traitors with death, and urge all men of good will to rally behind their leader and follow him wherever he might take them? It was a heart-warming concept, and worthy of María's beloved despite the dissimilarity of their idealisms. But the concept had no power.

The two young officers stood less than a meter from each other. The former cavalry lieutenant had discarded his cigarette after a single puff. They both had turned their heads toward the building. The sheen of the fixed searchlight lay on its roof. They both had put one foot forward. And suddenly Captain Loyarte was gripped by the eerie idea that the companion of this hour, this Doppelgänger, this rival kingmaker of Lorenzo Requesens, was put up here by the fates as a warning—or as a sign post, as a new promise and lure.

"Got a place to spend the night?" the apparition asked. "Rather over-crowded, you know."

XXX

"THEY'LL PIN IT on us, Don Basilio."

The Minister of the Interior nodded gravely.

"And you say the police haven't found out who the assassin is?"

"Was, Don Lorenzo, was! I told you he was lynched on the spot."

"Providence is not on our side, we might say."

"We might."

Requesens turned his swivel chair toward the window. He had folded his arms across his chest and merely waved a hand from the wrist, gesturing questioningly in the direction of the Palace.

"He is expecting us at eight," Basilio Gonzales said.

Requesens glanced at the silver clock on his desk. The enormous buttocks of Don Basilio who was perching on its edge, his legs precariously crossed, had displaced the small timepiece.

"Do you want your staff officers to be at the Palace at eight?" he asked. "If you do, you ought to call up the barracks."

Lorenzo gave a push to his chair. "I shall wait for *his* decision," he said, looking straight into his colleague's face. "My plan is known to him. It doesn't need the support of an officers' parade. I'll call the señores to the Palace as soon as *he* gives his consent to my plan."

"A proper way of procedure," Don Basilio muttered with an enigmatic inflection.

Requesens drew a deep breath. "How did he take the news?"

"I don't know. Honestly, I don't. He has talked to no one."

"At what time did he get the news?"

"About an hour ago. Six-fifteen, I'd say."

"Did *you* give him the news?"

"No. The broadcasting people did. He called me up. That's when I called up your place, Don Lorenzo, and was told you were on your way."

As this account elicited no visible reaction from Requesens, Don Basilio added in a key of minor concern, "The Palace happened to know that I was camping in my office. It was long past midnight when I was through with the Chief of Police. So I decided to stay here over night, and so informed the Palace. I informed young Olmedo who was on duty."

This mention of one of Dr. Zapeta's aides reanimated Don Lorenzo's expression. "Did you talk to young Olmedo this morning, too?"

"Yes."

"And what did he say? How did he say the President took the news?"

Don Basilio hunched his shoulders up to his ears.

"Was he sorry? Was he sorry Providence hadn't been on our side? Was he sorry the assassin missed?"

Don Basilio's protracted shrug upset his balance. He restored it by clutching the desk with both hands. He gave a short apologetic laugh before he replied, "Sorry? I don't know whether *he* was sorry. *I* wasn't. No, friend, I am not sorry the assassin missed. I am glad he did. I am glad that—according to my reports (reliable reports, for miraculously I still get such from Majamarca)—his bullet did hardly any harm to El Huérfano. Or would *you* wish to have a martyr to put up with?"

"They'll pin it on us anyway, no?"

Gonzales let his buttocks slide down from the desk. "I cannot bring myself to believe Fafreras will. There are limits even to propaganda." He fished a piece of candy from his wide trousers and began to munch it, while he walked up to one of the two windows and pushed the straight-hanging damask curtain to the side. The morning light fell into the room.

Across the mighty frame of his colleague, Don Lorenzo could see, at the southwestern approach of the Plaza, the President's pennant floating atop the Palace. Except for the monotonous cries of the early street venders, all was quiet in the square down below. He asked, "What orders did you give to the broadcasting people?"

"Jam . . ." Don Basilio mouthed, his speech a little impeded, "jam, jam those voices on the air."

"And how about *La Libertad?*"

"They won't print the story. Not today. And nothing went out from my office."

"Everything went out from the Voice of the People, so called," Lorenzo objected. The stoical pose of Gonzales began to irritate him, as

s

did his manner of addressing, as it were, the pane of the casement. "If *you* got the news on the air—"

"I didn't. The broadcasting people did, as I just made clear."

"Did you order them to keep their mouths shut?"

"I should say I did."

"Tomorrow being Friday," Lorenzo said, "we can thank the Lord we clamped down on that miserable printing shop last night."

Don Basilio's murmured assent was without enthusiasm.

It was Requesens who had taken the initiative in having the press of *La Semana* stopped right after the Fafreras pronunciamiento came over the clandestine radio. There had been some dissent about this measure in the Cabinet meeting, especially since the manifesto had created no disorders in the capital and as little restiveness as though it had reflected merely another inter-Army affair to be fought out among the colonels. The lower classes did not understand its nature, so Dr. Zapeta had suggested, and as likely as not the partisanship of Fafreras would make El Huérfano even suspect to them; and to gag the People's Party because of the treachery of Fafreras would only impress on the masses the seriousness of the incredible coalition. But Requesens' opinion had prevailed in the teeth of such arguments. As for rounding up the "functionaries" of the People's Party—this term, up to then never used, had sprung up in the meeting—Gonzales had stated that the only dangerous mob was an unorganized one, and that El Huérfano's sympathizers in Huacho should not be left without "their more responsible elements." Again it was Requesens who, not least by reminding Don Basilio of their salutary joint action on August eleventh, had won the Cabinet over to his point of view. Thirty-six individuals had been put into jail late last night; and except for one isolated scuffle in a public house, the night had gone by in complete quiet.

Lorenzo refrained from rubbing in this proof of his better judgment. He still sat with his arms crossed, his eyes on the fat man in the embrasure. "One other question," he said. "Are we going to stop trains? In case a state of siege is proclaimed, are we going to stop them?"

Gonzales extricated a no-longer-very-white handkerchief from his jacket. He wiped first his mouth and then the nape of his neck and his large fleshy ear lobes. Yet the morning was comparatively cool, and the western exposure of Don Lorenzo's office left it in the shadow. "I for one shall advise against stopping trains. You couldn't stop the

Northern Railway without halting the Majamarca-Huacho Railroad, unless you'd want a hue and cry to go up about the preferential treatment the British enjoy. On the other hand, it *would* be unwise to interfere with their business. That's the one thing Anglo-Saxons dislike, no? Of course," he continued with a moan, "events may force us to act irrespective of such considerations."

"Do you feel they will?"

The Minister of the Interior came back from the window. He tossed the crumpled wrapping of his candy into the wastepaper basket. "Feel? Feel, Don Lorenzo?" he countered, gazing at Requesens from under his heavy eyelids. But as he saw him reach for the telephone, and his arm get entangled in the cord, he gave to his smile a meaning of reassurance

"Would it not be wise to have our own people broadcast the news about the assassination?" Lorenzo asked.

"Let me think it over for another quarter hour. They must broadcast some statement, some bulletin that El Huérfano is definitely out of danger—"

"Is he?"

"Definitely. But some kind of bulletin from the authorities in Majamarca would be the thing to have when our people broadcast the news."

"What authorities?"

Don Basilio was buttoning the waistcoat of his dark suit. Then with some circumspection he rearranged the gold chain he wore across his immense stomach. His forehead was in creases. "Could you come over to my office when you've made your call, Don Lorenzo? I've arranged for an uninterrupted communication with the broadcasting station. They have some way of listening to the wildcat radio even though they jam it. Come over, will you?"

As he stepped out, a shuffle of hurried feet came to Lorenzo from the corridor.

He was about to lift the receiver when the telephone rang.

"Is it you?" asked Priscilla in English.

"Yes, of course."

"Any news?"

"No . . . Sorry, Pris, I had to leave so early."

"No news from Fafreras?"

"No, none . . . There's nothing wrong at the Casa, is there? How is it you're already up?"

"I wanted to talk to you. I wanted to last night, Lorenzo. Didn't Isabel tell you?"

"Isabel? No . . . Sorry I had to stay up so late last night with Loyarte. Your lights were out when I turned in. Isabel? . . . She did say something about you, Pris . . . but I could swear she didn't breathe a word about your wanting to see me."

"Where will you be during the day?"

Like a third party answering Doña Priscilla's strangely rushed voice, there was a knock on the door. Upon Lorenzo's impatient "Come in!" the orderly peeped into the room.

"Aren't you alone, Lorenzo?" Priscilla asked.

"I am . . ." he said, at once chasing the man back with a scowl.

"Don't you know where you'll be?"

"There'll be a meeting shortly. You better call back, Pris."

"What time?"

"In the early afternoon. Listen, Pris, I was just trying—"

"Where? Where do you want me to call back?"

"De la Torre barracks."

"Fafreras—"

"No, there's nothing yet."

"He's got time till tonight, hasn't he?"

"Yes," he said, his voice dropping low. He was staring at the door.

"Could you reach him before that?"

"I reach him?"

"Can't I talk to you sooner than in the early afternoon?"

"Ah, did your fairy queen pop up at last?" he asked with a little gasp.

"Who?"

"The Gracián girl. Did she?"

"I said I must talk to you."

"What is it, Pris?" As no further word came, he added that he would give her a ring as soon as he could.

"I'll be waiting, Lorenzo."

"Don't worry, Pris," he said, raising his voice to overcome the flurry of embarrassment that her last words, inexplicably, called forth in him, "everything will come out all right in the end. Look, nothing *real* can happen to us. I've seen to that myself in time. . . . And now, will you do me a favor, Pris? It's Ramón. Could you tell him to come here at once? He must wait for me. Yes, here. Will you tell him that?"

She said she would.

"And don't go out," he called into the telephone, "don't leave the Casa before you hear from me."

"I'll be waiting," she repeated, and he hung up, contemplating for well over another minute the receiver, whose handle had been clouded by his touch. Then he got up to open the door.

The orderly clicked his heels.

Where were the señores who had been here?

"Gone, Your Excellency," the man said. "They will be back."

The clatter of well-shod hooves called His Excellency to the window. A squad of mounted police, riding in twos, was coming out on to the Plaza. They carried carbines, holding them stiffly propped against the front pommel of their saddles. They trotted past the high green-white-blue platform in the center of the square, empty at this hour, and swung off in the direction of the Palace.

Some of the shops were already open for business; and their owners came forward from the shadows of the vaulted-over sidewalk, to throw a long look at the horsemen. A bevy of schoolchildren in tattered pinafores dashed out of the lane which had emitted the riders, and from afar watched them break ranks. A little aproned old man in front of the right-corner café put down the two cane chairs he had brought out, cocked his head, and took them back again into the house.

'Ramón . . . yes, Ramón!' Lorenzo said to himself, 'Ramón must go and get Philibert. The two are old acquaintants. They will get on well. I should have sent him a week ago to fetch Philibert. Still it isn't too late. Ramón must leave tonight.' No man on earth was more devoted to him, and few as determined to carry out orders.

Well, Loyarte was—and as of last night, with good reason, too! But he was needed here. . . . Lorenzo took out his wallet. He let his fingers run through the bank notes. Plenty. About a third of it should be plenty. Ramón would bribe the engineer with it easily, and have plenty left to buy tickets for himself and Philibert. . . . How long would it take Ramón to bring back his charge? Three days? Four? . . . Time aplenty in any case to inform the padre at Casaquiara! The thought of shipping Philibert to the monastery—to join his obstreperous countryman there—had come to Lorenzo as he was going to bed late last night; and to his comfort, this solution looked as sound in the light of the day as it had done in the dark. To Casaquiara with Philibert! Still . . . all sorts of things could be imagined happening within four, or even three, days. Things money could not be relied on to mend. Take, for instance, a stopping of the trains of the Majamarca-Huacho Railroad. Take only that . . .

Down below, a wagon drawn by an ill-matched team of oxen rattled over the cobbles. The children had disappeared. A group of employes of Government House was making for its portal.

All sorts of things, all sorts of things . . . In briefing Ramón, some emergency instructions must be added. "Very definite instructions," Don Lorenzo repeated, talking aloud through set teeth, as if to prove himself the earnestness of his maturing resolve. In case events in Huacho went in the wrong direction, Philibert must not be brought here. Nor must he stay out East, not even with Ramón watching his every step. Ramón would be quick to grasp the alternative orders.

Turning, Lorenzo felt a ripple of hesitancy creep over his icy decision. It was as though the final defeat of M. Philibert were arousing in him some new sympathy for the man whose last message—that overbearing, petulant, blackmailing letter—had imbued him with nothing but coldness. Sympathy? Nonsense! M. Philibert's defeat was irrevocable, whichever way the tide was to turn his protector's fortunes. It was final . . . and any finality was akin to the most irrevocable of all. It was as good as death. But for all this sophistry, Lorenzo did not relish the image of M. Philibert's end at the hands of Ramón—nor of the new blood spilled (as mercenary souls well might presume) over the old German treasure.

"To hell, to hell . . ." mumbled its present owner, breaking the current of his grisly imaginings. How late was it? He stood in front of his desk. He had just lifted the clock, without looking at it, when a din in the anteroom made him whirl round, to face the Minister of the Interior.

But instead of discharging the news that alone could explain his unbridled haste, Don Basilio took Lorenzo's arm, while with his other hand he beckoned behind him, apparently urging someone outside to quicken his steps.

"What is it? What happened?" Lorenzo called out. He felt Gonzales' short breath against his cheek, so close to his own was the purpled face, and then, beyond the wildly fluttering hand of the mountainous man, he saw the Finance Minister walk in.

He pulled the door shut with almost ironic composure.

"What happened?" Don Basilio echoed at last with profound indignation. "His broadcasts are attacking the Palace!"

"Fafreras?"

"Fafreras. He asks for *his* resignation—"

"The President's?"

"Fafreras contends that a chief executive incapable of protecting the life of a distinguished citizen—"

"Meaning El Huérfano," the Finance Minister threw in. A wry grin warped the small man's patrician face.

"I quote. 'A distinguished citizen hundreds of thousands pin their hope on'—Fafreras contends that such a chief executive has forefeited the right to his office, together with his entire Cabinet!"

"Did *you* not expect it?" the Minister of Finance addressed Lorenzo, who, unhooking his arm from Gonzales, faced his learned colleague with fascinated attention.

"I told you he didn't expect it," exclaimed Don Basilio, openly disgusted with the phlegm of the Finance Minister who had repeated his query. "Or *did* you, Don Lorenzo? If you did, if you really foresaw this insanity in Fafreras, then . . . then, by the Virgin, you did appallingly little to stem its outbreak. . . ."

Lorenzo had to support himself. Groping for the edge of the desk, he upset some of the metal knickknacks, which fell, like a peal of laughter, into the voices of the two gentlemen who had come with the incredible tidings. The realization of the full extent of Fafreras' audacity threatened to stop Lorenzo's heartbeat.

Incredible tidings? . . . Forgotten, ah forgotten—throughout these months he had forgotten the beginning, the true beginning of it all! He had forgotten that the person who gave birth to the thought of Fafreras' Majamarca command had been Fafreras himself! And he, Lorenzo, had allowed his delight in his own resource to erase from his mind the chance remark of Fafreras that had set the ball rolling. It had not been more than a light word, in one of their first talks in May, about the great charms of life in the Eastern province, which he, alas, had never had the privilege to enjoy. . . . Chance remark indeed! While boldly reminding the newly appointed Minister of his recent exile out East, Fafreras had implanted deliberately in his head the idea of sending "good old Fafreras" to Majamarca. He had played upon his superior's self-evident dislike for the kingmaker's continual presence in Huacho. He had played on his vanity. . . . What the señor had wanted was to prepare for his coup freed from any shadow of surveillance.

Thus it had been! The great coup had been on Fafreras' mind from the first. But unlike any of the ambitious colonels of bygone days, he had not enlisted the Huacho officers' corps to do the spadework for his putsch. He had bypassed the caballeros. He had bypassed the whole Army, pursuing his own, unheard-of, sinister, frivolous path. He had played the game of the Night-in-the-Palace group, lent it the weight of his age and rank, and bestowed upon it the fame of a formidable junta. He had endeared himself to the Palace through the modesty with which he—a mestizo risen from the ranks—pretended to further the ascendancy of a Requesens and watch the General's mantle being thrown round Requesens' shoulders. His, Fafreras', ambition had gone beyond it.

How clear was everything now, how crystal clear! Fafreras had entered Majamarca in June with the fixed design of winning over to himself the mob and its leader. Perhaps he had even himself invited El Huérfano to come East! Having made his pact with him, and conquered the mob through his fantastic scheme, that success had brought his officers into his fold. His shrewdness, his daring, the modernity of his plan, had conquered them. Nonetheless he might have postponed his coup. He might have recoiled from violence, and before striking out for his goal, tried to swerve the allegiance of the rest of the Army by underhanded means. The demand, surely bruited about, for the "undivided air force" had precipitated his direct assault. How clear, how trenchantly clear was everything now to Lorenzo! And how remote from his conjectures after overhearing the silly talk at the Club!

The two gentlemen had fallen silent. They seemed to withdraw from Lorenzo. Not altogether without the satisfaction of all bearers of shocking news, they watched his open consternation.

No sound came from him. What mortified Lorenzo was not the roguery, now unmasked, of Fafreras. It was the realization of his own blindness. His self-love, his conceit, and the never-tiring indulgence toward the picture he had drawn of himself, had befogged his vision throughout these months. He had lied to himself all the time.

XXXI

So STAGGERING A blow dealt to his self-assurance might have crushed many another man. It did not crush Lorenzo Requesens. At ten o'clock he could be seen, as he emerged from the Palace, bristling with energy.

The magnitude of his responsibilities must have restored it. The Army had been ordered to reinforce all police patrols. It was to guard the municipal entries of all highways, the two railroad depots, and the building which housed the broadcasting station. Notwithstanding his administrative subordination to the Ministry of the Interior, the Chief of Police had been advised to co-operate with Army headquarters set up, as of this moment, at the De la Torre barracks.

True, the President had postponed his decision on the state of siege. He had also rejected once more Lorenzo's plan of an immediate offensive; and even his suggestion that the air force would refrain from overt hostilities over Majamarca, merely staging a demonstration, had not changed Dr. Zapeta's negative attitude. He had, however, not objected to the security measures suggested by his Minister of War. Barbed wire was to be thrown around the Palace grounds, and a platoon of cavalry detailed there forthwith. And similar drastic precautions were to be taken with no delay in regard to all Government buildings and legations. True again, the Chief Executive had reserved for himself all future decisions about the use of large units of the armed forces. But Lorenzo felt confident that the course steered by the rebel in Majamarca would soon bring about what his own persuasion had failed to accomplish in open meeting.

Standing in the glaring light of the forenoon between the two Grecian pillars of the main entrance of the Palace, Lorenzo was flanked on one side by Colonel Villaroel—that new "commander" of the Majamarca garrison had been cooling his heels on the premises since the small hours—and, on the other, by the C.O.'s of the Sixteenth and the Third, who had both been summoned there as the meeting drew to its end. Behind them, a cluster of gaudy subalterns reduced to shadowy shapes the civilian Cabinet officers on the portico.

The handful of onlookers admitted to the gate observed Don Lorenzo speaking to the colonels at his elbow. He seemed oblivious of the Palace flunkies in earshot, so little did he lower his voice. The one figure that caught the spectators' eyes except for the military was the Chief of Police. Clad in immaculate white, stocky, chary of gestures, he stood next to Basilio Gonzales. In silence the two watched Requesens being driven off with his colonels while Villaroel was staying behind.

Silence also hovered over the three occupants of the limousine which rolled down the soft slope of the driveway. At the gate, the chauffeur checked the car to a second's standstill; and the three señores exchanged a forced glance of amusement at the antics of the mounted policeman who made his horse rear and paw the cobbles as he saluted. Then the automobile moved along the southern edge of the Plaza.

The sun in the speckless sky tinged the cool flagstones of the arcades. The groups of little swarthy men loitering on the sidewalks stirred a little at the approach of the car, staring at it with awe, or turning their backs. Children were buzzing about. Women emptied their pails in the gutter. Old men peeked from the shelter of black doorways. The smoke of smoldering charcoal drifted from back yards into the street.

As Requesens stepped out of the limousine in front of Government House, the tones of a string orchestra emanating somewhere from a loudspeaker at an opened window rose over the ordinary hum of the square; and this symptom of the unperturbed spirits of the official broadcasting station caused the two staff officers to return the contented nod of His Excellency. His placid expression cushioned their surprise at his asking them to proceed to the barracks without him.

His plan was ready. He must have his talk with Ramón before repairing to headquarters. The Majamarca-bound train was leaving at noon. He must inform Priscilla he could not possibly see her in the early afternoon. And he must get in touch with Loyarte at last. With Don Basilio and the Finance Minister in his office till the three of them left for the meeting, Lorenzo had not been able to communicate with his aide. He surely was burning with zeal to make his report: calling up at the appointed time, he seemed to have been advised that his master was at the Palace, for he had ventured to call over its wires; but Don Lorenzo had been in no position to step out of the President's chambers. These, then, were the three jobs he had made up his mind to attend to between the four walls of his office, undaunted by the early morning's cruel experience.

He did talk to Ramón. He briefed him most carefully. He handed him the envelope with the halves of the bills, and gave him more cash than he would need. He was closeted with the eunuch for almost half an hour. Then he spent at least another ten minutes in futile attempts to have his A.D.C. located at the airdrome. As to the intended conversation with his wife, it did not come off. For at eleven o'clock the troubles destined to taint this sorry twenty-third of August removed from his immediate cares all thoughts about Doña Priscilla.

It is significant of the confusion of this day that the silliest story of all came to Government House with the very first reports of new unrest. This story had it that ten, or twenty, or a hundred, of the inmates of Payapán, the leprosarium two hundred and fifty miles away to the north, had broken out of their compound, and forced their way on to the Huacho-bound night train. The truth of the matter was that a band of vagrants, Army deserters and beggars—"fourth class passengers"—after making a nuisance of themselves on that train, had been apprehended at Carjavel Station, locked up in a shed, and now were frightening the curious, quick to assemble before its barred windows, with their shouts and grimaces.

The police—an Army patrol arrived only much later—were hesitant to remove these prisoners, for no conveyances were at hand, and rumors about a brawl gathering momentum in one of the market squares they would have to cross on their march to the municipal prison had, by that time, reached Carjavel Station.

In that market, a score or so of women, haggling with some of the venders, had upset their baskets and flimsy stalls, and begun to obstruct the efforts of the lone constable on duty there to restore order. While this squabble was going on, a knot of ruffians (to use the language of officialdom) appeared on the scene and flung the news of El Huérfano's attempted assassination into the scrimmage.

It is a matter for wonder that the news did not reach the populace of the capital at a much earlier hour. Huacho Broadcasting Station was throughout the morning far from effective in its endeavors to jam the Voice of the People. But in 1945 whole neighborhoods could not boast of a single wireless set, and few of those which common people owned could be tuned to an out-of-town transmitter.

Be that as it may, once in the open, the agonizing news set the demonstrators in motion with the speed of an arrow released by a crossbow —or rather, a bundle of arrows shot out at random in rapid succession. El Huérfano's rescue from the murderous onslaught became known at once; but the deathly peril that had passed him by made his followers doubly aware of their love and inflamed their passions. Gangs sprang into action at widely separated spots in no time. Some of them —such as the "ruffians" darting to the support of those marketing women—had no arms save their fists and their uncouth howlings. Others, streaming from the archways of the Old City or the taverns of the northern slums, brandished machetes, axes, clubs, or huge knives. Not many carried pistols or guns.

Only about four hours later, when an intoxicated crowd, driven from the Old City, invaded the new residential section from its western end, stoned windows, and threatened to storm the Plaza, did the explosion of many firearms rend the air.

However, by that time the "throbbing heart of the Republic" had already been made impregnable. Chevaux-de-frise barred its every approach. Machine guns had been placed on a number of roofs. An entire company of the Sixteenth was deployed under the arcades. And the muzzles of automatic rifles lurking behind half-drawn curtains of the upper storeys of many buildings controlled the whole expanse of the square.

Yet neither in those crucial afternoon hours nor during the incipient phase of the disorders was anything like a revolutionary strategy to be noted. Public utilities suffered, on the whole, only such harm as was caused by wildcat walk-outs. The centers of communication did not appear to attract the mobs. Each one operated on its own. They had no common objective. No one purpose channelled their emotions. Perhaps they resented the absence of the functionaries of the People's Party, but the cries for their liberation, heard here and there, nowhere called forth a march upon their rumored place of detention.

What more than anything else robbed the rioters of a common goal was the gruesome mystery shrouding El Huérfano's assassin. According to the Voice of the People, the kicks and blows of those who witnessed the crime had pulped his face beyond all hope of identification. Hearsay about his identity grew by the minute. Now it was "the rich" who were supposed to have hired the gunman, now Requesens; the names of foreign legations were bandied about liberally; and in at least one cantina it was at one time maintained that Fafreras, at loggerheads over his Presidential aspirations with El Huérfano, had in cold blood arranged for his murder. The statement of the legitimate radio that the lynched assassin had been "a person of Communist affiliations" counted for naught in this turmoil of conjectures.

Thus completely in the dark as to their political aim, the revolters took to looting. They smashed the hastily put-up shutters of suburban shops, burst into them, emptied their shelves in a trice, and scared the wits out of the tradesmen, who quite often could be seen standing in a daze long after the plunderers had taken themselves to new pastures. In some of the embattled lanes, parts of the loot—welters of yard-goods, smashed crockery, splintered glassware, or cans trampled on and bent into fantastic shapes—were tossed on the pavement in a wanton lust for destruction. In vain did a handful of sober men, with dwindling vociferations, try to instill some revolutionary decorum into the waxing savagery of these scenes.

At 12:20 martial law was proclaimed. But how many of the frenzied offenders, one may well ask, heard the announcement while they were gutting some mart, cavorting about some booth set afire, or falling back, their eyes smarting and their shrill yells choked, before the fumes of a tear gas cartridge hurled at them by a desperate constable? Also, coming while the calamity was not yet being dealt with concertedly and on the large scale it called for, the Government broadcast may have sounded like a confession of fear to those who bothered to listen to it. Far from staying the lawlessness, it stoked its flames.

Rushing from one spot of disaster to another, outnumbered everywhere, the police were more often than not reluctant to interfere with the mobs. Only a few of them were equipped with tear gas pistols. Clubs were of small avail. Its fury fanned by the sight of cracked skulls, crazed by the shrieks of the women, the rabble closed in with amazing skill on the patrols. In several places, they were disarmed before they could—this was Gonzales' directive—discharge their revolvers over the heads of the attackers. Some policemen were manhandled, spit at, and ignominiously stripped. More were cut by machetes, not a few severely wounded. A couple of mounted inspectors had their horses knifed under them. At least five officers were shot in the northern sector of the town in these first hours. One died.

The Army detachments, joining the battle only belatedly in the most troubled areas and in insufficient numbers in most, sallied forth, wielding the butts of their rifles. Wherever the rioters were swaying back, the soldiers at once formed live chains. Even in the teeth of ever more bloody clashes, these brave men stuck to their orders to keep the scum from approaching the Plaza. In this they succeeded. But at what cost to life and limbs! At what an appalling price . . .

Afterwards, a great deal of the guilt for what the foreign press has called "the most shameful spectacle in the history of the Republic" was placed upon Lorenzo Requesens. It was said that the lack of timely communication between him and Army headquarters threw the President's strategy into a jumble; and it was implied that nothing but despicable cowardice kept the erstwhile Victor of Murcia from defying, on his road to the barracks, the dangers in the narrow streets of the Old City.

Now, even if one is to assume that he did not have the heart to expose his limousine to wild knots of men inflamed against him, the much-criticized delay in his leaving Government House cannot be accounted for by such a theory. For, acting of his own accord, the colonel of the Third dispatched one of its three armored cars from the barracks to fetch Requesens. It pulled up in front of Government House at eleven-thirty; and its grey-green top was under Lorenzo's eyes for most of the period of his indecision.

At eleven-fifteen, and then again at eleven-forty-five, Dr. Zapeta notified his Ministers that he would assemble them at the Palace again "shortly." Meanwhile he had summoned Gonzales for the final drafting of the state-of-siege proclamation. From that meeting, he called Lorenzo on the telephone to discuss some technical points involved. After Gonzales' return to Government House, Lorenzo asked for an immediate audience with the President. He was told that the President was conferring with the chief dignitaries of the municipality.

Already the confusion at Government House mirrored the chaos in the streets. Cabinet members could be seen flinging open the doors of their offices and vestibules at the merest sound of footfalls, dashing up and down the great staircase, secretaries behind them, or berating subordinates on frivolous pretexts. The clerks supposed to tabulate the incoming reports about the *tumultos*—that was the belittling term officially adopted—thought nothing of passing on what they learned, distorted by fancy or awe, to strangers who buttonholed them in the corridors. But what they did not hear alarmed the officials as much as what they heard. One thing they did not hear, while pandemonium was breaking loose, was the Voice of the People. It stopped its broadcasts at eleven. And since the Majamarca police had already ceased to communicate with the Ministry of the Interior earlier in the morning, no one could say exactly what was happening out there. On the other hand, it was—on the strength of scattered news—presumed that the Northwest was perfectly calm.

Meanwhile headquarters sought orders from Lorenzo. At twelve-fifty-five his patience was at its end. He lost his temper when the young aide at the Palace switchboard kept repeating that the President was "in conference." Finally he had Lorenzo talk to Colonel Villaroel. Did the President not realize that utter ruthlessness must follow the declaration of martial law? He did, said Villaroel; and the President would get in touch with headquarters "any minute now" . . . would Don Lorenzo be there? Lorenzo retorted that, like his colleagues at Government House, he had been waiting for the call to the Palace! For seventy solid minutes! He wanted the President to know that he for one had made up his mind to send two battalions into the northern suburbs. Salvos must be fired, machine guns brought into action, artillery, if need be, field-howitzers—

At this moment the two gentlemen were cut off. The line had gone dead. And the outcries resounding throughout the building in the following seconds disclosed the catastrophe (if not yet its full extent) which was to top the tribulations of Huacho officialdom on this never-to-be-forgotten twenty-third of August. Providence was *not* on Lorenzo's side! Only five minutes before his unsatisfactory talk with Villaroel—that is, ten minutes before the general breakdown of the telephone service—had he succeeded in getting the lieutenant colonel to the telephone at Carjavel; and the man had *sworn* he would find Captain Loyarte and have him call back His Excellency immediately.

(Subsequent investigations have established that the breakdown—which lasted for well over an hour—was not the result of sabotage. An accident, only partly caused but certainly aggravated by the panicky atmosphere that seized the personnel of the telephone company, paralyzed its wires. For years, graft had hindered the necessary overhauling of the company's machinery.)

Afterwards, Requesens' detractors at Government House loved to describe his inexplicable, his "altogether perverse" demeanor amid the "indescribable imbroglio" engendered by the collapse of outside communications. "There he stood," those critics were to say, pointing toward the oversized bust of the Liberator on the upper landing of the first-floor staircase, "his cap on his head, his revolver in his belt, all ready to leave. There he stood, two trembling armchair subalterns at his side (for his own A.D.C., this León Loyarte, as you may have heard yourself, was occupied elsewhere) . . . there he stood, and guess what he was doing! Lighting a cigar, if you please. Most carefully. Protecting the little flame of his British lighter against the draft. You simply cannot imagine the commotion in the whole building. It was Bedlam, friend, Bedlam! And he turning his back on it all! Literally Long after he had lighted his cigar, with his head stuck into the nook between the bust and the wall . . . long after that he still stood there, peacefully watching the smoke of his stogy rebound from the marble. It was obscene, I'm telling you. Obscene . . . Maybe he was collecting his courage in those ten or fifteen minutes—maybe. Maybe he was cooking up his unspeakable scheme in cold blood. Maybe he was just temporizing. And no consideration for the common man! Imagine, six or eight soldiers all that time had to line the three-meter stretch from the portal to the armored car waiting for him . . . and at that time scores of bullets had already come over from where the fighting went on beyond the Palace, ricocheting against the pavement. Stray bullets, I admit. Still . . ."

Another detail which observers indulging such fatuous afterthoughts would add to the puzzling portrait of the Requesens of that hour originated with the artillery sergeant at the wheel of the armored car. In recounting his nerve-wracking experience, this man would insist that Requesens first ordered him to drive up to the Palace. Then, about halfway across the Plaza, he asked the man to stop and inquired how long he reckoned it would take him to get to Carjavel Airfield. That, in the words of the artillery sergeant, was "a question none but the Evil One could have answered at that moment, with barricades known to have been thrown up in some alleys of the northern suburbs, and the débris of fallen masonry *this* high in some! It is not often," the man would go on with understandable pride, "that a simple non-com doesn't answer a question put to him by the War Minister. But that is what I did, friend, though he repeated his query four or five times, and not in a soft voice either, before he directed me to proceed to the barracks by the shortest route—which wasn't so short either, as it turned out, though the real clashes in the Old City were still to come then. . . ."

Contradictory though Requesens' orders sounded to the sergeant—then or later—they were yet dictated by one and the same purpose. A master plan had ripened in his mind, and he meant to carry it through.

If Dr. Zapeta, hiding his innate weakness under a cloak of leniency, still hesitated to bring into play all the ruthlessness at the disposal of the lawful powers, he, Lorenzo, was determined at last to unleash all its might. The task was more than the squelching of the stupid upheaval at hand. Brainless as it was, it was the vanguard of Fafreras. To put it down brutally, drown it in rivers of blood—this alone could deter Fafreras from going ahead, from mobilizing the barbarity of the Eastern masses, from coming here with his army! To dishearten the rabble in Majamarca, the Huacho rabble must get more than it had bargained for. It must get its fill of lead. Not in vain had he, Lorenzo Requesens watched from a Messerschmitt—nearly six years ago—the Warsaw rabble scamper like chickens. From above, from the sky, lead and fire must come down on the scum! This done, the town would be in the hollow of his hand. And so would the Palace.

The cigar in Lorenzo's mouth had gone out. Ensconced between his two subalterns, he glimpsed the devastation outside through the loophole in the armor. The smell of some burning hovels hung over the maze of the Old City. The foul odor seems to have pleased Don Lorenzo. He is said to have laughed out loud when the acrid smoke began to draw tears from his eyes.

But there is a certain amount of disagreement about his conduct on the ride. Two witnesses, or even (counting the driver) three, cannot be expected to establish historical truth. It is different with the telephone conversation Requesens had with Carjavel directly upon his arrival at the De la Torre barracks. The accidental wire-tapping resulting from the efforts of the telephone company to repair its apparatus gave to this talk—the first one to come off after the breakdown—any number of aural witnesses.

They all concur that Requesens' outburst, when he was told his A.D.C. could still not be located, defies imagination. And almost all of them maintain that he did not check his rage in the least on being informed that Loyarte had been driven off in an ambulance—an incident of whose peculiar nature he could not possibly have any knowledge at that instant—though his wrath abated somewhat after the lieutenant colonel relieved the ill-used non-com at the switchboard,

T

and asked for His Excellency's orders.

About them, those in the know speak only in whispers today. It appears that Requesens wanted a squadron—old planes, or new ones —to take off at once and machine-gun all centers of rioting as well as all spots "likely to become such." It also appears that he talked about a load of incendiary bombs stored at the barracks, and which he would get through to Carjavel in the armored cars, to be used in a second sortie, a third, a fourth. . . . Even so scrupulous an organ of contemporary history as Huacho's great newspaper did not print the whole story. It spread a veil of merciful inaccuracy over the blood-curdling details of that command. Thus it came about that the reply of the lieutenant colonel—"Will Your Excellency be kind enough to have the orders confirmed for me by the Palace?"—has not obtained, in the memory of his compatriots, the supreme place it deserves.

XXXII

Loyarte had been on his feet at six o'clock.

The first memory to come to his mind was the notion of that weird kinship to the equivocal first lieutenant. But on his way to the breakfast table of the lieutenant colonel, who had asked for his company, he already felt a renewed determination to do well by his task.

The commander of the air force did not inquire why he had spent the night at Carjavel. He was kindly and quite frank. He gave a brief outline of the security measures his staff had devised, and even showed Loyarte a sketch of the deployment of the sentries—"almost a cordon"—to take effect as of this hour. Would the captain, upon his return to His Excellency, assure him that the preparedness which he had demanded from all and sundry was a reality at Carjavel? The matter-of-fact faithfulness such talk implied gave Don León satisfaction. But no sooner did he mention the "unshakable confidence prevailing at the War Ministry," or, "Don Lorenzo's impatience to have the crisis done with in order to be untrammeled at last in his reform work," than the sobriety of the lieutenant colonel seemed to chill his own fervor.

A kind of instruction program was in progress on the airfield. Three of the new machines had been towed up to the runway; and there the old pilots had each assembled some of the young señores. There was a definite informality about their activities. The lieutenant colonel, who had stepped outside with León, did not comment on them. Soon he left him to himself.

León strolled forward. One by one, or in pairs, some of the caballeros came up to him, wished him a good morning, and inquired about the latest news. He said he didn't know more than anyone else did out here. On several occasions he started talking with studied lightness about the future wellbeing of them all. "Remember our situation four or even three months ago," he would say. "Being a subaltern officer was a hopeless occupation then, was it not? And so," he would go on with a smile meant to signify the ludicrousness of the mere idea, "so it would be again without Don Lorenzo."

The officers he talked to agreed. Their assent sounded oddly uninterested. Yet, in León's mind, it belied the image of their nocturnal gathering and challenged him to display the full strength of his passion. But whatever emotion was in him refused to transform itself into the force which his reason demanded.

At about eight o'clock the news of Fafreras' radio attack on the Palace reached the airdrome. From all Don León observed, it did not have the effect of a thunderbolt. Some of the young officers accused him, half teasingly, of having kept them in the dark. Others declared they had foreseen this development in the crisis; and pride in their alleged perspicacity appeared to supersede, for the time being, all other feelings. Also, everybody was called back to duty. The example of the imperturbable lieutenant colonel admonished everybody that this latest turn asked for still greater coolheadedness and discipline.

When León went to the telephone at nine, he imagined vividly the eagerness of Don Lorenzo to receive his report. Fafreras' flinging down the gauntlet to Dr. Zapeta could, on the one hand, be expected to strengthen the ties between him and Requesens. On the other, the men Requesens relied on most were at the same time those who still burned to have the disgrace of the Night-in-the-Palace avenged—a desire he had himself frustrated; and Requesens could not but fear that the bold attack of Fafreras on Dr. Zapeta might exert upon them a dangerous fascination. Don Lorenzo's question would no doubt be very explicit . . . and he, León, would not know how to answer it.

After being told, at Government House, where Requesens was, León let some time lapse before calling up the Palace. Don Lorenzo's failure to come to the telephone there did not trouble him. The aide on duty had no message for him. León understood him to assume that "His Excellency would get in touch with the señor captain on the conclusion of the meeting."

How the señor captain spent the subsequent hour was, later on, a matter of some wonderment to himself. He was to talk a great deal about Providence in relating to anyone willing to listen the story of his "instinctive decision" to remain at Carjavel. Of the instinct which

kept him most of the time away from the administration building and
its telephone, he was to talk less. At any rate he would, in those later
days, never omit a description of how "flabbergasted" he was as the
incident destined to influence the whole course of his life broke his
"involuntary idleness" on that morning.

He had just been sidling up to a knot of ground crew men about to
be equipped with carbines—another of the measures decided on in
great calm—when a motorcycle, driven fast, overtook him. He recognized at once the handsome lieutenant, his interlocutor of the past
night, who, riding in the side-car, was standing up and shouting at
him.

"You are wanted, Don León," he called out over the roar of the running motor of the nearby plane, and tapping his ears, beckoned to
Loyarte to step farther away from it. While León followed the request,
the lieutenant leaped out of the side-car and joined him. Still forced to
keep his voice raised, he explained that, being on duty at the gate, he
had had to deal with "this motorized sergeant." Although the man's
demand made little sense, the lieutenant had yielded to his entreaties
to find the señor *ayudante* for him.

Meanwhile the motorcyclist had dismounted. His bearing revealed
the professional soldier. He had a fantastic story to tell—so at least the
lieutenant was exclaiming, while León kept interrupting both men
with his questions.

Had the sergeant said he was needed? Where, *por Dios?*

The señor captain was needed at Carjavel Station. Among a band
of disreputable railroad passengers arrested this morning by the police,
there was one character who insisted he had some special business with
His Excellency, Don Lorenzo Requesens. The police, so the sergeant,
an intelligent man, went on, shaking his head, had paid that odd fellow
no heed. Most likely they had not even grasped what he said amid the
hubbub of those cursed lepers—

Lepers? Not lepers!

Not really lepers, the sergeant replied to the horrified outcry. Their
being fugitives from Payapán was nothing more than an ugly rumor
the police should have disproved to begin with. The police! As he was
saying, they simply ignored the fellow's request to be taken to His
Excellency on urgent business. Only upon the arrival of the Army detachment was attention paid to his clamor.

This was the point at which the two officers obtained knowledge of the security measures in operation throughout the town. The motor-cyclist also mentioned the disorder which had started "in one of the markets." But he did not dwell on this news. He proceeded to report that the captain in command of the detachment at the depot had questioned the obnoxious man, and had done what he could to communicate with His Excellency. But first His Excellency had been absent from his office, and then his telephone had been busy all the time—

"And what makes your captain think that the man has anything of consequence to relay to His Excellency?"

"That I do not know, señor captain," said the sergeant, squinting from León to the lieutenant and back again. "I merely know that someone in our squad happened to know that you were here at the airfield, sir. And so my captain sent me here to fetch you. He ordered me to tell you he did not want to neglect anything."

The first lieutenant broke in again. He had been listening with sharp attentiveness, his eyes returning to León all the time. "What *is* the business that vagabond asserts he has with the Minister?" he inquired.

"That is exactly it, señor lieutenant. That is it. He says nothing. Nothing except that my captain would regret it if he didn't get him to the Minister."

"And why doesn't he?" asked León.

"His words are that he'd leave the decision to you, sir."

"Ah, to me . . ." Surely the sergeant's captain had no right to give orders to him, no matter how flatteringly veiled! It was plain that he desired to pass on a responsibility.

"*Ayudante, ayudante . . .*" mumbled the lieutenant in an annoying singsong.

León looked at the sergeant, while he tried to twist his lips into a smile, to return the grin on the face of the lieutenant. No, this comrade-in-arms did not mean well. To ask for his opinion on the curious job offered here would lead nowhere. León could sense his reluctance to give advice. He did not care to take him into his confidence . . . as they all no longer cared to take him into theirs. His mission with the Air Corps officers had gone on the rocks. There was no mission. . . . The affair at the railroad station was most probably inconsequential. Yet there was a mystery about it which could justify his hurrying there. And his hurrying there would later account for his absence from the airdrome. The prospect of absconding, of becoming unreachable to Requesens, affected León's imagination with the sweet force of a drug. . . . Yes! he would go away with this sergeant. . . . He stepped up to the motorcycle and climbed into the side-car. The sergeant, taken somewhat by surprise, followed.

The vehicle started, turned, and rushed off. The lieutenant perched on the edge of the side-car, half on León's lap, who uneasily grew aware of the physical closeness of the erstwhile history-maker and man of questionable sexual habits.

The lieutenant spoke no word. When the gate came into view, he hopped down; and León, turning his head a moment later, saw him standing arms akimbo, leaning irreverently against the white stone block, that memento of a happier morning. . . .

The Carjavel stop of the Northern Railway lies a fifteen-minute drive from the airfield, at the farthest northeastern outskirts of Huacho. The neighborhood in between, in long-bygone times a place of upper-class summer villas and vast gardens, is today inhabited by folk of slender purses and an orderly way of life: clerks, minor professional men, teachers, local tradesmen and priests, besides a fair number of those people without a country who were driven overseas by the ruthlessness of a Europe that yet is so quick to voice its superiority over the "eternally unsettled political conditions of Latin republics." That peaceful neighborhood, then, remained so around the eleventh hour of this far from peaceful day. No echo of the unbridled violence rampant elsewhere in town was heard as yet in the streets the motorcycle was passing.

The sergeant was as taciturn now as before he had been loquacious.

The first shouts that came to meet León from the direction of the station resounded doubly loud in the quietness. The sergeant leaned down to León to say that these cries originated in the goods shed. As the motorcycle came out on the small square separating the station from the last row of houses, a freight car concealed the railway buildings. A gang of adolescents stood atop one of the box cars, and reciprocated the profanity emanating from the locked-up "lepers."

The greater part of the bystanders—so the captain, a man much older than Loyarte, informed him even before the latter alighted from the side-car—had dispersed by now. The captain asked Don León to come with him, and they crawled through, under one of the couplings, to the other side of the train. A row of rural Indios was squatting on the loading ramp, gaping at the grilled windows of the shed, and with taunts baiting the police who were trying to silence the locked-up men.

With bigger forces at his disposal, the captain remarked, he would chase away these vermin. He would do more. He would make sure they didn't get into the town. But he had his hands full already, had he not? He talked in a doleful key which revealed his anxiety to shift to others the blame for whatever might tarnish his record. He guided León past a picket of soldiers behind the freight shed.

"How about this man, señor?"

"I shall take you to him presently," said the captain. He was ahead of León now, and began to pick his path over the four pairs of rails of the freight yard. Behind them the vociferations became louder; possibly the hoodlums in their makeshift prison had been restraining their emotions at the sight of the two officers.

León asked, "Did you not succeed in getting in touch with the Minister?"

No, said the captain, he had not been able to reach him.

"There?" León inquired, pointing at the signalman's cabin which was ten or twelve feet away.

"There."

"And what is your theory about the man, señor?"

"These are troubled days," the other replied. He had halted, and stooped to flick away some dirt from his trousers. "You never know, you never know. . . ."

"Is he the ringleader of the gang?"

"Ah, no! In fact, they seem to have given him a rough time, and perhaps he is fooling us and merely wants to get away from the gang."

"Why? Why did they give him a rough time?"

"He is a foreigner. Did my sergeant not tell you he was a foreigner?"

León shook his head. "Do you think that gang has anything to do with—"

"With what is going on? Probably. Possibly."

"With El Huérfano?"

"Quite so."

"But they've come from the North. . . ."

"These are troubled days, friend." Neither the captain's manner of speech nor his posture suggested that he took any interest in Loyarte's mounting uncertainty. "Shall we go?" he asked. "If you prefer to question him without me, he is all yours, of course."

Don León nodded, and the captain advanced and knocked at the door of the cabin.

Inside, the key was pushed into the lock. It turned with a heavy rattle.

The captive man inside rose from the stool in front of the signal switchboard. He was manacled. Had it not been for his shackles, the soldier detailed to guard him would have seemed absurd. In spite of his bayoneted rifle he looked like a sickly child.

"Open the shutters," the captain ordered, "and stay outside till you are called."

The prisoner was a tall man. The small brim of his felt hat hung low across his forehead, nearly covering his eyes. When the shutters were thrown back, the light caught a long jagged scar glistening silvery beneath the reddish stubble on his face.

"This," the captain said, "is the aide-de-camp of His Excellency the Minister. Do you know what an aide-de-camp is?"

"I do. I must talk to him. To the Minister himself. To the Minister, Don Lorenzo Requesens." He spoke with precision. His foreign accent did not blur the impression of some intelligence.

It was very warm, and there was a stench of rancid grease.

"He is all yours, then, señor . . ." said the captain, and as León, contemplating the prisoner, gave no reaction, he withdrew.

"I must talk to Don Lorenzo Requesens," the man declared again as soon as he was alone with León.

"What is your name?"

"Don Lorenzo Requesens knows my name very well."

"Where do you come from?"

Ehinger tightened his lips. His fettered hands made a motion of defiance and shame. The experiences of the past two and a half days had reduced his whole inner life to a single burning desire. He must see Requesens! His existence hinged on his seeing Requesens!

"If you really wish to be taken to the Minister," León said softly, "you have to tell me first—"

"I must see him," Ehinger cut him short, "and he must see me."

"He must? Aren't you being foolish, my good man?"

Ehinger said in a deliberate undertone, "There is business between us. Important business."

"Come now. Come, tell me more about it. Tell me who you are, how you've come to associate with that crew out there, what your request is. . . . Cigarette?"

"No," said Ehinger rudely. The quivering scowl of reflection on the officer's face began to fortify him. His dogged intention ruled out all subtlety. Yet he was able to reason. He assumed that Requesens himself had dispatched this aide. Irrespective of this revolt, Requesens had been alarmed by the news that a foreigner had arrived from the Northwest and demanded to be taken to him. "Time presses," he remarked after a slight pause. "It does, believe me, señor aide-de-camp."

León eyed the fellow's dirt-caked boots, his breeches of good cut and an indistinct color, and the rumpled khaki shirt whose one torn sleeve bared a tattoo in the hollow of the elbow. The menacing tenor of his last words had at the same time stiffened his backbone. León no longer thought him to be an outright impostor. No longer did he dismiss his "business" as a crank's fancy. The fellow was a foreigner. A foreigner with some undeniable marks of civilization. He could not be prevailed on to disclose the secret, pretended or true, he shared with Requesens; and though León did not consider making him talk through some of the sharper methods of police interrogation, he was fairly convinced such methods would fail. Most probably he had gone without sleep for days; it could be seen that he was half-starved; manacled, he was unable to fend off the flies preying on him and yet did not writhe or wince. He showed no sign of weakness. He had discipline. The discipline of a well-trained man. A trained revolutionist . . . It was not likely that he was the foreigner reported to be working as El Huérfano's adviser. But he could well belong to that man, could be one of his collaborators, one of the henchmen of El Huérfano.

Something in Requesens' condemnation of the frivolity of Fafreras had aroused in León the suspicion that he was not entirely free of envy. This had been only a fleeting thought in the past night. Now the thought was back. . . . Hadn't someone at the airdrome said the latest pronunciamiento of Fafreras treated El Huérfano more as a protégé than as a partner? What if a misunderstanding had arisen between the two? What if El Huérfano was prepared to desert Fafreras against some promise, change sides in the eleventh hour? It would be fantastic! But surely the fantastic was not to be ruled out as a possible determinant of the three-pronged struggle now underway.

León looked through the window. An ambulance was backing up close by. The undersized soldier, whose bayonet had been visible all the time, stepped up to the white-painted car and started to talk with its driver. The driver climbed down, shoved the little soldier aside, and went round to fling open the back door of the ambulance. León recognized the sergeant who had brought him here on the motorcycle. A small group of railroad workers had gathered at a distance. But no casualty such as would have justified these preparations was to be seen. "Look here, man," León said—their common silence had lasted only a moment—"I can't just take anyone to the Minister. His Excellency is a very busy person."

Ehinger clicked his tongue. "Señor aide-de-camp, I may just as well let you know this. His Excellency will not be busy for long if he refuses to see me. This I may just as well let you know."

León gazed at the large red cross painted on the ambulance door. By now he attached true importance to the affair. The fellow had drawn closer. "I warn you," León said, turning, "I warn you. In case your so-called business with the Minister proves to be without interest to him—"

"It will not!"

". . . without interest to him, His Excellency is sure to become very angry, and this would have the most painful consequences for you. The most painful consequences . . . It would be different if you'd let *me* know first. . . ." The sentence died away half-spoken. It had occurred to León that to know what the man's business with Requesens was—if such there existed—might give him, León, power beyond the authority of an aide; and this thought, while making him try again to pump the stranger, came to him as an ambiguous incentive.

But Ehinger was deaf to persuasion and threats. He kept silent, and while Loyarte still spoke, walked to the door.

"Stand back, will you?" León shouted at him. Then he went to open the door himself.

The captain was standing beside the ambulance. "I've made arrangements for you, señor," he called to León.

"What arrangements?"

The captain stepped up to him. In a lowered tone he said it was getting rather uncomfortable in some of the streets, especially near the tanneries. The only other car he had here was an open coach, and he was afraid it would be impossible to get through to the Plaza in it, especially with a handcuffed man—

Don León slammed the door in the face of the captive behind him. "Who told you, señor," he asked, "that I wanted to get through to the Plaza?"

"It's up to you. I only made proper arrangements."

"Near the tanneries, did you say?"

"And farther south, yes. But the driver is a good man. The best I've got out here. He will get through to the Plaza. He will." The pudgy face of the captain was flushed.

León perceived his anxiety to have the matter taken off his hands. Yet it was not his pressing voice that caused León to agree to the proposal. It was the account the captain gave of the incipient riots. His words belittled them. But his nervousness revealed the scope of the peril. And to León, that peril sharpened the urgency of his self-chosen task. This was the eleventh hour indeed!

But no sooner were he and his new charge and the wretched little soldier in the ambulance than his courage began to sink. What if Don Lorenzo disapproved of his arbitrary action? What if he was more interested in the morale of the Air Corps still than in whatever this tramp was to bring him? "Back to the airfield first!" he called through the peep hole to the driver.

"It is a detour, señor captain."

"You heard me!"

"Yes, señor captain," came the voice from outside. Then the driver sounded the siren.

León drew the curtain of the small window above the folding stool on which he was seated. He was facing the two men who sat on the edge of the stretcher.

The soldier was next to the door. He held his rifle between his legs. At every lurch, the berth overhead, swinging in its straps, caught the point of his bayonet; and whenever he freed it, he glanced up to the shackled man by his side, as if he expected to be commended on his skill.

But not once did he draw a response from the prisoner.

XXXIII

Now THAT HIS objective appeared to be within reach, Ehinger's fatigue threatened to overmaster his body. He had not slept a wink on his flight from Murcia. The intensity of his hopes, his fears, and his doubts, had worn him out to the point of numbness.

He did not know what actual harm the two shots that he had fired had done in the guest house at the hacienda. He had seen Bundschuh take a sudden leap away from the plank table, and had heard his shrieks rise over Juana's outcries. But while the reports of his shots had still lingered, a tremendous silence had followed, emphasized by the sudden darkness. The lamp, tumbling over, had gone out.

Ehinger's memory refused its services as to the ensuing seconds. Not for the life of him could he remember how he had pocketed the revolver, or groped his way out into the passage, or picked up the two rifles, or stepped out of the building. Nor did he know for how long he had been standing behind the aloe hedge, telling himself that the storm must have deadened the detonations (which was good) and that it was futile (this was bad) to listen, in that storm, for the approach of Jacinto's footfalls. His hope for flight and rescue was, in those minutes, still tied to the person of Jacinto. He did not dare to think of what had happened. Nor why it had.

The man who for years had been reigning over a place so horrid that the civilized world, shuddering at its discovery, was incapable of retaining in its consciousness the pictures of torture both brutish and subtle, of wanton carnage, and unrelieved misery; the man who had considered himself the proud servant of so vast and novel an enterprise it could not but dwarf all concepts of human pity; the man who had come to taste the power in its least diluted potion—and yet had been sober and calculating enough to worm his way out of mortal danger before the cup of power was drained—this man did not have the heart to think of the girl who had misused his own call for human warmth. He had avenged her betrayal. But the very passion of his vengeance seemed to lend to his murderous assault the aspect of a personal deed which had been absent from the whole range of atrocities perpetrated in the line of his duties.

A shadow of similar compunction had entered Ehinger's heart on the day he had disposed of Roy. But then, it had, after all, been reason which guided his decision. This time reason had been far from counseling murder. Ehinger was not the man to examine his misgivings. Their incomprehensible trenchancy frightened and stultified him.

At last he had crawled out from behind the hedge, and advanced. Several times he stumbled. He made sure to tread the damp grass on the edge of the path. He strained his ears. But nothing save the howl of the wind came to him. Then there was the gate before him, and the sounds of his steps on the gravel. He slunk on, on tiptoe. From the corner of his eye he saw the light in the casa—the candle abandoned an hour before by Bundschuh—and its gleam thrust on him the lurid notion that someone watched him from one of the windows. But after the first steps on the dirt road, this imagined menace began to provoke his sense of self-preservation. It was like a command. He stopped listening into the night for Jacinto. He must flee without him!

The sight of the lorry braced his bearing. Jacinto had left the ignition key in the dashboard. Ehinger started the motor. He put on the headlights after he had driven a mile or so. A slight rain was coming down, and its monotonous rustle on the canvas soothed his nerves. His intelligence told him that Jacinto, coming to the guest house at the appointed time, would not know how to grapple with the situation. Instead of sneaking away from whatever he was to detect, he would succumb to panic. He would call the capataz. He would confess in no time. They would rush out in pursuit of the fugitive. He must stay clear of the town. He must change his direction. He must do the least probable thing. He must go south.

To his good luck, one of the maps of Juana's father had shown the township of Murcia in great detail; and though he had of course relied upon Jacinto for the right road, he had—attaching much importance to the first lap of their journey—studied that map carefully. This stood him in good stead now. He reached the Ulloa highway without entering the outskirts of Murcia.

It was an accomplishment that fitted the other, the far greater resolve he had formed. . . . He must go to Requesens! Requesens must protect him! The rumored revolt only steadied Ehinger's determination. Experience had taught him that the great ones were more likely than usual to yield to requests and do favors when in trouble themselves. Further, Philibert was with Requesens. Sick or in good health, he was in Huacho. He too must extend his rescuing hand. Philibert could not, he would not let him down. He would, to be sure, no longer treat him as a companion and comrade. He would give him orders. So be it. The prospect of receiving the right orders—or any orders, for that matter—looked in itself like salvation to Ehinger.

He drove on at great speed. A few leagues south of Murcia he encountered the first vehicle on the road. It was an old high-wheeled automobile with a canvas top, and it halted in the dark, dimming its light, to let the truck pass by.

Ehinger did not stop before dawn. He checked his fuel: Jacinto had provided plenty. When he started again, the sun rose in a sudden burst. He was thirsty. He got himself a drink in the fifth pueblo he drove through. He overpaid the Indio.

It was in the afternoon that he met the men. He had stopped his car at the distant sight of a settlement, and was just reflecting whether to buy provisions in the store he surmised the village could boast of, when he noticed, about five hundred meters to his left, an outcropping of tents in a clearing. But while he still kept his eyes turned toward that curiously silent camp, he heard human voices from the other side of the highway. And less than a minute later, a group of fierce-looking men trickled out of the bush, their appearance preceded by the rhythmical swishing of their machetes. Some of the marauders jumped on the running boards of Ehinger's car, and thrust their hands into the spokes of the steering wheel.

He was paralyzed by fear. All in all, there were a dozen shapes surrounding the lorry by now, with some stragglers still hiding in the thicket. Three or four carried carbines, and as they approached, were raising them in a clumsy manner. They all seemed bent on keeping their voices low; and their curiously whispered ejaculations rendered more uncanny still their encircling movement. Finally the man closest to Ehinger, breaking the spell, began to talk coherently. At the same time he urged his comrades with unmistakable signs to climb into the truck. There was no need for explanations. Yet their spokesman insisted on telling their story.

It appeared that one of the absentee landowners of the neighborhood, embarking on some construction venture, had secured himself the illegal co-operation of the authorities in recruiting labor. Thus these men had been pressed into virtual servitude, and had ever since been "worse off than debt-ridden peóns." Shunned by the villagers, they had been at the mercy of four heavily armed overseers, who, not content with lording it over the workmen, had quarrelled among themselves all the time. This morning another such altercation had resulted in a fatality. And the three surviving guards, drunk as they were, had at once shown their intent to pin the incident on the workers. Anticipating the futility of remonstrating with the village alcalde, they thereupon summoned the courage that all the injustice suffered for months had not been able to kindle. They managed to lay hands on the guards and disarm them. Now, they had left them behind in the camp, bound and gagged, trusting the pitiless sun to complete their triumph.

How all that could have happened without the interference from the settlement situated a bare two miles away, and why the successful mutineers had been roaming its vicinity instead of taking to their heels —these were riddles the tale of their spokesman did not solve.

But it was not these riddles which beset Ehinger's mind as, in silent obedience to the two men now ensconced by his side, he drove along the dirt road they had indicated to him. He was wide awake to the great dangers which the incident was adding to his flight. A troop of seasonal laborers on the road had not been an unusual sight near the Bundschuh hacienda; why should it be elsewhere? His unbidden passengers might even serve to make him appear less conspicuous himself. They might . . . under normal conditions. But there was this revolt. Had an echo of it come to that slave camp and readied these simpletons for their mutiny? Was he, in other words, transporting rebels? If he was, this would rob him, in case he was caught, of all hope of obtaining Requesens' protection. It might finish him off before he'd ever get to Huacho!

As it was, the mutineers were ignorant of all events outside their pale. El Huérfano's name touched no chord in them. Their initial bewilderment at the fulsome acclaim which their story got from three Indios picked up on the road was sincere; only after a great deal of talk did they discern a connection between what they had done and the praise the three newcomers engaged in.

Ironically enough, the three men—Army deserters, as it later turned out—had been taken on the transport at Ehinger's own suggestion. It had occurred to him that the more motley his crew, the better his chance of losing himself in case the lorry was stopped. Their increased number might also facilitate an attempt to get away from them in Ulloa.

After a four hours' circuitous ride the truck came out onto the highway again. It arrived at Ulloa after dark. There the original spokesman of the camp laborers directed Ehinger close to a railway siding at the southern limits of the town, and kept him under surveillance, while he sent two of the others out to get something to eat. Ehinger marvelled at the sudden discipline of his passengers. They were very still under the tarpaulin now.

But once the truck was in motion again, the men, reassured, fed, and content, began to enjoy fully the rôle of popular heroes the Army deserters had bestowed upon them. They goaded Ehinger to take on more such companions—wayfarers, tramps, beggars, and even a couple of cripples, whom the headlights singled out on the roadside—and presently gave to each of these men an increasingly embroidered account of this morning's exploit. The newcomers, in turn, contributed their brandy flasks, their tobacco, or a fistful of coca leaves, to the exhilaration which soon swept the band. One of them had a woman with him; and in no time ribald giggles rose over the din behind Ehinger's back. The two men who had shared the front seat with him joined their comrades. His vague plan to escape them in Ulloa having failed, Ehinger wanted to proceed as far as possible before daybreak. He accelerated the motor. Thus the lorry, spilling over with human shapes, whizzed through the night and the whirling dust, leaving wild yells, bursts of laughter, and shots fired in air, in its wake.

The truck broke down around midnight. By that time the reinforcements outnumbered the original mutineers. Wallowing in their newly acquired sense of importance, they had in the meantime all but forgotten the part which the docile taciturn man at the wheel had played in their rescue. Also, Ehinger had courted their disfavor by keeping apart from their frolicking and turning down their repeated requests to make a halt in one or another of the pueblos. Now the intoxicated gang refused to believe in the accident which stranded them in inhospitable open country; they suspected the foreigner of hatching some scheme to rob them of the fruit of their heroism and the pleasures foreseen in the capital. For they all were resolved by now to go to Huacho and "teach the blackguards *there* a lesson." They began to abuse

U

Ehinger, and already were closing in on him, stressing their threats by a display of their weapons, when one of the Army deserters, apparently a man with an inkling of mechanics, declared that the axle of the truck was in fact broken. They all should thank the Virgin for having escaped injury.

While to the majority of the thirty-odd men assembled (not to speak of the woman who had fallen into hysterics) that realization offered a new excuse for venting their high spirits, a small patrol which had gone off discovered that the track of the railway was less than a thousand paces distant from the highway.

Of the battle order on which the men then decided Ehinger gained no advance knowledge. Quite evidently, the color of his skin, his possession of so costly an object as a lorry, and above all his aloof conduct, disqualified him as an active partner in the enterprise which was taking shape in their heads. He was dragged aside, relieved of revolver and wallet, and from that moment on some handpicked bullies did not budge from his elbow. Already at that stage he was subjected to such blows and knocks as later deprived him of any use of his will, and turned him into an impotent witness of the misdemeanor that was to land the whole company in the goods shed of Carjavel Station. . . .

In his present condition, Ehinger did not care to recall his far from courageous thoughts throughout the men's preparations for their assault. Closely guarded, he had lain prone atop the embankment, observing them light a chain of fires on both sides of the track and barricade the rails with sleepers a pile of which they detected somewhere in the dark. He remembered distinctly the shrieks of the oncoming locomotive and its abrupt halt. He saw in his mind again the armed train personnel leap down and almost at once drop their weapons at the sight of the shapes springing out of the night brandishing their guns and machetes. Although Ehinger had quickly seen through their comedy, he could not forget the energy with which these inventive savages convinced their victims they had better move back and make room in the carriages for "three score lepers from Payapán."

Something, Ehinger told himself, had blunted his wits and turned him into a cur in those hours. Throughout, the girl in the guest house had seemed to mock him. She still defied the ever-increasing distance between them. The uncertainty of her death travestied his decision to take her life, to extinguish her betrayal, and with it whatever she had betrayed in himself. He had been taught that nothing could ever resist, nothing ever survive, the iron resolution of a man to extinguish life. Juana's bulletproof specter shattered this belief. How was he, without it, to cling to his trust in the ultimate power man had over man? . . .

"Cigarette?" asked León.

The prisoner shook his head. He had hunched up his knees and propped his forearms against them.

The driver was sounding his siren again. The ambulance, slowing down, took another bend. It was on the road to the airdrome.

Don León drew the curtain back from the window, and half rose. The macadamized road was empty. When the siren stopped, León thought he distinguished in the distance the sounds of a commotion.

"Is Don Lorenzo Requesens, the Minister, on the airfield?" the captive inquired. It was as if he had been brooding all the time over the change of direction.

"You'll see him," León answered. "In case we get through, you'll see him." Now he heard, far-off, a clangor. He no longer doubted its nature. . . . The dogged immobility of his charge began to bias him against this whole venture. He had acted on an impulse. He'd better bide his time. Better wait a while at the airdrome, make sure exactly what dangers were to be run on the ride to Government House and perhaps from there to the barracks. This ambulance, after all, was a death trap.

It stopped. León had just turned away from the window, and the sudden halt threw him off-balance, knocking him against the butt of the soldier's rifle. But before a word of reproof could come from his lips, he found himself face to face with the handsome first lieutenant who had thrown open one wing of the door.

"You, Loyarte!" he cried out even before he pushed his head inside. "Good God, are you hurt?"

"Go to blazes!" came León's answer, "don't you know better—"

"Loyarte? Not León Loyarte?" a loud Eastern voice broke in from somewhere behind the lieutenant.

All the saints together making an appearance on earth would not have startled León more than the man whose dignified figure rose to his eyes over the lieutenant's stooped shoulders. Jostling the lieutenant aside, León hopped down, and still gasping, made a move as though he expected his future father-in-law (if that he still was) to embrace him. At the same time he saw the lieutenant colonel.

"What happened, captain?" he asked, walking up to León briskly.

"I've to take a man to His Excellency, sir," León replied. His eyes were on the Senator from Majamarca.

"His Excellency's orders?"

"It is not quite clear, sir . . ."

The lieutenant colonel looked searchingly at the ambulance. A beam of the midday sun fell through the opened wing on the little soldier who had scrambled to his feet, a simian grin on his face. The manacled man behind him could not be seen from outside.

The lieutenant, sidling up to the three gentlemen, gave a low whistle.

"So you intend to proceed to Government House, captain?" persisted the commander of the air force. He was visibly vacillating between his deference toward the Senator and his curiosity about the unexpected assignment of Requesens' meddlesome A.D.C. But the Senator had already taken his arm and turned him away from the vehicle.

"This is it, friend!" he said with undisguised agitation, "this is it! I'll go with this ambulance. In this ambulance I *will* get through!"

"You didn't answer my question, captain," the lieutenant colonel said, beckoning to León. "Are you ordered back to Government House?"

"I shall try to get there, sir."

"You will, you will!" cried the Senator.

"Yes, señor senator," León agreed, "I will. . . ." He was still dumbfounded.

"You young men do not know your own country!" the Senator was exclaiming. "No matter how wrought up people are, they respect the sign of the cross. The Red Cross, too. Naturally. Yes, that they do, friends. Decency! Christian mercy . . . ah, they still have respect for its symbol in this country, no matter how the present absurdity may upset them!"

The commander of the air force had lapsed into silence. Most likely he would have pressed his investigation, or lent his ear to the lieutenant who made an attempt to catch his attention. But at this moment a man on a motorcycle came speeding out of the gate, and reported that the lieutenant colonel was urgently needed at the hangar. So he merely said, "The Minister has been trying to get in touch with you, captain. So you'd better rush along . . . Captain Loyarte, the señor senator has come to Huacho on a mission of the highest importance. He must get him to the Palace. I could not take it upon myself to have him driven there in an ordinary car. I might ask for an armored car. But the telephone, damn it, has gone dead, and the señor senator will not hear of delay. All right, then. You take him with you in that ambulance of yours. You take the señor senator to the Palace. May the Virgin protect you, caballeros. . . ." A wiry man, he swung his leg across the rear saddle of the motorcycle, and lifting his voice high over the hum of its motor, he added, "The Minister, I am sure, will appreciate what you do, captain. . . ."

"Friend—" the lieutenant tried to accost León, but the latter was already walking off, ahead of the Senator.

With all his excitement, the Senator seemed to have noticed earlier the two men in the ambulance. He barely wasted a glance on them while León ordered the little soldier to climb up to the upper stretcher.

Then he offered the Senator the folding seat, and pulling the door shut, dropped down himself at the prisoner's side. "To the Palace!" he shouted to the driver.

"I must go to His Excellency, señor aide-de-camp," the prisoner whispered.

Don León moved his head in a furtive sign of affirmation.

The Senator cleared his throat at some length. He stroked his wrinkled jacket. He plucked at his bow tie, which had half vanished beneath the triple folds of his chin. He smoothed his clipped grey mustache and his bushy eyebrows. He put his little finger to his ear, shaking his head, as people do after a plane ride. And all the time he seemed to be looking down at the tip of his strong aquiline nose.

León wished he had placed him on the stretcher, to expose his face to the light of the window. It came to him that the Senator had not looked in his face once, nor addressed one direct word to him. Still overwhelmed by his surprise, alarmed—without precisely knowing why —by the inquisitiveness of the lieutenant colonel and the unwonted sharpness of his attitude, and now finding himself compelled through the rapid shift of events to pursue a course whose wisdom he had questioned some minutes ago, Don León was not in the least the master of the situation. At the first sight of the Senator he had asked himself whether things had already come to such a pass in Majamarca that he had had to flee his constituency. But the lieutenant colonel had been far from treating the arrival as a refugee; and so León had rejected his first assumption. Alternatively no conjecture as to the Senator's "mission" had presented itself to his mind. He would have sold his soul to the Devil for an explanation from the Senator. He would have given a year of his life for one word about his María!

But the Senator's lips remained closed.

The driver went off the main road. He seemed to be taking a detour through the eastern section of the town. Almost continuously, the indistinct rumble of explosions rippled the air, now closer, now farther off.

León shifted his head past the short legs of the soldier dangling from above. "He is a shrewd man, the driver is," he said under his breath.

The Senator had his hands on the lapels of his jacket. He stared at the handcuffed man.

"Did you arrive on the commercial liner, señor senator?" León made bold to ask.

"I hope I arrived in time," was the reply. The Senator let his eyes run into the corners at León's side. "And who is this man, my son?"

"I am taking him to Don Lorenzo," León said with the inflection of someone discharging a duty as a matter of course.

The Senator pitted a prolonged look against that evasiveness.

"It's not a clear case, though. . . ."

"In what respect, Don León?"

The wail of the siren spared Loyarte an immediate response. He felt, creeping up in his breast, an urge, a child-like urge to throw himself on the neck of María's father, and admit to him the bizarre predicament in which, with waxing clarity, he saw himself trapped. "You!" he said harshly to the unmoving man by his side directly the shriek of the siren had abated, "you there! tell the señor senator what you told me. You there!"

A slow, imbecile-looking motion of his bowed head was Ehinger's only reaction. He could not make head or tail of the presence of this elderly civilian. The title of a Senator conveyed no meaning to him. Sensing the nearness of a peril he could not appreciate, he clung to a single thought: to keep the intruder at bay. "I must see Don Lorenzo Requesens, His Excellency," he said.

"You must? Today? Now?"

"And he must see me," Ehinger said, his teeth pressing on the lower lip.

Again the Senator cleared his throat. "Why did you have the man shackled, Don León?"

"Because I am not sure . . ."

"Of what?"

"Of the business he pretends he has with Don Lorenzo . . . of the acquaintanceship with Don Lorenzo he boasts of."

"He does? Is he one of the rioters?"

"In a way he is, yes."

"But he is not from our country, is he? . . . How is it you are not with Don Lorenzo, Don León?" the Senator continued, absently, almost sleepily. He did not permit his gaze to relinquish the prisoner. "You still are his A.D.C., no?"

"My duties took me to Carjavel this morning."

"I see, I see," mumbled the Senator. "And now you got hold of this ambulance to rejoin Don Lorenzo . . . and are taking this man along. I see. . . . And *where*," he addressed Ehinger, "did you say His Excellency met you, my friend? Was it in this country? Or abroad?"

A rattle of detonations could be heard. But the driver proceeded only the faster. Except for the little soldier who started to fumble with his gun, the men in the ambulance did not stir.

Then there was quiet outside. The air, with its odor of disinfectants, was stifling.

The Senator leaned forward. He asked, *"Sie sind ein Deutscher, nicht wahr?"*

Ehinger drew back his head. *"Nein. Kein Deutscher. Nix Deutscher.* A man from Switzerland," he said in Spanish, firmly, *"suizo, suizo."* He had quickly regained his composure. Don León's utterances had confirmed to his mind that he was being transported on Requesens' own orders. Whatever the authority of the civilian was, he would not dare countermand them.

"You do know El Huérfano, do you not?" León suggested.

But Ehinger had reverted to his former pose. He protruded his lip to blow away the beads of sweat that collected under his nose.

"Anyway, we shall see shortly," León uttered fretfully in the direction of his future father-in-law. "Don Lorenzo will make short shrift of this mystery. . . . Actually, it's not on account of this mystery that I am speeding back to him. As you were guessing so rightly, señor senator, I had to rejoin Don Lorenzo anyway."

The Senator reclined. "A mystery," he made himself hear. "A mysterious man. A mysterious foreigner, eh? Seems we both are wrong in our theories, Don León. But that is up to you, my son. . . ."

"To Don Lorenzo . . ." León said. He did not succeed in catching the eyes of the Senator, who after a pause added,

"Most things are up to a man himself in hours like these."

This was the last coherent remark of the Senator until he parted with León. The subsequent occurrences were not propitious for talk. To be sure, the Senator's trust in the symbol of mercy was, on the whole, not deceived; at one particular intersection the rioters even made a breach in their barricade to let the ambulance pass upon the plea of its driver, who proved to be a shrewd man indeed, besides being a brave one (far more so, incidentally, than the loudmouthed artillery sergeant who—at about the same hour—shied away from taking Requesens to Carjavel in an *armored* car). But the uncontrollable character of street fighting sets limits to humanitarian considerations. Several times the courageous driver had to turn round before some impassable mêlée. On one occasion—near the Cathedral, whose great bell was pealing—he had to dash through the crowd under a hail of rocks, throwing his car, as it were, into the fray. And more than once the four men in the ambulance were lying ascramble on the floor of their close quarters, faces down, while the bullets crashed through the splintering wood on both sides.

Withal, they made it. They reached the Plaza from one of its minor eastern approaches, after León, sticking his head out and yelling "War Ministry's special orders! War Ministry's special orders . . ." prompted the detachment on duty there to remove the cheval-de-frise for a couple of seconds.

"To Government House first," the Senator said to León, who, still somewhat shaken, transmitted the order through the peep hole.

Only then did he make a sign of courteous protest.

"Do not worry, my son, I'll get to the Palace," the Senator assured him grimly, "I shall get there if I have to crawl on my belly across the whole Plaza. This cannot go on. No, this *cannot* go on. It must be stopped. It will be stopped. Go now and take your mystery man to your Don Lorenzo." With a long screech of its brakes, the ambulance pulled up at the curb. The Senator pushed open both wings of the door.

The little soldier, clutching his rifle, jumped down first. As if changed to a hero by the trying half hour behind him, he clasped the elbow of his prisoner and pulled him from the car.

Ehinger staggered. His face was white as chalk. Perspiration drenched it. Blinking against the stark light and coughing, he permitted the ridiculous pigmy to drag him over to the portal.

"Go, Don León!" the Senator cried out, nearly shoving the captain down on to the sidewalk. "Go. . . . *She* is all right. She will be. And cured of her folly . . . This cannot go on. Go."

León turned his head to have one more glimpse of the crimson face of his future father-in-law. But he had to jump out of the way of a horseman galloping toward the sidewalk; and in the same split-second a pair of arms drew León behind the portal that already sheltered the prisoner and his guard.

"Is His Excellency upstairs?"

"Which one?" asked the officer of the guard.

"Don Lorenzo."

"Don Lorenzo has left."

"Left!"

The great door had been closed. The whole group, swelled by Government clerks, stood in the shadow. Everybody gaped at the manacled man.

Outside horses thundered by. "He left for the De la Torre barracks, so we presume," the officer said to León with a show of sang-froid. "You are his aide, are you not?"

León's mouth was dry with dust. He had to cough. He nodded emphatically in response to the officer's query. Over the hand he had brought up to his lips, he was observing, in the grey light, Don Lorenzo's acquaintance, the "man from Switzerland."

"What is going on down there?" an angry voice called from the top of the staircase. "To your desks, señores, if you please. Officer of the guard, what *is* going on there?"

León drew forward a step. He recognized the Minister of the Interior. His enormous figure all but erased the Liberator's bust from León's line of vision.

"Who is that shackled ragamuffin down there?" Don Basilio growled. "We can't have any of those rowdies brought here, officer of the guard. . . ."

León Loyarte walked on. He was aware of the tremendous import of this moment. Ever since the curt verbal exchange between the Senator and the "man from Switzerland" he had fought the suspicion aflame in his breast. Rumors about Nazi chieftains at large in some of the sister republics had been recurring throughout the past months. That one of those unwelcome men, expelled from one such country, or flee-

ing its territory, should be trying to take refuge now with Requesens
—the attaché recalled from Berlin in '41!—that was far, far from unimaginable.

Don Basilio Gonzales, amazed at the lack of obedience as he encountered, perhaps also frightened, frowned down at Loyarte who had
begun to ascend the stairs.

Close behind him, the "man from Switzerland" was being pushed
upwards by the soldier who more and more roughly applied the butt of
his rifle to the back of the helpless captive.

In the one minute left for his deliberations, León Loyarte repeated
to himself that Requesens had never, never opened his heart to him. To
the one friend he had in the country! He had never requited his love.
He had made use of his faithfulness, of his love. But his trump had
been vulgar bribery. No, for the sham that remained between them, he,
León, would not trade his patriotism, his honesty . . . and alienate his
María, to boot! Straight! He had to proceed straight. It was a gamble.
But it was the supreme gamble of his life.

Running after the three men, the officer of the guard seemed ready to
halt their advance. A new series of explosions outside, followed by
screams, drowned out his protests.

"Your Excellency," Loyarte called upwards, interrupting another outburst of Don Basilio, "Your Excellency! This man must be interrogated.
He says he has the most signal news for the Minister of War. For the
Cabinet. He *must* be interrogated, Your Excellency. His native tongue
is German."

XXXIV

It is a tribute to the Majamarca-Huacho Railroad that its noon train, on this never-to-be-forgotten Thursday, left the capital on schedule. As for railroad traffic on the two crucial days that followed, it has been pointed out that its non-stoppage was important to the solution of the crisis—or, in other words, that the Government, as of Friday morning, had no reason for blocking the avenue of approach from the East. But railroad men are an unruly lot and more often than not in the forefront of popular demonstrations. Thus it was only the discipline the management of the Majamarca-Huacho Railroad enforced on its personnel amid all the convulsions of public life that enabled the Government to pursue their tactics.

Be that as it may, the fact that trains were running contributed greatly to the calm prevailing in the towns and villages along the track of the railroad.

They were very calm on the whole. In spite of the unusual nature of the pronunciamientos and counter-pronunciamientos (which only spottily came to their knowledge), the rapidly moving events in the two big cities appeared most of the time as an Army affair to small-town people. El Huérfano's rôle in the conflict left most of them stunned. The news of his attempted assassination resulted almost nowhere in large-scale unrest.

The only township to experience something akin to it was Ollaytaytombo. Perhaps the clashes occurring there—on Friday—were a token of the special position that community fancied it held as El Huérfano's headquarters on the eve of his plunging into his unorthodox venture. Perhaps the perplexity and the dissensions that venture engendered were more pronounced and went deeper in Ollaytaytombo than anywhere else. In fact, this is very likely.

In M. Philibert, there was no doubt as to the person who must have guided the hand of the assassin in Majamarca. Throughout the trials and humiliations of his second captivity, the memory of the remarkable woman who had liberated him from the temple ruins had remained vivid in him. The image of her fanatic resolution to have El Huérfano done away with had in fact a special effect on the captive. To a proud man reduced to placating the ill humors of his kidnapper, and who in the loftiest of his dreams could conceive of his own future only as dependent on his wiles and his wits, the thought of someone fighting for the cause he believed in, if need be alone, could not but carry an agonizing fascination.

The woman must have been a great deal on Philibert's mind. When Ramón—shortly after arriving at the kidnapper's place—broached the news of the enigmatic incident in Majamarca, Philibert had been heard to refer in a loud exclamation to a "señora." Or so at least Ramón later said.

Still dazed by the unexpected sight of Ramón, and distraught by the hunchbacked kidnapper's bursts of joy at finding himself in possession of the complete ransom at last, M. Philibert had obviously been talking to himself. If Ramón had then and there asked Philibert who that señora was who so occupied his thoughts, M. Philibert might well have answered the query, bewildered and mollified as he was.

But the eunuch waited till he was alone with Philibert. And by that time, the freed man had grown conscious of the self-respect salvaged from his miscarried mission, and was no longer inclined to submit to the inquiries of a batman. Not that he was unappreciative of Ramón's courage and cleverness in locating the place of the old thief. In a mild way M. Philibert was even touched by Requesens' considerateness in dispatching his factotum here to shepherd him to Huacho. Ever since the envelope with the first half-bills came, proving Requesens' co-operative spirit, the captive had dreaded the prospect of having to pick his way back alone, exposed to unknown new perils. In that respect, Ramón was his rescuer. Yet M. Philibert stuck to his resolve to treat him with the same soft-spoken reserve which he had practiced throughout their former encounters.

To this decision, M. Philibert owed his life. He owed it, properly speaking, to this decision and to a brainstorm of Ramón's. . . .

On the crowded train which left the capital with such commendable punctuality, Ramón had gained the impression that the disturbances were taking an ominous course. One of the stories repeated among the passengers had it that the assault on El Huérfano's life, whatever the wider issues involved, was an act of Don Lorenzo's personal vengeance. Leaving the train at Ollaytaytombo—where the engineer, a man easily bribed, put Ramón in charge of a guide willing to sell the stranger his mule—Ramón noted the great tension of the assemblage on the platform; El Huérfano's name seemed to be in everyone's mouth, and so, if less loudly, were execrations on "this Excellency in Huacho." Thus Ramón had formed the opinion that his orders to put Philibert to death had become effective.

His guide, a curiously humorous one-eyed man, belonged, as it turned out, to the railroad thieves' gang himself. But he had great respect for the engineer who had given him directions, and could be trusted. Bypassing the restive town, he predicted to Ramón a six hours' ride on a very bad road.

Ramón's obesity and his short-windedness had long estranged him from physical exertions. He soon felt the strain of the journey, and the wooden saddle began to hurt him. Yet he did not consider giving up. He was a faithful servant, the unthinking instrument of his master's wishes. In the folds of his broad red sash, he carried, besides his old dagger, a length of rope and an army revolver. He would discharge his duty. Of course he would discharge it at a respectable distance from the kidnapper's place.

For all his fatigue, he did not stay there more than a couple of hours. He had been fearful lest the old thief, apprehensive of retaliation to come from the men he had fleeced and who now knew the way to his den, make an attempt to keep them from leaving. As it happened, a violent altercation started between Ramón's guide and the hunchback over a share in his spoils, and presently the two came to blows, and they did not let go of each other even when Ramón and Philibert mounted the mule and departed. Still—to keep the thieves off his track—Ramón shouted to them that he and "the señor" would return by way of Ollaytaytombo.

Once out of sight of the place, he proposed to turn east. He had got some information on the lay of the land from the one-eyed man. A small railroad station lay fifteen leagues to the sunrise. The Huacho-bound train was scheduled to halt there in the morning; and they would make that train—provided, that was, trains were running.

Philibert agreed. He was not anxious to show himself at Ollaytaytombo. Evidently the station for which they were heading was the same the "darling señora" had wanted him to reach on that long-ago morning. But the recollection of that morning had begun to fade in M. Philibert under the impact of his liberation.

Ramón sat behind his charge on the mule. He had asked him to take the reins, for there was an unwonted pain in his left upper arm and a recurrent heaviness in the shoulder. But it was not these discomforts which delayed the execution of Ramón's murderous plan. To slip a noose of his rope round the neck of his unsuspecting travelling companion, at the same time thrusting the dagger into his back, required no great strength or skill. Not for a second did he waver in his assurance that eventually he would go through with that scheme. But first he must find out who that "señora" was Philibert had been talking about. He figured—accurately—that Philibert, having some particular knowledge, connected that woman with the assassination in Majamarca. Public opinion, as Ramón perceived it, was pinning that crime on Don Lorenzo. If Philibert, then, could be induced to divulge his secret here and now, he, Ramón, might well be able to clear Don Lorenzo of the obnoxious accusation. Ignorant of the true state of affairs in Huacho, let alone its complexity, the loyal fellow imagined that thus he would—in the nick of time—turn the tide in his master's favor.

But something in the eunuch, joining that exemplarily faithful reflection, outstripped it. His ancient ambition to distinguish himself, his old yearning for proving his valor, had come to the surface in him. It was as though he were hoping to regain his manhood. He did not want to perceive that what he should do, under the circumstances he surmised, was to deliver Philibert to Don Lorenzo alive. Instead, he held fast to his idea that he must penetrate the man's secret himself, yet not permit that self-set task to interfere with his duties as executioner. As it was, he foretasted in his mind the sight of Philibert's lifeless body sliding down from the saddle. . . . He grew more impatient with every foot of the way. And so did his questions about that "señora."

The very inquisitiveness of the eunuch was sealing Philibert's lips. He did not suspect anything behind it. He simply did not wish to discuss his memories with the batman. He exasperated him by his silence, and then again, through a mere word he would drop, incited Ramón to relate what he knew of current political rumors.

They cast a sombre light on Requesens' chances. Yet all the adversities closing in on Requesens—including, perhaps, the loss of his office—were far from upsetting to M. Philibert. He argued very much the way Ehinger had four days previously, presuming misfortune would mellow Requesens, lower his will to resist and make him listen to reason at last in the one paramount matter, the one matter by now in Philibert's heart.

By now, Philibert's more high-spirited concerns had fallen from him as pustules do from a man who recovers from smallpox. He had done with the politics of the Republic and the imaginary gains crowning the fantastic, vainglorious designs of her great ones. But he had also done with his allegiance to his own world. Allegiance to a dead world was no more than an illusion. He had done with illusions. The one goal he conceived of was the recovery of his money. It was his. If ever there had been in his mind any question about that, the full awareness of his past sufferings had dispelled it. The money was his by dint of his martyrdom.

Approaching their destination long after nightfall, the two travellers heard a train's whistle and then its approaching thunder; and to Philibert's ears these dissonant sounds rang like the sweetest music. He felt confident he would get to Huacho. With trains running, the worst of the revolt must be over. He would get to Requesens. And it made no difference to their business whether he was still in office or out.

The two travellers—who thus were pursuing so widely disparate goals —dismounted at the foot of the embankment. It was pitch-dark, and only the reddish light of the semaphore indicated the station. Ramón seemed prepared to lie down on the bare soil.

Except for his one reiterated query—to which, at times, the eunuch would add vituperations upon all womenkind—he had been silent on the last lap of the ride. Sometimes his hands had reached out for Philibert's shoulders, or even the nape of his neck, as if groping for support. Now he was totally impassive. His lack of stamina did not displease Philibert. He had glimpsed the money bag Ramón carried. He would ask him to give him part of the money. It was not fitting that he should be at the batman's mercy, without a centavo; they also might become separated on the train.

Meanwhile the moonlight had pierced the heavy clouds; and Philibert went off in search of shelter. He ascended the embankment. No human being was to be seen, nor any animal to be heard. The unlit one-storey station was to the right. Philibert advanced to the left. After about two hundred steps he came upon a large lean-to. It was empty. A profusion of netting hanging down limply from the flimsy roof was the only sign of human habitation about the barren structure.

When Philibert returned, Ramón was sitting on the ground, the small of his back propped against the saddle, which he had managed to take off the burro. He could barely be moved to follow his companion. No sooner had they both reached the lean-to than Ramón dropped down on his poncho again and left it to the other to tether their mount.

"Listen," Philibert said sternly, "listen before you fall asleep. We better not let anyone find us here in the morning. The railroad people might not like it, and we don't want any arguments, do we? We want to get off on that morning train. So I shall wake you in two hours. Then I'll have an hour of sleep myself, and you'll wake me at dawn." Philibert waited for Ramón's answer, but he seemed already to have dropped off. So Philibert turned his back on the sleeping man and pushed the netting aside. He began to walk toward the station, keeping himself in the deep shadow of the high plants growing rankly on the ridge of the embankment.

The twin pairs of rails glistened in the light of the full moon. The semaphore stood at an angle of forty-five degrees. M. Philibert plunged his hands into the pockets of his too-loose-fitting jacket of Japanese silk, which he had boldly appropriated amidst the confusion of his departure from the kidnapper's place. He listened into the night. No one seemed to be around. Walking more slowly, he started whistling through his teeth. Suddenly he checked himself, struck by his own tune, one of the songs of the old days that extolled the community of bodies and souls. A parody, he thought to himself with a startling absence of bitterness, a ludicrous parody. Community, my eye! These were times to look out for oneself. And he would. . . . M. Philibert turned on his heels. Striding back, he halted at every other step. There was no hurry, no hurry at all. . . .

He did not know how far away he was from the lean-to, for a cloud was journeying past the moon, when he believed he heard the voice of Ramón. So Ramón did not sleep, after all! Or was he talking in his sleep? It did sound as if he were talking in a heavy dream. Or had something happened to him? Had someone come and started to argue with the intruder? This too, it occurred to M. Philibert, was not fitting —that this caricature of a man should be armed while he himself was defenseless.

"Where are you . . . where, señor?" he now heard Ramón distinctly.

Prudently slinking along the ferns, he had come closer to the shelter and to Ramón's calls. Now they trailed off in a hoarse moan. M. Philibert did not advance further before the moon was out again. Then he crawled up to the netting.

Ramón was alone. He lay on one side, his head tossed back. He fumbled about his stomach, his thighs. He was attempting to loosen the sash wound several times round his waist.

Philibert went down on one knee beside the prostrate eunuch. "What is the matter with you, eh?" he asked gruffly in response to his gasps. "Don't leave me, señor . . ." Ramón croaked in a convulsive endeavor to lend sound to his breath. "Where are you? . . . Ah, here . . . Help . . . Help me . . . I won't do it, señor, dear señor. . . ."

"Go back to sleep, friend," M. Philibert muttered. "Had a nightmare, eh? . . ." He had clutched the freed end of the sash, and pressing his other hand against Ramón's haunch, rolled him over. The thought of robbing his weary travelling companion had suggested itself to Philibert on his stroll in the most natural fashion.

"Sick . . ." Ramón wailed. "Heart . . . my heart, señor . . ."

M. Philibert rolled the wretch over once again on the poncho. A gurgling sob issued from him. "Orders . . . ah, my orders . . ." he breathed out in long intervals. "To kill you . . . Won't . . . No . . . Mother of God, help me. Help me, dear señor. . . . Do not go away. . . . You are safe. . . . I won't do it . . . no . . ."

So wild was Philibert's desire to lay hold on the money—hidden away, as he knew, in the folds of the sash—and so great the strain of his frantic efforts to unwind the broad band, that Ramón's words remained without sense at first. Only when his fingers felt the revolver's cold steel and—in this same lucky second—the leather bag with the money, did he comprehend Ramón's horrid confession. But at the same time M. Philibert realized that he was in the presence of a dying man.

The last push had landed Ramón prone on his back. Despite the feeble light, the rapid decay of his face was unmistakable. Its lumpy flesh quivered in contortions. The mouth stood open, obliquely, and emitted a high-pitched rattle. Ramón's right hand, on his breast, clutched the fat beneath the torn shirt.

There is no saying what, given the proper time, M. Philibert would have done to comfort Don Lorenzo's stricken henchman in his last struggle, or what cruelty he would have added to it to punish his treachery. As it was, he was given no time for either charity or retribution. The first scream of the locomotive found him still standing over the dying man, insensitive to his now fainter pantings, and fingering, as in a trance, the bag with the robbed money. The last that he saw of Ramón were the enormous whites of his eyes caught by the lights of the train, which had come to a halt.

Philibert stormed out from behind the netting. For a second he stood agape, as if benumbed by the fumes of the engine. Then, in a leap, he crossed the short stretch of gravel separating him from the rails. He was running. He ran along the carriages in one direction first, then in the other. He stumbled past men swinging storm lamps and shouting at the top of their voices. He tripped over a shape bending down in the dark, regained his balance, stopped, skidded on, stopped again, out of breath. He saw the thrown-open door of a carriage. At last he realized that this was an eastbound train—a train leading away from the murderous reach of Requesens—and, as though pushed by an unseen force, jumped onto the high steps of the carriage. It was all over in a minute, at the most.

The door was slammed shut behind him. He stood close to it in the corner of the corridor. The whistle blew uninterruptedly. He was soggy with sweat. Suddenly he felt chilled by the draft rushing in: the train was moving. The electric bulbs in the corridor dispensed only a shimmer of bluish light.

The compartments did not appear to be overcrowded. Perhaps this train had not come all the way from Huacho, Philibert wondered. He had turned about and was looking through the window. Then, for a long while, he did not move. At last he shoved Ramón's money bag into his pocket. It had been in his hand all the time. He also still clutched the revolver—in fact, he had been brandishing it while he ran up and down by the track—and now the weapon slipped on the floor with a hard clatter. He picked it up, trembling.

The sliding door of a compartment farther down the corridor was opened with a screech. Two men stepped out, talking in low voices. Philibert could not grasp a single word of their discourse. He did not look in their direction.

It came to him that, in the end, Ramón's sash had lain coiled up on the gravel in the lean-to: he distinctly recalled the scarlet shape as the onrushing lights of the engine scooped it out of the gloom. He must have stared at this spot of red in that second. Why think of it? He had escaped death. Requesens' assault had miscarried miserably, as it were, and the killer he had hired was dying instead. There was poetic justice in that, and its sense affected M. Philibert like a tonic. He no longer trembled. He was breathing evenly. He wiped his face. The wheels under him rolled in a softer rhythm. The train had gathered speed.

The murmurs at the other end of the corridor were resuming. In his new courage Philibert turned his head a little. The two men were walking back to their compartment. One of them threw up his arms and shook his head forcefully. It was a gesture of disapproval. Then Philibert heard Don Lorenzo's name pronounced in a key of awed knowledge. An uneasy little snicker followed which did not exclude some admiration.

That tone fixed itself in Philibert's mind. What had Requesens done to arouse such differing feelings at one and the same time? What had happened to him? Was he still in power—that meanest of thieves, that vilest of murderers? Nothing was inconceivable in this country.

He hated it, M. Philibert said to himself with profound conviction, nearly talking aloud. He had hated it from the very hour he first laid eyes on its territory. The very smell of the River wharf at Majamarca had been odious to him in that night in January when the steamship captain who was smuggling them into the Republic forced him and Ehinger and the ailing Belgian to swim ashore.

Yet that captain had not been a bad fellow. He had asked for only a small consideration. . . .

He must find that good captain again in Majamarca. . . .

There was no way of getting one's own from Requesens in his country. Not from a Requesens sunk so low as to send a bravo after the man he had promised to protect and whom he had robbed. In power or not, Requesens would try again to have him killed, and one day he would succeed.

To continue the battle, a man must stay alive first. Requesens must be fought from outside his reach, from abroad.

That was the thought which had pushed M. Philibert on to this train, no matter how many thoughts may have rushed through his head in that moment's confusion. Now he knew it for certain. Only now could he gauge the attainment of that split-second decision, appraise his own acumen. Only now did this man of so varied experiences (and who had made so many men experience so much)—only now did he realize how many hardships a human being could bear, how many humiliations, how much anguish, terror, despair, and loneliness, without losing that miraculous power, will, which alone, to M. Philibert's mind, lifted man above the animal kingdom.

XXXV

GOOD FORTUNE REMAINED true to the fugitive in Majamarca. He boarded the down-river steamer some time after midnight on Sunday—sixteen hours after his arrival in the city—undeterred by the rumors afloat there about the disgraced Requesens.

At about the same hour, a small sedan drew up in front of the Club Nacional in Huacho. The sentry at its main entrance had taken a step forward at the approach of the automobile, but in the light of the street lamp he saw the white plate with the letters "CD" on the bumper of the car, and relaxed. He was fairly proud of recalling his instruction that the curfew, which was still in force, excepted the personnel of foreign legations from all restrictions. He saluted the two gentlemen who got out of the car, and fell back into the shadow.

The gentlemen walked up the four steps to the bullet-speckled door of the Club without haste or stealth. The taller, slimmer, and apparently younger one stepped ahead. He lifted the hinged brass knob —a miniature effigy of a lion's head—and let it clang back. The knock, repeated after a pause, echoed in the still air. It was so quiet in the street, and down on the Plaza too, one could hear the barking of a dog somewhere very far off.

"Are you sure it was the secretary you talked to on the telephone?" asked the older man, forcing his naturally booming voice down.

"Positively," said the other. "You see I was right. No special guard here. *One* sentry!" He knocked for the third time. They both had turned their backs on the one street lamp which, bereft of its glass globe, was still diffusing its light.

At last there came the sounds of creaking shoes from behind the door. A chain was taken down. A crack was opened.

"This is the señor I talked to you about, *mi amigo,*" the younger man declared as soon as they were in the lobby.

"Did the soldier see you, señor attaché?"

"I told you you could leave such details to me, señor secretario," said the attaché, smiling. As far as could be seen in the rays of the flashlight he carried, the secretary of the club was as impeccably attired as ever. His frock coat—which had kept reminding the attaché of a sexton or undertaker in the two months of his membership here—was tightly buttoned.

His very small eyes went uneasily to the attaché's companion who advanced after returning with a move of his head the subdued welcome the secretary had extended to the late callers.

"You will excuse my not putting on the lights," he now suggested, clearing his throat.

"We will indeed . . ." said the attaché, while he thrust a hand into the pocket of his white jacket. "Here, *amigo*," he muttered, slipping an envelope into the rapidly opened palm.

"I only hope it is all right," the secretary said when the envelope had vanished beneath his somber coat.

"It is. And don't forget I promised you my protection. Did you tell your wife where to reach me in case you might not be able to do so yourself? Which I'm sure will never happen."

In a quick gesture of apology, the secretary raised his electric torch, and for a moment it looked as if he wanted to turn it on the attaché's face. But he curbed his hand, allowed himself a shrug, and said again in a muffled voice, "I'll call the waiter, señor attaché, the old fellow who is serving as a kind of valet to him." Rigidly erect, the bribed man strode past the other visitor. At the door to the reading room he hesitated. Then, with another nervous shrug, he left the two gentlemen in the dark.

"Simple, no?" asked the young attaché with a snicker.

"A waiter! This caricature of a secretary—or did you call him a majordomo?—and a waiter! It is unbelievable!"

"Not very dignified, is it?"

"Who is talking about dignity?"

"As for the rest . . . I told you so."

"Psh!"

They heard doors being opened, closed, footfalls coming nearer. At last a shaft from the flashlight trickled out from under the door of the reading room. There was an exchange of murmurs behind the door.

"Will *he* pay him off, or do you want *me*—"

"No, no," said the attaché, "*he'll* do that, or perhaps he won't. But don't tip the waiter yourself." They both stood near the door now, and they had to take a step back as it opened.

The old waiter wore only a collarless shirt above his black livery trousers. "He is resting, maybe sleeping . . ." he mumbled. But he was bowing to the two gentlemen.

The secretary gave a sound of impatience. He let his light play on the man's saffron-colored withered face, and the two visitors could see the protruding veins vibrate on his neck.

"Did you tell our friend he needn't worry in the least, señor secretario?"

"I did, señor attaché."

"But he's resting—" the waiter repeated.

"Never mind, my good man," interrupted the attaché, severely, "go and tell him Don Mauricio is here."

"Don Mauricio?"

"Don Mauricio."

"Don Mauricio will wait in the reading room," declared the secretary after a pause. "Can you light the old paraffin lamp?"

"Yes, I can light that lamp. Oh yes."

"Go on, then."

"This way, señor, please," the old man said, as Don Mauricio, misled by the shadows, took a step in the wrong direction.

He had brought up his arm to bid good-bye to the attaché who was making for the exit. Then Don Mauricio followed the waiter.

Profound though the quiet was, the noise of the automobile did not penetrate the upholstered doors. Mauricio Hojeda walked to the center table. The waiter had given him no second look. Hojeda watched him kindle a flame in the lamp on the shelf.

At last a trembling light filled the patterned porcelain shade of the lamp. But the man kept fumbling with the screw of the ancient contraption until an even cone of brightness blazed down on the mahogany of the shelf and on the green velvet of the huge armchair that stood with its back to the room. Low mouthings accompanied his efforts. Finally he went over to one of the shuttered French windows and drew out a chair. When he retreated, he was inaudible on his rope-soled shoes, and he disappeared, very much like a conjuror's trick, through the tapestried wall.

Mauricio Hojeda sat down in the niche the waiter had singled out. He stretched his legs. With a deep sigh, he began to unbutton his waistcoat. He thought of taking out a cigar. But the doctors had warned him against too much tobacco. He had eaten too much. His nephew, the attaché, had fed him too well at dinner.

Mauricio Hojeda had never been a great family man. Only his lucky star had years ago instilled in him a certain amount of affection for this one nephew. He had sent him to the right schools, had pushed him into the foreign service, and always provided him with ample funds. That generosity was paying dividends now—thanks, to be sure, to Don Mauricio's friend in the Government who, upon his suggestion, had attached the young diplomat to the Huacho legation in June. Whatever his record in that post would be in the long run, he had given a brilliant account of himself insofar as his uncle's special instructions were concerned. The inside story of the dismissal of Requesens from office could not have come to his knowledge before some time Thursday night or early Friday; and on Saturday at ten Don Mauricio had already had the telegram urging him to come to Huacho at once.

It was true that the nucleus of that inside story—the detection of Requesens' having sheltered a fugitive Nazi—fitted the contingency for which Hojeda asked his nephew to be on the lookout. Nevertheless it *was* an accomplishment to have winnowed an apparently accurate picture of the events from what must have been a whirlwind of diplomatic gossip.

The attaché had painted this picture with much gusto in the four-hour dinner talk with his uncle. There was so much in it a good neighbor ought to enjoy!

Take that "walking conscience of the right-thinking people," the wealthy Senator from Majamarca. It was he who worked out the compromise that saved the Republic from a full-fledged civil war. Yet it needed, in the words of the attaché, "the freakish incident" to have the Senator's endeavors and his personal courage crowned with success. "He is said to have beseeched Dr. Zapeta for many hours to get rid of Requesens first. For this was one of the prerequisites of the compromise. But Dr. Zapeta was adamant. Adamant. To us who've seen what went on a few blocks away from the Palace, his stubbornness seems all but incredible in retrospect; and today we all agree that there is far more strength than we used to assume in that *hombre de las leyes*.

And a great deal more ingenuity. Surely he had not an ounce of love for Requesens. The insane proposition of having airplanes machine-gun the town—I have it on good authority that the Senator was with Dr. Zapeta when Requesens telephoned him to that effect from the barracks—shocked and horrified him; the outburst with which he is known to have turned Requesens down leaves no doubt about that. Yet at the same time he kept procrastinating. He dreaded the appearance of yielding to Fafreras' pressure before Fafreras on his part should make some conciliatory gesture.

"And then—with the Senator still on the premises—the gods themselves threw the golden opportunity into the lap of Dr. Zapeta!

"There are all sorts of stories about how that German was caught Thursday morning and taken to Gonzales, the Minister of the Interior. The best guess is that Requesens had trusted his own A.D.C. a little too much, had told him about his German guest, or even used the A.D.C. as an errand boy to the man's hiding place—and that the A.D.C., realizing his master's star was on the wane and set on ingratiating himself with some other exalted personage, went to that hideout and dragged the poor devil of a German to Señor Gonzales (a Liberal who never had much sympathy for Requesens). This is the best guess. I've been told that the A.D.C. did not turn up for duty on Thursday morning, and that Requesens was trying frantically to locate him throughout the forenoon."

The amusing episode about Don Lorenzo's treacherous aide was outside the range of Hojeda's interests, appeal though it did to his sense of humor. Naturally, what he wanted to know above all was who the German was. But already on their ride from the airfield to his nephew's apartment, the latter had admitted that his intelligence on the man was meager except for his being a fairly young fellow "and astonishingly dull-witted." The attaché did not even know whether Gonzales had extricated a confession from him, or anything, for that matter, beyond the continual whinings with which he was said to have asked to be taken forthwith to Requesens. Neither had the young diplomat any reliable information on the questioning the German had been subjected to in the Palace. And since Friday morning the yanqui legation had been holding him in its custody. . . . This was an unkind cut for the hopes of Mauricio Hojeda.

But, "Imagine such presence of mind," the attaché had gone on, "the first thing Dr. Zapeta did—amid the orgy of lawlessness engulfing the city!—was to call up the yanquis and tell them he wished to deliver to them a German war criminal who, he was sorry to add, had had some dealings with the Republic's former (former!) War Minister. That done, he started to discuss the compromise with the Senator from Majamarca. You understand the President's tactics, Don Mauricio, don't you? Dr. Zapeta is of course well aware of the difficulties the great Allies meet with in their attempts to have any self-respecting country hand over such refugees to their questionable justice. So he offered one on a platter to them, and won the kind of support Fafreras could never hope to gain from those powers.

"And now comes the joke of it . . . As I said, Dr. Zapeta called up the yanqui Chargé d'Affaires. And who should be in his legation but the wedded wife of Requesens! She is of North American birth, as you may know, and an attractive woman she is, as their women go. What had happened was that their military attaché saw her on the Plaza at a moment when it was no place indeed for a woman to be. Probably she was panic-stricken by the riots starting at that time in the residential section. There also was a breakdown of the telephone. It seems she wanted to get to Government House to be with her husband. God knows why. In any case it needed, so I've heard from a good source, some persuasion on the part of her countryman to make her step into his car. Whatever the circumstances, this is how she came to be in the legation. And as the Casa Requesens came in for its share of the damage in the later part of the day and is as good as uninhabitable, she has remained in the legation ever since. A funny pair of guests—the señora Requesens and Requesens' scandalous foreign friend. Ha, ha . . ."

Don Mauricio had not interrupted the blithe young man. He had not shown him his disappointment at the scarcity of news about the "scandalous foreign friend of Requesens." Also, the attaché had made up for it by his amazing skill in arranging for his uncle's interview with Requesens.

Requesens was not free. But he was, so to speak, no one's particular prisoner. His dismissal from office was known to have taken place in a very informal manner. "They say that this Villaroel—that over-age colonel who's now in charge of the War Ministry as a stand-in for Fafreras—managed to get to the barracks late at night on Thursday. They say he had only a short talk with Requesens. The first news that reached *us* in the small hours of Friday was that he had shot himself. Naturally he didn't even make an attempt to do away with himself. A Requesens wouldn't, would he? What really happened in the barracks we still do not know.

"It is an established fact that the officers did not claim him as their prisoner. Dr. Zapeta's intercourse with the yanquis was far from pleasing to them; and because of it they even might have stood up for Requesens in spite of everything, if they had by that time not known Fafreras was in—and with what glory! Who finally, some time on Friday, devised the idea of having Requesens confined to the premises of the Club, we do not know. Last night someone said that a very old uncle of his (one of those 'distinguished elder gentlemen' who pass as aristocrats hereabouts) put in a word with Dr. Zapeta."

This reported leniency on Dr. Zapeta's part had been good news for Hojeda. Might the President not be glad to get Requesens off his hands altogether?

He might. In fact, some of the officers might have spirited Requesens out of the country already, except for the impending arrival of Fafreras and the uncertainty of his future politics. The prestige of the Huacho garrison was badly shattered; surely the last thing the officers wished for was to have Requesens—their man, after all—exposed to further indignities, whether they came from certain foreign legations or from the populace.

The populace . . . The attaché had not drawn an overly sombre picture of its temper. Some observers were making a fuss about the "miraculous influence" El Huérfano's Friday afternoon broadcast had exerted upon the municipal masses. More likely their fury had just about run its course. Two hundred and fifty, perhaps three hundred, dead to bury! And the unspeakable devastation! It was enough to sober even madmen! Don Mauricio's nephew gave only small credit to the stand the two infantry regiments had made on Friday morning under Villaroel's command, or the strict enforcement of the curfew.

When, returning to the matter nearest to the heart of his uncle, he suggested that probably even the yanquis would not mind having Requesens "somehow disappear into thin air," Mauricio Hojeda had no longer seen any reason for withholding his plan from the diplomat. He meant to rescue Don Lorenzo. Crudely speaking, this was the motive of his hasty departure from his comfortable offices at the Avenido de Mayo.

His relations with the government of his country had improved considerably since the end of the war in Europe. With the first flush of Allied victory paling, considerations for sentiment abroad no longer encroached upon the great respect a man of Hojeda's economic power commanded. No one would find fault with the hospitality he meant to grant to Lorenzo Requesens.

Señor Hojeda smiled to himself; and that smile relieved the strain which he felt as the sound of steps surely not emanating from the soft-shod feet of the waiter came toward him.

The former Minister of War walked in through the papered door far to the left of the lamp. "You have come to look for your money, no doubt, the money for your airplanes," he said immediately while advancing toward the bright circle of light. "Sorry, Hojeda. Wrong address."

The visitor rose with deliberate poise. A sidelong inclination of his body expressed his willingness to listen to some more inconsequential remarks, if this was the fashion by which Don Lorenzo chose to lighten his heart. "Do you want me to talk to you, *amigo?*" he asked.

"Talk to me? About what?" The voice was even a trifle hoarser than Hojeda had remembered it.

"Are you not a *bit* surprised?"

"Nothing can surprise me," Requesens said. He pretended to study a row of books.

Hojeda came out of the embrasure. "Actually, I was hoping you wouldn't be surprised. I hoped you would expect me. Subconsciously, as this new term has it. Subconsciously, yes. A man fighting great adversities—"

"I stopped fighting."

"A man in your situation is likely to review his friends. His subconscious, at least, is. And I do not think . . . No, *amigo,*" Hojeda declared in a louder key, "I do not think you've got many acquaintances of my caliber. That's why I hoped you'd expect me." He gave a deep soft laugh. "You have experienced human baseness. Who hasn't at some time or another? You should not allow that experience to blunt your common sense . . . your feelings. . . ."

Lorenzo had stopped, as if wanting to take out a book. "Feelings for you, Señor Hojeda, perhaps?"

"I was mentioning common sense."

"You were, were you?" Lorenzo retorted, swaying on his feet, so swiftly had he straightened and spun round to face this new tormentor sprung on him from Pandora's inexhaustible box. He knew that this monstrous businessman was after the German funds. He had come to make use of his lowered spirits, to extort the secret from him, as pirates would in prevailing upon a dying shipmate to hand them over the chart of his buried treasure.

"The world has not come to its end, Don Lorenzo," Hojeda said with calm, "and as long as it hasn't, common sense exists."

"Does it?"

"You aren't the first man to lose a job—"

"For how long have you been in our fair city, Hojeda? How much have you learned of what has happened? Not much, I'd say. Or else, you would be ashamed of indulging in such banalities. Nor would your confidence in the survival of common sense be so complacent. This—" he went on, his voice shaken, and striding quickly up to the oval table "—this should teach you that common sense no longer exists in this country!" He flung both hands into the piles of newspapers laid out on the table.

His vehement move had startled Hojeda. In ignorance of the goal of Don Lorenzo's lunge, he had drawn back and raised his arms in an instinctive gesture of defense. For a second he was tempted to question the man's sanity. But in the next, he felt a violent anger swell up in him. Why, this miserable has-been had actually frightened him! "Common sense," he said, raising his voice, "common sense demands of you that you stop pondering the past, man, and think of the future. Requesens! Listen to me. That German—"

"Stop pondering the past?" Lorenzo broke in. He was rustling a paper, holding it aloft with a flutter. "Common sense? You must permit a man who has become the victim of his trust in common sense to ponder the past, Hojeda. You may call my pondering remorse, if you wish, remorse . . ."

The tone of honesty underlying this outcry softened Don Mauricio, much as he wondered whether it was not a stratagem to put him off his track. Still he decided to humor the embittered man.

Lorenzo was returning to the light, all the time mouthing such words as "remorse," "negligence," "culpable negligence," or "stupidity." . . . He tossed the paper onto the armchair. "Come here," he exclaimed, sullenly. He tapped the pockets of his tunic. "Yes, come here. Read. I haven't got my glasses. Read for yourself. Read all about the past. And the future, too. Read for yourself . . ." He forced the crumpled paper on Hojeda who had stepped closer to him. Then he reached over Don Mauricio's shoulder to point out the most telling passages of the "outrageous pronunciamiento."

Except for its suave phrases, Dr. Zapeta's manifesto—issued the day before and reprinted on the front page of this morning's La Libertad —contained nothing Don Mauricio's nephew had not reported to him. He for one saw no outrage in Dr. Zapeta's offering "the mantle of the still lamented General to that proven friend of the common man and fighting democrat, Colonel Leandro Fafreras." The reference to next year's free elections, which they both had agreed were to decide on their respective "future services to the commonwealth," seemed ordinary enough to the great businessman who had lived through many political turbulences himself. The one item he gave a second thought to was the dexterity of Dr. Zapeta's handling of the "stricken leader of the People's Party." He extended to him, in this document, his best wishes for a speedy recovery—which would "enable him to lend his counsel to the Government in healing the wounds inflicted upon the country by the disaster of August the twenty-third."

This ambiguous invitation coincided with the story of El Huérfano's "curious defeat" as told by the attaché. It appeared that a sudden change in the mood of some of his followers had thrown El Huérfano on the discretion of Fafreras, or, to use the figure of speech picked by the diplomat, it had "turned El Huérfano into wax in the hands of Fafreras." Hojeda planned to present his Government friends with a good description of the "huachanazo"—this was the half-derisive term already applied on the shores of the River Plate to the Huacho upheaval— and he had made a mental note of his nephew's theory that "one particular European legation" ought to know a good deal about the defection of certain radical Eastern groups from the People's Party. He made another note now. . . . He was bending his head low over the newspaper. He replied with appeasing grunts to the inarticulate sounds of hatred, contempt, and acerbity, which came from behind him. Finally he folded the journal. "And what," asked he, "do you think is in store for you under the circumstances, mi amigo?"

Lorenzo dropped down on the arm of the huge chair. Unseeing he took the paper from Don Mauricio, who stood before him, one hand gracefully on the shelf.

"You are fairly safe here, I take it. But will you be safe here the day after tomorrow? Here in the Club, or anywhere else, for that matter? Do you assume the President has done anything about your personal safety in negotiating the peace with Fafreras?" He spoke with an inflection which left no room for an affirmative answer, and Lorenzo essayed none. "Who is he? Who is that German?" Don Mauricio went on without pausing. "I understand he is a young man, rather stupid. Now what is his relationship to your great friend?"

Requesens raised his head. A deathly stillness had petrified his features.

"I refer to a certain German colonel, an *Oberst,* with whom you conferred in Lisbon some time in '41."

Lorenzo did not stir. No sound came from him.

"His name I was told is von Klug."

"Von Klug . . . von Klug . . ." echoed Lorenzo in a pathetic effort to produce the impression of searching his memory. The blow was almost more than he could bear without shouting out his terror. M. Philibert's real name had assaulted him with so crushing a sense of irony that for a long while he failed to marvel at Hojeda's shrewdness.

The man from the Avenida de Mayo had hit the mark at one fell swoop. His calculation had been correct. The German financier in Spain had informed him accurately. Admirable old fox! Amidst the turmoil of the European collapse, he had ascertained that "a Colonel Requesens" had some time in '41 met *Oberst* von Klug, an officer "known to handle certain secret funds in those days." And undaunted by Hojeda's silence upon his first communication, he had passed on the fruit of his research.

"I don't remember an *Oberst* by that name," Lorenzo managed to say.

"And that poor devil at the yanqui legation—does he remember that *Oberst?* He couldn't be one of his henchmen, could he?"

"Why don't you ask him?"

Hojeda remained deaf to this rudeness. He went to fetch himself a chair. "So you do not know where von Klug is?" he asked, returning to Lorenzo.

Not knowing that gentleman, nor anything about him, Lorenzo said, he could not possibly know where he was. . . . He did not shun the eyes of Mauricio Hojeda, who sat down in front of him, his knees wide apart and his short-fingered hands reposing on them. Don Lorenzo was sure that von Klug—M. Philibert—was dead. He could not . . . no, he could not rise from his grave to exact another ransom!

"I seem to have read somewhere," Hojeda continued, "that people about to die are visited by the most amazing reminiscences. Now you are not about to die, good Lord, no, *amigo*. . . . Still it would be foolish to deny that as of the day after tomorrow your life is in jeopardy in this town. In this country . . . I hoped that fact would refresh your memory. In case you don't know where von Klug is, you may still know where his funds are. That man used to handle big funds. You might know . . . you might remember where they are. I don't say you do. I wish you did, though. It would be too bad if you didn't."

Inch by inch Lorenzo had been sliding down from the arm of the chair, as if to evade the heavy shadow Hojeda's figure was throwing on him. His buttocks touched the seat. One hand grasped the upholstery more tightly, while he extended the other up to the wing of the chair. He kept silent. He put his cheek into the hollow of this elbow. There was a juvenile abandon in his pose.

"It would be bad, Don Lorenzo. For, to put it squarely, I would not be interested in your further safety unless . . ."

From under his weary eyelids Lorenzo observed the hesitant gesture that took Don Mauricio's hands from his knees, and the slow shrug meant to convey the full idea of hopelessness. The former Minister was completely in the dark about the Government's intentions as to his person. He surmised that Dr. Zapeta did not wish to commit himself on that point before Fafreras' arrival, or before the foreign legations had had their say, or even—preposterous as this sounded—before taking counsel with the leader of the People's Party. Only now had Lorenzo heard precisely when Fafreras would take over his office. During the forty-eight hours of his stay at the Club, he had talked to no one. The two Palace aides escorting him here had made him promise on his honor not to leave the third-storey guest room. He could have broken his word, extorted under duress as it was. For all he knew, the Club had been as good as deserted. He could have tried to bribe the secretary. But where would he have gone? Throughout these forty-eight hours there had been no end to Lorenzo's dark imaginings. . . . Señor Hojeda had rigged his trap easily. Perfectly. But his trap opened an avenue of escape. The only avenue of escape! So Lorenzo asked, under his breath, "Does your legation know you are here, Hojeda?"

"Why?"

"Because . . . because without their help you would hardly be in a position to fulfill your part of the bargain you are proposing."

The businessman did not counter this at once. Victory did not take him by surprise. But a glow of vanity filled his breast with a great warmth; and this warmth threatened to give birth to some tenderness toward the foe so easily vanquished. He clasped his hands over his stomach and gave it a soft push. "Do not worry, *amigo*," he said amiably. "I'll get you out of the country."

"When?"

"I'd prefer to leave as soon as possible. As soon as possible . . . yes, yes . . ." he muttered dreamily, feigning not to hear Lorenzo's new query.

But he inquired again, more distinctly now, what Don Mauricio's price was.

"I did not come to sell my services," said Hojeda.

Lorenzo's head was erect.

"Where is von Klug?"

"I do not know."

"Does that man know? The man who is with the yanquis?"

"No."

"And von Klug's funds? Do you know where they are?"

"I've got access to some of them," Lorenzo Requesens said. The words came out quite mechanically.

"Where is the money?"

"I've got access—"

"Where? Where?"

"Is that of importance?"

"Of importance! Can't you see the danger? I am, after all, no wizard. What I've found out about your deal with that *Oberst* others will. May . . . No—will. The yanquis. They are on the spot overseas. They might catch von Klug any day!" Don Mauricio's upper lip tightened, uncovering his almost pointed incisors. His eyes roamed the room in growing exasperation. The danger, reference to which had occurred to him as a clever trick, began to awe him in earnest. His full rapacity was aroused. It made his heart beat fast. This stupid soldier of fortune! What did *he* know about money! His stupidity was actually disgracing the money in his hands! "Can't you see," the businessman cried out—he had got up—"that the most important thing now is to camouflage those funds?"

"They are camouflaged."

"How? Where? Where are they? Camouflaged! How much does

the man in the yanqui legation know about that 'camouflage'?"

"Nothing."

"And about the money as such? And about the access you have to it?"

"Nothing."

"Who is that man anyway?"

"An idiot."

"But how—"

An angry twist of Lorenzo's body expressing the immaterial nature of that point silenced Hojeda.

He had retreated from Lorenzo and from the light. He let a moment go by. Then he uttered in an undertone, "And your wife, Don Lorenzo?"

"She knows nothing about von Klug," Requesens said. "And you should know better than to drag *her* in."

"I apologize. But this is serious. We must see where we stand."

Lorenzo heaved himself up to a more comfortable pose.

"You cannot communicate with her, can you? That too, *amigo,* will be a simple matter once you are out of the country."

Lorenzo did not blame the great businessman for his caution. He did not blame him for inquiring after the knowledge Priscilla had of his transactions. It was natural that a wife should know of her husband's dealings.

"You want to communicate with her, don't you?" Hojeda persisted.

"Mind your own business, will you?" Lorenzo flared up. This vulgarian! this shopkeeper! playing on his sentimentality! Since Villaroel had told Lorenzo on Thursday night that Priscilla had "taken refuge with her countrymen," not one shred of news had reached him from her. He did not doubt but that his enemies enjoyed this cruel refinement of his plight.

"Be reasonable, Don Lorenzo, eh?"

He was reasonable. He was all reason by now. He *had* perceived the peril that someone else might be as resourceful as had been Hojeda in tracking down von Klug's funds. If he wanted to "camouflage" them—dissociate his name from them—this shopkeeper was the person to confide in. Confide! In reality, he, Lorenzo was at his mercy.
. . . His blood-shot eyes wandered downwards, and suddenly, to Hojeda's amazement, he broke into a laugh. It did not stop. It shook his

shoulders. It tossed back his head; and his profile against the lamp shade looked enormous—obscene—with its gaping black mouth and the long beak. He crossed and uncrossed his legs. "You win!" he cried to Hojeda, halting his guffaws at last, and lifted a rigid finger. "You win because I have learned that no man can stop the trajectory of a missile at a given point."

"Eh?"

"I learned that lesson last May. And from whom did I learn it, if you please? From Colonel Leandro Fafreras, the proven friend of the common man. It's his own coinage. Not bad. Not bad at all for an erstwhile mestizo sergeant. Here we are: you insist you must get all the particulars about that money—"

"I want to protect it!"

"Yes. But unless you're permitted to protect my money—"

"*Your* money!"

"—you aren't interested in my further safety. In other words, you are interested only in protecting—"

"Saving! Rescuing!"

"—in rescuing both my money and myself. This is the trajectory. I can't stop it. Fafreras was right. You win. . . ." It was an eerie sensation for Lorenzo to hear the name of his banker ascend from his own throat. He even repeated the name, as if to test the immensity of his defeat and the morbid feeling of release it seemed to entail.

Not in his most unbridled pipedreams could Mauricio Hojeda have hoped for so priceless a windfall. In his own country! The money was in his own country! And he was well acquainted with the provincial banker in whose care it was! . . . In whose account did the banker hold the money?

"Lorenzo Requesens," came the answer.

"Where can I get some writing paper?"

Lorenzo motioned Don Mauricio to one of the desks situated between the window niches. He said tonelessly, "If you want to send a message somewhere, I hardly think that will work, with the curfew. Or have you made your own arrangements? Of course I agree you'd better not use the telephone. . . ."

Hojeda was stepping up to the light, a sheet of the club's stationery dangling from between two fingers. He took out his fountain pen.

"Do you want to sit here?"

"Thanks," said Hojeda, already devoting himself to his writing. He had to raise his hand fairly high, for he had put the paper on the shelf beneath the lamp.

The wing of the armchair concealed his bulky shape from Lorenzo's vision. He did not turn. He went on to volunteer his advice on how to dispatch the message, and spoke of a "substantial tip" the secretary might be expecting. He was the corruptest of all corrupt men in this accursed city. . . .

Hojeda's pen was racing over the paper.

Lorenzo closed his eyes. His wrath against Hojeda began to evaporate. A businessman! *He* had not talked about friendship ever. Nor about fidelity. Nor about love. Those who had, had become traitors all. Fafreras! Bundschuh! That hypocrite of a priest who had sent the Nazi here. Loyarte! Priscilla . . . Priscilla? All of them! The Virgin knew he was not blameless himself (though surely it was the least of his sins that had brought about his downfall!), but he had always been loyal to others. To Fafreras whom he could have destroyed in May. To Bundschuh. To Loyarte. And even to Philibert whom he had spared the ghastly fate that would be his, had he, his protector, not chosen for him a shortcut to eternity. He had been loyal to them all—

"Dozing, *amigo?* Ah, a long sleep will do you much good, and you'll get it on my plane. It's a comfortable plane. . . . Read this. And sign it. I am taking a risk, I am aware of that. You may be trying to fool me. Think twice of it. People in my country do not fool Mauricio Hojeda. And you will be in my country soon. All right, *mi amigo.* Sign it. Meantime I'll give my nephew a ring."

"Nephew? What nephew?" asked Lorenzo, unhearingly. What he was looking at was a written instruction to his banker whereby he, Sr. Lorenzo Requesens, transferred to Sr. Mauricio Hojeda the balance of all his accounts and whatever stocks and bonds were held in deposit for him. "No, no, no!" he screamed, tottering to his feet. "I'll pay you, Hojeda! I'll pay you all right. I'll pay you a reasonable sum. A great sum! Five thousand dollars . . . No? Ten thousand, then . . . Twenty . . . You can't . . . you can't rob me of my last penny!"

Don Mauricio strode toward the door. "If I were you, Requesens, I wouldn't shout. Don't be childish. Wasn't our first consideration in drawing this letter to camouflage those old holdings?"

A ferocious impulse to tear to pieces the contract of surrender, come what may, flamed up in Lorenzo. But reasoning quenched his wrath.

Hojeda had sprung the trap. The avenue of escape he offered led to the bleakest of roads. The thief, the brigand! His savior . . . Before walking out of the room, he had handed his fountain pen to Lorenzo, and Lorenzo used it now in the prescribed manner.

Hojeda was back in the room.

Lorenzo straightened. The sputtering lamp threw wildly prancing shadows over one side of his face. The other was in blackness.

The great businessman took the sheet of paper from Lorenzo's icy hands. "Let us go," he said. "The car will be here any minute. Take this coat and hat. I just bought them both from the secretary. He *is* a corrupt man. Let's go."

The flame of the lamp was spouting a geyser of smoke up to the ceiling. But neither of the two señores paid any attention to the temper of the ancient contraption. The sound of its cracking chimney was lost in the bang closing the door.

XXXVI

"I DON'T BLAME you for mistrusting my motives," said the President's niece with a tone of exaggerated self-reproach. She had told Priscilla that Dr. Zapeta, having gotten the news an hour ago—at 8:30, to be correct—wanted Don Lorenzo's wife to know right away of his arrival in the great foreign capital. As Doña Priscilla showed no reaction, her caller repeated that she did not blame her for misjudging the reasons for this unexpected, late visit. She added, "You're justified, my God yes, in considering my solicitude rather sudden. I showed little of it when you probably needed it most."

Priscilla said, "These are difficult days for everybody."

Mrs. Partridge agreed. She stood in front of the daybed on which Priscilla was sitting. She kept her uneasy gaze on the purple school pennant fastened on the wall between two framed group photographs. It occurred to her that the wife of the Chargé d'Affaires, who in her husband's absence had received her, had been stressing her sympathy for "poor Priscilla" no doubt to give notice that the latter's presence at the legation was not as painful to her hosts as malicious rumor had it; the yanqui lady had made a point of Priscilla's occupying the room of her daughter who, as it happened, was staying abroad. Somehow the lady had intimidated Margarita. This, she admitted to herself, also made her so reluctant now to go ahead with her mission. "Yes, these are difficult days," she confirmed again. Her English sounded more hesitant than usual. "But God is my witness I was thinking a great deal about you throughout those terrible hours. Those terrible days . . . It was a tremendous relief for me to know you were with your own people. And when, this morning, we first heard of Don Lorenzo's abduction, I only hoped *you* wouldn't learn about it before getting news of his safe landing down there. For if I know one thing

342

well, much too well, it's the torments of waiting. That agony. Waiting for this sort of news, worrying about the man one loves."

Priscilla was clasping her tightly closed knees. Her eyes went past the young woman to the flower-filled vase on the bureau against the opposite wall. "Oh, Don Lorenzo wasn't exactly off to war, was he?" she murmured not without irony.

"That's true," Margarita conceded, thinking at the same time how well Priscilla's sullenness, her very pose, fitted this schoolgirl's room. "But not knowing who Don Lorenzo's abductor was—or did you know who he was? . . . I understand your Minister informed you this afternoon of what happened at the Club last night. Did he also tell you . . . ? No, he couldn't have. Until an hour ago not even *we* knew who the abductor was." She narrowed her eyes in a flurry of suspicion.

"I never heard Señor Hojeda's name before you pronounced it," Priscilla said simply.

"You didn't? Ah, he is a very well-to-do man. . . . You see, Don Lorenzo still has powerful friends in this hemisphere. He still has friends in this country. Believe me, if it hadn't been for his regrettable aloofness—"

"I appreciate your coming to see me," Doña Priscilla broke in determinedly. "I am very grateful for your uncle's thoughtfulness. But I've nothing to give in return. I've got no information about Don Lorenzo's dealings."

"Good heavens, you can't possibly think I came here to coax you for information!"

Priscilla watched the dimples on the round face come and go. "It could be imagined, couldn't it?" she replied. "In a crisis the interests of one's country supersede all other considerations."

"We'd better not think too much about the country's interests tonight, on the eve of Señor Fafreras' triumphant entry," the other observed bitterly—while Priscilla, only half listening, became aware that she had just been using the words the Chargé d'Affaires had used toward her. He had been fairly embarrassed when he told her that, even so, it was up to her whether she wanted to talk over the "obnoxious affair" with him, or with "someone back home," or not at all; and directly she said she knew nothing about her husband's contacts with that German—absolutely nothing—her host reassuringly patted her hands, saying he'd thought so himself from the first. And recalling his relaxed face, as he thus concluded their talk—the only one devoted to the "obnoxious affair"—and his expression of benevolence and of pity, Priscilla felt again the anger and shame that had colored her face and dried her mouth at that moment. But she merely asked, "So the colonel will be here tomorrow?"

"The general, if you please," affirmed the President's niece, pursing her lips.

"Oh, the general . . ."

"General Leandro Fafreras, yes." Doña Margarita sniffed. Then, tossing back her head as if to cast away that noisome image, she said, "No, my dear, I most certainly didn't come here to collect information. I am not anxious to get any. And frankly . . . frankly, I don't think you've got any."

There was a long silence before Priscilla, her voice dry and cold, replied, "I've got the choice, haven't I? I am free to assume that you're taking me either for a stupid little goose, a naïve foreigner, or for so hardened a hypocrite, it would be a waste of breath to ask me *any* questions?"

"About what? About that silly affair? For that's what it is—a silly, an absurd affair. It would be a waste of breath to ask *anyone* about it."

"But silly as it is, you don't think my husband took me into his confidence, do you?"

With a quick move Mrs. Partridge sat down by Priscilla's side. "Get this right, my dear," she said, unruffled. "What I meant to say was that Don Lorenzo's offense is far from being a crime to my mind—"

"It broke him, didn't it?"

"Politics broke him."

"*You* are saying that!"

"I am trusting you. . . . What I meant to say was that such fugitives as that chap Don Lorenzo is supposed to have gotten into the country illegally for some reason or another (or for no reason at all except for his own goodheartedness)—that such men surely are at large by the score in many countries. A year from today no one will bother about them. That's what I meant by calling the incident silly. Nevertheless Don Lorenzo took a great risk. He did—under the circumstances. He knew his position was not secure. He had to be very careful, hadn't he? More so than most men. Yet no man would have shared that secret even with his own mother. Not in these months. Later, a year from today, it would have been different. . . . And don't you think," she proceeded and slipped her arm round Priscilla's shoulders, "Don Lorenzo was also acting gallantly toward you under the circumstances? Imagine your embarrassment if you'd been in his confidence, as you put it. . . . Imagine your dilemma vis-à-vis your present host, who's bound by duty, for the time being at least, to regard Don Lorenzo's ridiculous indiscretion, his silly offense, as a crime. A crime against the spirit of democracy, I suppose, or something . . . Think of that."

It crossed Priscilla's mind that she should object to this. But she recalled at once the ambiguous inhibitions which—on Friday and Saturday and Sunday—had stifled her impulse to call Lorenzo over the telephone at the Club. With the Nazi in the legation, the Chargé d'Affaires could not possibly have permitted its wires to be connected with Lorenzo's quarters. But she had not thought only of the diplomat's sense of duty when she refrained from even trying to ask for his permission. . . . Had she not taken for granted he would turn her down— just as she had presumed Lorenzo would not be allowed to answer telephone calls at the Club—because she wanted both to be the case?

"Honestly," Margarita Partridge went on, withdrawing her arm, "I'd never have thought you'd resent Don Lorenzo's secretiveness in that absurd matter—and resent it *now!* I seem to remember your saying yourself—" An abrupt turn of Priscilla's head interrupted her. But she persisted, "Yes, I seem to remember your saying yourself how hard it was to assert oneself. You seemed resigned to it then."

"You are courageous, Doña Margarita. Reminding me of that talk of ours, you might also be reminded yourself of what we were discussing in that hour. And I take it you wouldn't be so pleased to be reminded of it, or would you? The gist of it . . . of that little intrigue, that plot of ours . . . the gist of it—remember?—was to have the People's Party crushed with the help of Lorenzo."

The President's niece was taken aback. She had not thought these translucent grey eyes capable of so hostile a glare. "Need I say," she said with an affected sigh, "how deeply I regret that the idea miscarried? How promising it all looked at the air parade that morning!"

"Did the idea really miscarry? Your idea? Your uncle's idea? When he sent you to get me to influence Lorenzo—his idea, his actual idea couldn't have been to keep his War Minister in line, could it?"

"Doña Priscilla!"

"It didn't work out so well for him, did it? The People's Party, I am told, and its leader—"

"Good Lord, I hope no one in *this* place takes the President's emer-

gency solutions seriously. Particularly not his policies in regard to that
so-called leader—the 'leader' of a party, by the way, which is miserably
weakened at this moment. No! I am sure no one in this place takes all
that very seriously. We don't. The right people don't. Some may pretend they do. The Senator from Majamarca may. He's more a businessman than a politician. Probably he wishes for peace at any price. And
then, there's that girl of his . . ."

'She tries to put me off the track,' Priscilla thought. 'She doesn't want
to admit that her uncle laid his plans to trap Lorenzo and got trapped
himself. She's loyal to her uncle.'

The President's niece was talking on, her voice thickened by pent-up
scorn.

'She tries to confuse me with her pointless stories,' Priscilla thought.
It was simple to look through this young woman. She had come to gloat
over her misfortune, over that utter helplessness that sooner or later was
the foreigner's lot in the Republic. Perhaps she was still in love with
Lorenzo, and enjoyed humiliating his neglected wife. Nothing short of
that intention could have induced this supercilious, purse-proud Gracián girl to expose herself to arguments and rebukes.

Some young fools in Majamarca, she was saying now, might actually
hail that union as a symbol of the compromise, of the new order—

What union?

"The marriage of the Senator's daughter to Captain Loyarte."

Doña Priscilla got to her feet. "Oh, Captain Loyarte . . ."

Mrs. Partridge failed to notice the impression the news made on Don
Lorenzo's wife. Perhaps Doña Margarita was, even in this hour, only
yielding to her inveterate delight in gossip; perhaps she was also carried
away by what she now termed the "more freakish aspects of the much-
hailed compromise." At any rate she began to repeat what Priscilla had
not listened to: that the Senator had talked Dr. Zapeta into making
Loyarte a Palace aide . . . that the Senator was hastening his daughter's
marriage to gloss over her political escapade . . . that the girl was terribly in love with Loyarte. . . .

Priscilla paced the room. She had never heard of the girl's escapade
and recalled but hazily having heard of Loyarte's betrothal.

"Terribly in love, yes," Doña Margarita said with a shrill laugh. "I
have it on good authority that she's been calling her beloved a victim of
his idealism."

So Loyarte had been doubly rewarded for his betrayal, Priscilla registered in her mind. When exactly, she wondered, had he in his heart begun to betray Lorenzo? How did betrayal begin in a human heart? Was indifference alone strong enough to breed treason?

Suddenly Margarita's rapid voice stopped.

Priscilla glanced over to her from the other end of the room, and her faraway look must have struck the young woman, for her tone sounded deliberately calm and even grave as she suggested,

"Don't you think we should cease to review the sorry history of the past week? My coming to see you . . ." She straightened her legs which had been tucked up on the couch. ". . . it has a purpose. Another purpose than the news I brought you."

Priscilla let a moment go by. Then she said, "The sorry history of the past week! Is that what the right people have dubbed it already? Never mind. That history might have taken a different course. You would be surprised to learn that *I* could have changed its course, wouldn't you? Yet that is the case. I could have brought Lorenzo into an alliance with Colonel Fafreras. I could have. I could have influenced him—and that's another thing I didn't know I could do before you tricked me into playing your game. . . . Do you recall the Day-of-Independence reception, and how Fafreras was lying in wait for me on that rear balcony? He asked me there . . . he virtually asked me to transmit an offer to Lorenzo, an offer of the closest possible friendship. I didn't understand it at the time. He said a man must have *one* friend, and so the friendship he was suggesting obviously excluded others. Do you follow me, Doña Margarita? That friendship excluded the Palace. And assuming, as I did, that *you* had maneuvered me into facing Fafreras on that balcony, his proposal made no sense to me. But it did later. It *did*. Yet instead of advising Lorenzo of it, I allowed your plot to seduce me, and I played the game of your uncle—"

"It was no game. There was no game. Up to Thursday afternoon—"

"On Wednesday night I decided to tell Lorenzo of Fafreras' offer. Perhaps it would have been too late anyway. Still I tried. I tried again on Thursday morning—"

"My dear, you forget what happened in the afternoon."

"Didn't you just say Lorenzo still had many friends?"

"Gonzales didn't belong to them. And he met the German first—"

"Oh, the German! Isn't that merely a silly affair? Wasn't it politics that broke Lorenzo? But for me, Doña Margarita, politics might have broken your uncle instead!"

Margarita Partridge did not counter that assertion. She had allowed this talk to slip away from the purpose of her visit. She had even encouraged this useless controversy. The other's unavailing excitement called her back to the realities of this twenty-seventh of August and to her mission. Without raising her voice, she said with a sigh that it was futile to reconstruct a hypothetical past.

"Is it?" asked Priscilla. But her intonation no longer carried a challenge. She stood with her back to the room, facing the dresser; and in the wall mirror hanging above it obliquely, Margarita could see the top of Priscilla's head, its somewhat dishevelled auburn hair set off against the faded flowers over which she was bending. Her shoulders sagged.

And suddenly the Gracián girl realized that to Priscilla the alleged abortive plot of Fafreras meant more than a political chance missed by Lorenzo. Her feminine intuition told Margarita that this woman who had just accused her husband of a lack of confidence in her—of secretiveness, insincerity, if not outright deceit—was accusing her own honesty now of having failed him. "Doña Priscilla . . ." she said and got up. "My uncle is offering you the use of an airplane to rejoin Don Lorenzo."

Priscilla turned round. "If this is an order, I'll have to take it up with my Minister first. I am an American citizen."

"It is not an order. Nothing even resembling an order. To my uncle, your North American citizenship makes no difference in this instance. He would offer you the same facilities if you happened to be born in this country."

"Does the President feel it would be dangerous for me to return to the Casa?"

"Most assuredly not. Peace is restored. Fafreras' peace, to be sure. But even if (which no one thinks will happen) new disturbances should break out, you wouldn't be more endangered in any way than the rest of us would."

Priscilla was very pale. Her hands clutched the dresser behind her, disarranging the lace spread over its top. "What then . . ." she started to ask.

"What then prompts my uncle to make you this offer? You may be inclined to call it a *beau geste*. But *beaux gestes* aren't in his nature, you see. He is a simple man. What prompts him to make you this offer is a simple thought. He feels you want to be with Don Lorenzo. You proved once before that you knew when he needed you. In '41. Didn't you?"

No reply came. All was quiet in the unscathed building of the United States legation.

"A short while ago, Doña Priscilla, you said my uncle had been playing a game. An unfair game, as no doubt you implied. I won't argue about that. I'm bringing it up only to admit once more that I don't blame you for questioning my uncle's sincerity. Or mine, for that matter. But think of it. What ulterior motive could he possibly have for sending me on this errand? And suppose he has such a motive . . . suppose he'd rather not see for some time the wife of the man he had to throw overboard by whatever means were at hand (*had* to, Doña Priscilla!) . . . suppose such a thought did enter his reflections—can it change your wish, your natural wish to be with Don Lorenzo when he needs you?"

"Does he?" murmured Priscilla. She knew the answer in advance. She expected none from the young woman facing her across the whole length of the light-colored rug, her features sharpened by a frown of scrutiny and demand. She too . . . little Margarita Gracián too would vanish in the haze sure to descend upon the image of years grown senseless, Priscilla was saying to herself with trenchant clarity. Yes, little Margarita Gracián too would step back onto a stage doomed to shrink in one's memory—until its revolts, flaring and dying, the clamor of its glorious aspirations, its betrayals, and its sordid silences, would lose themselves in the distance, together with the unfulfilled promise of a great love.

"And you—"

"And I . . ." Priscilla said, looking unseeingly into the jet-black eyes of little Margarita Gracián. For a moment—a moment so wild and so dark, it already seemed part of a life not hers—Priscilla had found herself wishing she had known of Lorenzo's secret dealings, of all the shoddy and scandalous affairs which, without discerning them, she had always known were there. For that one incredible moment she had wished indeed she had been an accomplice in all these affairs, in his offenses, his crimes, his sins . . . as though that complicity might have established an unbreakable bond between them and afforded her the sweetest of satisfactions. But imagining her return to the guilty man—where had it begun, that guilt, where would it end?—Priscilla knew that she could not have shared his guilt for any satisfaction in the world. Not for the sake of being loved, and not for the sake of loving. "The President has been very gracious to me," she declared with a steady voice. "Please tell him I'm planning to go back to my country. I guess I'll be staying with my mother for a while."

"I hope you're doing the right thing, my dear," Doña Margarita said frigidly. But then, with a brisk motion, she relaxed her erect posture, and walking up to the immobile woman at the schoolgirl's bureau, embraced her and kissed her on both cheeks. "This too . . ." she said in her mother tongue, as she disengaged her soft body from Priscilla, "this too, this destroyed happiness of Don Lorenzo's and yours, this shattered love . . . this too belongs to that silly, that absurd, that ridiculous affair! How . . . oh, Mother of God, how can life be so ridiculous and so tragic at one and the same time?"

THE END